THE PASSION OF A MARQUESS

LINDA RAE SANDE

Twisted Teacup
PUBLISHING

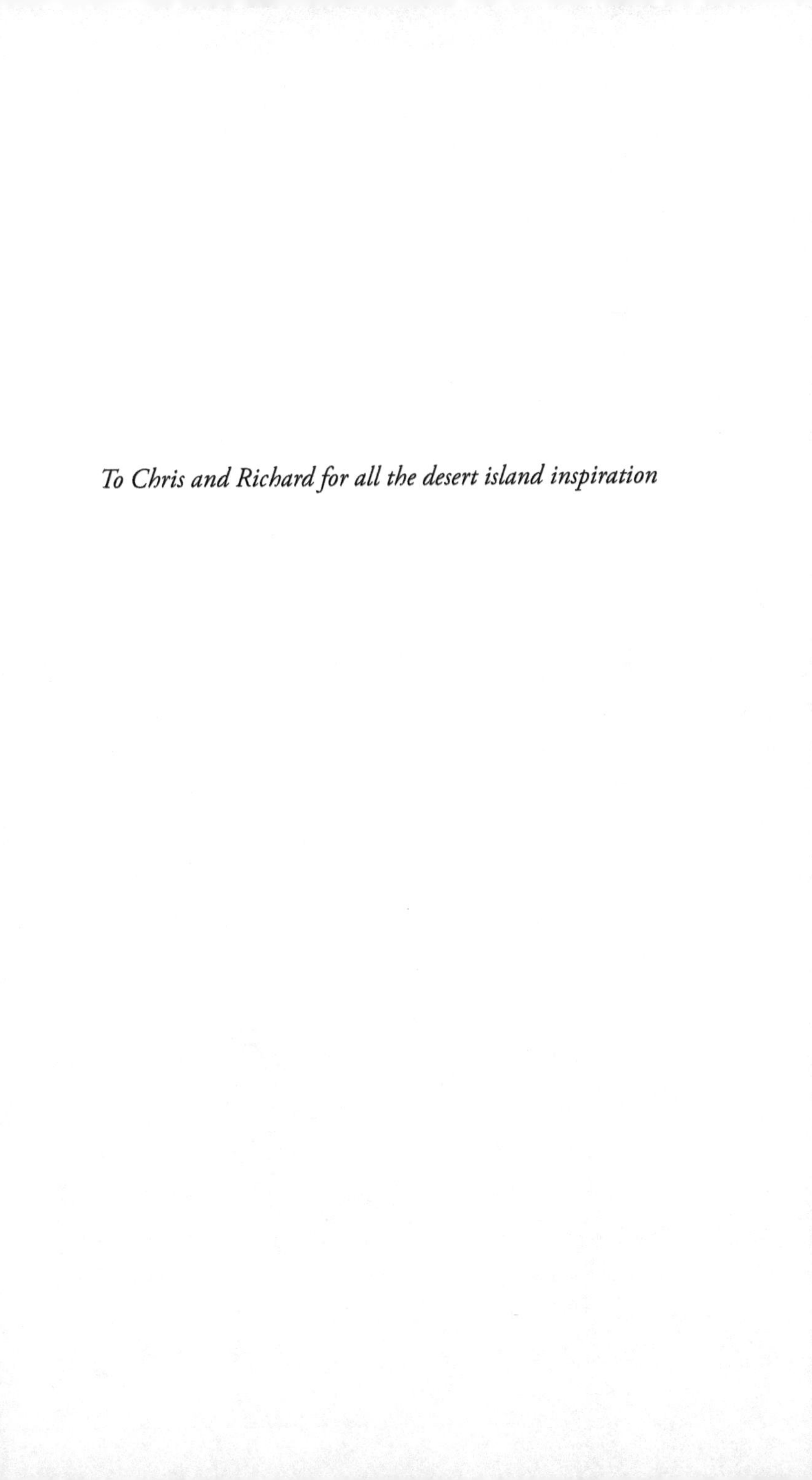

To Chris and Richard for all the desert island inspiration

ALSO BY LINDA RAE SANDE

The Daughters of the Aristocracy

The Kiss of a Viscount

The Grace of a Duke

The Seduction of an Earl

The Sons of the Aristocracy

Tuesday Nights

The Widowed Countess

My Fair Groom

The Sisters of the Aristocracy

The Story of a Baron

The Passion of a Marquess

The Desire of a Lady

The Brothers of the Aristocracy

The Love of a Rake

The Caress of a Commander

The Epiphany of an Explorer

The Widows of the Aristocracy

The Gossip of an Earl

The Enigma of a Widow

The Secrets of a Viscount

The Widowers of the Aristocracy

The Dream of a Duchess

The Vision of a Viscountess

The Conundrum of a Clerk

The Charity of a Viscount

The Cousins of the Aristocracy

The Promise of a Gentleman

The Pride of a Gentleman

The Holidays of the Aristocracy

The Christmas of a Countess

The Knot of a Knight

The Heirs of the Aristocracy

The Angel of an Astronomer

The Puzzle of a Bastard

The Choice of a Cavalier

The Bargain of a Baroness

The Jewel of an Earl's Heir

The Vixen of a Viscount

Beyond the Aristocracy

The Pleasure of a Pirate

Stella of Akrotiri

Origins

Deminon

Diana

CHAPTER 1

ON A CLEAR NIGHT

June 1817

Anyone living in London was probably denied the scene that greeted Lady Samantha Fitzsimmons as she made her way up from her cabin on *The Fairweather*. A sky full of brilliant stars drifted overhead, their lights winking like diamonds on black velvet. The ship rocked so gently she could imagine she was still on dry land. Her aunt, Lady Chamberlain, was probably wishing they were. The poor woman was below deck with a case of seasickness she claimed prevented her from joining her niece on her nightly walk on the deck.

"You would feel better if you took the air," Samantha said as she offered her aunt another damp cloth.

Caroline Fitzsimmons, Viscountess Chamberlain, regarded her charge with a shrug. "Probably," she agreed. "But the mere idea of climbing those stairs is not the least bit appealing. You go on ahead," she urged Samantha. "It's not as if you'll be accosted by anyone at this time of the night."

Samantha considered the older woman's words. Her aunt did have a point. The ship's captain had assured the ladies his men would be below deck after dark most nights, although one was always behind the wheel if he wasn't.

Still ruminating on her aunt's words, Samantha didn't realize she'd been joined by another of the ship's passengers until he cleared his throat. "A pleasant night for a stroll," he remarked as his gaze swept the heavens above. The clear sky was a rare sight for those used to London's usual fog and smoke-shrouded skies.

Samantha regarded the intruder for a moment. If the Marquess of Plymouth could somehow parlay his handsome good looks with his disagreeable manner, he might be a tolerable guest at dinner. Why the man sported a continuous scowl every moment of this trip—or at least those moments she had been in his company—was beyond Samantha's comprehension. Any aristocrat who could claim a title and lands as rich and varied as his, even if they were in a remote part of Yorkshire, should be displaying a permanent smile, she thought.

Samantha turned from where she had paused at the rail, her attention caught by the sky's sudden change in color as the effects of the sun disappeared completely. Wondering if the marquess expected a response, Samantha turned to face him. "The fair weather has been a blessing on this trip," she agreed. Suddenly nervous at being alone on the deck with a man, she added, "I trust you're faring better than the viscountess. She's still overcome by seasickness." Fighting the urge to roll her eyes at the image her not so pleasant comment created in her mind's eye, Samantha turned to make her way to the stairs and her cabin below.

"I apologize if I disturbed you," the marquess replied, taking a step in the direction she was heading, as if he intended to intercept her.

Pausing in her retreat, Samantha blinked. *Had the man actually apologized?* she wondered. And without any evidence of the sour face he had worn for the four days they had been on the open seas?

In a few days, *The Fairweather* would dock near Rome, and she and her aunt would embark on an abbreviated version of the Grand Tour. Not having gained the attention of any marriage-minded men during the past Season, and realizing her best friend's brother wasn't yet ready to propose, Samantha had announced her desire to travel. Anxious to be out of London during the summer months, her aunt Caroline had whole-heartedly agreed. "Perhaps we'll find you a suitable count in Italy. Or a Russian prince on his travels in Greece," her aunt enthused.

Samantha had merely nodded. If she hadn't been able to land a husband after four Seasons in London, she rather doubted a foreign aristocrat would show any interest in her. If Harold Tennison, Earl of Everly, didn't propose in the next year, she would be officially declared on the shelf. Well, not *officially*, perhaps. But in the minds of most members of the *ton*, she would be on her way to spinsterhood.

The prospect wasn't as daunting as it should have been, she decided. Other unmarried women tended to exploit their independence to their advantage, taking lovers and traveling on a whim. But Samantha found herself wanting a husband. Wanting children. Wanting a life beyond the one she had at Fitzsimmons Manor with her aunt and uncle.

"Oh, you didn't disturb me," Samantha claimed as she stilled herself and decided she really didn't want to go back to the cabin. The warm night, occasionally cooled by a slight breeze, seemed almost magical. Moving to the opposite rail, she gripped the worn wood and gazed out over the ocean.

"It must have been quite a shock to learn your maid was Trenton's sister," the man said then. A brief, bright light split the darkness as he scratched a match. The blaze grew larger as he lit a cheroot and inhaled.

What a rake! Samantha thought as she regarded the marquess. *He dares to smoke in the presence of a lady!* She managed to keep her voice light, though, when she responded. "A very happy one, indeed."

For a moment, Ethan Range, Marquess of Plymouth, seemed surprised. His face returned to its passive expression of boredom almost immediately. So quickly, in fact, Samantha was left wondering if he had displayed any reaction at all or if she merely imagined her simple words had done the trick.

The bastard! Lily Harkness had been her lady's maid since

before her come-out. There had never been any scandal surrounding the girl, nor any suggestion she was other than what—or who—everyone thought she was. And then, just last year, Gabriel Wellingham, Earl of Trenton, appeared at Fitzsimmons Manor and announced Lily was his illegitimate sister. He was there to see to it Lily enjoyed the life and comforts of being an earl's daughter.

Samantha had assisted with Lily's come-out, such as it was, at Lord Mayfield's ball. Although Lily had been nervous, the young woman soon realized her new sister-in-law, Sarah Cumberbatch Wellingham, had far more reason to be nervous. The manager of a coaching inn in Staffordshire, Sarah had captured the earl's attention—and heart—and was now the Countess of Trenton.

Lily, her short blonde curls the *au currant* in coiffures, had spent the evening dancing with every young buck at the ball, and offers of marriage were made every week until the end of the Season. At least Lily had enough sense to declare she was still too young to marry just then, thinking to wait until the end of this past Season to make a decision. *Perhaps she is considering an offer this very moment,* Samantha thought with a wan smile.

She couldn't feel a bit of jealously, however. Samantha had shepherded the girl's education in the ways of the *ton* and had seen to it she was able to attend the very best balls and soirées.

"I hear she's already betrothed," Lord Plymouth said before taking a long draw on his cheroot.

Smiling so her straight and perfect teeth shone in the twilight, Samantha nodded. "I have heard the same." She hadn't, really, but given the number of gentleman callers in the past few months, she wouldn't be surprised if Lily had finally made a decision to accept an offer.

The marquess frowned. "You seem ... pleased," he said in a quiet voice.

"I am. I was her sponsor this past Season," Samantha replied, her chin rising just a fraction. *I might not have made an impression on the men of the* ton, *but at least I could see to it Lily had two successful Seasons,* she figured.

"Rather sporting of you," the marquess commented. "How is it then, traveling with your mother?" Ethan took another draw from his cheroot, suddenly realizing he was smoking in the presence of a lady. He blew the smoke off to one side, knowing he should apologize. Having spent most of this life sequestered at his estate's home, Castle Keys in Yorkshire, he found his polite society manners were somewhat forgotten. *Unused*, he thought, feeling a bit sorry for himself. He rarely socialized—Castle Keys was nearly a mile from the nearest village, and none of its denizens could be counted among his friends. From there, it was another four miles to any town of decent size. A town he no longer visited considering Daisy lived there.

London wasn't much better. He was rarely in London, and when he was, he eschewed the *ton* events in favor of spending his evenings at Boodle's. The men's club, far more sedate than White's, featured a clientele of landed gentry and his favorite son-of-a-duke, Sir William Burroughs. The former banker, recently retired from the Bank of England, had managed to help his clients, including Ethan, amass small fortunes in a number of trades including imports, real estate, coal mining and textiles. Although, at the moment, the coal mines were costing him more than the income they generated.

Samantha frowned, her eyebrows drawing together at Lord Plymouth's odd question. "I am traveling with my *aunt*, Lady Chamberlain, in fact," she stated, sure Caroline had been introduced as such when they had dinner with the captain their first night on board. "And it's quite fine. We get along rather well considering our age difference," she added, remembering the gist of the question.

It was Ethan's turn to frown. *After all these years, did Lady Samantha not know the truth about her so-called aunt?* "You needn't pretend on my behalf, my lady," he finally said, ignoring the warning bells going off in his head. "I know what really happened. It's certainly nothing to be ashamed of, being a bastard and all." He took another draw from his cheroot and took a moment to glance up at the blackening sky.

Samantha tamped down the anger she felt in response to his

impertinent remark. *Being a bastard and all?* What was the man talking about?

"I assure you, my lord, I have nothing to be ashamed of because I am *not* a bastard," she insisted, one gloved hand turning into a fist. *How dare he?* "Wait. What is it you think you know about me?" she asked then, her curiosity piqued.

Ethan Range regarded Samantha for a long moment before taking a deep breath. *So this is how it's going to be*, he thought with derision. Were the Fitzsimmons passing off Samantha as their niece rather than Caroline's illegitimate daughter? Perhaps he should just drop the subject, keep his mouth shut, and carry what he knew from his youth as his own secret. He had been doing so for over twenty years. But at that moment, he was incensed. "Your mother is Caroline Fitzsimmons. You were born before she married your ... *uncle*," he said the word with a sneer, "And apparently she's been passing you off as her niece ever since. I'm surprised. I would have thought she would share the truth with you around the time of your come-out, if not before."

Samantha stared at the marquess, stunned by his words and even more stunned by how ... *sure* he seemed to be of them. "How can you ... what makes you think any of what you claim is true?" she asked, her spine stiffening for a fight. *The impertinent bastard!* How dare he claim she wasn't who ... or whom ... she was!

Ethan sighed and allowed his eyes to scan the heavens again before he leaned against the railing. "I was there," he said in a voice so quiet Samantha had to take a step closer to him in order to hear his words. A breeze had begun, the slight wind sending the loose tendrils of her hair flowing across her cheeks.

"There?" she replied, her voice pitched to show her annoyance.

"Yes," he responded. "I was ... seven, I think. And Caroline's sister, Elizabeth—Liza—was expecting ... I don't know, her third baby, perhaps? She never actually gave birth to a living babe, as I recall. Rather a shame, because I remember Edward saying he wanted an heir. He was Matthew Fitzsimmons' cousin, I think, and spoke often of his good fortune at being married to an earl's daughter."

Samantha nodded, although she wanted desperately to counter the man's claims. She had been told of Liza's miscarriages, but she had also been told she was the one surviving daughter—the only child of a couple prone to mishaps and mayhem. She also knew Liza and Edward had perished in a carriage accident shortly after her birth. She wondered if the marquess knew the same story. "Go on," she said carefully, giving him another nod and suddenly wondering if the story about how the Fitzsimmons died in a carriage accident was a tale of fiction or if the accident had really happened.

What am I thinking? Of course, it really happened! Everyone she knew in London seemed to know of it.

Ethan took a breath. "Well, your *mother* showed up in Yorkshire—already with child. She intended to have the baby ... you," he stammered, "And then claim you were her sister's babe. Maybe even have Liza and Edward raise it as their own, although everyone knew they were the last people on earth capable of seeing to a babe ..." Ethan stopped his tirade when he realized Samantha was staring at him, her expression one of shock. Dismay. *Good God, she knows nothing about this!* "I ... I'm sorry. I rather thought you ... knew all this," he said in a hoarse whisper.

Samantha shook her head, ignoring the breeze that had torn another lock of her dark hair from its pins to send it trailing in front of her neck. "Almost none of it," she whispered, never allowing her gaze to leave his face, sure she would catch him in a lie or discover his story was made up to confuse her. To demean her.

But for what purpose? To what end?

The marquess didn't know her. Until she and Aunt Caroline had boarded *The Fairweather* earlier that week, she had never even heard of the Marquess of Plymouth—at least, not this one. She had only ever heard of his father and the dominion over which the tyrant ruled.

So, it was entirely possible—probable even—that the

marquess was telling her the truth. Or his version of it, which meant her world was suddenly upside down.

My aunt is my mother!

And if that were really true ... *I am illegitimate.*

Samantha couldn't allow the marquess to see how his words affected her, though. Not now. Not when her immediate future held such promise. Not when she was about to take a tour of Europe. Not when she might finally find a man who would consider her to be his wife. "What else do you believe is the truth about me?" she asked, annoyance in her tone. *Why is he doing this?* she wondered again.

Ethan swallowed, suddenly questioning if he should really be the one to tell Samantha Fitzsimmons how she came to be in the world. *I was only seven, after all.* But the conversations he had overheard seemed so important—because they were, he soon realized—and so he had remembered them. Just as he remembered everything his father had taught him about the lands and properties he would one day inherit. About the people who tended the farms or worked in the mines or operated the businesses in the marquessate.

He regarded Samantha for a moment before allowing a shrug. "Well, when the Fitzsimmons died in that carriage accident, shortly after you were born, well, I guess your mother had the perfect story to explain your existence. She obviously took you back to Chamberlain and claimed you were her niece," the marquess stated, not sure what had really happened upon Caroline Harrington's return to London. He knew she wasn't yet married to Matthew Fitzsimmons, but Ethan rather doubted the viscount would accept Caroline as his wife knowing she had borne a child—some other man's child—out of wedlock.

Or maybe he would.

The Fitzsimmons seemed a rather loving couple, he thought as he recalled the viscount's prolonged 'good-bye' to his wife on the dock in Wapping. Their marriage seemed far different from the one shared by Liza and Edward Fitzsimmons, a union that was troubled more often than not and survived as long as it did simply because the two were so flighty and careless.

Ethan took another draw from the cheroot and tore his gaze from Samantha's, wondering at the sudden change in the wind. Only moments before, the air had been still; now, the wind had increased so standing on the deck was no longer pleasant.

Moving to the rail, needing it for support as much as needing to be closer to the marquess in order to hear him, Samantha took a breath. And another. "You say you were *seven?*" she asked, suspicion evident in her voice. "How do you even know if you're remembering any of this correctly?" she asked with a shake of her head.

The Marquess of Plymouth sighed, frowning when he suddenly turned to his right. "I remember many incidents from my youth," he countered. "Back to when I was three, in fact." Knowing she would ask why the son of a marquess would be anywhere near the Harrington's summer estate, he added, "I used to play with the servants' children at Darbing Manor. Didn't have any siblings, so I sought playmates where I could. And little pitchers have big ears." He didn't add that he had overheard much of what he knew because he hid in cabinets or closets while he spied on the residents. *I should have worked for the Home Office,* he thought with a bit of dismay. *Probably would have made a better spy than a marquess.*

Not *probably,* now that he gave it some more thought. *Definitely.*

Though he had finally made a bit of headway with the Plymouth marquessate. Until the previous year, when there had been no summer and most of the crops had failed, the farmlands had produced more than they had when he inherited. His investment in textiles had certainly paid off, which helped to overcome the losses in the fields. But it didn't matter how well anything else did when compared to the state of the coal mines.

'Money pits' was probably a better term to describe the mines. He couldn't afford another accident. Couldn't afford to lose another man because supports weren't properly installed or had rotted, or because miner's lights were so dangerous. If everything went as it should on this trip, he would be going home with a crate of new devices that should mitigate that problem.

"So, if Edward Fitzsimmons isn't my father, then who is?" Samantha wondered aloud, her arms suddenly crossing over her chest. The action had the tops of her breasts mounding above the edge of her dinner gown's bodice, and she felt a bit of satisfaction at have drawn the notice of the marquess in that regard.

Ethan was reminded of Daisy when she was cross with him. How she would stand to her full five-foot, one-inch height—in her high heeled shoes—and argue with him about fripperies or jewels or some-such. She was rather beautiful when she was riled, he remembered fondly, before he suddenly remembered he no longer had any claim to the mistress. Before he remembered he was annoyed with the witch and wouldn't be seeing her again.

Ethan realized he was staring at Lady Samantha's rather plump charms and forced himself to look away. *What had she asked?*

Something about her father. *Who is her father?*

"How am I supposed to know?" Ethan answered with a shrug, tossing the remains of his cheroot onto the deck with a flick of his fingers. He planted the toe of his boot over the embers and gave it a quick twist. "I'm quite sure your 'aunt' could tell you, though," he said with a cocked eyebrow.

As far as he could remember, Caroline Harrington was a proper lady. She was an earl's daughter. An earl's sister. Ethan had never heard a word of scandal associated with her, nor her husband, although that was to be expected given Matthew Fitzsimmons' position at the Foreign Office in Whitehall.

"In fact, I'm quite sure she could tell you a good deal of what you claim you don't know," he added in a rather harsh tone.

Incensed by his last comment, Samantha stepped forward and slapped the man hard across his cheek. The impact sent a shock down her arm and a sting through her palm, but the sound of the hit gave her an immense sense of satisfaction. "How *dare* you?" she said in a voice filled with menace. She curled her hand into a fist, fighting the urge to shake off the impact of the hit in the man's presence. She was tempted to hit him in the jaw with the fist, but a sudden thought of propriety stilled her arm.

Barely.

The marquess stared at Lady Samantha for several seconds—or at least what he could see of her through the white stars that danced in front of his eyes.

Good God! The chit could throw a hit with the best of them! He almost—almost—made a comment about when her next boxing mill might be scheduled at Gentleman Jackson's salon, but thought better of it. He had already inflamed her anger with his claims, and rubbing salt in the wound would do him no good. Nor her.

Poor thing.

"I ... deserved that," Ethan said with a nod as he regarded her, his hands pressed against his breeches in an effort to still them. He wanted desperately to rub his cheek, if for no other reason than to assure himself nothing was broken. Had the chit used her fist on his jaw, it might well have broken a tooth or two!

He glanced again at the sky, a frown replacing his passive expression. "Jesus," he breathed, noting how the stars had been replaced by low clouds. Was that rain he smelled? The sky to the west suddenly lit up when a lightning bolt flashed near the horizon.

Curious as to what had the man's attention, Samantha turned to peer in the direction of his gaze, spanning the horizon. The breeze, suddenly blustery, picked up in intensity. "What is it?" she asked as she tried to make out what had captured the attention of the marquess. Glancing up, she realized she couldn't see a single star in the sky. The ship, until then seeming to float on its course, suddenly rose as a swell passed beneath it.

"We need to get below deck," Lord Plymouth announced suddenly, tearing his gaze from whatever had him spellbound only the moment before.

"What is it?" Samantha asked again as she continued to stare to the west. The ship lifted again, this time higher, so that the main mast wavered above them. She had to take a step to the right to keep her balance, even though the marquess had taken her upper arm in a grip that would surely leave a bruise.

The sky to the west lit up with blue-white intensity as a lightning bolt seemed to strike the ocean.

Struggling to keep her balance as she made it to the companionway, Samantha was about to descend when a wave crashed over the rail and sent seawater washing over the deck. Several barrels suddenly lost their footing as the water lifted them and sent some over the side of the ship. When the wave of water hit the wheelhouse, it rolled back over the deck, grabbing Samantha and nearly upending her. Seawater poured down the companionway as the ship suddenly tilted.

Lord Plymouth kept his hold on Samantha, jerking her away from the stairs just as the water would have caught her and probably sent her head-first through the opening.

"Hang on!" he managed to get out as he gripped a railing.

Samantha reached for anything to grab onto, one gloved hand grasping the marquess' lapel while the other tried to hang onto the railing.

"Christ!"

The curse had Samantha following the Lord Plymouth's startled gaze.

Damnation!

Although she was fairly sure she didn't put voice to her own curse, Samantha Fitzsimmons would remember it for all the days of her life. For directly in front of them, a wave of monumental proportions descended on the ship. The roar was deafening. The impact of the water was far more than her tenuous grip on the railing could withstand. Within a fraction of a second, she was forced to let go and move her hand to the only body she could hang onto.

That of the Marquess of Plymouth.

In the cold, black, swirling water in which she suddenly found herself, Samantha was forced to hold her breath and hang on for dear life. Years of spending summers in the Isis River had her kicking with all her might, her half-boots fighting the water's drag on her skirts, on her petticoats, on her lungs as she struggled not to take the breath she desperately needed to take.

Just when she was quite sure her lungs were about to explode, her head cleared the top of the water and she gulped air. And just as quickly, she was below the surface again. Her entire body seemed to go numb all at once, the cold water permeating her very being. The desire to simply let go and allow the water to take her down was almost more than she could fight.

But then an arm wrapped around her waist and she kicked as hard as she could. For what seemed an eternity, she treaded water the best she could given her half-boots and sodden gown and undergarments. At some point, the marquess had disappeared below the water, and she was suddenly aware of his arms around her thighs, of a hand grasping at fabric, of her petticoat ties coming undone. A moment later, her efforts at staying above the water's surface suddenly seemed easier.

Good grief, she realized as her teeth began chattering. The marquess had removed her petticoats! But even as she could more easily move her legs, the water's cold seemed to suck the very life from her.

Lord Plymouth, having surfaced several feet away from her, swam in her direction and captured one of her hands.

"Hang on!" he managed to get out. In the darkness, his face was barely visible until lightning split the dark. For a moment, she was sure his lips were blue and wondered about her own.

"To what?" she managed to croak, almost wishing he had removed her gown when he had been seeing to her petticoats.

"Me!" he shouted as he held her hand out of the water and moved it to his neck.

Samantha nodded as best she could and grasped the back of his waistcoat, her gloved fingers barely warm enough to take hold. *Had the man shed his topcoat whilst he was underwater?* she wondered.

When he moved to swim, she did so as well with her free

arm and treaded water as hard as she could, hoping her feeble attempts were helping more than hindering him.

When they seemed to swim into a solid mass, Lord Plymouth let out a shout and everything went black.

CHAPTER 2

SHIPWRECK

*E*than Range hauled Samantha onto what he thought might have been the door to *The Fairweather's* wheelhouse, it's thick planking barely floating on the rough seas. Once he was sure she was secure, he made his way around the edges to the opposite side and lifted himself enough to get his head and shoulders entirely out of the water, his weight counteracting hers on the planks. Pausing a moment to catch his breath, he glanced at the young woman's prone body. She could obviously swim, he realized just then. If she hadn't been kicking the waters as hard as she had with her half-booted feet, they might both have found themselves at the bottom of the sea.

His pair of Hobys were probably there now. Despite their custom fit, the boots had quickly filled with water and made treading water nearly impossible. Kicking them from his feet had seemed the logical thing to do at the time—now he missed the warmth they would have provided. The seawater was cold in a way that made it very easy to simply give up the fight and allow the ocean to take him.

Samantha's sudden cough had him opening his eyes. "Behind you," she said, weakly pointing beyond his shoulder.

Ethan followed her direction and realized what had captured her attention. A larger length of wooden planks floated behind him, a raft that looked as if it could provide a far sturdier area on which they could both rest. Reaching around, he captured something that jutted from the edge and guided the raft until it came to rest against the one on which Samantha was perched. Despite the weight of her drenched gown, she was able to move of her own volition, crawling until she was positioned in the center of the larger raft. Reaching out, she beckoned the marquess to join her.

Ethan lifted himself over the edge, cursing when his added weight caused one corner to sink beneath the water. Samantha shifted her own weight to counter the effect and then reached out with both hands to grasp the marquess' arm and pull him farther up onto the raft.

Once he was aboard, Ethan quickly moved to the center to sit next to Samantha, swiping a hand through his wet hair and over his face. "Damn it! Damn it all to hell!" he shouted, not intending for his curse to be heard by anyone but the gods above.

Giving the marquess a quelling look, Samantha dared a glance at their surroundings. Even though everything seemed almost black around her, her other senses took over. The swells had lessened in their rise and fall, and the wind had died down as well. The odor around her was no different than it had been when she was on deck, although there was no longer the hint of cheroot smoke nor the scent of the amber cologne the marquess seemed to favor. The clouds above seemed to light the area in a gray wash, with the occasional bolt of lighting providing a split second of light that allowed them to better see their surroundings.

Barrels and other wood objects from the deck of the ship bobbed on the water near their raft. And one by one, stars reappeared above. Shivering more than she had in the water, Samantha wondered about the fate of the ship, of her aunt, of the other passengers and the crew. *Had anyone else managed to get clear of the ship before it broke apart in the sudden storm? Or* were she and the marquess the lone survivors?

Tears pricked the corners of her eyes as desolation and loneliness settled on her. She might have allowed herself to become one with the sea, for what good would it do her to fight for her life when her aunt was no doubt taken by Poseidon himself?

Or did he take my mother?

Was Caroline Harrington Fitzsimmons really her mother as the marquess seemed to believe?

Does uncle know?

The sudden thought of her uncle had her reconsidering her fate. Matthew Fitzsimmons, Viscount Chamberlain, was a dedicated man who refused to leave London when he still had work to do on behalf of the Foreign Office and Parliament. She couldn't give up for his sake, she decided.

That last thought had her reaching for the marquess, for the slight bit of warmth he could surely supply if she could only get herself close enough.

She found him on his back, one arm above his head. His almost lifeless eyes stared at the now-clear sky above, with its host of brilliant stars stretched out from horizon to horizon. After another moment, his eyes closed.

Samantha wasn't sure if she, too, fell asleep or if she merely dozed, but she inhaled sharply and tried to sit up, immediately regretting the sudden movement. Moaning, she moved a gloved hand to the back of her head and gingerly touched it, wincing at the sharp pain her slight pressure incited. She winced again when she realized her hair was damp. And again when she realized nearly everything she wore was damp.

Chilled and suddenly woozy, she lowered herself onto her side, aware of a large prone body that offered warmth and a pillow for her head. She wrapped an arm over its middle and snuggled her body against it, allowing sleep to take her into oblivion.

Samantha wasn't sure if only a few minutes had passed or if it had been hours since she had fallen asleep, but she raised herself onto one elbow, her movements slow as to not rock the makeshift raft.

When she dared a glance toward Ethan, she was a bit startled to find the marquess close—so close, she could make out the dark stubble of his beard, the whorls of his ear, his close-cropped hair where it merged with his long sideburns. His square jaw and chin seemed to rest in his cravat, the once-crisp fabric now limp from its soak in the seawater.

She studied his face, remembering how he always seemed to display a scowl, as if he were angry at everyone and everything. But now, in the dim light from the moon and stars, the planes of his face were softened, his mouth framed by lips that appeared firm but kissable, a nose that was long and a bit broad, dark eyelashes that barely curled where they rested against his lower lids, and nearly black eyebrows without a hint of the furrows that usually separated them. Samantha sighed. The man looked positively at peace.

So when one of his eyes suddenly popped open to stare at her, she let out a shriek and jerked away, causing the raft to bob and water to slosh onto her nearly dry gown.

Ethan took a deep breath and let it out slowly. "What the hell?" he whispered hoarsely, opening the other eye to glare at her. *What had the chit been about to do?* He had felt her soft breaths on his face as she seemed to hover over him, been aware of her staring at him for some time. Despite her dowsing in the sea, she still managed to smell better than the surrounding air, which now invaded his nostrils and reminded him where he was. Or, at least, of the situation he found himself in.

He rubbed one jaw with the flat of his hand and regarded Samantha for a moment. "Were you about to kiss me?" he accused, startled that his voice could sound so unreasonable.

What would have been the harm if she had kissed him?

"Of course not!" Samantha replied, a bit indignant. At his look of disbelief, she straightened and pulled a knee up so she rested on her hip and lower leg. "I thought you might be dead!" she countered in her own defense. "I just wanted ... wanted to be sure you were still breathing," she added in a quieter voice, realizing just then that it really did feel better knowing he was alive, even if it meant he was back to being the scowling marquess. And in a foul mood.

Except that he wasn't scowling just then. He was grinning at her. "And if I'd been dead, what would you have done?" he wondered in a teasing voice, surprised he could find any humor in their situation. *Good God! They were floating on a few planks of weathered wood somewhere in the Mediterranean!*

Samantha frowned, not sure what she would have done. The mere thought of being stranded on a raft with a dead body was more than she could abide right then. She shook her head. "I've absolutely no idea," she murmured in reply, tears suddenly pricking the corners of her eyes.

Moved by her sudden show of emotion, Ethan reached over and took her hand, angling his torso so he could reach to kiss the back of it. "Thank you for your concern, my lady," he said before carefully lowering himself back to a prone position. "And for helping me to get on this damned raft."

Embarrassed by his gratitude, she felt a blush warm her face. "I believe I am the one whose life you saved this evening," she said quietly. "You nearly drowned on my behalf."

Ethan shrugged as he felt exhaustion settle over his entire body. "Thank the gods you can swim, or you would have drowned," he replied before falling into a deep sleep.

About to counter his claim with an annoyed 'huff ', Samantha stopped herself.

The man had saved her life.

The least she could do was be gracious about it.

Feeling chilled in her wet gown, Samantha shivered and settled herself back down onto the rough wood. The promise of warmth had her pressing her body against the side of the marquess, one ungloved hand buried under his waistcoat and her head firmly tucked into the small of his shoulder.

Samantha closed her eyes and allowed exhaustion to take hold, for she was quite sure when she woke up, the entire night's events would turn out to be a very bad dream.

CHAPTER 3

ON THE FAIRWEATHER

"How bad is it?"

The *Fairweather's* first mate stood up from where he had been examining the pedestal of the ship's wheel. "It's intact," Rodney announced in awe, his gaze taking in the part of the deck that had held the wheelhouse. Three walls of the structure, including the door and its frame, had been torn away and tossed into the ocean along with several instruments and the captain's collection of maps. Only the wheel and the back wall of the structure remained. Most of the barrels that had lined the starboard side of the deck—tubs of brandywine—were gone as well. If they withstood the beating they must have taken, their contents would be a valuable find for whomever discovered them when they finally washed ashore. Although passenger fares were funding most of this voyage, the profit from the brandywine would have been a welcome bonus.

Captain John St. John furrowed his brows. "You're telling me I can still steer?"

Rodney nodded. "Aye," he replied, turning his attention to the main-mast. Despite a vertical crack radiating up from the base of the conifer, the mast still stood, although most of the sails were gone or hanging in tatters from the rigging. "I wouldn't want to take any chances with this, though," he warned as he shook his head. "But the fore-mast seems intact."

St. John followed the man's line of sight to the topgallant mast. "Get someone up there to cut the lines. I don't want this thing coming down on us out here on the open water," he ordered. *Or anywhere, for that matter*, he nearly added aloud.

What the hell had happened to cause the ship to tip so far over it nearly capsized before suddenly righting itself? When the main-mast cracked, he had felt it deep in his bones, the sound so loud it managed to be heard above the sudden squall that sent what must have been a solid wall of water cascading down on his ship. The fore-mast had probably only survived because its sail had suffered a tear on their last voyage and was still being repaired.

Only one man on his crew had been injured, his arm sprained when he was tossed out of his hammock. Although St. John hadn't yet had a chance to speak with all the passengers, he was fairly sure they had all survived. Two had come from their cabins soon after the rough seas had subsided, wondering what had happened.

Good question, St. John thought in dismay.

For four years he had managed to sail the Britain to Rome route without so much as a few storms—and certainly no loss of inventory—and then suddenly ... this. He shook his head.

The first mate nodded to his captain and began shouting orders. A bucket brigade had already been formed from the lower levels of the ship, water coming up a bucket at a time on the two flights of steep stairs that made up the companionway. As their contents were tossed overboard, the buckets were snatched by his youngest crew member and tossed to a waiting man below decks to be refilled. Another half-hour and most of the water that had flooded the lower deck would be back in the ocean. The hull was intact, and the mid-deck seemed to have survived, although its passengers were complaining of wet floors and an especially rough night. He hadn't allowed any of them to leave their cabins. The last thing he wanted was for anyone to panic anymore than they already had the night before.

John St. John moved to the bow of the small ship and surveyed the horizon. As was common for the mornings after a storm at sea, the sky was clear. The water was relatively calm. The breeze was so slight as to be barely noticeable. Until its sail was repaired or one could be fashioned from the remainder of what hung above and rigged to the fore-mast, they would require the help of the ocean currents to get to land.

"You ready for a bit o' breakfast, capt'n?"

St. John shook himself from his reverie. "Breakfast?" he repeated, turning to find the ship's cook and sometimes sail-maker holding a cup of coffee in his direction. "Did the stores remain intact?" He hadn't given a thought to their food supplies.

Doyle Watson frowned, apparently insulted by his captain's comment. "Of course. I secure the cupboards at night, capt'n, so even most of the crockery survived. The bigger pots, well, they might have gotten loose and bounced around a bit, but I can still cook in 'em," he said, sounding a bit defensive.

The captain nodded, noticing the bucket brigade had finished baling water. He could already tell the ship sat taller on the water. And his own stomach grumbled, reminding him it was past the normal time for his morning meal. "Breakfast it is, then," he said as he took the proffered cup. "See to it the men get a bit extra this morning. Salt pork, if you have it," he added, knowing they had more than enough food in the stores down below.

One of the reasons St. John had such a loyal crew was due to the amount of space in the hold devoted to their food stores. Nothing would be gained by starving his men. They worked far better and longer on full stomachs.

"Aye, capt'n," the cook replied as he headed for the companionway.

Watson might not have been the best cook for a ship like *The Fairweather*—he had been a cook on a British warship during the skirmishes with Napoleon's navy and didn't have much experience in pleasing the palates of paying passengers— but his fare was well seasoned and his coffee was far better than anything served in London coffee houses.

Thinking of his passengers, St. John realized he had better

check on them. Although the cabins didn't offer much that could have been damaged—the furnishings were bolted to the floorboards and lanterns were hung from hooks so they wouldn't fall over—people were wont to bring along some comforts of home. After last night, those would no doubt be scattered all over their cabins.

St. John made his way down the companionway and to the farthest passenger cabin. Mr. McCulvey, a tradesman from Kent, had kept to himself on the trip, taking his meals in his cabin and only coming top-side a few times to smoke a cheroot. At the captain's knock, there was a pause before he heard, "Come."

St. John turned the knob and peaked around the door's edge. Although he expected to find the room in disarray, everything seemed fine except for the wet floor. "Good morning," he said with a nod.

The tradesman gave a grunt. "Finally," he said, getting up from the table in the center of the small room. He offered his hand. "Everything ... all right?" he wondered, surprised to see the ship's captain checking on his well-being.

St. John nodded as he shook the man's hand. "For the most part. We'll get a sail up and be on our way before long," he said, hoping he wasn't being too optimistic. *Don't promise more than you can deliver*, he remembered his father telling him. "Cook should have breakfast ready within the hour."

Mr. McCulvey nodded and returned to the table, his attention on the ledger he had spread out on the table. "I look forward to it," he said with a wry grin.

Even before St. John had closed the door, the couple in the next cabin were standing in their doorway. "So ... we're not sinking?" the young woman asked, her fair skin nearly white with fear.

The captain shook his head and gave the Fullers his very best smile. "Not today. The hull is intact." When he realized they had probably paid witness to the bucket brigade, he added, "We just took on a bit of water when a wave landed on the deck." He watched as the woman's hand went to her bosom and she seemed to take a breath of air—perhaps her first since the storm hit.

"It's her first time aboard a ship," Mr. Fuller said quietly as he rested a reassuring hand on his wife's shoulder.

St. John was about to say something like, "Mine, too," but thought the attempt at humor wouldn't be appreciated. "And now you've experienced the worst a trip aboard a ship can offer," he said instead, nodding as he moved on to the next cabin. "Mr. Range?" he called out, waiting a moment before knocking on the next door.

Although the man was always impeccably dressed and seemed comfortable aboard ship, St. John couldn't help but think Ethan Range was hiding something. He sported what could only be described as a permanent scowl, as if this trip were an unpleasant chore. And yet during his one conversation with the man—he had hosted him at his table on their first night after leaving the Thames—Mr. Range had mentioned looking forward to the trip as it would mean he could finally acquire some devices he needed for one of his mining concerns up north. *What had he called them?* Batteries.

When there wasn't a response from inside the room, St. John knocked again. Perhaps the gentleman had gone up on deck whilst he was talking to the other passengers. He moved onto the next cabin, rolling his eyes before he finally knocked. He wondered if Viscountess Chamberlain still suffered from seasickness. Although her younger companion seemed just fine on this trip, her first aboard a sea vessel, the older woman had been sick from her first moments aboard ship. "But I will be fine after a day or two," the viscountess had insisted, her pleasant nature at odds with her station.

St. John had always found it difficult to deal with the members of the aristocracy who had been aboard his ship in the past. Besides their snobbery, they were hard to please when it came to food and even harder to please when it came to the tiny accommodations.

The door opened to reveal the viscountess herself, her face the epitome of a sunny disposition. "Why, good morning,

Captain St. John," Caroline Fitzsimmons said brightly, her eyes moving from him to give a glance down the hall. "Oh, I thought perhaps you were returning my wayward niece," she said, her smile disappearing.

St. John followed her line of sight, wondering what she meant. "My lady, I have not seen Miss Fitzsimmons this morning," he replied, thinking he certainly would have noticed the chit had she been on deck—not that she would have been allowed—at least, not until they had determined the extent of the damage done by the storm.

Viscountess Chamberlain leveled a gaze on him that reminded him she was an aristocrat, but that same gaze suddenly held a look of uncertainty. "Oh, dear," she murmured, glancing back into the cabin. Although the floor was damp and a slight odor of vomit still hung in the air, everything seemed to be fine. "I haven't seen her all morning," she said.

Suddenly alarmed, St. John's first thought was Mr. Range. Perhaps he was a rake. Had he lured the young lady into his cabin for a tryst?

Without so much as giving the viscountess a bow, St. John hurried back down to the door of Mr. Range's cabin. He didn't bother to knock but simply turned the knob and walked in as if it were his right. Ready to do battle, even if he didn't have his firearm in his coat pocket and hadn't strapped on a sword in the four years he had captained *The Fairweather*, John St. John was almost disappointed to find the cabin empty. The blanket and linens on the bunk were neatly arranged, suggesting the man had either made it or hadn't slept in it.

St. John moved farther into the room. The man's trunk had tumbled over, it's lid opened at an awkward angle. Clothing and papers were strewn nearby, the water having soaked some of it. Reaching down to pick up the closest parchment, St. John noted the seal embossed at the top and scanned what remained of the letter where the ink hadn't smeared. *Marquess of Plymouth?* he wondered, noting the seal. A sound at the door had him turning.

"Why, where is the marquess?" Lady Chamberlain asked, her slightly wrinkled hands clasped together in front of her.

John St. John stared at the viscountess and attempted to hide his surprise at her question. *Marquess?* "I take it Ethan Range is the Marquess of Plymouth?" he countered, feeling a bit of a fool. How had he missed the man's title? But the marquess hadn't introduced himself as a peer that first night over dinner. Hadn't said a word about being an aristocrat.

"Why, yes," the viscountess answered with a nod, her brow suddenly furrowing. "May I inquire as to why *you're* in his cabin?" she asked, her voice taking on that tone he had come to associate with those in power. He suddenly realized just what a chameleon the viscountess could be. Despite having been rendered helpless by a bout of seasickness only the day before, she was certainly displaying her title with aplomb today.

"I ..." The captain sighed. "I was afraid I was going to find your niece in here," he finally admitted, feeling even more foolish than he had upon learning of Ethan Range's title.

A mix of surprise and was that ... *delight?* ... appeared on Lady Chamberlain's face. "As much as I would welcome Lady Samantha's association with a marquess of Lord Plymouth's means and good looks, I rather doubt she could be that lucky, Captain St. John," the viscountess said with a shake of her head.

St. John's head jerked to stare at the viscountess in surprise.

Was that a twinkle he spotted in her eye?

St. John blinked. And blinked again.

Was the viscountess trying to be funny? Or was she just teasing him? For Lady Samantha was a rather pleasant young woman. Not as pretty as some, but she was handsome with her golden brown hair and peaches and cream complexion. Smart, from what he recalled of their conversation over dinner. And tall. A nice change from the petite milkwater maids the aristocracy usually produced.

Remembering the marquess' scowl, St. John arched an eyebrow. "I should think a lady of Miss Fitzsimmons' good humor deserves a man of similar disposition," he countered, his manner most serious.

It was Lady Chamberlain's turn to give a look of surprise. "'Tis kind of you to say so, Captain," she replied with a nod. "Now, I should think I need to find her. Breakfast will no doubt be served at any moment, and I should like to join her for it." With that, the viscountess gave him a curtsy and took her leave.

St. John managed a quick bow in the direction of the door, giving the cabin another quick glance.

If the marquess made his bunk, why would he have left his trunk in such disarray? Or did he even stay in the cabin? Perhaps he stayed in ... St. John considered the other passengers. *In whose cabin would Ethan Range have stayed in if not his own?* Not with the viscountess and her niece, certainly, nor the Fullers. McCulvey had been by himself in his cabin.

That just left his own.

Well, he knew *he* hadn't spent the night with the marquess!

St. John reached down and gathered up the papers that lay on the wet floor, depositing them on the table. Perhaps they would dry and still be of some use to the marquess. He dared a glance at the papers, rather pleased to see the ink hadn't smeared too badly. The top letter held an address in Italy.

He moved back to the door when a thought struck him.

Perhaps the marquess hadn't spent the night in any cabin because he was no longer on the ship.

A bit of panic gripped the captain. He rushed to the companionway, climbing the steep stairs as quickly as he could. Two crewmen were at the base of the main-mast whilst one scampered up the cracked conifer with a knife in his teeth. Another man was tightening the ropes around what remained of their brandywine barrels. Two more were preparing the rigging for the fore-mast. St. John took another look around. No sign of the marquess.

But he caught sight of the viscountess as her head poked up from the companionway, her gaze one of worry. "If she's not up here, Captain, where can Lady Samantha be?"

John St. John shook his head before daring a look at the horizon. "Where, indeed?"

CHAPTER 4

WAKING UP TO REALITY

Used to being up well before dawn, Ethan woke and wondered at the warmth that covered half his body and the chill that had the other half nearly numb. He turned his head and wrapped his cold arm around the source of heat, absently wondering when his mistress had decided to return to his bed.

Daisy had thrown him over months ago in favor of a tradesman whom she claimed would double her compensation. To add insult to injury, the rake had apparently given her a piece of jewelry worthy of royalty.

The slight bobbing beneath him had the events of the night before bringing him to full consciousness. *Christ! Where the hell am I?* he wondered as he dared a glance at the pink horizon. *East*, he thought suddenly. He turned his head the other direction, his nose colliding with damp hair that smelled of seawater and ... *lemon?*

Christ!

Lady Samantha Fitzsimmons, he remembered suddenly. The wall of water. The sound of a mast cracking. The water as it tried with all its might to drag him beneath its surface.

His free hand moved to Samantha's cheek and then to her neck, his finger feeling for a pulse. She had to be alive if she were providing this much warmth, he thought, finding her thready pulse somewhere beneath her ear. Although she stirred, she did so only to cover more of him with a leg betwixt his and half of her torso over his chest. With the top of her thigh providing warmth to the one part of him he was just beginning to feel again, he felt compelled to wrap his free arm around her back and hold her in place.

Despite the unfortunate situation, he nearly laughed. If the chit had any idea of what she was doing—and with whom—she would certainly be mortified. His mirth changed to near-panic when he remembered more, though.

Shipwreck, he thought, sobering fast. His topcoat was no longer on his body. His only possessions of note might still be in his waistcoat, although he doubted his timepiece would have survived its drowning. His purse, usually in an inner pocket, contained all the money he'd brought to complete his purchase of the batteries and his passage home. As for his trunk with all his papers, well, it was no doubt at the bottom of the ocean with the rest of *The Fairweather.*

Fairweather, indeed.

He wondered if anyone aboard knew what had taken down the small ship. The rogue waves had come out of nowhere, although they had done so with other ships in the same vicinity with enough frequency he shouldn't feel too surprised at having been caught in one. The Countess and Earl of Everly had died in such a wreck, their ship on its way back to England after their Grand Tour. One of his mates from his days at Oxford had gone missing while on just such a trip. He was attempting to think of another when he realized the warm body he held was moving. The bent leg, nestled between his legs, seemed about to bend more. "Stop moving," he ordered, hoping his stern words would still Lady Samantha's movements.

They had the desired effect, for if they hadn't, he was quite sure he would be speaking in a much higher voice for a while.

The knee between his legs slowly straightened, and the head that rested in the small of his shoulder relaxed. Within moments, the marquess joined Lady Samantha in a fitful sleep.

CHAPTER 5

LAND, HO!

"Sail's up on the fore-mast!"

John St. John raised his eyes to the single cloud overhead and said a prayer of thanks. The sail, although not completely repaired, was already filling with the bit of breeze ruffling the sea. "Let's see if we can't make it to …" He had to stop and think of where they might find a dock with the capability of replacing a mast. He knew they were well beyond Cartagena, but probably not as far as Barcelona. Perhaps they were within easy reach of Valencia.

"Valencia?" Rodney offered from where he stood at the wheel.

St. John glanced up to where there should have been a wheelhouse—and all his maps and instruments. A few had been found strewn about the deck, but with three walls of the wheelhouse missing, he knew his maps were probably littering the bottom of the Mediterranean. "Valencia," he said with a nod. He raised his one remaining spyglass to his eye and slowly scanned the horizon for at least the tenth time that day. Although he thought he might have spotted something bobbing on the surface, he couldn't make out enough detail to determine just what it was. With six casks of brandywine missing from the deck, it could have been one of them.

A thorough search of the ship had determined Lady

Samantha Fitzsimmons and Ethan Range—*Lord Plymouth*, St. John corrected himself—were indeed missing. After his conversation with Lady Chamberlain, he was hoping the two would be found having an illicit *affaire* in the lower hold.

"She can swim," Lady Chamberlain had said, her lower lip quivering while her eyes brightened with unshed tears. "And I'm quite sure Lord Plymouth can as well," she added with a nod. "How far to the nearest land mass?"

The captain of *The Fairweather* stared at the viscountess, somewhat dumbstruck. Did she actually believe her niece had survived being tossed off a ship in the middle of a squall? But he dared not take away her hope—at least, not yet. "The Balearic Islands are fairly close," he offered.

Caroline Fitzsimmons' eyes widened. "Minorca? Majorca?" she countered.

St. John had to maintain an impassive expression despite being surprised by her knowing of the two nearby islands. "Yes. Have you ...?"

"The Earl of Everly recently returned from having spent a couple of months on Minorca. He's a bit of an explorer," the viscountess explained, a handkerchief pressed to one side of her nose. "Studies the birds, I think. Sam spent hours in his company, learning all about his discoveries."

Nodding his understanding, the captain considered the information. He glanced at where the walls of the wheelhouse used to stand. Realized they had been torn from the deck without having caused undue damage to the boards. And no damage to the wheel. They had to have landed in the water either as a U-shaped structure or ...

No. He considered the wall with the door near the middle. Perhaps the door would have been forced open by the water, allowing the wheelhouse to suddenly flood and the force of the water to lift the walls off the deck. That meant that two walls were probably still intact. Made entirely of wood, they would float, perhaps act as rafts.

Before he could allow himself the chance to consider what

might have happened to their missing passengers, his first mate called out. "Land, ho!"

Stunned, St. John stared at the man. "Rodney, so help me, if you're ..." He raised his spyglass to the west and suddenly quieted. "I'll be damned." Almost directly ahead, land appeared on the horizon.

So the storm *had* pushed them closer to land. Far closer than he had estimated earlier that morning. "Put up the flags," he ordered, knowing his men would raise the pennons indicating they were in distress.

"Aye, Cap'n."

St. John turned his attention back to Lady Chamberlain. Although she had followed his gaze to the west, she now regarded him with a raised brow. "Will you at least send word of their disappearance? Employ a courier? I would be willing to pay for news to be sent to my husband."

Nodding, Captain St. John said, "I will do that and more, my lady."

CHAPTER 6
NOTES FROM SPIES

"A courier from our northern route just delivered this, my lord," a clerk stated as he handed Matthew Fitzsimmons, Viscount Chamberlain, a neatly folded missive. Sealed with wax and stamped with a nondescript emblem, the note gave no hint as to its author until one noticed the feminine script on the front.

The viscount frowned. Not having any females agents under his supervision in the Foreign Office, he wondered who might have sent the note. "It's not addressed to me," he replied as he read the strange writing.

"Grenville is out this week. Some house party in Kent required his attendance. He asked that any missives from Yorkshire be directed to you," the clerk replied as he flipped through several more notes. "Oh, and here's another."

Matthew took the second note, an eyebrow arching when he recognized the writing as one of his agents in the Mediterranean. In the course of only six months, Alex Bradley, a former British naval officer, had managed to gain the trust of his fellow sailors and had been elected captain of the ship, *Molly*. Matthew wasn't particularly surprised by Bradley's quick promotion—he was trusted by his crew and was an excellent navigator—but the fact that the man could pass as a pirate was still a bit of a surprise to the viscount.

He opened the captain's note first, reading the scrawl that described Bradley's acquisition of several shipments of French liquor apparently destined for England.

I've reason to believe this batch would have made the trip via the Straights to the Channel and onto English shores as far north as Yorkshire.

Yorkshire?
Matthew wondered why a shipment—or several, it seemed—would be intended for a county so far north of London.
He read on.

Although I have no names to pass along at this time, I have reason to believe smugglers were to intercept the shipments and deliver them to a third party somewhere north of Scarborough.

Matthew sighed. No names meant the intelligence was just hearsay. Or information gleaned from having strong-armed a midshipman or cook on the ship from which the liquor was taken.

It was better than no information, though.

He gave a quick thought to what might be north of Scarborough. A bay where smugglers might have a hideout, he considered. A contact nearby who would see to the transfer of the liquor. A client for the liquor.

Whom could that be? he wondered. Someone running a gaming hell? A large pub? A public house? Or perhaps someone who could resell it at a tidy profit.

Setting aside the captain's note, he broke the seal on the second note and caught a whiff of perfume as he unfolded it. There was no salutation, but the feminine script didn't require the nicety.

After nearly a year, I can say with complete certainty that Plymouth is not our man. I have turned my attentions on another, a tradesman of some recent wealth from Whitby. Am working to gain his trust. Pillow talk to follow. D.

Blinking at the odd missive, Matthew raised his head and motioned for one of his clerks to join him. "Who the hell is 'D'?" he asked, *sotto voce*.

The clerk, Andrew Higgins, furrowed his bushy brows. "Home Office agent, I think." He held up a finger and returned to his desk, rifling through some papers before returning to Matthew's desk. "Daisy Albright. She's in the field. Yorkshire. Working on determining the head of a smuggling operation," he recited from the sheet he held up. "Her cover is ..." The man suddenly colored up. "She's a ... a mistress, my lord," Higgins finally managed to get out.

Leaning back in his leather chair, Matthew regarded the clerk for a moment. "Does this involve illegal liquor, perhaps?" he asked with a quirked lip.

The clerk nodded. "Indeed. Did you wish to send a response to Miss Albright?"

Matthew considered the question for a moment. He glanced over Alex Bradley's note and wondered if the two situations were related. "Find out who Grenville was reporting to," he ordered, once again wondering why the note from 'D' was given to him instead of someone in the Home Office. The coincidence seemed too good to be true. "I think this is one of those situations where the Foreign Office and the Home Office will have to work together."

"Yes, my lord," Higgins replied, hurrying out the door to complete the errand.

Rereading Daisy Albright's note, Matthew realized the 'Plymouth' she referred to had to be the Marquess of Plymouth. Why anyone would suspect the marquess to be involved in a smuggling scheme was beyond the viscount's comprehension. Ethan Range, Marquess of Plymouth, was the last man Matthew would implicate in anything illegal. The marquess rarely ventured to London, and when he did, he favored Boodle's over White's, eschewed the races and probably never set foot in a gaming hell. The owner of several coal mines along with thousands of acres of agricultural land and his estate home, Castle Keys, Lord Plymouth certainly wouldn't risk it all by becoming involved in the illegal importation of liquor.

Would he?

Plymouth had been at the docks in Wapping less than a week ago, boarding *The Fairweather* just as Matthew was saying his farewells to his wife and niece. "A bit too late to be taking your Grand Tour, wouldn't you say?" Matthew asked as he held out his hand to Ethan Range.

"Rather wish I was, but it's business. I need to see a man in Como about some batteries for miners' lamps."

Matthew furrowed his brows. "Certainly you could have Wellingham see to importing them for you. Save you the trip," he suggested, realizing the marquess referred to the devices that allowed a miner's lamp to provide light without the need for an open flame.

Several years earlier, Italian Count Allessandro Volta had developed the voltaic pile, a battery that could provide power for lamps. Matthew wondered if the marquess intended to transport the devices back to England and hoped he had other plans for their delivery—the viscount had heard they could be quite hazardous.

Plymouth seemed surprised by the suggestion. "Wellingham?" he repeated.

"Wellingham Imports," Matthew responded. "Earl of Trenton's cousin runs the place. Takes orders for products from all over the world and arranges for their acquisition and delivery."

Ethan paused then, as if he were reconsidering his trip to Italy. He shook his head, though, and sighed. "I can at least get the process started," he replied. "And I shouldn't be gone long. Thank you for the suggestion." He gave the viscount a nod and continued on his way up to the ship.

Matthew watched the marquess before turning back to his wife and niece. "Ladies, it seems you'll be in the company of a marquess on this trip." His arched eyebrow was directed in Lady Samantha's direction. "Not too much flirting now, or I'll have to join you in Italy sooner than planned," he warned with a grin. He pressed his forehead to his wife's forehead and finally kissed her on the lips, shocking her and Samantha. Then he gave Samantha a hug. "Take care of my love, won't you?" he said *sotto voce.*

His niece had grinned and nodded as a blush colored her face. "I will, Uncle Matthew."

Matthew took a deep breath, wishing he had simply joined the two women onboard right then and there instead of assigning Charles Fuller to keep an eye on them. The agent had recently married and wished to take his wife on a wedding trip; the assignment proved a boon to both parties.

Needing a few more days to clear up some matters, Matthew had returned to Whitehall and his duties. In a few days, he would be on a ship bound for Rome to rendezvous with the ladies. The week until he arrived would allow the two women to spend some time together shopping and sight-seeing.

The viscount was pulled from his reverie by the clerk who had taken his leave only moments before. "You wished to know to whom Grenville was reporting, my lord," the short man began in preamble. "He reports directly to Mr. Branaugh."

Matthew didn't bother to hide his surprise. "The Home Secretary?" he replied, straightening in his chair.

"Indeed, my lord. I believe he's expecting a visit from you."

Giving the clerk a nod to dismiss him, Matthew wondered what had William Branaugh involving him in a matter clearly of a domestic nature. "I'll make my way there now," Matthew promised, reaching for the missives and the dossier he had on Alexander Bradley.

Matthew made his way out of the Foreign Office building and headed down Whitehall. He had an appointment with the Home Secretary.

CHAPTER 7

WAKING UP TO WATER,
WATER EVERYWHERE

Fingers delved into her hair, a thumb caressed her cheek and a sudden movement beneath her right cheek had Samantha slowly opening her eyes. She really would have to have a word with her new maid as to the proper way in which to wake her in the mornings. *Simply opening the drapes would do the trick*, she thought as she regarded her counterpane.

Except that it wasn't her counterpane.

The brocade of intricate design had her blinking awake, and the fingers in her golden brown hair suddenly pulled out. Lifting her head, she realized to whom the waistcoat belonged just before she felt the rolling motion beneath the wood on which she and the marquess rested.

"I would say, 'Good morning,' but I am not yet sure if it will be," Ethan managed to get out in a croak, his vocal chords obviously protesting the gulps of seawater he had tried to avoid swallowing. "No sudden movements," he added in a whisper, "Or we'll have seawater washing over us."

Samantha's green eyes widened, but she nodded her understanding at the same time she realized where her left knee was—indeed, where her entire body was with respect to the hard body she was molded against. "Where ... where are we?" she whispered, suppressing the urge to cough. The back of her throat felt dry and abraded.

"I'm hoping somewhere near Spain," Ethan replied, daring to lift his head. In the gloom of early morning, it was hard to distinguish where the water met the sky. "Do you see ... anything?" he asked, realizing she had a slight advantage. Despite how Samantha had nestled against his chilled body and provided enough warmth to keep him drowsy but awake, Ethan was so stiff he could barely move his limbs. The air temperature wasn't the least bit cold, but his damp clothing made it seem so. He hoped that once the sun climbed higher, the heat would warm him enough so he could see to getting them to a land mass. From what the captain had said the day before, they shouldn't be too far off the western coast of Spain.

Samantha slowly lifted herself on her elbow, conscious of leaving her knee exactly where it was or risk the marquess noting her impropriety. Her quick glance around their makeshift raft—deep blue water as far as she could see—had her feeling a bit queasy. Closing her eyes, she tamped down the sensation and was suddenly aware of bird song. "We must be close to land," she said as she turned her attention to the marquess, his face mere inches below hers. His lower face was covered in dark stubble, and his hair was matted, but his eyes were open and nearly black in the dim light.

She reached out with her free hand and gently combed her fingers through his silken hair, forgetting for a moment who he was. Who she was. What he had called her only the night before. She had never in her life been this close to a man, never been pressed against one in such an intimate manner. Despite his layers of clothing—he still wore his shirt, waistcoat and breeches—she was quite conscious of her missing petticoats. At least she still wore her gown and corset, and as near as she could tell, her stockings and half-boots. *Pantaloons?* She wasn't yet sure and probably wouldn't be until she had an opportunity to shake out her skirts. Her sodden silk gown would no doubt appear translucent once the sun lit the sky, but there was nothing she could do to hasten its drying, especially since she needed the warmth of his body. "I hear birds," she said in a quiet voice.

Ethan moved his free hand to wrap around her wrist, but he

didn't move it from where it pressed against the side of his head, leaving her fingers threaded in his hair. He closed his eyes a moment, thinking he had merely had a nightmare. When he woke up he would find his mistress nestled against him.

Except he knew he wouldn't.

Daisy had accepted someone else's offer of employment. Despite his having offered to continue to pay the lease on her townhouse and see to some pin money and her modiste's bill every month, another man—Myles Longburn, a man engaged in trade—had apparently offered Daisy enough jewelry and a larger townhouse to lure her away from him.

He had felt betrayed by her unexpected traitorous act, of course. Although he could have made a counteroffer for her services, he was so offended she would throw him over for another, especially for a man who was wealthy because of his coal mines, Ethan had simply bid her farewell and reminded her she needed to be out of his townhouse within the week.

The look of hurt on her face had transformed to one of hate so quickly, he wondered how he had allowed her to warm his bed for nearly a year. So stunned was she by his response, she had pulled her shoulders back and stalked out the door of Castle Keys as if she had received the cut direct. Which she had, in a way, he supposed.

He thought almost immediately he might miss her, that he might yearn for her slight body in his bed, for the touch of her slender fingers over his chest and abdomen, for the feel of her tongue on his nipples and along the whorls of his ears, but he found he felt a bit of relief at her departure.

Too hard to please and too demanding, Daisy Albright was better off with her wealthy tradesman, he decided.

A few moments on the pisté with his manservant—Ethan had been careful not to skewer the poor man with his foil— and a glass or two of scotch, and he was quite over the ungrateful bitch. At least, that's what he told himself.

The sound of a gull brought him out of his reverie. The woman he held against him now wasn't mistress material, of course. In fact, when he suddenly remembered who she was, how she had slapped him only the night before, he nearly jerked from her grasp. But then her warmth would be gone, he realized, as would her slender fingers and the look on her face that had him thinking she might be about to kiss him. *This isn't exactly the time or place for seduction,* he thought, *but I certainly wouldn't mind if she made the attempt.*

What else did he have to do at the moment?

Until the bird song was closer or the sky was lighter, he wasn't about to raise himself from the raft to look for land. He rather doubted he had the strength to swim just then.

Samantha regarded the marquess for a long time, wondering why he hadn't said anything in response to her comment. Certainly the sound of birds was a sign they were near land. Harry Tennison, Earl of Everly and Lady Evangeline's brother, had described in great detail his recent trip to the island of Minorca. She had listened to his recitation, amused at how excited he could be about the flora and fauna —especially the birds—of a small island off the coast of Spain.

She wondered if she could ever share in his excitement at having discovered something new and different. If she would ever be invited to join him on one of his scientific expeditions. Be invited because she was his wife, and he would have decided to take her with him instead of leaving her behind in London for months at a time. Take her with him because he valued her company. Longed for her to spend his nights with her by his side.

Samantha wondered why Evangeline Tennison Sommers was so sure Lord Everly would one day propose to her. The young matron did claim her brother appreciated Samantha's intelligence and interest in his adventures. Perhaps Evangeline thought Samantha's willingness to join the earl on his travels and assist him with his scientific studies would endear him to her.

But after the earl's return from Minorca, Lord Everly still treated Samantha as a younger sister—and despite trying to imagine him as a partner on future adventures, as a lover and as her husband, Samantha found she could think of Harry Tennison as nothing more than an older brother.

Stunned by the realization, Samantha had shed a few tears. The sense of loss had been transformative. After four Seasons and not a single proposal—at least, none that she could take seriously—spinsterhood loomed for her. *On the shelf,* she was sure she heard in the whispers overheard at *ton* events.

"Who are you thinking about?" Ethan whispered, his sore throat preventing him from saying the words louder than a whisper.

Startled from her thoughts about the earl, Samantha brushed her thumb along Lord Plymouth's temple, smoothing an errant hair from his face. "Lord Everly," she replied with a shake of her head.

The mention of an aristocrat wasn't what he expected her to say.

Everly?

"Harrison Tennison?" he whispered in reply. He knew the man from Oxford. *A couple of years younger than me and a rather odd duck.*

A clever, odd duck.

Samantha nodded. "He's an earl."

Ethan stared at Samantha for a moment, schooling his features to remain as impassive as possible. No need to have the chit guessing he disliked the Earl of Everly. *Wasn't he an explorer now? Why ever would she be thinking of him right now?*

"He just returned from Minorca," Samantha explained, unaware of his uncharitable thoughts of the earl. "He told me all about the island." When she noticed his grimace in the brighter light—the sun had just cleared the horizon—she added, "He's my best friend's brother ... rather like a brother to me, as well," she murmured.

Rather surprised at the sense of relief he felt, Ethan raised his eyebrows. "And what, pray tell, does Minorca have to do with *us?*" he wondered, his voice cracking from dryness.

Samantha allowed a wan smile. "You were the one who said we were probably off the west coast of Spain."

Ethan furrowed his brows and then his eyes widened. "I take it Minorca is an island off of Spain?" he half-questioned. Geography hadn't exactly been his favorite topic at Eton or at Oxford.

Samantha nodded. "There are many islands, however," she warned with a careful shake of her head. At the sensation of dull pain, she remembered the bump on the back of her head. At least it didn't have her feeling too queasy. The gentle motion of the water beneath them was doing a fine job of it all on its own.

Ethan raised his hand to the side of her face, threading his fingers into her golden brown hair and pulling her down so their foreheads touched. Although her lips barely made contact with his, he lifted his head and captured hers in a kiss. Gentle at first, he pulled her closer with his other arm, moving her so she was nearly atop him, his lips continuing to caress hers in light, feathery kisses. "I should apologize," he whispered against her lips, expecting at any moment she would come to her senses, pull away suddenly and slap him across the face for his rakish behavior. If he hadn't been so chilled, he was sure he would feel the lingering sting of the slap she had landed on him the night before.

"Oh, please, don't," Samantha replied in the same manner, capturing his lips with her own to return the favor. She felt his heart hammering beneath her breast, and reveled in the sensation of warmth that spread throughout her entire body.

Ethan ended the kiss but left his forehead touching hers. *Christ!* How had she known what he needed just then? The warmth of a soft woman pressed against him, the excitement of an impromptu kiss? Daisy would never have allowed him the intimacy.

Especially first thing in the morning.

But Samantha? *She was an enigma.* Gently bred, niece of an aristocrat, long out of the schoolroom and yet still unmarried. A bastard.

And ever so willing!

Her kiss had his entire body feeling warm, even his feet, which for some time he thought might have suffered from frostbite given how cold they had been when he lost his boots. His cock, until then a part of his body he couldn't yet feel, was suddenly making its presence known in how it throbbed against the fall of his breeches and into Samantha's soft belly. Her arched eyebrow told him she was well aware of his reaction to her. Her lips on his told him she was ... *thankful?*

Well, probably not, but he could allow himself the pleasant thought for just a moment more. Another moment before the sun completely lightened the sky and he would have to devote his attention to getting them to dry land.

And finding fresh water.

"Who has been the beneficiary of your kisses in the past?" he wondered, moving his free hand to slide along her neck, one finger tracing its way to her collarbone.

Samantha smiled, her eyebrows arched in surprise. "I have never kissed anyone before. At least, not like this," she said with a slight shake of her head. A curtain of golden brown hair slid down one side of her face, hiding them from the sun's rays.

The marquess gave her a look of disbelief. "You expect me to believe I am the first man you have ever kissed?" he countered, his manner more teasing than serious.

Her green eyes darkening, Samantha's smile turned sultry. "You are an excellent instructor," she whispered before capturing his firm lips with her own.

How easy this is! she thought, feeling joy for the first time in months. The tip of her tongue touched his teeth, pulling away when his tongue suddenly joined hers to taste and tease. She tensed at the same time his hold tightened on her waist, as if he thought she might push away from him. But she relaxed against him, felt her insides turn to liquid and her breasts swell. Her breaths, nearly ragged as her excitement increased, sounded loud in her ears. Or perhaps that was her pulse pounding. She found she didn't care. As long as she could keep her lips angled over his, she felt warm. Welcome, wonderful warmth.

A gentle pressure from his hand against her shoulder brought her back from the pleasure.

"My lady, I ..," Ethan whispered, breathless.

I ... what?

I won't be able to control myself for one moment more if you do not cease your kissing? Christ! He had almost thought his body on the verge of death before she suddenly brought it back to life with her gentle kisses. His entire body seemed to heat from the inside, warming his feet and hands so he could once again feel them.

"Mmm," Samantha murmured as she finally pulled her lips from his and dropped her head to his shoulder. "Had I known how warm that would make me feel, I would have tried it hours ago," she murmured with a slight chuckle. After a few seconds, she suddenly gasped and her eyes widened. "Oh, do forgive my impropriety," she whispered, her arm once again settling over his chest despite her words.

"Oh, I do," Ethan panted, giving her a reassuring tug about the waist. *I'm not sure anyone else will, but then who would ever know what we've been doing whilst floating on a makeshift raft somewhere in the Mediterranean Sea?*

Memories of the sudden storm the night before brought his mind into focus. The wave that had crashed over the small ship had been so high, and yet the wind hadn't yet been strong enough to set it off.

What else could have caused it?

A giant sea creature? A whale or a squid? He shuddered when he realized they could have ended up like Jonah.

He had heard tales of rogue waves, of ships suddenly swamped when the ocean rose up and dumped itself atop the deck. *Like that of The Earl and Countess of Everly's, when they were on their way back to England from their Grand Tour.* Perhaps their ship had sunk when struck by the same kind of wave as *The Fairweather* suffered.

Or perhaps *The Fairweather* was merely hit by the first wave from the brief storm that had already blown over and left a clear sky in its wake.

Ethan stretched out, testing his limbs to determine if anything hurt more than it should. His left arm, a bit numb, was trapped beneath Samantha. He bent it and pulled her against his body again. He kissed her on the forehead. "I have to beg forgiveness. I really must sit up and look about," he said, carefully lowering her to the wood planks as he reclaimed his arm from beneath her.

Samantha gave a nod and lowered her back to the solid raft. *My, but the man was an enigma.*

Raised an aristocrat, obviously well-educated, probably rich as Croesus and yet still unmarried. One minute a bastard and the next as polite as can be.

Her attention turned to the sky overhead, her gaze spanning the blue from horizon to horizon. Clear except for a few wisps of clouds, the day promised to be as warm as any they had experienced so far on their trip.

Ethan slowly raised himself on all fours and then onto his knees, conscious that any sudden movement might cause part of the raft to dip under the water's surface.

Scanning the horizon to his right and then to his left, he watched a bird as it flew nearby and then circled above them, its cry a welcome sound. When it flew off, Ethan followed its flight path toward the east, finally spotting the tops of a land mass above the waterline.

He smiled and turned his attention to Samantha. She was on her back, watching him with a smile that held more promise than it had any right. *Good God!* Did she have any idea how wanton she looked just then?

"What do you see?" she wondered, her eyelids heavy.

Desire rammed into Ethan. "Our immediate future," he said simply.

CHAPTER 8

WHEN MISSIONS COLLIDE

William Branaugh, Home Secretary, waved Matthew Fitzsimmons into his spacious office as he signed a series of documents held out to him by a bespectacled clerk. "Chamberlain. So good of you to join me," Branaugh said in greeting as he indicated the tufted leather chair facing him. The clerk gave the Home Secretary a bow and quickly took his leave of the ornately decorated office, closing the double doors behind him. The gold and scarlet Aubusson carpet, velvet drapes and mahogany furnishings reminded Matthew of a men's club without the haze of cheroot smoke in the air.

"Seems our offices may be investigating two sides of the same coin," Matthew replied as he took the proffered chair. He sat back and regarded the secretary with an arched eyebrow, the notes and dossier he had brought with him landing on his lap with a *thud*.

Branaugh nodded and leaned forward, his elbows resting on the edge of his modest mahogany desk. "I rather doubt Grenville would have made the connection as quickly as you did," he replied. "So it's just as well any missives from Albright landed on your desk."

Matthew angled his head to one side, wondering if the note from the female agent had been deliberately directed to him on the secretary's direction. "According to her current assignment, she's working undercover as a mistress," Matthew said, almost making the statement a question.

Leaning to one side to grab a crystal decanter of scotch, the Home Secretary nodded. "And rather effective in the role," he replied as he splashed a bit of the scotch into two tumblers. He offered one to Matthew, who took it with a nod. "Last I heard, she was doubting our original supposition that the Marquess of Plymouth was involved in a smuggling operation. It seems the rascals are operating off the Yorkshire coast somewhere near his lands, bringing in brandy and wine and apparently storing them in a sheltered cove."

Matthew shook his head. "Plymouth would never ..."

"Is that her latest letter?" Branaugh interrupted, holding out his hand.

Handing over the missive, the scent of perfume wafting through the air as he did so, Matthew took a deep breath and nodded. *Thank the gods Caroline doesn't wear that scent,* he thought as he wrinkled his nose in disgust.

Opening the note and giving it a quick read, Branaugh tossed it on his desk, oblivious to the cloying scent. "I agree. The marquess was an unlikely target, but we had to be sure. Daisy has obviously managed to gain a new contract with another person of interest." He pointed toward the dossier Matthew still held on his lap.

The viscount offered it to the Home Secretary, hoping he wouldn't regret sharing the information about his pirate in the Mediterranean.

"One positive about this operation is how inexpensive it is for us," Branaugh went on. "Plymouth paid for a townhouse for Albright. Gave her pin money. Been doing so for nearly a year now. It will be interesting to discover what her new target might be providing in the way of housing and compensation," he said as he wiggled his eyebrows.

Matthew frowned, wondering if Lord Plymouth had any idea the woman he had employed as a mistress was actually an agent of the Home Office. "Do you know the identity of this tradesman she refers to?" Matthew asked. He opened the note he had received from Alex Bradley and quickly reread it to himself.

"Not yet," Branaugh replied, as he briefly glanced at Alex Bradley's dossier. "Ah, our pirate," he commented before perusing a bit of the information. He tossed it back to Matthew and then reached over to take the letter Matthew offered. After a moment, he looked up suddenly. "Are you thinking Bradley has found the source of whatever is ending up in Yorkshire?" he asked as one eyebrow arched up in surprise.

"It would seem the two could be related," Matthew agreed. "But I'm not about to jump to any conclusions. Listen, I'll be leaving for Italy in a week. I can make arrangements to intercept Bradley and pass along any intelligence he might ..."

"No," Branaugh interrupted, his head shaking. "We'll allow him to continue raiding ships for their alcoholic cargo. See what he discovers about the intended clients," he stated. "He's bound to come across a shipment meant for Yorkshire."

Matthew bristled at the Home Secretary's words. The man spoke as if Alex Bradley worked for him rather than for the Foreign Office. "*I'll* see that he does then," the viscount agreed with a stiff nod. "In the meantime, should Miss Albright's 'pillow talk' reveal anything about this smuggling operation, could you see to it her missives are passed along to me? I'll be sure to give them back, of course."

Branaugh took a sip of his scotch, savoring the smoky flavor before giving the viscount a nod. "Of course," he replied. "So glad our two offices can cooperate on this little matter."

Nodding, Matthew stood up and gave the Home Secretary a bow. *Little matter?* If it were a 'little matter', their two offices wouldn't be involved at all! "Likewise, Home Secretary," he said as he took his leave of the office.

He was halfway back to the Foreign Office when he realized he hadn't even touched the glass of scotch.

CHAPTER 9

SAILING ON A SEA

"Are we moving in that direction?" Samantha asked as she slowly raised herself on her elbows in an attempt to see whatever it was that had Ethan's attention. She winced when she caught sight of the condition of her gown. Having been soaked with seawater and now partially dry, lines of salt had discolored the sapphire fabric. The ruffle at the bottom edge was torn a bit from the skirt, one sleeve had come loose from her bodice, and it was evident she no longer wore any petticoats beneath her skirt. A slight breeze caught her hair, sending tendrils in the direction of Lord Plymouth's gaze.

"I won't be able to tell for a time," he answered, positioning himself so he faced due east, silently cursing when he realized he would have preferred to find land to the west. Any land to the east of them meant an island rather than the mainland.

Samantha slowly sat up straighter, careful not to rock the raft. Reaching for the hem of her gown, she freed it from beneath her ankles and pulled it up, allowing the slight breeze to fill the fabric much like a sail. She would have gathered up more and held it higher, but she dared not expose her legs above the knees where the tops of her stockings were still tied. The ribbon ties had since become knotted, which she supposed was a good thing. At least they hadn't come loose in the water. She couldn't imagine what it would have been like to have her stockings fall to the tops of her boots.

"We're moving," the marquess announced suddenly. He looked down and realized why. "Oh," he remarked as Samantha raised her eyes to meet his. "Have you done this before?" he wondered, working the buttons open on his waistcoat, thinking he could spread it open. He noticed a bulge behind an inner pocket. *My purse? Is it possible there are still some coins inside?*

Samantha had to bite back a giggle. She supposed she had allowed her skirts to billow about her whilst running in an open field as a child, but she had never done it on open water before. "Not quite like this," she finally admitted, wondering what had his attention. "What do you have there?" she asked when she noticed him take something from his waistcoat pocket.

"My purse," he answered in a quiet voice. He pulled open the strings and let out a whoop of joy. "Seems we've some coin. Should be more than enough to get us back to England should we find someone willing to take us," he murmured. He tucked the purse back into the pocket and tugged the waistcoat back onto his body. He spread it open, hoping to achieve a bit of a sail effect much like Samantha was doing with her skirts.

Something solid landed against his thigh, and he looked down to find his pocket watch dangling from its chain. Lifting it carefully, afraid it might come loose and drop into the water, Ethan popped open the hinged lid. Although the timepiece no longer worked—it had stopped at eight-thirty—the crystal wasn't broken. Allowing a wan smile, Ethan slipped it back into its pocket, ensuring the chain was still clipped to his waistcoat. He had lost his boots, lost his topcoat, but somehow his purse and chronometer remained with him.

Feeling a bit of relief, he glanced back down at Samantha, surprised at her lack of fear, even more surprised by her sense of humor. Did she realize *The Fairweather* was no more? That her aunt—her *mother*—had no doubt perished in the cabin they shared?

He couldn't even be sure they would find a way to get back to the continent. Perhaps they would be set upon by highwaymen. Or perhaps they would be stuck on the approaching land mass for the rest of their lives. Although the thought should have chilled him, he didn't find it as daunting as he probably should have. So he wouldn't be in Yorkshire to oversee his marquessate. So he would be declared dead, and having no heirs, his title would simply revert to the Crown.

Would that really be so bad?

His responsibilities would belong to someone else. As would his lands and his home and all that mattered to him. Well, that would be a sorry loss, he considered.

And what of his companion in survival? Would Lady Samantha break down in a fit of vapors and waste away at the loss of her life in London?

Ethan glanced down at her, noted how she seemed to regard their situation as just another day in her life. He wondered if she was the sort of chit who simply took everything in stride. Perhaps she did.

Or perhaps she's in shock, he thought suddenly. Once she realized their dire situation, she would probably panic. Maybe turn into a blubbering idiot. Possibly get them both killed.

He dared another glance in her direction. She seemed ... fine. Alert and interested, in fact.

Ethan glanced back toward the island, surprised to see there was more land than he first realized. In the growing light of dawn, a curving white sand beach spread out before them. Some kind of greenery lay beyond the beach, and rocks jutted up beyond that. It was then he realized that the land mass he had first spotted was actually north of the island they approached. "I think there's another island," he said, excitement tingeing his voice.

"If we're truly west of Spain, there will be an entire chain of them," Samantha replied, turning her attention to the water below. Now that the sun had come up completely, she could see the ocean's bottom not far down. An odd movement caught her eye, and she followed a translucent creature as it undulated, moving in the same direction as their raft. Lord Everly had described just such a creature when he told her of the wonders of Minorca. "Jellyfish," she breathed.

"What?" Ethan wondered as he tore his attention from the horizon. He followed her line of sight, swallowing hard when he noticed the strange movement. And the round blob with white tendrils streaming behind it. At first glance, he thought it looked like a mushroom.

"Jellyfish," Samantha repeated. "They sting, though," she warned suddenly, remembering Lord Everly's words. "We must take care not to startle them or step on them," she explained.

Ethan sighed. He was barefoot. He didn't relish the thought of having to wade through water that might contain stinging creatures. "I suppose Lord Everly told you about them," he commented with a hint of annoyance.

Samantha frowned at his tone of voice and wondered why he might sound cross. *Was the man jealous of the earl?* She allowed a shrug. "He did," she admitted finally. "He told me about the fish and the shrubs and the strange rocks and the freshwater springs and ..."

"Water?" Ethan repeated, his eyes widening. "How ... how will we find it?" he asked, his sudden movement causing the raft to dip down a bit. He moved backward on his knees and then slowly stood up.

"Careful," Samantha whispered, noting how his side of the raft angled downward. "I expect we'll hear the springs before we see them," she said in answer to his question.

When the forward motion of the raft suddenly stuttered, Ethan nearly pitched forward. "Damnation!" he cursed. He caught himself before falling into the water, but when the raft stopped completely, he was forced to step forward. He landed calf deep in the icy water, the bottom of the wood planks catching in the sand and sea grass.

Samantha dropped her skirt and scooted to the edge of the raft. "Is it truly only that deep?" she wondered, concerned because the beach still seemed a long way off.

"Well, it is right here," Ethan said with some hesitance. He took some tentative steps, his gaze settling on the sand just ahead of him.

Without his weight, the raft once again moved freely, continuing on a course toward the white sandy beach. Ethan walked alongside, carefully placing his feet so as to not step on a sea creature. Once the raft caught again on the sea grass that seemed to grow in round patches out of the sand below, he paused and regarded Samantha.

"Stay there," he ordered, setting off to continue toward the beach. Twice he stopped as jellyfish moved by. A fish startled him enough that he nearly pitched sideways, his arms flailing at his sides as he did his best to keep his balance.

Once the water only covered his feet, he turned to motion to Samantha. She was already in the water, though, her skirts hitched up to her thighs, carefully picking her way toward the beach. *At least she's wearing boots*, he thought as he watched. With her hair down past her shoulders and her gown in disarray and the tops of her stockings peeking below the edge of her ruffled gown, she looked like some kind of nymph. *A rather naughty nymph*, Ethan thought with a grin.

"Watch out for the jellyfish," he called out, suddenly conscious of several taking interest in his own feet. He continued onto the dry sand, his feet welcoming the warmth of the pristine beach, and he said a prayer of thanks.

CHAPTER 10

A VERY LONG BEACH

The first day on the island
        Ethan stood on the strip of beach, its pristine white grains of sand so fine they shifted easily beneath his feet. He regarded their surroundings with a good deal of disappointment. Although the white sand of the beach was beautiful—it stretched in a wide arc in both directions and would have been a welcome sight for any aristocrat visiting a summer retreat— it offered nothing in the way of shelter. Beyond the beach were small shrubs that seemed to give off a familiar scent, and beyond them ... well, he would have to hike a bit to discover where this land mass ended and how far it might be to the one beyond it.

"We may find a spring nearby."

The marquess turned to find Samantha at his side, one gloved hand lifted to her brow to shade her eyes from the sun as she surveyed the horizon. Her reticule still hung from her other hand, its handle wrapped about her wrist. If any pins had remained in her hair after its thorough soaking in the ocean, they were now obviously out of her hair and probably tucked away in the reticule. The golden brown locks, nearly dry, hung well below her shoulders in waves, waves that turned into soft curls at the ends. And despite her dinner gown's dunking, the dress didn't appear too badly damaged, although salt water streaks were faintly visible in the sapphire blue silk.

Ethan wondered at her half-boots. Slippers would have been more appropriate with the dinner gown, he supposed, but who was he to wonder about women's fashion? He only knew what he knew because of Daisy.

"I put them on after dinner for the walk on the deck," Samantha said, realizing the marquess was staring at her feet and probably wondering why she was wearing footwear more suitable with a walking ensemble. Realizing her lower legs were still exposed, she hurried to untie the skirts of her gown and shook them out, a blush coming over her face as she did so.

"You needn't have done that on my account," Ethan said with a smirk, his attention back on the landscape.

Samantha regarded him for a moment, wondering what he thought of the sight of her bare legs. *Did he find them offensive?* From his comment, she thought perhaps he didn't.

She was about to ask—she often wondered how her legs might be viewed by a member of the opposite sex—when the marquess seemed to read her mind. "I admit to liking the sight of a well-turned ankle. Since you're wearing boots, I can only imagine them, but given the length and curves of your limbs, I'm imagining ..." He stopped, suddenly aware the topic of conversation was most inappropriate. *Good God!* What was it about the chit that had him saying things he had no business saying?

"Something like this?" Samantha asked as she presented a bare foot from beneath the hem of her gown. She had pulled off the wet boot with the help of her other booted foot, anxious to get her feet into what she thought would be warm sand. Lord Everly had regaled her with stories of the fine, white sand that rimmed the island of Minorca, telling her of his long days spent barefoot as he studied the birds and plants. Judging from the pleasant sensation created when the sand pushed up between her toes, she could understand why he would elect to go barefoot. She worked to remove the other boot without bending over, temporarily pulling her foot from view.

The Marquess of Plymouth blinked at her, stunned by her brazenness. "Indeed," he remarked with an arched brow, wondering if she were teasing him. He was suddenly aware she was removing her other boot behind the ruffle of her skirt. "Are you sure that's wise?" he queried, staring down at his own feet half-buried in the pristine sand.

"Lord Everly claims he spent most of his time on Minorca barefoot," she countered, giving the marquess a quick glance. Although his dark hair was a bit ruffled from their ordeal and his feet and lower legs were bare, he appeared every bit a gentleman, she thought. His chronometer, attached to a chain and secured to his waistcoat pocket, even looked undamaged.

"I'm afraid it's no longer functioning," Ethan said as he reached for the gold disc, pushing the small catch that allowed the lid to pop open.

Samantha gave a start. Could the man read her mind? It was if he had a ready answer for anything she was thinking!

"I saw you looking at it," he added when he noticed her surprise at his comment.

Lifting an eyebrow, Samantha allowed a grin. "I didn't mean to stare. I was just ... surprised to see you would still have it after ... after what happened," she said by way of explanation.

Ethan gave a nod and motioned to her reticule. "I see you didn't seem to lose anything," he countered.

Samantha turned her attention to her handbag, unwinding the tie so she could remove it from her wrist. She, too, had been surprised at finding it hanging from her wrist, the handle so twisted it had nearly cut off her circulation. Once she had it open on the raft, she found everything intact, although soaked. Thank heavens for her comb. She had pulled out the remaining pins from her hair and managed to get the snarls out of her wet hair before the warming air dried it completely. She had intended to pin it back up, but without the benefit of a way to balance her small looking glass, she rather doubted she could do a decent job of it. "I didn't seem to," Samantha agreed, pulling the gathers open. "But there's not much, I'm afraid, although I do have a pair of embroidery scissors, a small mirror, a comb and a couple of handkerchiefs. Oh, and a knife," she added as she pulled out a folding knife, its handle made of rather ornate ivory.

Stunned by the comment, Ethan furrowed his brows. "A *knife*, did you say?" he wondered as he reached for it.

Samantha sighed. "My aunt ..." She stopped, suddenly remembering their conversation from the night before. "My mother insisted I keep one handy, in case I was ever set upon by footpads."

Ethan gave her a nod. "Smart woman," he murmured, forgetting he was speaking of a woman who was no doubt in Poseidon's possession.

Glancing about, he spied a wood cask drifting toward the far edge of the beach. *The brandywine?* He supposed it made sense that a tub or two of the liquor would end up in the same place as they had. If there was one ... he surveyed the beach to the left and discovered two more barrels firmly ensconced in the sand.

"It must be low tide."

Ethan turned to find Samantha staring at the tubs. "If so, then those barrels may wash out sometime tonight," he replied.

"We should roll them up farther onto the beach," Samantha suggested, "Just in case we're not able to find water right away."

Ethan nodded his agreement, and they made their way to the casks.

"Rosemary," Samantha said as she detoured to one of the many bushes that dotted the landscape. Leaning down, she sniffed the leaves and plucked a twig. When she noticed Ethan regarding her with a quizzical expression, she said, "Definitely rosemary."

Ethan arched a brow, realizing it had to be the scent he recognized when he had first come ashore. "If we find something to eat, then I suppose we'll have seasoning," he remarked, leaning down to place a hand against one of the brandywine casks. He gave an experimental push. Although it was heavier than he expected, he was able to push his shoulder into the wood and roll the barrel a few feet farther up the beach and into a thicket of bushes loaded with berries. A few birds squawked and flew off, startling him.

Samantha bent over and regarded the berries, taking one between her thumb and forefinger. She pulled it from its branch and studied it in the palm of her gloved hand.

"Is it edible, do you suppose?" Ethan wondered, his stomach grumbling at the thought of food.

Before she answered, Samantha popped the berry into her mouth and bit into it. A tart juice sprayed over her tongue, the flavor not at all unpleasant. "I think so. The birds eat them, so we should be able to," she surmised.

Frowning, Ethan helped himself to a couple of the berries and hesitated before popping them into his mouth. "Here's to hoping these aren't poisonous," he said. He walked back to the other brandywine barrel and struggled to move it.

"May I help?" Samantha asked as she moved to stand next to him.

Ethan sighed, thinking she might be hurt should the tub roll forward. But before he could put voice to his concern, she lowered herself, placing her hands where the barrel rested in the sand. When he realized she was going to help whether he allowed her to or not, he put his shoulder into the barrel and pushed at the same time she lifted. With a creak, the cask rolled a quarter turn before coming to a halt. The two worked it free to roll it up next to the other. Even before Ethan could catch his breath, Samantha was plucking berries from the bush. She offered him a handful.

"Thank you, my lady," he said as he finished them off. He watched as she helped herself to a few, although she ate only a few at a time.

"Do you fish?" Samantha asked suddenly.

Ethan blinked, wondering at the odd question. "I have on occasion," he replied.

"Hmm," she replied, glancing around. Not finding any branches long enough to use for a pole, she said, "I'll keep a lookout for something you can use. If we can't find anything more substantial than berries, we'll need to eat fish," she explained.

About to remind her they didn't have any string to use for line, Ethan thought it better not to dissuade her from the mission. If she had projects to occupy her time, she would be less likely to ruminate on their situation, less likely to realize they might be in danger or that they might have to stay on the island for a few hours before being rescued by a passing ship.

He turned around to concentrate on the horizon. As Ethan slowly scanned the line where the turquoise and deep blue water met blue sky, he was certain he would see a ship pass by. Even if he did, though, he wasn't sure how he would signal it. Although the island was covered in plenty of small shrubbery, he wasn't sure it would burn. And, on that thought, he wondered if there might be something he could use to start a fire.

"Will these work, do you suppose?"

Startled from his reverie, Ethan turned to find Samantha with one hand held up. On her palm were two stones, one clearly suitable for use as a flint. Had she read his mind?

"Probably," he answered with a nod. "Where did you find these?"

Samantha pointed farther up hill from the beach. "There are rosemary bushes everywhere, and some wild garlic, too," she said with some excitement.

Ethan dared another glance at the water, realizing he would have better luck spotting a ship if he were higher up. "I suppose we should do a bit of exploring," he said as he took the stones and shoved them into his pockets. "Put your boots back on, and be careful where you step," he ordered as he turned to climb up the beach.

Grimacing, Samantha lowered herself to the sand and started to pull a boot back onto one foot as a wave washed up within a few feet of where she sat. The water moistened the sand and brought with it what appeared to be flotsam. Reaching out, she captured a parchment before the wave retreated, but in the process, part of her gown was doused by the wave.

Damnation!

She nearly said the word aloud. Her gown, nearly dry, was now once again wet. She hurried to pull on her other boot. As she did so, she noticed another parchment floating nearby. Once she had her boots laces tied, she captured the other piece of parchment and hurried up onto dry sand.

"What do you have there?" Ethan asked as he turned to find his fellow castaway once again wet but holding two sheets of soaked parchment.

"I think one is a map," she answered, holding out one of the dripping sheets for Ethan to take. She bent down and spread out the other on the sand, careful so as not to pull the edges too hard or risk pulling the fibers apart. Ethan sat on his haunches and did the same with the one she had given him, grunting when he had the corners spread out.

"Are these the islands you spoke of earlier?" he asked as he waved a hand over a string of land masses drawn out in colored inks. Around them were lines and arrows. The word 'Spain' was written at the top, but if a coastline had been included on the map, it was no longer visible.

Samantha turned her attention to the map and looked for the shape of Minorca, thinking she might be able to identify it from Lord Everly's drawings. Nothing looked familiar, though. "I'm not sure," she said with a shake of her head. "Although this could be Minorca," she guessed, pointing to one of the uneven circles. A small 'm', faded to the point of almost being invisible, was written in the middle. A larger shape nearby had a similar capital 'M' in its center. "Majorca," she guessed as she pointed to it. Dozens of other shapes nearby had no such identifying marks, either because they hadn't ever had them or because the ink had washed away.

Ethan glanced around, wondering if they could be anywhere near those land masses. Without a scale, though, he couldn't be sure how far away they might be. "What's on that one?" he asked after a moment, waving to the one Samantha had spread out on the sand.

"I'm not sure, but what do you make of this?" she asked,

indicating a series of numbers. "They look like they might be dates ... or times."

Ethan frowned and shook his head, squinting as he tried to make out what might have at one time been plainly printed on the sheet. "A diary, perhaps?"

Whatever information the sheet held was mostly washed away, but Samantha was able to make out a few entries. "Docked at Gilbraltar. Something ... provisions," she recited, shaking her head when she couldn't read the rest of the line. After a moment, she sighed. "It's a captain's log," she said with a hint of surprise.

"For *The Fairweather,*" Ethan guessed, noting the date next to the entry she had read matched the date when they had docked at the Straights of Gilbraltar. "We took on provisions there," he added.

Samantha shrugged. "Not much help for our situation, I'm afraid," she murmured as she moved to stand up. Ethan was quicker, though, holding out a hand to help her up. She took it, surprised by his firm grip and by the frisson that passed through her arm at his touch.

"Thank you, my lord," she said with a nod.

"Ethan," he responded, wondering why she would be surprised by his offer of assistance. "Given our circumstances, I think we can forgo the formalities."

Samantha regarded the marquess for a moment and then held out her right hand. "Samantha," she replied with a nod. "Or Sam, if you must."

The marquess shook her hand. "Samantha, then," he said with a grin.

She gave him a wan smile and shook out her wet gown, showering sand on her boots and on the captain's log. "Should we take them with us?" she wondered as she indicated the drying sheets.

"Probably not," Ethan replied with a shake of his head. "We best get going. We need to find water," he said.

Samantha noticed what appeared to be a clam shell and bent down to pick it up. Admiring the pattern of the scallops, she was about to toss it aside but thought better of it. When she noticed Ethan's quirked lip, she said, "You never know.

It might come in handy," she said as she shoved it into her reticule.

When Ethan's back was turned to begin the walk up the beach, Samantha reached down and picked up another.

CHAPTER 11

A MARQUESS REMEMBERS A VISIT

Twenty-three years before

"You stay away from the Fitzsimmons' place," Charles Xavier Range, Marquess of Plymouth, ordered, a thick finger pointed at his son. "They're bad *ton*, I tell you," he said, his head shaking as much as his finger.

Ethan Range regarded his father with wide eyes.

Bad ton?

Lady Elizabeth and her husband, Edward Fitzsimmons, seemed like genuinely nice people, although a bit on the eccentric side. Their modest estate abutted the lands of the Plymouth marquessate, the manor home in the middle of it known as Darbing Manor, although no one could remember anyone named 'Darbing' having owned it in the past. From what he had overheard when the adults spoke of it, Ethan was certain it was part of the property associated with a viscountcy. Since Edward Fitzsimmons wasn't a viscount—he wasn't anything as far as Ethan could tell, given his limited understanding of titles and such—he could only deduce Lady Elizabeth's family owned it and allowed the couple to live there.

Ethan thought perhaps the 'bad *ton*' reference was due to the couple's predilection for swimming at night in the small lake next to their manor house, a lake Ethan enjoyed on warm days in the summer. He had arrived a bit late for dinner, claiming he was detained because he had taken a swim with Lady Elizabeth. The news was not well received by his father, however; he had just suffered a dressing down as a result of his tardiness.

But his real reason for being late was because he had hidden for a time when Lady Elizabeth's sister, Caroline, arrived at Darbing Manor. Far prettier than her older sister, Lady Caroline was a young widow who had come to Yorkshire to, and Ethan was very sure he had heard this correctly, "Have my baby and claim it as yours."

Ethan had puzzled on this news for some time, for when he had asked as to why Lady Elizabeth seemed to be growing larger in front and no where else, his mother had explained Lady Elizabeth was expecting a baby before Christmas. "But you mustn't get your hopes up," she had whispered, knowing he would welcome a future playmate. "Mrs. Fitzsimmons has had a rough go of it and may lose the baby."

Lose the baby? As if she couldn't keep track of it? Ethan considered the Fitzsimmons behavior and decided that, yes, they would be capable of misplacing a baby.

Now that Lady Elizabeth was expecting a baby, she seemed prone to flights of fancy, skipping about her dining room as if she were some fairy princess. She did this wearing nothing more than her chemise and a tiara her husband had purchased for her because, and Ethan was quite sure he had heard this correctly, "You might be the mere daughter of an earl, but in my world, you are the queen."

The reason Ethan had heard the endearment was because he was hiding in the Darbing Manor sideboard at the time, one of his favorite places to stay when he visited the Fitzsimmons. Depending on how often his mother took him on calls, there were some weeks when he paid a call on the Fitzsimmons nearly every day. And sometimes he merely visited without telling anyone. It was on days such as that when he hid in cupboards and sideboards or under furniture, secretly pleased at how the adults never seemed to notice him as long as he remained very quiet in his hiding places. And they never seemed to notice him as they shared news or intimacies or secrets never intended for a young child to overhear. Learning Lady Caroline was expecting a baby was just such news. Ethan was rather pleased he seemed to be the only one to know of it.

"Oh, Plymouth, really," Margaret scolded her husband, "Ethan hardly understands matters of the aristocracy. He's only seven."

"Six," Ethan corrected his mother, almost immediately regretting having done so when his mother cast him a look of annoyance.

The marquess straightened at his carver and regarded his wife with a raised gray-streaked brow. "'Bout time he learned, don't you think?" he countered. "Seeing as how he'll be in charge of this God-forsaken place in not so many years."

Margaret Fitzwilliam Range straightened in her chair at the other end of the dining table and suppressed a sigh of frustration. Having been raised the daughter of an earl, she had been educated from an early age on the history of the royals and the peerage, and had spent many afternoons in the schoolroom at Fitzwilliam House in London poring over the pages of Debrett's *The New Peerage*. She was older than Ethan's age at the time, however.

Now the Marchioness of Plymouth and sequestered in a castle far from London, Margaret could barely remember the chits in whose company she had been presented to the queen. "I'll see to it when he's old enough to read, Plymouth," she assured her husband. She held his gaze a moment longer, giving him a cheeky wink and a suggestive grin.

Margaret knew exactly how to erase the scowl that was almost—almost—a permanent fixture on Charles' face.

Charles blinked. He blinked again, his sullen mood seeming to fall away with the prospect of bedding his wife later that night. Although he usually spent his entire day locked away in his study as he dealt with matters of the marquessate, Charles knew he could look forward to a good dinner—he claimed to employ the best cook in Yorkshire—and more often than not, a tumble with his willing wife.

The days he wasn't in his study were spent at the coal mines or in the fields with his tenants, and his late return often found the house quiet and Margaret asleep in her bed. A few kisses on her shoulder and neck, and soon Charles would be invited to join her. Once there, he spent the entire night, relishing in the warmth of her body pressed against his.

Charles often wondered what might have been had Margaret not agreed to be his wife. If she had to do it over again, he was quite sure she would elect to remain in the Marriage Mart in the hopes of landing a husband who would spend time in London for at least the Season each year. By agreeing to be his wife, though, she had relegated herself to life in a gloomy pile near the rocky cliffs and the promise of only sporadic trips to London. She made his life tolerable by giving him something to look forward to, and she had already given him an heir. But best of all, she never complained about living at Castle Keys.

Other than whatever it was his mother implied with her wink in his father's direction, Ethan soon learned he had nothing to look forward to in terms of his inheritance. Hearing his father's frequent rants and paying witness to the man's almost permanent scowl, Ethan realized the marquessate was riddled with problems, from the frequent accidents at the coal mines to the issues with the tenants who farmed the lands.

At least their home, Castle Keys, an entailed structure in the Plymouth holdings, seemed in good repair. Despite its age—his mother claimed it had been built over several decades sometime in the Middle Ages—Castle Keys had housed generations of the Range family. From the portraits that lined the gallery in the west hall, though, none of the previous marquesses seemed particularly happy to hold their titles. Indeed, from the blank stares and familiar scowls depicted in the paintings, Ethan realized his portrait would probably appear a copy of those already there.

"Do you like living here, mum?" he remembered asking his mother one afternoon, a particularly gloomy day when rain threatened an already chilly day.

Margaret Fitzwilliam Range set aside her embroidery, an

exquisite rendering of a floral arrangement, and regarded her son with a wan smile. "Of course, darling," she had answered, spearing her fingers through his dark hair to ruffle it. "What girl doesn't dream of living in a castle?"

But Ethan couldn't help but notice her wistful expression, as if she said one thing but meant quite another. "I like Darbing Manor better," he murmured, his voice kept low so as to not be overheard by a passing servant.

His mother smiled then, understanding her son's comment. "It is a bit ... brighter, isn't it?" she replied with a sigh. "How is Lady Elizabeth doing these days?" she asked then, wishing she hadn't been forbidden from paying calls on the woman who sometimes behaved like a Bedlamite.

Ethan's eyes widened as he wondered if he should share one of his secrets. "She's expecting a baby again, so her sister came from London," he replied finally. "A widow."

Margaret's expression changed suddenly, her brows furrowing as if she were concerned. "Again?" she whispered. "Poor thing." Elizabeth had never delivered a living child, most of her pregnancies ending in miscarriage or, in one instance, a stillbirth. "At least she has her sister. Do you know which one came?" she wondered, thinking she would attempt to arrange a meeting somewhere other than Darbing Manor.

"Lady Elizabeth calls her 'Caro'," Ethan replied carefully, not having been formally introduced to the young woman with the golden brown hair and green eyes. He had only spied her from his hiding place beneath a Grecian chaise lounge.

A mix of surprise and sadness crossed his mother's face just then. "Lady Caroline," she whispered. "Married for all of a week, I think." Certainly not a marriage approved by her father, given the man was in the military.

"Is she bad *ton*, too, mum?" Ethan wondered, hoping she wasn't so he could use her as an excuse to continue visiting Darbing Manor without having to hide whilst doing so.

The Marchioness of Plymouth gave her son a wan smile. "Since she didn't marry an aristocrat, then I suppose she is," she said with a heavy sigh, her head shaking.

Ethan thought perhaps his mother wished Lady Caroline had married an aristocrat, if for no other reason than she, too, could pay a call on the woman without earning her husband's wrath.

Given the situation, he didn't tell his mother Caroline was expecting a baby. He figured she would simply hear of it while paying calls on others in the area.

So, it was a bit of a surprise when a few months later, word came to Castle Keys that, with the help of Lady Caroline, a girl had been born to Lady Elizabeth and her husband.

Nothing more was said about Caroline's baby. However, when Ethan spied her walking with her sister around the small lake as Elizabeth cried and lamented the loss of her baby, Ethan couldn't help but notice Caroline no longer appeared as overweight as she had the week before.

CHAPTER 12

EXPLORING AN ISLAND

*L*ater, on the first day on the island

"I cannot imagine why women dampen their gowns for balls," Samantha said as they made their way inland. Despite her half-boots, she was careful where she stepped, afraid a slippery rock might cause her to fall, or a shrub might catch on her gown and cause it to tear more than it already was. The silk was already damaged enough from seawater.

"They do it to show off their limbs," Ethan replied, not realizing Samantha meant the comment to be rhetorical. "Knowing the male of our species are usually attracted to females with long limbs," he added at her look of annoyance.

Are you? she almost asked, curious as to what the marquess found attractive in a female. And then she found herself wondering if her limbs were considered long. She was about to ask when Ethan suddenly grinned. "Yes, and yes," he said with a nod.

Samantha frowned. "What?" was all she could think to say in response, her face suddenly colored with a pink blush.

Ethan allowed a smirk. "Yes, I am rather attracted to women long of limb, and yes, yours certainly seem to be," he remarked, noting how pretty his companion appeared with a slight blush on her cheeks. That pink blush would no doubt turn more red as the day progressed if he couldn't figure out a way to create some shade for her. The June sun would burn her peaches and cream complexion in a matter of minutes.

Jerking her head to regard him, Samantha wondered how the marquess could have known what she was thinking. And she couldn't help but notice he didn't actually come right out and say he was attracted to *her*. "I would have thought men preferred a more ... *petite* woman," she replied, deciding the marquess hadn't meant to offend with his remark. Nor provide a compliment, either.

"Some do, I suppose," he replied as he noticed a bent Y-shaped branch among the low shrubs. Lifting it up, he regarded it with a critical eye and then began undoing the knot of his cravat. "Here. Hold this, if you would," he said as he gave her the branch.

Samantha took it, wondering what he intended to do with it. She didn't think it would work well as a fishing pole. She watched as Ethan first unpinned and then unwound his cravat, wincing a bit at the ruined length of silk. Once it was free of his neck, he spread it open and wrapped it around the V part of the branch, winding it several times and then securing it in place with the pin. "There," he said as he angled it so it shaded her from the sun.

Blinking, Samantha looked from the marquess to the sunshade and back again. "Why, thank you," she said, allowing awe to sound in her voice.

"You're welcome, my lady," he answered, rather liking how appreciative she seemed of his effort. His grin disappeared when he stared beyond where she stood.

"What is it?" she asked before turning around to follow his line of sight. Off in the distance, the larger land mass they had seen from their raft was more evident—as was the stretch of water between them.

"I rather hoped that was part of this island," Ethan said with a sigh. "And it appears the water is too deep to simply wade over to it," he added, realizing it was considerably farther than he originally thought.

Samantha scanned the other land mass, not seeing any evidence of human occupation. Then her gaze swept their island, stopping suddenly when she realized there were trees, and behind them, a structure. Too far away to determine what it might be, Samantha continued her sweep of the horizon all around her.

Watching her with a bemused expression, Ethan was about to ask if she had discovered anything when she lifted an arm and pointed straight east. "A ship," she said quietly. Then she redirected her finger toward the structure. "A tower." She lowered her finger a bit. "Trees. Pinewoods, I think," she said, remembering Lord Everly's list of plant life on Minorca. "And steam."

But Ethan's attention had already turned to where she had indicated a ship. Sure enough, the white sails of a vessel were barely visible on the horizon. *How had she even been able to notice it?* he wondered, thinking her eyesight must be far better than his own. Without a means to signal the ship, though, Ethan knew there was no way they could be seen. "Damn it!" he said under his breath, not bothering to apologize for his curse.

"I have a mirror," Samantha murmured, thinking they could reflect the light of the sun on the mirror and perhaps capture the attention of someone on board. "But it's rather small." She opened her reticule and pulled out the tiny looking glass, its handle barely large enough to be held between a thumb and forefinger.

Ethan glanced down at the mirror, realizing he didn't know the code required to summon a ship. He took the mirror from her and angled it toward the horizon, wiggling it up and down in an attempt to cast a reflection. After a moment, the ship disappeared from the horizon and he gave up. He wondered how long the ship had been visible, thinking that if they had already spotted one, there would certainly be others. In the meantime, they needed to find water. "Wait. What did you say about steam?" he asked suddenly.

Samantha pointed to where wisps of steam curled up, not

too far from where they stood. When the breeze kicked up a bit, a hint of sulphur assaulted her nostrils.

"What's that smell?" Ethan asked then, one hand coming up to his nose.

"Brimstone," Samantha remarked, not sure if the marquess would be familiar enough with chemistry to recognize the word 'sulphur'.

"Sulphur?" he responded with an arched brow.

Samantha had to suppress a smile. "Yes. Which means a mineral spring," she said as she headed off toward the steam. "Now, if we had some sort of container ..." She allowed the sentence to trail off as they made their way south, disappointed she didn't have anything in her reticule that could hold water. At least, anything larger than clam shells.

From Ethan's estimate, they were about half-way across the island when he suddenly had to stop or end up in a lagoon filled entirely with mud. Disappointment settled over him when he didn't immediately see a source of water.

"Over here!"

He glanced to his right. Samantha was bent over something, her face lit with a smile.

Hurrying to her side, Ethan gave a sigh of relief at seeing water bubbling up from the ground. The basin in which it was briefly held drained into the muddy lagoon. Gingerly, he lowered his hand into the warm water and lifted it to his mouth. He smelled the foul odor before he finally dared a taste, deciding it wasn't as bad as he feared.

Samantha pulled one of the clam shells from her reticule and rinsed it out under the burbling water. When it was filled, she pulled it to her lips and sipped, her face scrunching up at the odd flavor. She offered the shell to Ethan, who took it as she stood up and continued her trek around the lagoon. Ethan went about filling and draining the shell, his thirst obviously worse than hers.

Looking up, he found Samantha farther along the shore of the lagoon. Bent down, she seemed intent on whatever she had found. "What is it?" he asked as he joined her.

"More berries!" she said with some excitement, wondering if they were the same as the ones she had found down by the beach. She held one up to her lips. She crushed it between her tongue and the roof of her mouth, surprised by the tart flavor that filled her mouth. "Rather tart," she said, "But good." She offered a handful to the marquess, who took them and popped the entire bunch into his mouth. When he noticed her look of surprise, he said, "I'm hungry."

Giving him a wan smile, Samantha went about picking the rest of the berries off the bush, deciding to tell him about the wild garlic she had found if he was in need of good news.

Ethan lowered himself to the sandy beach, his elbows coming to rest on his bent knees, his hands clasping together in front of him. As promising as the day had begun, what with finding water and shrubs with enough berries to stave off hunger, the end of the day wasn't proceeding as he hoped. He thought they would have spotted another ship—at least one much closer to the island—by now. He thought perhaps someone else might be on the island and provide a means to get them to the mainland. Instead, the part of the island they had explored proved to be deserted. Although he had seen evidence of rabbits, he hadn't actually spotted one. Even if he had, he didn't yet have the means to capture it or shoot it. Perhaps Samantha had something more in her reticule that could help in that regard.

The marquess had also come across some kind of reptile that looked like a miniature dragon. He had seen the creature sunning on a rock just as Samantha had walked by, her attention on what appeared to be a man-made structure south of their location—the tower she had mentioned earlier. He wondered if she would have screamed at seeing the odd animal or if she would have simply taken it in stride as she seemed to do for everything else they had encountered on their first day.

"I suppose finding food and water is as much as we can expect for only having been here a few hours," he said, his gaze on the distant horizon.

Samantha didn't immediately respond, thinking they might

have shelter as well if they had just made their way to the structure at the other end of the island. For some reason, the marquess had seemed reluctant to begin the trek. "I suppose," she finally said with a sigh, her attention on the sand in front of her. She held a short stick in her left hand and was using it to draw patterns in the fine grains.

"We'll get off this island, I promise you," Ethan said, his brows furrowing as he wondered at her reticence. The chit had barely said a word since their return to the beach.

Samantha angled her head to one side and finally turned to regard him. "I believe you," she acknowledged, her words sounding sad.

Ethan's frown deepened. "You don't seem particularly pleased by the prospect," he accused.

"That's because I'm not," Samantha replied, continuing to draw in the sand in front of her feet.

"Why ever not?"

Sighing, Samantha continued her work with the stick. "I have nothing to look forward to. My aunt ... *mother* ... is gone, I've no prospects, my best friends are married and already expecting babies." She suddenly realized how maudlin her words sounded. "I must admit I have looked forward to life as an independent woman. Lord Chamberlain has arranged a dowry on my behalf. I could use it to buy a townhouse, pay a companion, travel ..." She allowed her words to trail off, a wan smile replacing her look of sadness.

"No children?" Ethan asked as he brought up his knees to his chest and rested his arms on them.

Samantha shrugged. "Of course, I would like them," she answered, "But I certainly wouldn't want to have them out of wedlock," she said with a shake of her head.

Ethan gazed out at the sunset, the blue sky taking on pink and orange hues. "I suppose not." *Despite the fact that it was exactly what your mother did*, he thought. He glanced down at the patterns she had created in the sand, realizing she had drawn a landscape of the island that lay beyond the one they were on, including intricate details such as the shrubs and other plant life. "Where did you learn to do that?" he asked as he indicated her artwork.

"Oh, I have painted for years. I don't know that I *learned* how to paint so much as I just ... did it," she said with a shrug.

Ethan thought of the portraits in the gallery at Castle Keys. "Do you paint portraits?" he asked, thinking he might commission her to do his. Perhaps she wouldn't have to include the scowl that seemed to dominate the portraits of his ancestors.

"I have, but I prefer painting landscapes," Samantha replied. "Especially if I can set up an easel and do them while I'm there, instead of doing them from memory."

Thinking she might have traveled extensively, he asked, "Where haven't you been that you'd like paint, do you suppose?" he asked.

Samantha looked up from her creation. "Somewhere in Scotland. In the spring or summer," she said wistfully.

Surprised by her answer, Ethan frowned. "How do you know you want to paint there if you've never been?"

Shrugging one shoulder, Samantha replied, "I have heard it's beautiful. And I like to paint beautiful settings. Someday I shall paint this," she said as she waved a hand to indicate the island.

Ethan considered her words, realizing just then that Samantha wasn't at all what he had expected in an aristocrat's daughter. He wondered what other surprises she might have in store for him.

CHAPTER 13

TRUTHS BE TOLD

First night on the island

"How are you holding up?" Ethan asked, tearing his gaze away from the small fire he had managed to build using the flint stones and bits of kindling Samantha had gathered in her skirts while on their way back from the spring. Seeing such a familiar sight in such an unfamiliar place had him mesmerized. Despite the flames dancing above a completely different fuel source than what could found in a typical English home— coal or wood—the fire still looked the same. He wondered if he would be able to keep it going through the night. If not, he thought any animals on the island would be more likely to pay them a visit, and he didn't relish the thought of waking up to something crawling on him. Or eating him.

Samantha straightened, realizing she had begun to slump as she watched the fire. "Fine, I suppose," she replied brightly, not sure what else she could say. If she kept her mind on matters other than her aunt—or her mother, if Caroline Fitzsimmons truly was her mother—she found her spirits higher than they had any right to be. She was stuck on a deserted island with little in the way of food, water that tasted of minerals and probably glowed in the dark, and her only company was a marquess who no doubt considered her a burden.

"Would you like more?" Ethan offered, lifting his clam shell to indicate the brandywine.

At her earlier suggestion, Ethan had rolled one of the brandywine tubs to where they had begun building the fire on the beach. He had then used her knife to tap the cask and drink from the small hole he had made. Remembering the shells she had picked up from the beach, Samantha pulled them from her reticule and filled the bowl of one with brandy. She offered Ethan the other shell. "I rather wish I carried a necessarié about," she said as she lifted her reticule. "At least then we would have a cup to drink from." Not to mention a fork, knife and spoon should the marquess have any luck fishing.

"The shells work," he replied with a shrug, his mood lightening as the alcohol gave him a slight buzz. "About tonight ..."

Samantha stilled herself, wondering what he would say. They hadn't discussed where—or how—they would spend the night. "Go on," she said before taking another sip of the wine.

"I ... I don't know how cold it's going to get ..."

"It's June. Not very," Samantha said with a shake of her head.

"Or where the best place would be for us to ... sleep," he went on, wishing they had made the trek to the only structure evident on the island. He had every intention of exploring it on the morrow. "But I should probably ..."

"You needn't keep watch, if that's what you're about to offer," Samantha said with a shake of her head, aware her cheeks were reddening in response to the wine. "We can ... sleep on the sand. According to Lord Everly, the tides in the Mediterranean aren't very pronounced as the sea is almost completely landlocked, so we needn't be concerned about the waves coming up this far." She couldn't help but notice Ethan's look of contempt when she mentioned Lord Everly's name. "May I ask why you don't like Harry?"

Ethan visibly jerked at the mention of the earl's given name. "*Harry?*" he repeated, a bit incredulous. "Oh, so now you're on a first-name basis with him, are you?" he asked rhetorically, bending his legs so he sat cross-legged before the fire.

Samantha's eyes widened at the man's ire, her mouth opening to respond before she closed it and reconsidered what she was about to say. "He is my best friend's brother," she finally said. "I've known Harry Tennison ... almost my entire life."

And I thought he would have asked for my hand by now.

Even Evangeline had thought Samantha would be her sister before the year was out. But given Lord Everly's ambivalence—oh, he was nice enough, and rather attentive when Samantha showed an interest in whatever he was research-ing—it had become evident to Samantha that the explorer and adventurer wasn't about to ask that she join him on any future endeavors. He just didn't seem interested in her in that way.

"He can't be a very honorable man, though, can he?" Ethan retorted.

Her brows furrowing, Samantha watched as Ethan refilled his shell for at least the tenth time since he had tapped the cask. "What makes you say that?" she asked, getting up to move to the wine barrel. She allowed the marquess to refill her shell before she sat down next to it, careful to keep her skirts beneath her and away from the flames.

She had given up on trying to keep her gown in good repair, deciding the silk was long past its prime. At least it provided coverage despite her missing petticoats.

Ethan rolled his eyes. "Seems to me, any man who has spent as much time with you as he apparently has over the years should have married you by now," he said, sounding rather incensed. "Have you given him some reason to believe you'll still be available when he finally decides to ask?"

Gasping at his impertinent question, Samantha stared at the marquess, replaying his words in her head. He hadn't exactly offended with his remarks—at least, not her—but he hadn't exactly implied she was biddable, either.

"I ... I have not. Not directly. But I hardly think it's any of your concern," she added before drinking every bit of the brandy in her shell. A warmth spread through her belly, made more potent due to her lack of a decent dinner. She and the marquess had dined on more of the tart berries, cleaning off at least two of the bushes they had come across on their way back from the spring. There was some thought that one of the larger birds that seemed to frequently fly over the island could be made into a meal, but they hadn't yet managed to capture one.

"You're absolutely right, my lady," he answered, his words a bit slurred. He brought his knees up and wrapped his arms around his legs, his head leaning forward to rest on his hands. Despite the early hour, he thought he could simply close his eyes and fall asleep.

"What about you?" Samantha asked, breaking the sudden silence she found disconcerting. Having grown up in London, she was used to hearing noises throughout the night—hackneys and horses, shouts of link boys as they led their customers down dimly-lit streets, revelers out too late at their clubs and gaming hells—but on the island, the quiet was deafening.

"What about me?" Ethan countered, lifting his head from his hands.

"Do you ... have a wife?" She was quite sure Caroline had mentioned the marquess was still unattached, but given the man lived in Yorkshire, he could have been married for a couple of years and word wouldn't have necessarily made it to London. Had the man married in London, the entire town would know within a couple of days.

Ethan shook his head. "No," he replied. "And, no, there is no marchioness in my future," he added, thinking she would press the issue.

"No prospects?" Samantha asked, rather surprised a man of his age wasn't yet betrothed. He had to be near thirty!

Clearing his throat, Ethan straightened and stared into the dying fire. "None."

Samantha angled her head as she regarded Ethan for several minutes. Was he angry that he had been stranded on the island with her? That he was forced to provide protection despite not liking her? He had been rather polite to her the entire day, even turning his cravat into a sunshade that later had doubled as a scoop to capture water so they could bathe at the spring. And he seemed genuine in his concern for her well-being as they made their way back to the beach.

"I wish to apologize," she said quietly.

Ethan tore his gaze from the fire, one eyebrow arching at her words. "For what?"

Samantha sighed. "I'm quite sure you despise me for even being in this situation ..."

"Despise you?" he repeated in surprise. "My lady, I wouldn't even be *alive* if it weren't for you," he said with a shake of his head.

Stunned by his statement, Samantha stared at the marquess. "I'm quite sure you have that backwards," she countered. "I am the one ..."

"Who can swim," Ethan interrupted. "Who had enough sense to keep your head about you and not panic," he went on. "Even when I was ready to give up, you didn't," he whispered, his gaze back on the fire.

Samantha stared at the marquess for a very long time, astonished by his words. "Oh," she said quietly, not sure what else she could say to his comment.

She remembered how she had awoken that morning, her body resting atop his, one leg betwixt his, her head in the small of his shoulder. Despite how awkward it was to wake up pressed against a man she had barely known for less than a week, the marquess hadn't made her feel more so, although there had been his question about her intent to kiss him. Truth be told, she had considered it, but then she had also thought herself still in a dream. "Do you suppose we could ...?" She felt a wash of embarrassment color her face.

Ethan stared at her, wondering what had her so tongue-tied. *Do you suppose we could ... go hunting? Go fishing? Go for a walk on the beach? Go for a swim? Kiss? Make love?*

I have had entirely too much to drink on an empty stomach, Ethan realized suddenly.

"Spend the night ... much like we did last night?" Samantha finally got out. "Well, not on the raft, of course," her attention suddenly directed toward the water where their makeshift raft was still bobbing in the shallow water. "Here on the dry land."

Ethan stared at her, his alcohol-addled brain not quite comprehending her words. *Did she just ask if we could sleep together?* "You're not going to try and kiss me?" he replied, his brows furrowed in mock disappointment.

Samantha swallowed, wondering just how drunk the man had become in the short time they had been on the beach. "Would you mind if I did?" she asked, feeling rather bold just then. *I have had entirely too much to drink.* Never had her head felt this fuzzy when she had drunk champagne. Usually she just felt it in her knees.

Ethan allowed a chuckle to burble forth. "My lady, if you kissed me, I would hardly know what to do," he answered with a shake of his head. "Since I haven't been kissed by a member of your sex in, oh, I can't even tell you how long," he said, mirth still lighting his eyes.

Samantha blinked in an attempt to clear her blurry eyes. Hadn't she just kissed him this morning? *My kisses must not have made much of an impression if he's claiming he hasn't been kissed recently.* Allowing a wan smile, Samantha dipped her head. "At least you've been kissed," she countered, catching a tooth in her lower lip. "I have not." She wondered if he would remember having kissed her.

The marquess stared at Samantha for a long time, his breathing shallow and his eyes glazed over from too much drink. "You're not missing much, my love," he managed to get out before he suddenly lay down—or perhaps he fell—Samantha wasn't entirely sure—on his side on the dune. He bent the arm beneath him to act as a pillow, closed his eyes and, within seconds, fell asleep.

Samantha stared at the marquess for a long time. Well, in his inebriated state, he apparently didn't remember having kissed her on the raft. *You're not missing much.*

My love?

Well, that seemed rather odd. She had heard such wonderful stories of kissing. Of first kisses and second kisses and those shared in the gardens of Lord Weatherstone's estate. Of the kisses Evangeline had described with her baron in the library and every other room of Sommers Place, and Julia's whispers of kisses with Alistair in the stables at Harrington House. Although, she couldn't imagine a kiss in the stables would be particularly memorable, what with all the horses as witnesses and the odors generally found therein, but Lady Julia had certainly enjoyed it.

Rising from where she sat next to the brandywine, Samantha leaned over and placed a few more pieces of wood on the fire and then moved to where Ethan slept. Glancing around, as if she thought someone might be watching her, she lowered herself to the sand behind the marquess, rested her head on her reticule, and molded the front of her body against the back of his. She moved her free arm to rest atop his body and was asleep within minutes.

Ethan opened his eyes and allowed a sigh, wondering if he was going to regret this night. Feeling the warmth at his back, he rather hoped not. Feeling the effects of the brandywine, though, a hangover was probably in his future.

CHAPTER 14
A TOWER TO EXPLORE

*S**econd day on the island*
"You're awfully quiet," Ethan said as they made their way toward the island's only structure. From their current vantage point, it appeared to have been made of smooth stone blocks. Squat and cylindrical, it reminded Ethan of the defense towers sometimes seen at the corners of castles. There were even battlements at the top.

Samantha had paused to pick berries from a bush filled with them. Apparently the birds hadn't yet discovered it. "Does the quiet bother you?" she asked as she caught up to where he stood looking out over the horizon and held out a handful of the berries.

She knew he was concerned about not having seen a single ship on the horizon since they woke up on the beach that morning. That and his pounding head and dehydration from having had too much brandy the night before, a condition Samantha knew from experience with her uncle could be mitigated with water. Although Matthew rarely drank to excess, there were times he did while at his men's club, especially when he was in the company of several friends.

The two had made their way to the spring first and had their fill of the odd-tasting water.

Ethan accepted the berries. "Thank you," he said, his

stomach grumbling. He had never before had to forage for his breakfast and found himself missing his usual bacon, eggs and Yorkshire toast. "And, no, I'm not bothered by the quiet. Castle Keys is actually rather quiet. Usually," he added giving the horizon another quick scan.

"Usually?" Samantha repeated, stepping around a rock on which a lizard was perched. She thought about stopping to give it a closer look, but she wondered what the marquess might think of such a creature. *No need to frighten him*, she thought, knowing from Lord Everly's description the creature wouldn't bite. *They look positively hideous, but they're harmless*, he had said, *unless you're an insect or a cricket. Then you're dead.*

"If I'm to believe my butler, apparently the servants are prone to speaking rather loudly when I am not on the premises," Ethan answered. The man had said it as if his master should do something about it, but Ethan was at a loss to why that would be. So what if they talked? Loudly? It wasn't as if Castle Keys was a mausoleum.

"Do you require them to be especially quiet?" she countered, giving him an arched eyebrow.

Ethan wondered if he was being teased. "Not at all. They just have always ... *been* rather quiet."

Samantha stooped to pick some more berries. "Ours sing sometimes, or hum whilst they work," she said as she formed a bowl with the fabric of her skirts and filled it with more berries. "I rather like that our house doesn't sound like a ... mausoleum." This last was said with a shiver and mock fright, as if she found the silence associated with a cemetery something to be avoided.

Furrowing his brow, Ethan wondered if Castle Keys would seem like a mausoleum to Samantha. There were times it certainly seemed like it to him, which had him wondering why his servants didn't sing or hum while they worked. "I don't forbid my servants from singing or humming. Or talking, for that matter," he countered, thinking it important she know that about him. *But perhaps my father did*, he thought suddenly. *Good God!* Did his servants think him as brutish as his father?

Probably.

He would have to remedy that situation just as soon as he returned to Castle Keys.

Gathering her berry-filled skirts into one hand, Samantha stood up and faced the marquess, her sunshade held in the other. "Would you like more? I rather think you're used to a more substantial breakfast than this."

Ethan nodded and helped himself to another handful of the tart fruit. "Truer words were never spoken. And what about you? Aren't you used to something a bit more than fruit?" Or perhaps she was one of those women like Daisy, who ate like a bird, pushing their food around their plate and claiming they were full after eating only a few bites.

Samantha continued on toward the tower. "Indeed. Eggs, bacon, Yorkshire toast ..." With Ethan following her just then, she didn't see his look of surprise. "Chocolate. And sometimes an orange. Mmm."

"That does it," Ethan announced with a shake of his head.

Turning around to discover what had the marquess suddenly sounding angry, Samantha gave him a questioning look. "What?"

"There shall be no more talk of food. Especially of my favorite breakfast."

Samantha gave him a brilliant smile. "Agreed," she said before continuing the trek.

As they got closer to the tower, the number of pinewoods thinned. Rosemary bushes were scattered about, their distinctive scent making her stomach grumble. Having found wild garlic earlier, Samantha was disappointed they hadn't come across a food source that could use the seasoning.

Samantha stopped walking when they reached an apron of clear ground around the base of the tower. "Well, it's not as large as I thought," she commented, lowering her sunshade so she could look up the side of the two-story tower.

"No, but it's shelter. Come on. Let's see if anyone is at home," Ethan said as he made his way around the building to an arched doorway.

"How old do you suppose this is?" Samantha wondered. The

blocks didn't appear to be as ancient as she had first thought, but rather made within the past century.

Ethan shook his head. "I've no idea." His hands on his hips, he regarded the doorway and allowed his gaze to travel up the side of the tower to the top. "Anyone home?" he called out, his voice echoing inside the stone structure.

He didn't expect an answer, and he didn't get one. Stepping through the arched opening, he stopped and allowed his eyes to adjust to the dark. Although there were small windows—or rather rectangular openings high up in the stone walls—the cool space was dimly lit. His bare feet seemed to stand on the very same ground as what was outside, which meant no wood floor. The space also smelled a bit musty, as if it hadn't been used in a while.

Walking carefully, he moved toward a staircase leading to the upper story. Samantha followed behind, noting a small rustic table, a chair that looked as if it had seen better days, and a shelf. "Cups!" she whispered as she quickly moved to the shelf. Setting her sunshade on the table so she could reach for the utensils, she was about to take one from the shelf when a movement behind the cup startled her. Her cry of alarm had Ethan at her side in an instant.

"What happened?" he asked, grabbing onto her arm to pull her back.

Samantha stilled herself. "Something ... moved," she said as she pointed to the cup. "Probably just a mouse or a spider," she added, hoping she didn't seem like a scaredy cat to the marquess.

Ethan lifted the cup from the shelf and found himself staring into the eyes of one of the islands' indigenous creatures. He took a steady breath, wondering if the thing was going to attack or simply stare back at him. *Here there be dragons,* crossed his mind, along with the image of a dragon shooting a stream of billowing fire out of its nostrils.

"Oh, it's just a lizard," Samantha said with a sigh. The reptile regarded them for a moment before its herky-jerky movements took it across the shelf and down the wall to the floor.

Stilling his thumping heart, Ethan turned and nodded. "Did Everly tell you about this, too?" he asked with some derision.

Samantha gasped at his question, rather annoyed at the implication that everything she knew was because of the earl. "Yes, if you must know. He said they eat insects, so we have nothing to fear from them."

Tamping down his sudden ire—why did the thought of the earl have him so angry?—Ethan hurried to the stairs and made his way up to the second story. The wood floor creaked, but seemed solid enough to hold his weight. A cot, a chamber pot and what might have been a wash basin were the only furnishings. If the wash basin could hold water, it might come in handy at the spring.

The stairs continued up the curved wall through an opening in the roof. Popping his head through the hole, Ethan realized almost immediately what had at one time been installed behind the battlements—a canon. The gun was long gone, though the means to make a fire in a stone cauldron were still there.

Shaking his head, he wondered what the tower was meant to defend against. Marauders? Invasion from a foreign army?

He suddenly remembered how close they had to be to the coast of Spain and realized what the invaders had been.

Pirates. Barbary pirates.

He glanced out beyond the battlements, stunned at the sight of other nearby islands and water as far as he could see. Surely if the towers were meant to defend against pirates, there would be someone nearby who watched for some kind of signal from this tower. *Fire*, he realized, which could be seen well at night, but probably not as well in the daylight. He wondered if they used some other signaling method during the day.

"What a beautiful view."

Ethan swung around to find Samantha scanning the horizon, her skirts still bunched up to hold her cache of berries. He reached in and helped himself to a handful. "I hadn't noticed, but since you mentioned it, it is ... rather beautiful," he breathed before tossing several berries into his mouth. The water nearest the island was a deep turquoise and so clear, he could see to the sea's bottom. As it stretched out toward the horizon, it turned a brilliant blue.

"Do you think it would be safe for us to spend the night here?" Samantha asked. Although she had seen the cot, she had no intention of sleeping on it. The covering was rotted, and there weren't any blankets or pillows.

"I think we should. With this view, we'll have an easier time spotting a ship," Ethan replied. He didn't mention the means to make a fire, nor had he decided if he would. On the one hand, someone might see the fire and think an invasion was occurring. The false alarm would no doubt bring someone to investigate, someone who might not find their need to be rescued an excusable reason for using the defense system. On the other hand, whoever came to investigate might provide them with the means to get to the mainland. *I have money. I can pay for passage.*

"Do you plan on building a fire in the cauldron?" Samantha asked as she continued to survey the top of the tower, occasionally leaning through the batttlements to survey the surroundings.

Ethan sighed. So much for keeping Samantha in the dark. "I don't think so. At least, not yet. We may not want to attract that kind of attention," he added when he noticed her arched eyebrow.

"Smoke would certainly be more noticeable than my little looking glass," she commented before eating some berries. Giving her a look of surprise, the marquess seemed to realize something just then, but he didn't make a response.

Samantha regarded the marquess as he stood looking north, deciding he really would be far more handsome if he didn't scowl all the time. Just seeing him like this, standing under the noonday sun, had her wondering why he had claimed to have little experience with kisses.

She was certain the man had kissed a woman before yesterday morning when he had kissed her on the raft. And she was sure he had been kissed by a woman before she kissed him. Had probably spent many a night with a woman in his arms, the afterglow of lovemaking bringing on even more kissing. Perhaps, if she asked him, he would show her more of how it was done.

The kissing.

Not the lovemaking, of course.

Then she suddenly remembered what he had said about her being a bastard, and all thoughts of kissing him left her head.

CHAPTER 15

A MESSAGE TO THE VISCOUNT

*M*atthew Fitzsimmons, Viscount Chamberlain, made his way out of the doors of the Foreign Office and was forced to shade his eyes from the bright afternoon sun. He quickly donned his top hat as he made his way down the steps to Whitehall, determined to find a hackney and be home within the hour.

"My lord!"

Matthew turned his attention to an approaching servant, hiding his annoyance at being accosted outside the building where he had performed his duty for King and Crown for over twenty-five years. Recognizing one of the footman from Fitzsimmons Manor, he stopped and waited until the man reached him. "Conroy?" he addressed the young man, a bit surprised at the appearance of one of his household staff. One who appeared as if he had run the entire distance from Fitzsimmons Manor. "What is it?"

Gasping for air, the thin man gave a bow and held out an envelope. "I apologize, my lord, but I was told it was imperative you read this at your earliest convenience," Conroy managed to get out between gulps for air. "A courier delivered it only an hour ago."

Frowning, Matthew reached for the missive and noted the rough parchment and the odd seal on the back. *What could be so important that a courier would be making a delivery this time of the day?* he wondered, sliding a thumb beneath the seal and popping open the folded note. He angled the writing so the sun lit it, his eyes immediately drawn to the signature at the bottom. *William Nattersley.* Not recognizing the name, he scanned the writing.

> *An incident aboard* The Fairweather *during inclement weather has resulted in the loss of two passengers, one a Lady Samantha Fitzsimmons. I am led to believe Miss Fitzsimmons is a relation of yours. Also reported missing is a Mr. E. Range, who may be a man of some importance from Yorkshire. The Fairweather made its way to dock at Valencia where its main-mast is to be replaced. Viscountess Chamberlain insisted she be allowed to remain. She is understandably bereft at the loss of her daughter and has refused an offer of immediate transport back to England. Captain St. John writes that she has been offered accommodations at a local convent, one of St. Augustine's. We can arrange for your transport to Valencia at your soonest convenience. I have a ship at Wapping ready and bound for Spain and Italy. I await your reply. My sincerest regards, William Nattersley.*

A rock seemed to settle in the pit of Matthew's stomach as he read and reread the letter. At least Caroline was alive. But Samantha? What kind of 'incident' would have her and ... he glanced at the name of the other passenger. 'E. Range' had to be Ethan Range, Marquess of Plymouth. He had spoken to the marquess and watched him as he boarded the ship.

"Good God," he murmured, raising his eyes from the missive for the first time since unfolding the parchment. He glanced around, searching for someone he knew, and when he didn't see anyone, he turned back to Conroy. Digging a coin from his pocket, he pressed it into the footman's hand. "Find a hackney. Get back to the house and have my valet pack a trunk. We'll leave as soon as he's ready to depart."

His eyes widening in alarm, Conroy nodded. "May I tell him the nature and length of the trip? So he might pack the right clothing?" he added when he realized his query might seem inappropriate for one of his station.

Matthew took a deep breath and nodded. "Tell him ... Spain. Three weeks." The amount of time was only a guess. He didn't know how long it would take to find Caroline, how long it would take to determine Samantha's fate.

The footman nodded, gave a quick bow and hurried off toward Whitehall as Matthew made his way back into the Foreign Office building. Although he had already left word he would be traveling to the Continent—he had intended to join the women in Florence—he hadn't intended on leaving London for several days.

He was already in the building and on his way back to his office when he remembered another line of the note. Unfolding it again, his eyes scanned the script until he saw the words, "She is understandably bereft at the loss of her daughter ..." Raising his eyes to the ornate ceiling, Matthew took a deep breath and let it out slowly. *Finally,* he thought with a mix of relief and a stab of jealousy.

He had always known Caroline Harrington had loved another. She had been married to a military man soon after her come-out—at her mother's insistence—and was a widow within a month. Matthew always thought Caroline had only married him because first her father and then her brother had thought the two of them would suit. Her dowry had been more than generous, allowing Matthew to pursue his passion for strategy and planning for the Crown at the Foreign Office while an estate manager saw to his poor excuse for a viscountcy. And although he had been smitten with the younger woman from the moment he first met her, he had simply known her heart belonged to another.

At least, that's how it had been for the first few years of their marriage. At some point, though, Caroline had changed. Matured, perhaps. Seemed to accept ... embrace, even ... her position as his viscountess. As his wife.

As his lover.

Samantha was her daughter. There was no doubt now, he

realized as he reread the note. He had suspected as much, always wondered at how Caroline could be such a doting aunt to a babe supposedly her sister's. Well, he loved the girl as he would his own, even if she was merely his niece. If she had somehow survived 'the incident' mentioned in the missive, he would find her. Find her and return her to Caroline, if for no other reason than to see a look of joy on his wife's face. To be her hero.

Matthew allowed a grimace at the thought as he continued to his office. *Hero, my ass.*

"Where's our man in the Mediterranean? Somewhere near Spain, I hope?" Matthew Fitzsimmons asked as he entered the office next to his own.

The startled clerk at the front desk regarded the viscount with a blank stare before comprehending the question. "That would be Bradley, my lord. Alex Bradley. He's ..." The man gave a shrug, not quite sure how to describe the spy's current assignment. "On the search for contraband," he finally managed to get out. "And he concentrates his travels from the Straights to Marseilles."

Matthew's brows furrowed. "Still playing pirate, is he?" There was no need for those in this office to know the man had been discussed only a few days ago in the Home Office.

The clerk gave a shrug, his manner making it evident he was uncomfortable divulging any information about an officer in the field, especially to someone who didn't work in his office. "Something like that."

Sighing, Matthew figured a man with a ship was better than any other alternative at that moment. If Samantha and Lord Plymouth were still alive, it would be because they had either been found at sea by a passing ship or they had somehow made it to an island or the mainland.

He opened the missive he had received from the shipping company and reread the details.

"I need a courier dispatched to Bradley's location immediately," he ordered.

A clerk at another desk straightened. "We have one going

out tonight. He's to intercept Bradley at the port in Marseilles in two or three days."

Three days?

Christ. It had already been at least two days since Samantha had gone missing! But what else could he do? His own travel arrangements couldn't get him to Valencia any quicker. "I have a mission I need to have added to his manifest."

The clerks exchanged glances, obviously wondering how to proceed given their supervisor had left the building along with most of the other employees. But Matthew Fitzsimmons had been a fixture at the Foreign Office far longer than most. The two nodded, waiting for him to provide his explanation.

"A marquess, Lord Plymouth, is missing. Lost at sea. Given the location of where he was apparently tossed off a ship—along with some rather valuable cargo—it's possible he has made it to one of the islands off the coast of Spain."

Matthew hoped the naval navigator with whom he had spent the past half-hour was right. Given the winds and currents this time of the year in the Mediterranean, and the apparent location of the rogue wave—the captain of *The Fairweather* had provided a rather detailed accounting in his report to his company—it was probable anything tossed off the ship would end up on Majorca or one of its neighboring islands. But there were dozens of islands in the chain to the east of Spain. Looking for a castaway would be like looking for a needle in a haystack.

The mention of a member of the aristocracy had the clerks straightening at their desks and suddenly busy conferring with others in the office. If the man was alive, it was imperative he be found, for if the Marquess of Plymouth was declared dead, his marquessate would revert to the Crown.

The man had no heirs.

CHAPTER 16
FISHING FOR INFORMATION

Second afternoon on the island

Samantha closed her eyes and recognized the scent of rain. Lifting her face, she felt her golden brown hair fall from her shoulders—she had given up trying to keep it pinned— and it ruffled in the slight breeze. She turned to the east to see the horizon darkening, low, dark clouds roiling while the sky nearby was still clear. "Rain is coming," she murmured.

Ethan glanced up from where he was attempting to use her sunshade as a net to catch a fish. "Rain means fresh water," he said, cursing under his breath when his latest attempt to snag a good-sized fish failed. Earlier, Samantha had reconfigured the makeshift sunshade so the cravat was wrapped looser around the Y-shaped branch and formed more of a net. Ethan had to suppress a grin as she completed the project by securing the fabric to itself with his diamond-tipped cravat pin.

"The diamond should help to attract a fish," she said as she handed him the net. "At least, it would in an English river," she added when she noticed his look of doubt.

"Something tells me you would be better at this," Ethan said as he waded into the shallow waters. The clear water made the sand below seem as if it were mere inches below the surface when it fact it was a foot or more down.

Smiling, Samantha shook her head. "I've watched my uncle

fish, of course. But I've never done it," she countered, not about to admit to having fished even if she had. The marquess already thought the worst of her with respect to her parentage. She didn't want him thinking she was a hoyden, too.

"What makes you think I have?" Ethan asked as he managed to get a fish into the net. When lifting it from the water, though, the fish flipped out and swam away. "Damnation!" he cursed, not bothering to excuse himself.

Samantha wondered if he would have apologized had she not been a bastard. "Don't you live on the coast? And you must have a lake or two near your home. I would expect you to go fishing every day," Samantha replied, her attention once again turned to the east. They had been on their way from the tower to the spring when she suggested the attempt at fishing. The pristine beach they found was on the opposite side of the island from the one where they had landed. Not nearly as long or as deep, it was still a beautiful setting with a few palm trees at the end of the stretch of white sand. Samantha could imagine spending a night here, but not in the rain. They could stay in the tower; from the condition of the interior, it appeared to be a solid shelter from rain.

She glanced down at the wash basin they had taken from the tower. Intending to fill it at the spring so they wouldn't have to make frequent trips for water, she now hoped to use it to catch the rain. The water was sure to taste better than what they had been drinking. And it probably wouldn't glow in the dark.

The marquess waded farther out, scooped up a fish and immediately tossed it toward the beach. Flopping about as it sailed through the air, the fish landed with a *thump* in the warm sand. It continued flopping about for several seconds, forcing Samantha to dodge out of the way as she giggled with excitement.

Watching from where he stood in the water, Ethan said a prayer of thanks and grinned at her enthusiasm. Emboldened, he continued his search for fish, slowly moving the branch through the water. By the time the rain started, there were three fish on the beach.

"We'll need to get wood for the fire," Samantha said as Ethan returned to the beach, his hair glistening with water droplets. His shirt, open at the top and mostly untucked at the bottom, was nearly drenched, the fabric clinging to his skin and shifting over taut muscles as he moved to retrieve his catch. He tossed the fish into the makeshift net and stood up, the muscles of his thighs showing in relief through his damp breeches.

Samantha sucked in a breath as a frisson shot through her body, the pleasant sensation leaving her rather stunned. She dared another glance at Ethan, smiling when she noticed how handsome the marquess appeared when an expression of joy was lighting his face.

Realizing she was staring, Samantha shook herself. "I'll get the basin," she said as she stooped to pick up the ceramic bowl, its bottom already filling with rainwater. She swished it around in an effort to rinse it.

"Here," Ethan offered. "I can get that," he said as he took it from her hands, hefting it against one hip as he held the fish-filled net in the other. "There's wood in the tower. And flints, too. And I'll need your knife to the clean the fish," he said as he nodded toward her reticule, still hanging from her wrist. He wondered if she slept with it—he hadn't seen her without it since their arrival on the island.

"Thank you," she said with a nod as she gave up the bowl, turning to lead them back to the tower. By the time they reached the stone structure and had placed the basin where it could collect rainwater, the shower had increased in intensity, and the two were drenched as they ducked through the arched doorway.

"It actually felt good to get a bit of a shower there," Ethan said as he moved to put his catch on the table. His clothes were dripping wet. With nothing to dry himself, he wondered about removing his shirt in the presence of Samantha. She was already busy with bringing wood down from the second floor, her damp gown clinging to her legs as she did so. He remembered how those legs had been wrapped around his when they were on the raft. He had to tamp down the sudden arousal he felt in his loins. "Actually, I think I'll take these outside and clean them in the rain. I don't want to stink up the place," he said as he picked up the chair and the net full of fish.

Samantha dropped the wood and dug into her reticule for the knife, placing it into the net with the fish. She watched as Ethan disappeared through the doorway. Shrugging, she felt a bit of relief at having a moment alone. Throughout the day, she had been confused by the marquess' behavior. Usually he seemed aloof, polite though guarded. And yet there were times it seemed he wanted to be friends, conversing freely with her about matters of no import .

Shaking her head, Samantha moved to an area opposite the stairs where it appeared from the darkened floor that a fire might have been made there in the past. Given the small openings at the top of the walls, she hoped the smoke would be drawn up and out and not collect in the structure. She worked with the flints until she managed to get a spark to light some kindling. Blowing carefully, a flame soon erupted. Adding a short branch and some of the wood from above stairs, she had a fire going when Ethan returned. His hair was matted to his head, and his clothes were dripping wet. "I intended to do that," he said with some surprise when he saw she already had the fire started.

"Goodness. We need to get you dried off," Samantha said with concern.

Ethan wiped a hand over his face. "The shower felt good, actually. I feel like I've taken a bath in my clothes," he replied with a grin. He moved over to the shelf where the cups sat and took them down. "I'm going to rinse these out and let them fill with water," he said. "No sense you getting soaked, too." He left again, and Samantha busied herself with finding something on which to place the fish while they cooked.

Once outside, Ethan leaned against the tower wall and took a deep breath. Seeing Samantha in the dim light had him unnerved, aroused in a way Daisy had never made him feel. *What the hell is happening?* he wondered as he allowed rain to fill the cups before he swished the dirty water around and dumped them out.

The woman was an enigma. If he considered her a lady, he found he could tamp down his desire. He knew she wasn't truly a member of the *ton*, though. Why that made any difference—why his arousal was suddenly more intense—he didn't know.

He wanted her—wanted her stripped bare—beneath him or on top of him or pressed against a wall. And he was quite sure she would accommodate him, although he wasn't yet sure she would do so because she truly wanted to or because she would willingly sacrifice herself in order to help him.

When they had been at the top of the tower, he wondered for a moment if they might kiss—she had given him a look that suggested she would be willing before something suddenly darkened her visage.

What had she been thinking that had her clear green eyes changing to storm clouds? That had her spine straightening and her manner suddenly all business?

Ethan suddenly slammed the back of his head against the stone exterior, rainwater pouring down the curved wall and soaking his entire body more than it already was. *I called her a bastard.*

Christ!

Stupid, stupid, stupid!

Even if it were true—and it *was*, he reminded himself—everyone in the *ton* believed her to be the daughter of the Fitzsimmons of Darbing Manor. Why was it so damned important who her parents were if, for propriety's sake, everyone accepted her as the daughter of Eliza and Edward?

Because I know better.

I know the truth.

Had he been raised by anyone but a father who believed in the importance of pure bloodlines and a clear delineation between the peerage and commoners, he might not feel this way, might not feel as if Caroline Harrington had somehow cheated the *ton* and gotten away with it, the evidence of her cheating just inside the very tower he was leaning against for support.

Damnation!

She doesn't even know who her father really is, he remembered, his anger slowly ebbing. He regarded the fish as they lay on his ruined cravat. They wouldn't be there if she hadn't encouraged him to try fishing with her makeshift net. They might not even have shelter from the rain if she hadn't suggested they use the rainwater instead of going back to the spring at the other end of the island.

Ignoring the streams of water tracing down his face, Ethan took a seat in the chair, picked up the knife and expertly gutted each fish. He wondered if she would notice. He had meant to leave her with the impression he didn't know how to fish just so she might be impressed with his effort. It was true he had never fished using a net like he had this day, but he certainly knew how to use a rod and reel.

Allowing the rain to rinse each fish as well as the makeshift net, Ethan leaned his head back and allowed the rivulets of water to run down his body. When he was sure he had all the evidence of the fish rinsed away, he gathered everything and returned to the darkening interior of the tower.

CHAPTER 17

DINNER IN A GOWN

*S*econd night on the island

Samantha looked up from where she was fashioning a grill on which to cook the fish. "Oh, goodness! You're soaking wet!" she cried as she stood and hurried to his side, taking the cups from one of his hands. Brimming with clear water, they would provide enough water to get through the night. She carefully placed them on the table. "I found some linens upstairs in that little cupboard," she said as she moved back to the table to pick up a small stack of folded fabric. "They appear fairly clean," she hedged as she offered them to him.

"Thanks," he said with a nod, watching her to determine if she was still angry with him. *If she was, she wouldn't have been concerned about how wet you are, you dolt,* he thought. *Although maybe she's just concerned about how you're making the floor into a muddy mess.*

"What do you have there?" he asked when he noticed a metal grate set up on four rocks and positioned over the fire.

Samantha allowed a shrug. "A means to cook the fish, I hope," she replied, moving back to where he had found her. Although small, the fire crackled and popped and had already warmed the interior. Ethan glanced up to see that smoke had pooled at the ceiling but was slowly making its way out of several of the windows.

He squatted opposite from her and pulled one of the fish from his cravat. He placed it on the hot grate, setting off the sounds of sizzling as the wet fish made contact. He tossed the other two fish onto the grate and then used a linen to dry his hair and face.

"You've done this before."

The comment wasn't a question, but Ethan felt a bit of satisfaction at having her notice. "Yes. As you mentioned, I do live near lakes and ponds and the coast," he said with a nod. Pointing to the grate, he said, "As have you."

Samantha inhaled sharply, ready to deny ever having cooked fish. "I've only watched it being done," she countered. "I found some plates," she added. "Will you keep an eye on the fire while I rinse them off outside?"

Ethan shook his head. "I can do it. No need having the both of us soaking wet. Besides, I still need to bring in the chair," he said as he stood up. He hoped the sorry excuse for furniture would be cleaned of its years of dust.

Back outside, he was surprised to find the sky darkening faster than he expected. Looking toward the east, he realized the rain would probably last through the night. To the west, the low clouds stretched to the horizon. *So much for looking for ships*, he thought with some dismay.

The scents of wood smoke, cooking fish and garlic reached his nostrils, and he inhaled slowly. His stomach suddenly growling in anticipation, he went back into the tower, the seat of the chair resting against his hip as he held onto the back. The plates dripped from their rainwater rinse. Seeing Samantha crouched amidst her sapphire blue skirts, carefully turning the fish with a makeshift spatula, Ethan had to tamp down the sudden desire he felt for her just then. "Your chair awaits, my lady," he said with aplomb. "Although it's rather wet."

Samantha giggled. "There's a stool next to that cupboard over there," she said as she pointed to an area in shadow.

Ethan wondered how they had missed it during their earlier exploration of the tower. The three legs seemed solid enough, although the wooden seat was a bit cracked. He brushed it off with the damp linen and placed it next to the table. "It smells delicious," he commented.

"Hand me a plate and you can start eating," she replied, using the flat metal to scrape the fish from where it had burned to the metal. Although she had a hanky wrapped around one end of the hot metal, it was still difficult to hold onto.

"Here," Ethan said as he took the spatula from her and managed to get all the fish onto the plate. "I don't want you burning yourself." No sooner had he said the words when he sucked in a breath between his teeth. "Damn, that's hot," he cursed, shaking his hand.

Samantha managed to grab the plate of fish before it landed in the fire. "Are you hurt?" she asked, her eyes wide with concern.

Ethan nearly sucked in another breath, stunned she would care so much about his welfare. "I'll live," he murmured, not able to take his eyes off of her.

Glancing down at the two fingers he held out, Samantha saw they were a bit red. She carefully lifted them to her lips and kissed each turn.

"Kiss and make it better," they both said in unison.

Blinking, Samantha angled her head. "My ... mother used to say that," she whispered.

"My mother still does," Ethan said with a smirk. The sound of his stomach grumbling brought them out of their reverie. "Let's eat." He stood up and held out his hand to help her up, his burned fingers forgotten.

The two took turns using the knife to separate the flakes of fish from the bones. Eating with their fingers, they finished the fish in only a few minutes, both agreeing it was rather pleasant tasting—the wild garlic Samantha had found earlier that afternoon made up for the lack of salt given the mild flavor of the fish.

They spent the rest of their meal occasionally popping berries into their mouths until they were gone. With nothing to do—the rain still fell and the only light was from the dying fire, Samantha wondered about the sleeping arrangements.

"Perhaps you should go upstairs," Ethan suggested as he moved to put the plates and empty cups just outside the arched doorway. He figured the rain would rinse the plates and fill the cups for the morning. The basin was already full again. He had used it to clean up earlier and now brought it in, the bowl filled with rainwater.

Samantha dared a look at the stairs and shook her head. "I'd really rather not," she said with a quick shake of her head. She found the room above them rather creepy, and was sure small animals had made their nests in the cot.

Surprised at her response, Ethan looked about the small circular space available given the table, chair and fire circle took up so much of it. "I don't like thinking of you sleeping in the dirt," he replied with a shake of his head.

Samantha arched an eyebrow in surprise at his comment, but felt a bit of satisfaction that he felt some concern on her behalf. She considered their options and decided she would need to be a bit bold. "If you don't mind, we could sleep in my gown," she suggested.

Blinking, Ethan angled his head. "Excuse me? I'm not sure what you mean." How was he supposed to fit inside her dinner gown when she was already in it? "And I would rather not sleep in my wet clothes," he added, giving her an arched eyebrow that suggested he was daring her to say it was entirely acceptable for him to do so.

Sighing, Samantha said, "I can remove my gown and lay it out ... upside down. Then you can open up the bottom of the skirts and slide inside. I'll ... sleep on the outside. It's warm enough. I can use my reticule as a pillow, and you can use the linens as yours."

Ethan regarded Samantha a moment, one hand rubbing the side of his whiskered face as he considered her suggestion. Her plan was practical, although not exactly ideal. But what choice did they have?

"All right," he finally agreed. "But ... do you have anything on ... underneath your gown?" He felt a rush of warmth cover his throat and face at his sudden discomfort. *Christ!* The two had slept next to one another the past two nights. *Why was tonight any different?*

"Of course," Samantha replied, a blush coloring her face. Leaning down, she removed her half boots and turned her back to him. "If you could just undo the top two buttons," she said, "I can pull this up and over my head."

Sighing, Ethan fumbled with the fastenings and then found himself helping to pull the yards and yards of sapphire silk up and over her hair. As Samantha shook out the gown and carefully spread it out on the ground, Ethan felt a rush of desire. Dressed only in a corset, pantaloons and stockings, she reminded him of the young ladies that worked in a brothel he had frequented whilst at university in Oxford.

"Could you loosen the ties just a bit?" Samantha asked as turned her back to him again.

Ethan swallowed. *Loosen the ties?* He realized after a moment that she meant the ties of her corset, and chastised himself for his clumsy attempt. What was wrong with him? He had undone Daisy's corset many a time. But Daisy was a mistress. Not much better than a prostitute when all was said and done.

He heard Samantha's sigh of relief as her corset seem to unglue itself from her body, leaving behind red marks in her skin just below her shoulder blades. "Thank you," she said as she stayed where she was, her back still turned to him.

When Ethan realized she was expecting him to undress, he moved to get the chair and place it near the fire. Hanging his damp shirt on the chair back and then his breeches over the seat, he wondered about his smalls. Although they were nearly as wet as his breeches, they were the only thing left on his body. He quickly doffed them, deciding it better they dry by the fire than dry on his body. He was about to open up the skirts of her gown when he remembered the linens. She had suggested he use them as a pillow, and he found he rather liked the idea. They were on the table, however.

The table she was facing.

"Close your eyes," he suddenly ordered.

Samantha did so, unsure of what the marquess was doing. "Is everything ...?"

"I just need to get my pillow," he said as he scooped up the pile of linens from the table.

Opening one eye just a bit, Samantha was blessed with a vision of Ethan's muscular and very naked back—and backside. In the firelight, his broad shoulders very nearly rippled as he reached for the linens. His torso, tapered slightly to his waist, ended in buttocks that had obviously spent a good deal of time on a horse. A frisson passed through Samantha as an image of him atop her flashed in her mind.

Suppressing the urge to gasp, she quickly closed the eye and stood patiently as she heard him move back behind her. The rustle of the silk told her he was opening up the gown and getting inside.

"Well, it's not ideal," he murmured, "But I suppose it will work."

Samantha dared a glance down and found the marquess covered to his chest while his feet protruded through the bodice. Unable to suppress a chuckle, she said, "The blue really brings out your eyes."

"No doubt," he replied, rather shocked to find she didn't have her arms wrapped around the front of her corset in an attempt at modesty. The ruffled cups above and to the sides of the busk barely covered her breasts, and in the firelight, he could see the silhouettes of her nipples. "Are you ... cold?" he asked, feeling a bit embarrassed that she wouldn't have the benefit of her gown to cover herself while she slept.

"Not at all," she replied with a shake of her head, trying with all her might to tamp down the arousal that had her breasts swelling and her nipples tightening into buds.

Despite her words, she moved around him to put another branch on the fire before considering on which side of the gown she should arrange herself.

"Here," he said as he patted the fabric. He had pulled the fabric around one side of his body so his outline shown in relief while the rest of the silk was flat next to him.

Samantha lowered herself onto the gown and stretched out, remembering too late she was going to use her reticule as a pillow. Ethan's arm was suddenly beneath her head, bending to pull her shoulders so her head lay in the small of his shoulder. Moving her arm over his bare chest, her hand ended up beneath his breast, her thumb resting on his flat nipple.

In the dim light, Samantha could make out the outline of his arousal in the silk fabric. She was tempted to move her hand down, move it down and cover the bulge and use her fingers to explore its shape, but she dared not. Ethan's free hand suddenly moved to her arm, his thumb brushing the side of the ruffled cup of her corset as he did so.

Unable to suppress a gasp at the frisson his touch had set off, Samantha moved her hand over his and guided his thumb back to her breast.

A bit surprised by the inherent invitation, Ethan lifted himself onto one elbow, forcing Samantha's head off his shoulder. His hand moved to cover her breast, his finger tips grasping the edges of the ruffles to pull them down. Leaning over, his mouth took her breast, his tongue laving across the puckered flesh in an assault that had Samantha so stunned, she almost couldn't breathe. Her chest arched up as his mouth released its hold and then blew air on the damp breast. His fingertips pulled down the ruffles on the other side, exposing her breast to his fingers and then his tongue.

Gasping her surprise at his boldness, at the frissons of pleasure that skittered beneath her skin, Samantha felt suddenly emboldened and moved her hand down his silk-clad body to where his arousal was evident. He gave a start and a groan as her hand covered it, as her fingers wrapped around the hardened shaft and pushed and pulled. Three fingers moved to the base and below, cupping his sac and lifting it through the silk.

Ethan sucked in a breath as his body jerked. Samantha was sure he cursed, but she could barely hear him through her own labored breathing. When she moved her fingers back up along his shaft, she mewled as his mouth took her breast again, as his teeth gently bit the flesh, his lips sliding off the mound until her nipple was between his lips.

Samantha cried out as a wave of pleasure passed through her torso, her fingers tightening their hold on his manhood in response.

Moving his fingers to the ties of her pantaloons, Ethan had them undone in an instant. Samantha gasped as his warm palm caressed her belly beneath the muslin fabric. When his middle finger reached her dark curlies, it paused a moment before continuing its descent, parting the curls and sliding between her slick folds. His other fingers splayed open, his thumb and forefinger pressing against the inside of one thigh in an effort to move it aside so he might caress her womanhood.

With Ethan's sudden shift onto his side, Samantha lost her hold on his manhood. His body suddenly lay angled atop hers. Flat on her back, Samantha could do nothing but allow his lips to continue their worship of her nipples and his hand to explore her most private place. When one leg bent slightly in response to the intimate touch of his fingers, she allowed it to fall to the side, thinking herself rather wanton just then.

Suddenly open to his ministrations, her swollen womanhood met his touch. The explosion of sensation had Samantha crying out, her body tensing and giving into the swirling void that suddenly surrounded her.

Her right hand sought something to hang onto, something to provide an anchor as she felt tossed about. The flat of her hand landed beneath his chest and slid down the front of his body, her fingers deftly caressing as they trailed down his body. Once she had his erection pressed into her palm, felt his wet tip pulse against the base of her thumb, she folded her fingers around him and held on.

She reveled in how his body responded, in how his manhood seemed to come alive at her touch, in the sound of his moan as he suddenly spasmed, at the sight of his face as he raised it from her chest and regarded her with furrowed brows before he seemed to lose all strength and collapse onto his back.

Not knowing what to do—she still held onto his pulsing

erection—Samantha simply allowed her breathing to return to normal before lifting herself onto an elbow. Ethan's torso was entirely uncovered, his manhood held in her fist as it rested in a nest of dark curls. His breathing, still labored, seemed on its way to normal. The pool of his seed was smeared on his belly, glistening in the light from the fire.

Leaning over his body, Samantha touched the tip of her tongue to it and was forced to pull away when Ethan suddenly reacted to the touch, his body jerking, one hand flailing in an effort to find her. When it settled on her shoulder, he suddenly grasped her and pulled her entire body up along his body. He only let go to reach for and pull the silk gown over the top of them.

"You minx," he accused in a whisper before his body went slack beneath hers.

Samantha swallowed, thinking she should have argued. Not sure of what to say in response or even what to do, she took a deep breath and let it out slowly.

Finding her position half atop his body, it reminded her of when they were on the raft. Settling one leg betwixt his, she relaxed her head into the small of his shoulder and was soon asleep.

CHAPTER 18

THE IMPORTANCE OF BEING

*I*n the middle of the night

"Do you ever think of the effect your existence has on the people who make up your marquessate?" Samantha wondered as she stared up at the stars. She and Ethan were standing in the top of the tower, the room below having collected too much smoke from the fire to make it possible to sleep comfortably.

Ethan frowned at the question, never having given his existence much thought, let alone that of those who lived on his lands.

"Well, I didn't before just now," he murmured, leaning against one of the battlements. "I suppose I would hope they are better off working my lands than they would be if they lived elsewhere," he added after a moment. "What about you? What effect has your existence had on those who you know in London?"

Samantha allowed a grin, a bit surprised the marquess would turn her question on her. She thought for a moment, wondering who besides Caroline and Matthew may have been affected by her existence. Her face suddenly lit up.

"I know. I believe something I said may be the reason Julia Harrington is married to Alistair Comber," she said with delight.

Ethan shook his head. "Who?" The last names were familiar, but he didn't recognize the first names.

Samantha leaned on the opposite battlement. "Julia Harrington is Caroline's niece and the daughter of the Earl of Mayfield," she clarified. "And Alistair is the second son of the Earl of Aimsley."

"Christ!" Ethan said just then. "I thought he'd died on the Continent," he said in surprise.

"I think he almost did," Samantha said. "How do you know him?"

Despite the warm air, a breeze had begun, and Ethan found himself moving toward Samantha. She was honey to his bee, and after what they had done downstairs, he wanted her nectar as near as possible. "We attended university together," he murmured, his arms wrapping around her shoulders so he could pull her against the front of his body. "I take it he returned to England. Is he ... well?"

Pleased by the man's hold on her, Samantha smiled. "He did. He is. But he had made a promise to one of his soldiers that he would see to the man's widow and family. A payment of fifteen pounds a month." Ethan's sudden hiss had her pulling away a bit. "What?"

The marquess shook his head. "A rather expensive promise for an officer to make," he said with concern. "But I suppose for the Aimsley earldom, it would be but a drop in the bucket."

"Except his father wouldn't honor the promise," Samantha countered. "Alistair was forced to sell his commission," she explained, glad the marquess was quick to understand the problem.

Ethan hissed again.

"Exactly!" Samantha said. "His father found out and disowned him, which meant he had to find a position, which is how he came to be employed as a groom in the Harrington House stables."

Wrapping his arms around Samantha's back and pulling her against the front of his body, Ethan fought the sudden fatigue he was feeling. "He was always rather good with horses," he murmured. "Should have worked at Tattersall's."

Samantha wondered if she should mention that he already did—he had been hired as a consultant by the horse trading company—but instead, she said, "And he's rather handsome, which ..."

Ethan was suddenly standing up straight and regarding Samantha with a look that suggested he might be offended. "Come again?" he interrupted.

Samantha giggled at his expression. "Which *Julia* noticed one afternoon whilst she watched him from her bedchamber window," she went on. "He was brushing the earl's horse, and Julia said he was too handsome to be a groom. She said that with a bit of help from her brother's valet and some dance and elocution lessons, she thought he could be made into a gentleman."

His frown turning into an expression of bewilderment, Ethan shook his head. "But ... But he is already a gentleman," he claimed.

"But we didn't know that," Samantha replied. "We had no idea who he was. So I dared Julia to go through with her plan."

"You dared her?" Ethan repeated, wondering if tiredness was the cause of his slow comprehension or if it was due to having just been pleasured that had him beyond his ability to reason. Perhaps his ability to think straight would return in the morning.

"Double-dog dared her, actually," Samantha amended, rather liking how the warmth from his body was keeping hers so comfortable despite the slight breeze ruffling her hair just then.

"Double-dog dared? To do ... what, exactly?" he wondered, his lids feeling as if they weighed far too much.

Samantha sighed. "To make him into a gentleman. In time for the Mayfield's ball. Julia accepted the challenge, had three weeks to complete it, and, of course, Alistair passed with flying colors. They were married shortly thereafter, and I am very happy to report a baby is on the way."

Ethan's chuckle turned into laughter. "All because you double-dog dared her?" he whispered.

"Mmm," she replied with a nod, his kiss swallowing her response.

"Then I believe, my lady, that your existence is far more important than mine, for I cannot claim any such feat," he murmured.

Samantha regarded the marquess for a long moment, knowing they would need to get to where he could lie down before he fell down. "Oh, I beg to differ, my lord," she replied, her eyes darkening with her words. "You saved my life."

Ethan finally nodded. If that's what she believed, he wasn't going to argue.

CHAPTER 19
REUNITED

*M*atthew Fitzsimmons regarded the front of the hotel, a bit surprised by the ornate plasterwork decorating the tops of the arches along the front of the building. Located near the center of Valencia, the hotel seemed to be the only establishment offering rooms for the night. Apparently the building was actually the residence of a local aristocrat but served as a hotel when the noble was out of the country.

According to the captain of *The Fairweather*—Matthew had paid a call there first thinking he would find Caroline still aboard the ship while it was under repair—his wife had stayed at a convent for two nights and had just secured a suite at the hotel. Caroline had told the captain she intended to stay in the port city until the ship's mast was replaced.

Captain John St. John promised he would make the trip back to England just as soon as repairs on *The Fairweather* were complete. Since the other passengers had made their own arrangements to travel onto Rome, he had more than enough room to accommodate the couple.

Matthew's arrival had been noticed, he realized, when the tall front doors opened before he reached them. A butler bowed deeply and bade him enter.

Matthew did so, stepping into the large foyer and admiring

the rich decor. From the marble floors beneath his feet to the gilded ornamentation on the walls to the chandelier dripping with crystals above him, he realized no expense had been spared in the decoration. On any other occasion upon entering such a hotel, Matthew might have wondered how much it was going to cost him.

Not on this occasion.

He didn't care if it cost every pence of his viscountcy. He just wanted to find his wife and spend the rest of his life with her.

"Matthew Fitzsimmons, Viscount Chamberlain, here to claim my viscountess," he stated with a nod, not intending for his words to sound quite so brusque.

The butler's eyes widened. "This way, my lord," he said in thickly accented English.

Climbing the wide staircase to the second floor, Matthew felt as if he were at court. A half-dozen servants scurried about, keeping their eyes averted and their footfalls as quiet as possible. At just the second room from the top of the stairs, the butler stopped and indicated a set of double doors. "Viscountess Chamberlain, my lord," he said before giving a deep bow and then hurrying off.

Furrowing his brows, Matthew watched as the butler made his way back down the stairs, apparently leaving him to announce himself to whoever he found behind the doors. He gave a tentative knock, wondering if a servant would answer or if he should simply enter on his own.

"Come in," he heard from within. His heart gave a stutter at the sound of the voice. *Caroline!* Matthew had the door open in the next heartbeat, his gaze sweeping the elegant apartment.

Caroline Fitzsimmons, looking every bit the aristocrat in a deep green silk dinner gown, stood up from a settee, a book held open in one hand. She turned to see who her visitor might be. "Matthew!" she cried out, rushing toward him.

The viscount barely had the door shut before she had her arms around his shoulders, her face pressed against the side of his face. "Caroline, oh my sweeting," he whispered. He hadn't known what to expect. Hadn't known if she would welcome him or simply acknowledge his arrival with a polite nod or, God forbid, shun him. He could have joined her and Samantha on their trip. He should have, he told himself for at least the tenth time since leaving London.

"I didn't know if you would receive my note," Caroline replied, tears pricking the corners of her eyes. *Haven't I cried quite enough this past week?* If only there had been some news— even bad news—she would at least know if she should continue holding out hope for her daughter. *She cannot have perished*, she kept thinking. *I didn't have a chance to tell her the truth.* A truth she had every intention of telling the girl once they had reached Rome. *She deserved to know.*

"I received the news from someone in charge at the shipping company. They made arrangements for my travel here," Matthew explained, rather liking how his wife hadn't given up her hold on him. "I just came from the docks. I spoke with Captain St. John. He said you spent most of your time on board in your cabin. Said you were quite seasick," Matthew spoke as he held her, his arms wrapped around her waist and shoulders like steel bands. He wasn't going to allow her out of his sight anytime soon. "Are you ... recovered?" he asked in a whisper, his lips brushing her hair and then her ear.

Caroline sighed and gave into his hold, pressing herself into his welcoming embrace. "As much as can be expected, I suppose," she murmured, allowing another sigh. She felt him stiffen suddenly before he pulled his head from next to hers.

"What does that mean?" he asked in alarm, his brows furrowing.

Allowing a wan smile, Caroline regarded her husband of twenty-two years for a long moment. Without his usual powdered wig, he appeared at least ten years younger than his fifty-six years. He looked so much like his brother George, Caroline was briefly reminded of the few nights she had spent in the other man's company.

Despite their age difference, she had fallen in love with George Fitzsimmons, a widower with a daughter. She had met him at his hat shop. He seemed smitten with her from the moment they met. She loved the attention the hat maker had showered on her, loved how he was so dedicated to his trade—to making hats better than any others on the market—despite him being the son of a viscount. She loved how he had held her in such high esteem and yet teased her about being a Harrington, how he had finally—almost reluctantly—taken her to his bed when she had insisted he do so because she thought herself in love with him.

"I wish to know what it's like to make love to a man who loves me, for I will never have that once I am married," she had said that first night they were alone together. And George had kissed her so sweetly, tears had come to her eyes. He continued to kiss her, to barely touch her, as if his slightly calloused fingers would somehow damage her skin as his caress incited such pleasure. His kisses had continued as he slowly removed her gown and petticoats, to untie the new corset she had purchased for the occasion, to slowly strip her of her translucent silk chemise and stockings until she was naked. His lips had continued their journey over her body, sending shock waves of pleasure in their wake until she begged him to take her, to take what she had promised would be his for the rest of his life. The look on his face betrayed his lust for her as well as what she later realized was his knowledge that the rest of his life would be but a few years.

She was sure Samantha had been conceived that night— her first night with the man she swore would be her only love. They would have only two more nights together before reality would force them to part, force them to acknowledge that what they shared could no longer be allowed. And so Caroline Harrington had accepted her duty as the daughter of an earl and agreed she would wed a viscount.

What a cruel irony to be in love with the brother of the man to whom she would wed only a year later!

She had never told Matthew of her love for his brother, but

she often wondered if he simply knew. And despite her vow, in the intervening years, she had grown to love the man who held her so tightly just then, grown to appreciate how kind he had been, how accommodating he had been to allow her to bring into his home the baby she had claimed was her sister's. To raise her as a daughter of an aristocrat believing she was merely a niece.

Did he know? At some point, had Matthew guessed the true identity of Samantha?

"Are you well?" Matthew questioned, watching his wife as she seemed lost in thought.

Caroline sighed and nodded her head. "I am ... sad, and I am happy," she finally responded.

"Happy?" Matthew repeated.

His wife lifted her head from his shoulder and nodded again. "I've never been so glad to see anyone in my entire life," she whispered, realizing she meant the words. At his arched eyebrow and look of astonishment, she added, "Oh, and I rather think it has something to do with the baby I'm expecting."

Having worked at the Foreign Office nearly his entire adult life, Matthew Fitzsimmons thought there wasn't anything that could surprise him. News of wars, of political intrigues, of royal *affaires* and matters of the heart and all manner of life's minutia could not have prepared him for the words his wife had just spoken, as if she were commenting on the weather. He blinked, thinking of the nights they had spent together these past months. It was if they had discovered they loved one another, and not just the sort of love they had shared earlier in their marriage, as if they were siblings who simply shared a home.

He blinked again. *A baby?*

"I do hope you're ... all right with it?" Caroline said, her brows furrowing at his lack of reply. "I'm hoping for a boy, of course, seeing as how you need an heir ..."

Her words were cut off by his mouth, which had suddenly captured hers in a kiss that was both urgent and tender. When he pulled away, it was to take a breath and leave his forehead pressed against hers. "You wicked, wonderful woman, you," he whispered before kissing her again.

Caroline allowed a moan to escape as she reveled in the sensations her husband's simple kiss and tentative tongue created against her lips and teeth. George had never kissed her like this. Never kissed her as if his very life depended on it. She was quite sure if Matthew continued, she would have to undo the fastenings of his breeches—she could feel his erection pressing into her belly.

He continued.

Excited, she pulled away and moved her hands to his cravat, undoing the intricate knot before moving her fingers to the button that held his shirt closed at the top.

"Whatever are you doing?" Matthew asked as one hand wrapped around her wrist.

Undaunted, she moved the other hand to the placket of his breeches and slipped a fastening through the hole. "Undressing you," she replied, a bit breathless. "As you should be doing to me," she added as she pulled her wrist from his gentle hold and finished what she had begun below. His manhood sprang from its nest of curls and into the palm of one hand while her other moved to cup his sac.

Suddenly breathless, Matthew swallowed and did her bidding. With her sleeves rather low on her arms and little in the way of buttons down the back, he could simply pull the gown up and over her head. For a moment, the green silk separated them, and she was forced to give up her hold on him. Once her arms were free of the gown, though, she reclaimed him, arching an eyebrow as the gown floated to the floor.

"Jesus, Caro," he breathed, his lips taking purchase on the tops of her shoulders before moving down to one breast. "You'll forever be my undoing." Despite her forty-three years, Caroline still excited him in a way no other woman could. Her hourglass figure was nearly the same as the day he had married her, although her breasts were now a bit larger and her hips a bit wider. Her brunette hair was streaked with gold but no silver, and her legs, long and shapely, would be the envy of every other woman at a ball if she ever dampened her silk gowns. Just the thought of her calves wrapped around his thighs had Matthew hardening even more than her hold on him had managed just then. His breaths coming in short pants, Matthew moved his lips to her other breast, suckling the nipple until he heard Caroline's soft mewling.

His boots long since removed from his feet, he lowered his hands to his breeches and pushed them down until they fell in a heap at his feet. Sliding his hands back up her thighs, he moved his palms to her derriere. He lifted her, forcing her legs to wrap around his body, and carried her to the bed.

Once she was on her back, Matthew had her legs spread wide. He lowered his head to the apex of her thighs. Even before his tongue made contact with the soft folds, already glistening with her anticipation, he heard her gasps and slid his hands along the inside of her thighs, grinning when her torso seemed to rise from the bed. A simple flick of his tongue across her engorged womanhood had her body trembling. Another flick had her begging him to impale her, and the last had her saying his name in a sigh so welcome to his ears, he nearly obliged her right then and there. But he waited until he heard her sob before capturing the bud with his lips and suckling it until he felt her body shiver and shake beneath him.

At that point, he pulled her derriere to the edge of the bed and thrust himself into her welcoming cocoon, nearly losing himself in the process. He forced himself to hold on, to deny himself the release his body had demanded since the moment he had walked into the room and had her in his arms.

Her thighs were suddenly gripping his, her calves already wrapped around his buttocks. Feeling the undulating waves and then the sudden clench on his manhood was his undoing, and he stiffened his body as the pleasure took him under.

Could anything ever be as good as being in the arms of Caroline? Being inside her sweet haven? Being on top of her soft body as oblivion took him away? Matthew collapsed atop his wife with a final groan, only aware of her murmured, "I love you."

He would have responded in kind had he still been conscious, but satiation and exhaustion combined to put him to into a deep slumber.

Sighing at her own sense of satiation, Caroline closed her eyes and slept well for the first time in days.

CHAPTER 20

ON THE MERITS OF A MISTRESS

*T*hird night on the island
Daisy.

Ethan had spoken the word several times in his sleep, once as if he were angry and once as if he were very sad. Samantha wondered why a flower could have him so upset.

"She's not a flower, I assure you," Ethan said in response to Samantha's carefully worded question. *Deflowered, to be sure,* and he often wondered by how many different men. "She was my mistress," he finally admitted, realizing if he didn't offer the information, Samantha would probably ask who she was.

"From the sound of your voice, I would assume you did not much care for her," Samantha murmured.

For a long moment, Ethan didn't respond, his chest merely rising and falling with his breathing. "She was not an honorable woman," Ethan finally spoke, realizing for the first time what had bothered him so much about Daisy Albright.

He and his mistress had had more than a simple understanding. They'd had a contract. Daisy broke it by attempting to play him against another client. *Badly played, Daisy,* he thought as he took a deep breath.

Samantha felt Ethan's body relax and wondered at his words. "Did she ... lie with another?" she whispered, raising herself up onto an elbow so she could see his face. Twilight had descended, and the shadows around them had nearly disappeared.

Ethan regarded the woman whose virtue was in serious danger. "After she tried to extort more from me than we had agreed in our contract," he answered. "Larger house, more pin money." He furrowed his eyebrows. "And why would a gently bred lady such as yourself be wondering about a *mistress?*" he asked suddenly. "It's hardly a proper topic for conversation," he admonished her, his manner not as serious as it probably should have been.

Still supporting herself on her elbow, Samantha regarded the marquess for a very long time. "I cannot imagine making a bargain with you and then breaking it," she said quietly, her voice full of awe. "She must be such a fool!"

A burst of laughter erupted from Ethan, the rich baritone rending the quiet night. He lifted a hand to her shoulder and pulled her down, meeting her lips in a gentle kiss. "She thought she had a better bargain with my replacement, I suppose," he murmured then, saying the words to prevent her from asking the question he expected she might ask next.

"Did she? Get a better bargain, I mean."

Ethan blinked.

Well, that wasn't the question he expected her to ask.

"What do you think?" he countered, not sure how to answer her. Of course, Daisy ended up with a larger townhouse—or at least, she was promised one. He hadn't cared enough to discover if she had larger living quarters now or not. He only knew she had vacated the townhouse he had let on her behalf.

Samantha placed a hand along Ethan's face, her fingers caressing his stubble-lined jaw down to his neck, her gaze following the trail of her fingers. "I think I would take whatever you offered, no matter how grand or how small," she murmured before touching her lips to his.

For a moment, she wished she was stripped of everything she wore and that he was naked as well. She craved him. Wanted to feel his warm flesh against her own. Wanted his arms to hold her tighter to his body. Wanted ... what else, she did not know just then.

His chest suddenly tightening, Ethan wrapped his other arm around her waist and pulled her hard against his body, his mouth taking hers in a kiss that was both bruising and possessive. He had never thought of himself as a bargain before, but if Samantha Fitzsimmons thought him one, well, then so be it. For he couldn't imagine another woman with whom he would rather be stranded on a deserted island at that moment. All the others would be complaining about the heat or the sand or the lack of facilities or of hunger. "You sound as if you're offering yourself as my mistress," Ethan teased, nipping her lower lip before moving his kisses to her neck.

Samantha suppressed a giggle when the soft stubble on his face caressed her cheek and neck. "I rather doubt any man would *want* me as his mistress," she replied in a whisper.

Pulling her away from him so he could see her in the dim light, he wondered at her words. "I beg to differ, my lady," he said, reclaiming the base of her neck with a soft kiss.

Her gasp of surprise couldn't be helped. Samantha slid her fingers into his hair, holding his head in her hands and tilting it up so she could see his face. "Beg all you want, but ..." She shook her head, surprised to see the marquess sporting an expression so unlike the scowl he seemed to wear all the time.

"Why cannot you believe a man would want you as his mistress? Not that you could ever *be* one, since you are a lady," he added, as if he thought it important to make the distinction. "But, still."

"I have no idea what to do to please a man!" she claimed. Although, that wasn't entirely true, she considered. Both Evangeline and Julia had told her some of what their husbands found especially satisfying, but other than what she had done the night before through the silk of her gown, Samantha had certainly never tried such things on a man. Her eyes widened in an effort to make her point. "It's not as if we are allowed to take lovers before we are married so that we may ... learn lovemaking skills," she argued.

Ethan let out a snort. "I should hope not!"

"But, *you're* allowed," she accused.

"So we can sow those wild oats," he countered, his manner still one of amusement.

"But how are we to know if we're doing it ... right?" Samantha countered, readjusting her position atop his body so one knee rested between his thighs. The hard ridge of his manhood was suddenly pressed against her thigh. She felt more than heard his sudden intake of breath and wondered if she had hurt him.

"I shouldn't think there are any *wrong* ways," the marquess countered, his amusement mixed with something bordering on lust.

Samantha had certainly known what to do the night before. He had been so stunned—so surprised—she would be willing to hold onto his manhood and bring him such sudden and unexpected pleasure. How long had it been since he had felt such a satisfying release? How long since his entire body had been racked by a spasm of pure pleasure?

Probably since he last visited Daisy's bed, he supposed. Although the last time hadn't been that satisfying.

"So, what should a woman do when she is in her lover's bed?"

Ethan stared at Samantha for a moment. He couldn't help but notice she had said 'lover' rather than 'husband'. Had the chit truly given up on the idea of ever getting married? She wasn't yet old enough to be considered on the shelf! There must be some young buck in London who could appreciate the young woman's sense of humor, her easy-going, forthright manner. Someone who wouldn't care that she was the illegitimate daughter of an earl's sister?

"There is much to be said for willingness," he finally replied, his eyes darkening.

Samantha's own eyes suddenly widened, his words sounding as much a challenge as a recommendation. "And if I am willing ... are ... are you?" she whispered, stunned at how bold she sounded—how positively *wanton* she was behaving. Her breasts felt as if they were swollen well beyond the confines of her corset, their nipples already pebbled into points behind the fabric cups. An ache deep in her abdomen demanded that something be done, something much like he had done to her the night before, but more ... just more.

Ethan Range arched a brow, realizing he had a decision to make, one he needed to make before there was no choice. For given another minute or two, he was quite sure the chit would have no choice—he would take her virtue over having to endure another night of a constant erection, another night of fighting the battle he found himself fighting this very moment. *She's a lady,* he reminded himself. *A gently bred ...*

A thought struck him suddenly. She wasn't *really* the daughter of a viscount, he remembered. Niece, yes, but merely by marriage. Who knew the identity of her real father? Perhaps only her mother. Had Caroline Harrington's lover been another aristocrat? Or just a commoner, perhaps?

And did it really matter?

Samantha was still a young woman. A virgin. Stranded on a deserted island with a man nearly thirty years of age who hadn't had the benefit of a bedmate in months.

The thought didn't have the same effect as being doused in cold water, which it should have had at that moment. In fact, he realized he should be picking up Samantha and setting her aside. He should be heading for the other side of the island so he wouldn't be tempted to do more than he already had done with the chit. He should be ...

When her lips captured his, Ethan suddenly knew he wouldn't be spending the night on the other side of the island or diving into the cold Mediterranean Sea to douse his desire. For Samantha Fitzsimmons had come to a decision—she had made her choice—and her choice was obviously him.

Here.

Now.

Ethan returned her kiss, gently at first, and then with more passion, more pressure, as Samantha writhed against him. Her fingers had already made their way to the fall of his breeches, fumbling with the fastenings already straining from the hard bulge behind them. He felt one side give way and heard her mewl of delight as she moved her fingers to the other side. He was surprised when she managed to free the placket in mere seconds, relieved when his manhood sprang free and collided with the silk of her gown.

Moving one hand to the buttons at the back of her gown, his fingertips barely skimming her skin, Ethan felt a bit of satisfaction as her body shivered in response. The top button gave way with the slightest pressure. The next required a bit more agility. In only a moment, though, he had as many undone as was required for him to push the bodice down past her shoulders.

Samantha pulled her lips from his at the same time she pulled her arms from the sleeves of the dinner gown, allowing the marquess to take in the sight of her bare shoulders and arms. The sapphire silk bodice still covered her corset, but Ethan pulled it down with a simple stroke of one hand. About to return her lips to his, Samantha inhaled sharply as Ethan's lips instead took purchase on the top of one of her breasts. One of his thumbs brushed down on the gathers of the cup, allowing the aching breast to pop free of its confines.

Stunned at the sight of her already erect nipple, Ethan growled and moved his mouth over it, swept the blade of his tongue across the pebble, reveled in the sound of Samantha's sudden inhalation and her whispered, "Ethan!"

Moving his attention to the other breast, he found it was already exposed. Arching an eyebrow, he glanced up at Samantha's face, a face filled with desire and yearning—for him, he realized. He had never seen such a look on Daisy's face. His mistress had always affected an air of boredom, as if she challenged him to make her appear otherwise whilst in bed.

"I couldn't help myself," she whispered in her defense, thinking he meant her whisper of his name.

He shook his head, one lip curled up in a smirk. "You may say whatever you wish, my lady," he murmured, reaching his hands down to her hips and lifting her so she was before him on her knees. "If you want me to stop, though, you had better say it soon, for I fear I will be unable to comply after …"

He had to stop speaking when Samantha leaned over and kissed his mouth, her tongue suddenly tangling with his. He took the opportunity to gather up the hem of her gown and pull the yards of silk up and over her head, breaking their kiss to allow the fabric to pass between them. Using both hands, he lifted and lowered the gown so it spread open in the slight breeze and finally landed on the sand. Ethan turned back to Samantha, a bit surprised to find her still on her knees, the cups of her corset well below her breasts, her pantaloons the only impediment to what he intended to do next. What surprised him most, though, was how wanton she looked, how positively seductive she seemed as she regarded him.

Her hands were suddenly at his sides, pulling up on the fine lawn fabric of his shirt until she had it over his head. Like he had done with her gown, she allowed it to spread out in the breeze and lowered it over the bodice of her gown. When she turned her attention back to Ethan, a shiver passed through her entire body, a shiver of anticipation or of fear or excitement, she knew not. She merely knew she had to have this man. Turning her body so her back was to him, she whispered, "Untie me, please."

Ethan thought he had never heard such erotic words in his entire life. He nearly cursed when his fingers fumbled with the ties of her corset—he had just retied it this morning, after all.

Once it was finally loose enough, Ethan pulled the corset up and over her head, worried by her sudden hiss when the corset abraded her nipples. He leaned over and kissed each of them in turn. "I apologize, my lady," he whispered, closing his eyes and shivering as her fingers speared his hair and held his head against her breast.

"Apology accepted, of course," she responded, her voice so breathy he nearly chuckled.

"You're quite good at this," he murmured, moving his lips over her breasts and up to the hollow of her throat. His hands, meanwhile, had moved to the top of her pantaloons and were now sliding down her thighs, up and around the globes of her bottom, sending shivers of delight through Samantha.

"I've really no idea what I'm doing," she replied, her breaths coming in pants. She let out a squeak when he suddenly pulled her against him, one arm wrapping around her back and the other behind her knees. Lifting her slightly, he rolled her onto her back, onto the silk blanket of her gown, and settled her there.

Still on his knees, he regarded her with heavy-lidded eyes. Good God, she was beautiful on her blanket of blue silk, wearing only her pantaloons and an expression that could only be one of invitation.

He would see to the pantaloons in a moment. Right now, he needed to get his breeches off his body. "I have had a bit of experience, I'll grant you that," he managed to get out between gasps for air. "But never out of doors," he added, deciding he needed to slow down. Slow down or risk allowing his release before he had seen to her pleasure.

It's her first time, you idiot.

The reminder had his cock settling down a bit, his ardor cooling so he could think with his other head.

Ethan glanced at her bare breasts, at how her slim waist led to her wider hips. His hand moved to the pantaloons still covering most of her lower body, his fingers fumbling with the ties that held them closed around her waist. Once they were loose, his hand moved to the globes of her bottom, grasping the fine muslin fabric and gently pulling it down her legs until she lay naked before him.

Forcing himself to slow down, Ethan regarded Samantha for a long time, marveling at her long torso, her even longer legs. At her swollen breasts, which would nearly fill his hand. Daisy's weren't nearly as impressive, nor would she have allowed him to look upon her like he was doing right now.

Gazing and hungry with a need he hadn't acknowledged for some time, Ethan allowed a low groan to escape.

Samantha realized at that moment she should be afraid. She should be reaching for something to cover her body, pushing herself away from the man who suddenly looked at her as if he were a hungry animal and she was his next meal. At the man whose rigid cock hovered very near her body, near enough to impale her, to claim her maidenhood as its own. But she stilled herself, reminding herself that Ethan was a man, a man who seemed to relish the banquet spread out before him, a man who *desired* her. No other man had ever looked at her quite the same way. No other man had kissed her breasts, and undressed her and gazed with such reverence upon her. No other man had undressed himself to reveal his naked body to her, his throbbing manhood ready to enter her wet, welcoming folds. She was his to claim, she decided, no matter the consequences.

So Samantha was a bit surprised when Ethan reached for the back of her knees and spread them wide—not for his manhood to impale her, but rather for his head to suddenly descend and his tongue to take purchase on the feminine folds she was sure were throbbing with anticipation. The raspy feel of his rough tongue over the tender flesh had her arching her back in response, a cry forced from her throat. When the blade of his tongue struck again, her hips quivered and her hands flailed, desperate to capture something to hold onto. Finally gripping the silk of her gown, Samantha gasped and tried to hold herself still as the next thrust of his tongue caught her by surprise. She cried out, mewled and wept as the sudden waves of pleasure brought stars to her eyes and immense pleasure to her lower body. "Ethan!" she whispered, sure there was something she needed to do for him but not sure how to do it.

"Sam," he whispered in reply, moving his body up over hers, his throbbing cock finding her wet folds. He held himself over her, kissed her on the lips and lowered his forehead to hers. "I cannot stop now." And with those words, he sank himself into her, barely aware of her hiss as he breached her maidenhood.

Tight and warm and suddenly clenching around his rock-hard shaft, Samantha's warm, wet haven seemed to welcome him, draw him in and then imprison him. The intense sensation had Ethan grunting as he attempted to pull out. Unable to do so—his strength had suddenly left his body—he ground himself into her deeper, aware he would not come out, at least not until her body was willing to give him up. Moaning as he allowed his release, Ethan slowly lowered himself atop Samantha's body and passed out.

Unsure of what had just happened and still smarting from the rather uncomfortable pinching sensation she had just experienced, Samantha lay beneath the marquess and allowed a sigh of frustration. The weight of his body made it difficult to breathe, but she dared not try to move him. Not while he was still inside her. Not while his cock was still so hard and filled her until she was almost uncomfortable. Her lower body spasmed a bit, causing her to clench around the foreign body invading her most private place. She wondered at Ethan's sudden inhalation of breath, as if he had felt the very same sensation she had.

A sense of disappointment settled on Samantha just then. She hadn't experienced any particular pleasure when he entered her; indeed, she had felt as if she had been stabbed by a blunt instrument.

His tongue had been far more satisfying. Far more intimate. Far more pleasurable as it brought her waves of intense pleasure, intense pleasure so sharp, it was almost painful. The memory of his tongue sliding over her womanhood had it reacting again, though, clenching involuntarily around his still-hard cock.

Ethan groaned, his body finally lifting from hers to fall at her side, his hands still grasping her bottom so her body was forced to follow his. Samantha ended up atop him, her legs straddling his hips and her breasts pressed into the crisp, dark curls covering his chest.

Wondering if she could simply lift herself from his body, she found his hold on her absolute, his thumbs pressed along her hip bones while his fingers still gripped the globes of her bottom. His eyes were closed, and his face appeared almost serene, his expression making him appear rather handsome just then. Despite his groans and what had looked like an expression of pain on his face, he had obviously experienced something rather pleasant at the same moment Samantha had felt a rush of warmth fill her lower body.

The memory had her wondering if he had felt the same sort of pleasure she had felt when he had touched his tongue to her. His entire body had stiffened so suddenly, the cords of his neck evident behind the stubble of his beard, the muscles of his arms rippling beneath his skin.

Samantha was tempted to touch his face, to slide her fingers over the short beard that had both caressed and abraded her thighs as his tongue had worked its magic. The memory had a frisson passing through her entire body, the sensation of pure pleasure causing her to inhale sharply.

Was this the pleasure her friends alluded to when they spoke of making love to their husbands?

If so, she had to admit it was ... pleasant, but certainly not earth-shattering. The stars hadn't exploded into fireworks, filling the sky with streaks of light. Her body hadn't felt as if it had come apart into a billion pieces. Ending up atop Ethan's body was somewhat comfortable, but not in a way that made her feel as if she was loved, as if she would be protected for the rest of her life.

No, this wasn't at all what Julia Harrington Comber alluded to when she spoke in quiet whispers of her nights with her husband, Alistair. And it wasn't anything like what Evangeline Tennison Althorpe described of her frequent couplings with her husband, Jeffrey, when the baroness last paid a call at Fitzsimmons Manor. Who would have ever thought sweet, innocent Evangeline capable of having intercourse in nearly every room of Sommers Place? Although, to be fair, Sommers Place wasn't *that* large a home. Samantha supposed when they ran out of rooms, the Althorpes would simply turn their attention to the varied pieces of furniture ... Samantha shook her head to clear the image.

Better the furniture than out-of-doors, she supposed.

The thought had her remembering where she was— very out-of-doors and rather exposed atop an unconscious marquess.

Pressing her hands into the silk gown on either side of his chest, Samantha pushed up her shoulders. She gasped as the motion sent a tendril of pleasure shooting through her abdomen. The effect was obviously felt by Ethan, for she watched as his face displayed what looked like pain before a slight grin appeared. Curious, she pushed up again and this time pulled her knees up to the sides of his hips. They took purchase on her gown, the soft ground underneath the silk cushioning them somewhat. Once again, her lower body suddenly spasmed, and Ethan sighed, the grin widening on his face.

Aware that one of his thumbs was moving to where their bodies met, Samantha concentrated her attention on the feel of his hand as it made its way over her sensitive flesh, anticipation tightening her warm haven's hold on him. When the thumb suddenly made contact with the swollen bud he had so expertly pleasured only moments before with his tongue, Samantha tensed as the exquisite pleasure took hold, passed through her and back again, seeming to toss her insides into jumbles of perfectly timed waves of wonder. She cried out, her back arching as her chest lifted and her head angled back with her ecstasy.

Watching from below, Ethan thought he had never seen anything quite so erotic—Samantha, naked, her body taut and her spine bowed, her head thrown back in ecstasy, her neck and collar bones held in relief in the pale moonlight. "God, you're beautiful," he managed to get out as her sweet, warm wet haven clamped around his manhood once again.

How does she know what to do? How could she continue to incite such pleasure in him? To continue to force his manhood to stay so hard despite his having already spilled his seed in her?

The last thought nearly had him frowning, but her body once again shivered and shook, and rational thought left his brain as she gripped him with her honeyed folds. He was spent, he was sure, so how could she continue her assault of pure pleasure?

His eyes roamed her body, taking in the dew-covered, smooth skin. Her upturned breasts, their nipples ruched and fully aroused, begged to be held, to be kissed. Lifting himself onto one elbow, Ethan managed to get himself into a sitting position while Samantha still straddled him. He captured one breast in his mouth while a hand smoothed over the other and continued up to the side of her neck. He only let go of her breast when her body jerked suddenly, her soft cry the only other evidence of the pleasure that had coursed through her body. Ethan had his mouth over her other breast in an instant, his teeth and tongue teasing the tight bud until her body spasmed again. He felt her tighten on him, tighten and release and tighten again, her waves pulling him into her as deep as he could go. Groaning, he buried his face above one breast and struggled to catch his breath.

Although Samantha struggled to hold onto something—one hand gripped his shoulder while another was braced on his thigh behind her, the sensations he created with his touches and kisses had her losing her grip on sanity. Sure she couldn't take any more, Samantha moved the hand from his thigh and reached out for his other shoulder, grabbing onto it so her fingernails left half-moon indents in his skin.

Straightening her body and then finally slumping against the front of him, she gasped for air and whimpered quietly.

Ethan moved his hands to her back, holding her, rubbing the area below her shoulder blades as he considered what he had just done. What she had just done. He was quite sure this had never happened with Daisy. His mistress had never given—nor taken—so much during their tumbles. Had never prolonged his pleasure beyond his release. Had never held onto him as if her very life depended on him.

Tightening his hold on Samantha, Ethan eased her into a more comfortable position atop his body and lowered his head to the silk covered ground below. Kissing her hair, he closed his eyes and allowed sleep to take him.

CHAPTER 21

STAR GAZING

The fourth day on the island

Four days into their ordeal, Samantha and Ethan explored the southern coast of the island. The rocky terrain proved treacherous for Ethan, however, for without boots, his bare feet were unable to withstand the heated rocks. They both ended up in the sea, the clear, cold water providing relief as well as an opportunity for Samantha to wash her gown and undergarments while Ethan fished for their dinner.

Their clothes having dried in the sun, the two found a high spot in the dunes and watched the stars wink into existence. When one suddenly streaked across the inky darkness, Samantha gasped. "Make a wish!" she whispered.

Ethan gave her a sideways glance. "Why?" he asked, apparently not familiar with the superstition surrounding shooting stars.

Samantha regarded him with a frown. "You needn't be a spoilsport," she scolded, returning her gaze to the heavens above.

"I ... I wasn't. I assure you," he replied with a shake of his head. "Why would I make a wish?"

Hearing the sincerity in his voice, Samantha wrapped an arm around his. "When you see a shooting star, you make a wish."

Ethan glanced down and saw how her arm looped around his, saw how her hand lay wrapped around the front of his tricep, her slender thumb resting along the line of the muscle. The gesture seemed rather intimate, and something clenched in his chest. *I wish ...*

What?

What could he wish for that had any hope of happening? What wish could possibly come true?

I wish for batteries for all the coal lamps in all the mines in the marquessate.

There. There was a wish that could come true, he reasoned.

"Oh, look! There's another," Samantha whispered, pointing to the bright trail left by another shooting star. "Make another wish," she said, her body very nearly vibrating with excitement.

Ethan angled his head and leaned over to whisper in her ear. "I wish you would sleep with me tonight."

Samantha stilled herself before finally turning to regard the marquess. Her look suggested she was a bit disappointed. "Of course, I will," she murmured. "But ... But I would have anyway. You wouldn't have had to waste your wish on it."

Staring at her for several seconds, Ethan finally took a breath and nodded. "If my wish comes true, then it wasn't a waste, was it?" he countered. Out of the corner of his eye, another bright trail streaked across the sky. "Make a wish," he whispered.

Samantha's breath caught, and she finally nodded.

"What did you wish for?"

She shook her head. "I cannot say, or it won't come true," she claimed.

Ethan's shoulders suddenly slumped. "You might have mentioned that when you were explaining the rules," he chided her.

Samantha giggled, allowing a small smile. At least one of her wishes would come true that night.

As for Ethan's second wish, had they been watching for shooting stars on the other side of the island, they might have spotted not one, but two ships that passed close by the small island. It was rather doubtful the crews on board would have seen the castaways, however. They hadn't yet built a fire for the night.

CHAPTER 22

A MARQUESS REMEMBERS
A BABY

Twenty-three years before ...

After news of the birth of the Fitzsimmons' baby had made the rounds of the nearby village, Ethan paid a call on Darbing Manor and asked if he might be introduced to the new addition. The ancient butler gave him a bow and bade him enter, and another servant escorted him to the nursery where he had his first look at the dark-haired babe.

In her mother's arms—Caroline Harrington Smithson's arms—she smelled of mother's milk and powder and lemon laundry soap. Wrapped tightly in a blanket and sporting a scrunched up face, Samantha Anne Fitzsimmons was just about the ugliest thing Ethan Range had ever seen in his entire life.

Knowing what he did about the whimpering bundle, Ethan sighed and took his leave of Darbing Manor, never to return again. For it was mere months later when Elizabeth and Edward Fitzsimmons suffered a horrible carriage accident and both died before a physician could be summoned. Those in the village spread the word of their demise along with the good news that the baby was safe at the manor with her aunt, Lady Caroline.

A fortnight later, Caroline left Yorkshire, taking her baby with her back to London, and Darbing Manor was locked tight, its furnishings covered in Dutch cloths.

Denied his usual place to hide out, Ethan Range took to

playing in the castle and forever remembering the scrunched up face of baby Samantha.

"You were an ugly baby," Ethan announced from where he lay flat on his back, one arm resting on his forehead as he gazed at the stars overhead.

Samantha lifted herself onto one elbow and regarded her fellow castaway with a look of surprise. "Indeed?" she answered, her jaw slack before she remembered to close her mouth. "Well, aren't all babies ugly?" she countered finally, not sure what else she could say to such an odd comment.

Ethan chuckled as he wrapped an arm around her shoulders and pulled her against his body.

Then Samantha realized the implication of what he had said.

"You *saw* me? As a *baby?*" she asked as she stared at him, forced to suppress her own mirth at the simple words that conjured such a comical image.

The man looked so happy just then. Not a hint of a scowl, nor the furrow between his brows—just a grin of good times remembered. *He looks so young,* Samantha thought as she resisted the temptation to kiss him.

He had just claimed she was an ugly baby, after all.

Nodding as he continued to smile, Ethan lifted his head to plant a kiss on the top of Samantha's head. "You were all pink, and your face was ..." He screwed up his own face in an attempt to imitate what he remembered of her scrunched face. "But you smelled *wonderful.*"

Samantha lifted her head from his chest, stunned by his words. "Where? *Where* did you see me?" she wondered in a whisper, rather liking that he remembered she smelled wonderful. Perhaps she would kiss him after all.

Ethan took in a deep breath and let it out slowly. "Darbing Manor," he finally replied. "A couple of months before the Fitzsimmons crashed the carriage on the road to Scarborough."

Darbing Manor. Samantha forced herself not to gasp.

He really was telling the truth.

Her aunt ... *her mother* had told her many times of her first months in the home of the eccentric Lady Elizabeth and

Edward Fitzsimmons. Of how they danced about the dining room during dinner, or swam naked in their lake under a full moon. Of how they doted on one another one week, and then fought like cats and dogs the next.

How had the two found one another? And known they were perfectly suited for each other?

"Kismet," Ethan murmured, as if he knew exactly what Samantha wondered.

When she regarded him with a questioning eyebrow, he added, "When two people are supposed to be together, and they both know it, it's kismet."

Samantha nodded, wondering for a brief moment if she and the marquess were meant to be together.

He had said nothing about what they would do once they were back in England. Although Samantha thought she could spend the rest of her life with him, she rather doubted he felt the same about her.

She was a bastard, after all And had apparently been a particularly ugly baby.

CHAPTER 23

CONFESSIONS OF A VISCOUNTESS

*C*aroline let out a sigh of contentment as one of her fingers slid through the graying curls on her husband's chest. She had known from the start that if she seduced Matthew, he would respond, reciprocate and redirect her thoughts from Samantha's fate—and he had. The blessed oblivion of pure pleasure had made her forget everything for a time. Even now, she found she couldn't allow thoughts of Samantha to intrude. Not yet. Not while Matthew held her atop his body, one hand holding her bottom while his other cradled her head against the small of his shoulder. She smiled when she felt him kiss the top of her head.

"I was such a fool to think I could only love one man my entire life," she whispered, the words coming out on another sigh. She felt Matthew's body stiffen beneath her and she raised her head to regard him. "Especially when the second one is so much ..." She stopped, realizing to what she was admitting. *More loving? More lovable?* Did she truly love Matthew more than she had his brother?

Matthew frowned, a pang of jealousy gripping him at the very moment he realized what her words meant for him. "Are you speaking of me, I hope? As the ... second, I mean?" he wondered in a quiet voice, tempted to hold his breath until he heard her answer.

A smile appeared to lighten Caroline's flushed face. "Of course, I was referring to you. I've been in love with you for years."

The admission had Matthew lifting himself onto one elbow, the movement causing Caroline to slide from his chest and end up on her back next to him. "Truly?" he asked, a strange sensation filling his chest.

Caroline wrapped an arm around his shoulders and pulled him down for a kiss. Before she allowed his lips to leave hers completely, she said, "I do love you, Matthew," her lips caressing his with the words.

Matthew moved a hand to her cheek, holding it in his palm as his lips recaptured hers, his kiss as possessive as it was passionate.

When he finally came up for breath, he supported himself on one elbow and rested his head in one hand. He gazed at his wife. Her bee-stung lips were the color of berries and tasted as sweet, but the words they had just said were the most welcome he had heard in a very long time. "And your first love? Your husband, no doubt," he said in a quiet voice. Although he had never met the man—the second son of an earl who was an officer of the British Army—Matthew knew her first husband had died fighting on the Continent shortly after they had said their vows.

"Oh, I cannot claim to have ever loved Alfred," Caroline countered with a shake of her head, the arranged marriage having been her mother's idea to appease a distant relative.

Matthew frowned. "If not Alfred, then who was your first love? Do you ...?"

Caroline shook her head. "I made a vow when I married you," she replied, wondering at his questions. She reached up to stroke several fingers through his close cropped hair, secretly glad when she felt his scalp shiver beneath her fingernails. "And I promise, I have honored that vow." She had never given him any reason to doubt her fidelity. "Besides, death took him some ... twenty years ago," she added in a whisper, finding the thought no longer had her mourning George.

Matthew's brows furrowed at her mention of her marital vows. He knew she was telling the truth. Having arranged for her to be watched—as much for her safety given his position at the Foreign Office as to determine if she paid calls on another man—Matthew knew she had never done anything to embarrass him, and she certainly hadn't cuckolded him. Perhaps she knew a man in his position couldn't afford a hint of scandal.

As for her second comment, Matthew wondered if he wanted to know the identity of the man who first held her heart and decided that, yes, he wanted to know—he *needed* to know. "He was an older man then?" he queried, hoping she might divulge the man's name with her answer.

Moving his hand from her cheek to her lips, Caroline kissed the palm and rubbed her thumb in circles over the deep lines. "Younger than you," she murmured with a quirked lip. She shook her head in the pillow. "But only by a year. You really want to know, don't you?" she whispered, a mix of sadness and fear building in her. "Promise you won't ..."

"I won't," Matthew replied, not sure what he was promising but fairly sure it had something to do with reining in his anger or at least a promise not to seek retribution. After all, what could he do to a dead man?

"Your brother, George," Caroline finally admitted, a tear sliding down one temple. "After he was widowed, of course," she added, hoping he wouldn't think the absolute worst of her.

Matthew stared at his wife for some time, his face devoid of expression. He blinked twice, a bit stunned by her answer. "Why?"

His simple question had Caroline blinking several times herself before she could think of a suitable response. "I ... I don't know *why* exactly. I mean, why do any of us fall in love?"

"Caro," Matthew protested, forcing his face to remain impassive. "Did he ... approach you? Dance with you at a ball? Kiss you in Lord Weatherstone's garden?"

Caroline shook her head at his questions and finally lifted a finger to his lips. "I ... met him at his hat shop when I was there to buy one for my brother." She stopped, wondering if she should continue. Matthew's face was still impassive, giving her no hint as to how he felt about her simple explanation.

"Go on," he encouraged her.

"Well, his daughter, Emma, was there, and although she was still rather young, she was already doing his books so he had the time to make hats. George was so ... *passionate* about his hats. He described how he made them in great detail. Talked about the beaver skins and the patterns he had designed himself because he didn't like what other hat makers had created. And while he was showing me the various styles, I noticed his hands ..."

"His hands?" Matthew repeated, one eyebrow arching up.

"Yes. They were just like yours," she commented, still holding onto the one she had kissed. "I remember wondering what it would feel like to have those hands touch me. To be touched by hands that he used to make his creations, hats he was quite proud of. My entire body must have betrayed me at that moment, for I didn't say anything, or do anything, but perhaps he just *knew*, because the next thing I knew, he was holding one of my hands in his, and kissing the back of it and then turning it over to kiss the palm.

"I don't remember removing my gloves, but I must have because he was holding onto my bare hand as if it were something very precious." She paused as she swallowed a sob. "He asked if ... if he might be allowed to call on me."

Matthew allowed her a moment before asking, "And what did you say?"

Sighing, Caroline shrugged in the pillow. "I said I would like that very much. Only ... he didn't. At least, he didn't the next day. I went back to the shop the following night ... just before closing." She closed her eyes in an effort to stave off tears. "I was such a fool. I had spent that entire day waiting for him. Didn't even consider he couldn't simply leave his shop to pay a call on me. I was so smitten. Emma was staying at your sister Christine's apartment for a couple of days. And ... that's when our ... *affaire* began, such as it was."

Matthew had always thought Caroline Harrington could

have been an earl's wife, even a marchioness, but she had instead agreed to be his wife. She was thirteen years younger than Matthew and had agreed to her father's suggestion that they be betrothed, despite Matthew being a mere viscount, despite his being so much older than Caroline. Did her father think she was no longer biddable? Because she was a widow?

He hadn't expected Caroline to be a virgin when they married—he knew she had been married for what had probably amounted to a week before her husband left for the Continent —but her father, the Earl of Mayfield, had implied she was still an innocent. "Then, George was the one who took your virtue," Matthew whispered, still rather stunned that her lover had been his brother.

Caroline frowned. "'Remember, I was married before George. Alfred had that honor, if you will," she replied with a roll of her eyes. "But if I had still had it to give, it would have been George's." Another tear streaked down her cheek. "I loved him, you see."

Despite knowing she had loved another, Matthew still winced at hearing the words. "How long did it last?" he asked, his words quiet in the growing gloom of twilight.

Caroline didn't answer right away, but Matthew heard the unmistakable sound of a sob. "A few weeks," she finally managed to get out.

"That's all?"

Stunned by the question, Caroline nodded. "You and I were betrothed by then. I ... I kept in touch with George, of course. Wrote him letters about Sam ..." At his sudden hiss, Caroline squeezed his hand, knowing he would be concerned about someone else reading the letters and starting a scandal. "Emma knows—she found the letters in his desk more than a dozen years ago—but she agreed to keep my secret, and she has," she assured him.

Although Matthew wanted to feel anger at his brother for having taken what might have been rightfully his—her heart— Matthew found he couldn't muster the emotion. George had been dead a long time.

Matthew considered the repercussions of her brief *affaire*, though, and swallowed hard. "Samantha is truly my niece, then, isn't she?" he half-asked as he gathered Caroline into his arms and pulled her back atop his body. "Not just by marriage."

Caroline's eyes widened in alarm. "How ... How did you know?"

Matthew allowed a chuckle. "Besides the fact that she looks just like you when you were that age? And that you dote on her as if she were your daughter and not just a niece?" he asked rhetorically. "I have known for many years that she is your daughter. I just never knew ... the rest of it," he said quietly. His kissed her forehead. "Thank you for telling me."

Astonished by his calm reply, Caroline frowned. "I ... I should have told you years ago," she whispered, another tear making its way down her cheek. Matthew caught it with a thumb and wiped it away.

"Perhaps," he replied. "Especially so that we could tell Samantha about Emma. It seems to me Sam would have enjoyed knowing she had an older sister," he remarked. Realizing his comment made it sound as if Samantha would never have the chance to meet Emma because she no longer lived, Matthew quickly added, "We'll tell her just as soon as we find her. Agreed?"

Caroline regarded her husband as one of her teeth captured her lower lip. "Agreed," she finally said with a nod. Lowering her head to his chest, she allowed a wan smile and closed her eyes.

CHAPTER 24

OF ALL THINGS CONSIDERED

The fifth day on the island

On their fifth day of being castaways, the threat of rain in the morning sent Ethan and Samantha racing to the tower. Laughing as they made their way into the structure, the two regarded one another for only a moment before undressing one another. Not a word was said as Ethan lifted Samantha onto the table, her gown covering the rough, cracked wood.

Ethan took his time as he kissed his way down her body. He reveled in hearing her quiet whimpers as he teased her to readiness with his lips and tongue. When he finally stood at the end of the table and wrapped her legs around his waist, Samantha was begging him to hurry.

Impaling her in one thrust, Ethan growled as she clenched on him, growled again as he pulled nearly all the way out of her. From there, his movements quickened, his thrusts deepened. When he was sure she could keep her legs around him of her own accord, he leaned forward and cupped his hands around her breasts, flicking his thumbs across the ruched buds until Samantha's whimpers turn to cries and her chest arched up. He moved one arm beneath her and lifted her torso from the table, pulling her against the front of his body. When her upturned breasts suddenly pressed into the hairs of his chest and she gasped at the sensation, he allowed his own blessed release.

His body spasming with the intense pleasure, he found he had to hold onto her or risk losing himself in the swirling abyss that had every one of his nerve endings sending out signals of pure pleasure.

He knew not how long he stood holding Samantha against him, wasn't completely sure he was standing at all, when he felt her fingers work their way up his back and around his ribs, her thumbs brushing over his nipples and setting off an entirely new sensation beneath his skin. He gasped and jerked, his hold on her tightening.

When he felt her entire body sag against his and heard her happy sigh, Ethan dropped a kiss on her head. "If I don't lie down, I fear I shall fall down," he murmured, his breathing still labored.

Samantha sighed again before slowly unwrapping her legs from around his waist and allowing them to slide down his thighs. "At least let me spread out my gown for you," she whispered, her lips curling up as she planted a kiss on his sternum.

Ethan helped her from the table and turned her around, keeping one arm wrapped around her waist as she pulled the silk from the table and shook it out. "I owe you a new gown," he whispered, his nose tickled by her hair.

The blue silk floated to the ground next to the table and Ethan nearly dropped onto it. Giggling, Samantha followed him down, sighing as she ended up with her back pressed against his front, his knees behind hers and one of his arms wrapped over the front of her body.

"I'm going to miss this," Samantha murmured, a sense of melancholy settling over her just then.

When Ethan didn't make a response, she listened carefully and realized he had probably fallen asleep. Placing her hand on the back of his, she pulled it to her breast and sighed.

Closing her eyes, she wondered what he might be dreaming, or if he even dreamed at all. Did she ever appear in his dreams? She remembered him saying Daisy's name while he slept, remembered the feeling of jealousy she experienced when she found out Daisy was his mistress and not simply a flower. She wondered if he would ever say her name in his sleep, hoping that if he did so, he would say it when no one else could hear him—especially another woman—for she couldn't abide the thought of him lying next to another woman. Not like they were doing at that moment.

Ethan stilled himself, appalled at himself for what he had just done and surprised at how Samantha had simply allowed him to take her on the table, as if she were some tavern maid, always ripe and ready for a tumble. Even now, she held his hand so it cupped a naked breast. Five days away from civilization, and she had turned into a wanton, willing and ready for him whenever he wanted her, which was nearly all the time, he realized.

She's bewitched me, he thought, thinking there could be no other explanation for how Samantha had thoroughly and completely replaced Daisy in his dreams. The thought of his former mistress, which might have angered or saddened him only a week ago, now brought only ambivalence.

He listened closely, realizing almost at once that Samantha wasn't sleeping. "What are you thinking?"

Samantha stiffened, his quiet whisper sounding loud next to her ear. "What ... What do you mean?" she replied, leaning back into the front of his body so she could angle her head to see him.

"Your last thought. Before I spoke. What was it?"

Samantha was sure he could see her blush in the dimness. "I wondered if you would ever say my name whilst you slept, and if you did, I didn't want you to be lying next to another woman."

Ethan stared at her for a long time, one brow furrowing at her unexpected response. He thought she might mention something about London or her best friends, or God forbid, Lord Everly. But he certainly didn't expect her thoughts to be on what he might say in his sleep. "Oh," he finally responded, swallowing. "Is this because I said Daisy's name in my sleep?" he finally ventured, wondering if she were offended or jealous, or simply concerned for the next woman he bedded.

Christ!

He hadn't thought of Daisy since they last spoke of her. And he certainly didn't have anyone in mind to share his bed when he finally returned to Yorkshire.

Samantha nodded. "Something like that," she replied.

Ethan lifted himself on an elbow, realizing there was more she wanted to say. "What's this about?" He backed up a bit so Samantha was no longer on her side but on her back, staring up at him with eyes bright with tears.

"Why do you employ a mistress?" she asked, suddenly aware his hand still rested on her breast.

"I don't," he answered.

Samantha rolled her eyes. "Why did you employ Daisy?"

Furrowing his brows, Ethan realized he wasn't going to deflect her question. He could just tell her it was for sexual intercourse, but he guessed she wouldn't be satisfied with the response. Despite her upbringing, she seemed to want to know all about Daisy. "She met me in Scarborough. A chance meeting, I think. Someone pointed out who I was, she introduced herself, she took my arm, and we proceeded to walk into a park."

Her eyes widening, she shook her head. "And, just like that, she's your mistress?"

"Of course not!" Ethan countered. "We spoke of many things before she mentioned, rather on the sly, that she was looking for a new paramour, and would I be in the market for someone to ... 'warm my bed' is how I believe she offered herself." He was watching Samantha's face change as he spoke when he suddenly wondered if she was considering offering herself as a mistress. "Do not even think for a moment about being someone's mistress, Sam," he suddenly added.

Samantha blinked at his order, rather shocked he would think she would consider such an occupation for herself. "I wasn't," she answered with a shake of her head.

"Although, I must say, you would be rather good in the role," Ethan said with a teasing arch of his brow.

Now she was positively sure he could see her blush. "Tell

me, then. What kind of agreement did you have? Is there a ....
contract, or a simple handshake? What if you're not ...
compatible?"

Ethan allowed a chuckle before sobering. "A contract. For a
year. I arranged for a townhouse for her to live in and gave her
enough pin money to pay for gowns and fripperies and such.
She demanded a bauble here and there." He considered her
other question and let out a breath. "As for compatibility ... it's
just sexual intercourse, Sam. She was obviously experienced. She
was good for a couple of tumbles a week and some conversation.
Enough to take my mind off all the problems of the marquessate. Probably not very different from having a wife."

Samantha winced at his last sentence, and Ethan noticed. "I
meant no offense," he said quietly.

"I shouldn't think you would want a woman who makes
demands of you, and then only beds you when you buy her
jewels," Samantha said quietly. "But I suppose for a mistress,
well, she would see it as payment for her services, whereas a wife
would see it as a gift, as a sign of your affection."

Ethan frowned at comment. "But couldn't that be seen as a
payment as well?"

It was Samantha's turn to frown, "What do you mean?"

"For ... For being a wife. For being a mother," he struggled
to explain.

"I should hope not," she replied, raising herself up on her
elbows.

Suddenly aware his hand still rested on her breast, Ethan
pulled it away, and then, at her pretty pout, he put it back.
"Why not?" he countered, his look of confusion aging him to
how he looked when they first arrived on the island.

"I do not believe a wife expects payment for anything in a
marriage, for then it wouldn't truly be a marriage, but rather a
... *business transaction*."

"Isn't that what a marriage is?" Ethan questioned with a
shake of his head.

"I should hope not," Samantha repeated, her own head
shaking. "At least, not a marriage borne from affection. From

mutual respect." When she noticed he didn't seem convinced, she added, "I understand there are marriages made from arrangements ... business, political ... but we are not speaking of such marriages. Are we?" she countered, wondering at the wrinkle that had formed between his brows. After so many days of its absence, Samantha was a bit dismayed to see its return on Ethan's forehead. She reached up with a finger and touched it, hoping to smooth it away.

Ethan stared at her for a time, not acknowledging her touch nor her explanation. "I suppose not," he finally agreed, lowering himself to the silk. He stretched out and took a deep breath, aware Samantha still held herself up on her elbows. "You do realize that if I say your name in my sleep, I rather doubt I will say your name in its entirety. Whoever hears it will hear only 'Sam'."

A huge smile split his face as he pictured the possible ramifications—*What would Evans think if he heard me say 'Sam' in my sleep?*—until Samantha pinched him and settled herself next to his prone body. "Don't you dare," she whispered, her own smile widening.

CHAPTER 25

THERE BE PIRATES!

The seventh day on the island
        "I'm starving."

The simple words had Samantha opening her eyes and inhaling sharply. Another night on the dunes of the small island had she and Ethan nearly naked and their limbs tangled. The memory of their frenzied lovemaking brought a sudden smile to her face. "Good morning, grumpy," she murmured, lifting her head to glance around.

Although the tower provided shelter from rain and was a good place to eat their dinners, they found it almost claustrophobic for sleeping. The odor of fish and smoke from the fire hung in the air, a situation that had Ethan deciding that on clear nights, they would be more comfortable sleeping on the sandy dunes rather than on the hard ground of the tower.

They had selected the most secluded patch of land in which to make their bed the night before, covering the dune with Samantha's tattered gown and using Ethan's rolled up breeches as a pillow. Surrounded by the small shrubs, the space provided them some privacy and a good vantage point from which to see a passing ship.

Ethan scrubbed his face with a hand and groaned. How many days had he gone without shaving? "I must look a sight," he replied, lifting himself onto one elbow and surveying their surroundings. The early morning light reflected off the clear blue water, the color of the horizon making the sky appear to merge with the sea. In the other direction, the larger island promised more food sources, but they would have to fashion an oar and figure out a way to get there on their makeshift raft. He had decided today would be the day to do just that.

"If handsome is a sight, then yes, you do," Samantha said as she bussed his cheek. "I, however, am sure I am in need of a comb."

Ethan grinned as he watched her open her reticule and pull out her ivory comb. Her tousled hair, with its glints of gold reflecting the sunlight, made her look every bit as wanton as she had been the night before.

And the night before that.

Christ! As much as his morning erection demanded relief in her more-than-willing body, he was quite sure he didn't have the strength. Despite the constant diet of berries they had been able to find in the various shrubs covering the island, he couldn't live on them. His stomach growled in protest at the thought of having to breakfast on even more berries.

He had also had his fill of fish, despite the many varieties he had managed to catch in his makeshift net. Although Samantha had the cooking down to an art, with only rosemary and wild garlic as seasonings, Ethan was quite sure he would never eat another fish once he returned to Yorkshire.

The gurgle of the nearby spring was a welcome sound. He stood up and pulled on his breeches before helping Samantha with her corset and pantaloons. Given the heat during the midday, she had spent the day before wearing nothing but the two pieces of clothing, a situation Ethan found as amusing as he did arousing. She had even removed her stockings and half-boots, preferring to walk in the sand barefoot. Although she always carried her sunshade in an attempt to keep the sun off her skin, it had taken on a golden glow, making her look like some misplaced sun goddess.

Ethan scooped water into his hands and lowered his face into it, glad for the heat this particular spring provided. He soaked his shirt and then rubbed it over his body, wincing when he realized how dirty it had become in only a few short days. Rinsing out the shirt until the water ran clear, he was about to pull it over his head when Samantha called out from where she was still combing her hair. Within a moment, she appeared, a startled expression on her face.

"What is it?" he asked, rising slowly, thinking a small animal might have scared her.

Samantha pointed behind her. "A ship."

Ethan was on his feet in an instant, staring over the small rise of the island. Indeed, a ship was nearby. So near, in fact, it appeared to have dropped anchor just beyond the half-circle of the bay. The shallow water of the morning's low tide wouldn't have allowed it to come any closer to the island.

He was about to make his way toward the beach when he stopped and studied the pennons waving from the mainmast. Squinting in an attempt to make out the colors of the flags, a stab of fear had him swallowing when he noticed the black flag bearing a skull and crossbones.

Samantha came up alongside, one hand held to her forehead to shade her eyes. "Is that ...?" she stopped and inhaled sharply.

"Damn it," Ethan said under his breath. He glanced at her. "Get dressed. Now," he ordered quickly. "Boots, too." He dared a glance back at the other island, wondering how deep the water was between the two land masses. If they could get to it, they could hide—there was far more shrubbery covering the larger island. They would be exposed for nearly a mile if they headed to the tower.

Samantha cursed as she tried twice and failed to get her stockings over her feet. Slowing down her movements, she dared a glance at the ship. A packet had already been lowered to the water. Three men were climbing down the side of the ship's hull, their voices occasionally making their way to her ears. Pulling up her stockings, she tied them above the knees with their ruined ribbons. She grimaced as she shook out her gown, the sapphire silk stained and covered in dirt, the skirts hopelessly wrinkled. Pulling it over her head, she was pushing her arms into the sleeves when she realized she was being watched.

Turning around, she followed the packet's progress as it made its way over the shallow bay, two of the men manning the oars. The third man held a spyglass to one eye.

Aimed directly at her.

Samantha stared back, wondering what she should do. *Wave?* As if she welcomed the men whose ship was clearly marked as that of a pirate? Or stick out her tongue? Which is what she felt like doing just then.

Deciding to act as if she hadn't seen them at all, she hurried off to the spring to join Ethan.

Captain Jack Crawley readjusted the focus on his spyglass, not quite sure he could believe what he was seeing. *Was that a woman?* he wondered, bringing the glass in alignment with the dark-haired human wearing almost all white ... undergarments.

He inhaled sharply and dared a glance at his ship's quartermaster.

"Capt'n?" the man wondered, lifting his oar from the water and turning around in attempt to see whatever it was that had his captain so confounded.

Crawley shook his head. "I do believe we'll have some luck on this island," he said, giving Russell a wink when he was sure the other oarsman's attention was on his oar. The ship's carpenter had agreed to come on this endeavor, claiming he hadn't been on dry land for over two months. Their brief stop in Marseilles hadn't afforded much in the way of shore leave for the crew of the *Molly*.

He lifted the spyglass again, stunned when he realized he was watching a woman as she pulled a blue gown over her head —a rather poor looking excuse of a blue gown, he realized as she shook out the skirts and then suddenly disappeared over the rise. "I'll be damned," he breathed, excitement building in him. "I do believe we'll find what we're looking for," he announced as he stood up and allowed the packet to slow before stepping into the shallow water. "Gentleman," he said as he motioned to his fellow crewmen, "Time to collect some treasure."

"What are you doing?" Samantha asked as she watched Ethan make his way down to the opposite beach. From this vantage, they couldn't be seen by the ship.

"Testing the depth of the water. Something I should have done the first day we arrived," he said as he walked into the water.

"Be careful of the ..." Before she could finish her warning about the jellyfish, Samantha heard Ethan's sharp curse.

"Shite and damnation!"

Samantha hurried to the water's edge, hissing when she spotted the red slash across the marquess' ankle. "Rinse it in the saltwater. To get the poison out," she instructed quickly.

"I would rather rinse it in the *clean* water," he countered, heading for the spring while keeping his voice down.

"No!" Samantha argued, giving her head a quick shake. "Fresh water will only make it worse," she claimed, matching his volume.

Ethan frowned and regarded her for a moment. "It *stings*, dammit," he countered, still moving toward the spring.

"Fresh water will only spread the poison. Urine will stop the sting."

Blinking, Ethan turned and regarded Samantha with a raised eyebrow. "What did you say?"

Samantha sighed, realizing how unconventional the treatment sounded. "You have to ... pee on it," she stated as her tanned face took on the pink cast of a blush.

Shaking his head, Ethan stared at her. "You know this ... how?" he wondered, a bit irritated. There were pirates on their way to the island, and she was telling him to urinate on his ankle!

"Lord Everly. Whilst on his visit to Minorca," she explained.

Everly! Damn the man. A stab of jealousy had Ethan rather angry at the moment. Despite Samantha's comment about the man not showing interest in her *in that way,* he was quite sure Samantha would end up married to the earl once he managed to get her back to England, and the thought had him feeling more than a bit annoyed. The earl might be an adventurer, frequently off exploring various lands to learn about their flora and fauna, but Harry Tennison, Earl of Everly, wouldn't have the first clue about how to explore Samantha Fitzsimmons.

However, everything she had told him about the earl's visit to the Spanish island of Minorca had been somehow useful during their stay on this small island. If urinating on his ankle would somehow stop the rather painful sting he had suffered at the hands—or rather, tentacles—of a jellyfish, then so be it.

He quickly unbuttoned his breeches and pulled out his cock, aiming a stream of urine to intersect with the red slash cross his ankle. He took some satisfaction when, suddenly embarrassed, Samantha whirled around and faced the opposite direction—the direction in which a rather amused man stood with his hands on his hips, staring down at them. Within a moment, two more men, dressed in black pantaloons and open shirts, appeared and flanked the black garbed leader of their band.

Unaware of the appearance of their visitors, Ethan finished his business and rebuttoned his breeches. "Your unconventional cure seems to have worked. I no longer feel the ..." He stopped, his gaze settling on the man regarding him with a quirked eyebrow—an eyebrow decorated with a gold ring, which brought attention to the pierced ears with gold rings. To the myriad gold chains hanging from a rather tanned neck. To the large hands with beefy fingers encircled by even more gold rings. And to the gold front tooth on display due to the man's rather happy expression, which at the moment, was aimed entirely in Samantha's direction.

To her credit, the chit didn't seem the least bit intimidated by the black-haired, black-eyed rogue with the black goatee who stood before them. Ethan wondered how long she would keep up the brave face.

"It's rather rude of you to watch a lady dress," Samantha piped up suddenly, her arms crossing in front of her chest, the move forcing her breasts to mound up above the bodice of her ruined gown.

Startled by her words, Ethan turned, intending to shush her.

Had the pirates already been on the island when she put on her gown?

"I saw you watching me through your spyglass," she accused with a huff.

Their intruder seemed even more amused by her sudden outburst. "True. And I would have watched far longer, but I prefer to watch a lady *undress*," the man countered as he took a step forward, the same moment Ethan stepped closer to Samantha.

The man held up a bejeweled finger and angled his head in warning. "I'll deal with you in a moment," he said quickly before turning his attention back to Samantha. "But first, I think I should like to finish my conversation with your ... *doxy*," he added with a raised eyebrow.

Samantha's jaw dropped in indignation. "I am no such thing," she stated in anger. "I am a *lady*, and you'll treat me as such," she ordered, rather surprised at how haughty she could sound when pressed to do so.

The pirate regarded her with a quirked eyebrow before directing his eyes to travel from her face to her toes and back up again. "And yet, you're wearing a very *used* dinner gown when it's clearly time for breakfast," he replied with a hint of amusement.

Samantha didn't have a chance to argue when the man suddenly turned to Ethan and said, "I can understand why you would bring her here. Your own private island retreat, where you can have your way with the chit." He turned back to Samantha "Why, the idea of one of my hands filled with one of her breasts ..."

Gasping at the man's implication, Samantha's hands went to her hips just as Ethan took two steps closer to the pirate, his hands formed into fists. He stopped, though, when the man pulled out a dueling pistol from inside his black cape coat and calmly aimed it in Ethan's direction.

"As if *that* could ever happen," Samantha stated suddenly. She edged closer to Ethan, suddenly frightened for him. If he was shot, she knew she would end up on the man's ship, and

Ethan would be left for dead. She couldn't allow that to happen. Not after everything he had done for her.

To her.

The pirate regarded her with a look of surprise. "You doubt me?" he replied, as if he was uncertain about how he should respond to the impertinent chit.

"Your hands are entirely too large. I couldn't begin to fill one of them," she retorted, her chin thrust out with her indignation.

To her right, Ethan struggled to keep an impassive expression on his face, but he was failing, a chuckle burbling out. The pirate, similarly amused, burst out laughing, and his two henchman finally allowed smiles and chuckles of their own.

"My dear, you are a jewel," the pirate announced when it became apparent the tension had been thoroughly broken. "Captain Jack Crawley, at your service," he stated as he bowed before her and reached for one of her hands.

At first not willing to give him her hand, Samantha frowned. She finally allowed it, rather shocked when the man brushed his lips over the back of it. Almost automatically, she gave him a curtsy. "Samantha Fitzsimmons," she said before waving a hand in Ethan's direction. "And this is Ethan Range." She almost—almost—added his title, but thought better of it. No use giving the pirate the idea he was a valuable man.

Jack Crawley regarded the two people before him, trying to decide just what to do with them. They were obviously stuck on the island, and not of their own volition. "I take it you arrived here via that raft I saw near the bay," he ventured, his eyes glancing between the two of them.

"We did. We were on *The Fairweather* when it took a rogue wave and sank somewhere near here," Ethan said by way of explanation.

Samantha watched the captain as Ethan made his statement, wondering at the way the man's brow quirked, the way his eyes seemed to register recognition and then return to their previous appearance. *Had he heard of the sailing ship?*

Perhaps he had robbed it at some point!

"May I inquire as to your destination?" Samantha wondered, her embarrassment over the comments about her breasts clearly in the past.

Captain Crawley gave a nod. "I go wherever there is promise of financial gain," he replied, the gold tooth gleaming in the sun. "Seems your ship may have been hauling some rather ... valuable cargo."

Ethan acknowledged Crawley's statement with a nod. "Brandywine, I think. There were barrels of it all around the deck," he said. The three they had managed to roll onto the island were in some shrubs, but anyone looking for them would easily find the barrels.

The pirate angled his head and glanced between the two of them. "And you know where some of these ... barrels are located? Surely they arrived with you," he intimated.

Samantha exchanged a glance with Ethan. "After we lead you to the barrels, could you transport us to your next ... port of financial gain?" she wondered.

Captain Crawley threw back his head and laughed, his attention going from Samantha to Ethan. "That would be Valencia," he said finally, "And, I suppose, if my men are in agreement, we can make some sort of accommodation. But first, the brandy."

Ethan nodded. "Of course." It wasn't as if they were hiding it. They had merely rolled the barrels up and out of the water in case they would have need of them. He could use a glass of the stuff right now, he considered. "This way," he said as he trudged up the hill.

As he crested the hill, Ethan noted the position of Crawley's ship. Anchored just beyond the bay, its sails lashed to the masts, the ship was rather close to the island. Ethan understood how the pirate had been able to watch Samantha get dressed.

"Tell me, does this island have a name?" Ethan wondered as they made their way to the thicket of shrubs in which the barrels were nestled.

"S'Espalmador," Crawley answered simply. "At low tide, you

could have waded to Formentera," he added as he indicated the island to the south.

Ethan silently cursed, wishing he had known. "Here are the three barrels that arrived with us. You'll need to take care with that one. I already tapped it," he said as he indicated the wooden casks resting on their sides. "It's possible there are more nearby. As I said, the ship's deck was lined with them."

Crawley directed his men to roll the barrels to the water's edge. "We found two yesterday along with some wreckage," he replied with a cocked eyebrow. "Which is why we came here. Like following a string of pearls."

Ethan winced, wishing their rescuer could have been a more respectable man. He wasn't completely convinced the captain would simply take Samantha and him to Valencia and drop them off without demanding something, perhaps a ransom, in return. "Do you have just the one packet?" he asked, thinking it would take several trips to get them—and the brandywine—to the ship.

"I'll have the men send another out when they get these to the ship," Crawley replied, using his spyglass to survey his ship. "Ah. Seems my first mate has noticed your presence," he added, lifting an arm and forming an upside-down 'L' and then straightening it again.

Wondering as to the signal the pirate had just made, Ethan glanced in Samantha's direction. She was watching the men roll the barrels and occasionally daring a look at the ship. He beckoned for her to join him, thinking it better if they stayed close to one another.

"I don't have much in the way of accommodations on board. Certainly nothing suitable for a lady," Crawley explained as he made his way to the packet.

Ethan followed, glad to find Samantha at his side, his waistcoat gripped in one hand, her reticule hanging from her arm, and the sunshade resting on her shoulder. *Thank the gods she had remembered to retrieve the waistcoat!* Now he had to hope the pirate wouldn't suspect it contained his purse.

When Samantha saw that the pirate's attention was elsewhere, she slipped Ethan a handful of berries. He gave her a wink and nearly swallowed them whole. "How long to Valencia?"

Crawley gave some instructions to his men while a shout from the ship had his attention directed there. "If the wind helps, we'll be there before morning," he said, once again giving the strange arm signal. "Finally," he said with an impatient sigh.

Ethan glanced out to the ship. "What is it?" he asked.

"They're lowering the other packet. It means we can be on our way shortly. If you can man an oar, it will go that much quicker," he hinted, one black eyebrow arching at Ethan.

Giving the man a reluctant nod, he said, "Of course."

Once the boat was in the shallow water, Samantha hiked up her skirts much like she had done when they first arrived on the island—had it already been six or seven days?—and made her way to the boat. She took a seat near the front and watched nervously as the captain and one of the new men took their places. Ethan was left to push the boat farther out and then jump in at the last minute, wincing as his injured foot caught the edge of the packet.

"Good idea, that was," Crawley said as he indicated the red slash on Ethan's ankle. At Ethan's questioning glance, he added, "Peeing on it. Most don't know to do such a thing. Damn jelly-fish. Beautiful to watch, but ... damned nuisance, they are."

"Oh," Ethan responded, deciding not to explain that it had been Samantha who had insisted he actually urinate on himself. He took up an oar. Timing his movements with those of the other oarsman, he began to row.

Ethan couldn't help but notice Samantha at the other end of the packet. Facing his direction and looking every bit the lady with her hair pinned up in a simple bun and the makeshift sunshade held over her head, she displayed an expression of sadness as they left the island. If he hadn't been so damned hungry, Ethan might have shared in her sadness at having to leave the island. But it was past time he got to Rome. Past time he got back to England and to Yorkshire.

Back to duty.

CHAPTER 26

SIZING UP A PIRATE

Once on board the ship Captain Jack Crawley had christened 'Molly', the captain led Samantha and Ethan down the companionway to a deck with rows and rows of hammocks. "They're all spoken for," he warned, leading them to another steep ladder to the cargo hold below. "But at least it's only for a night," he said as he motioned to the dark hole in the floor.

"Any chance we can remain up top until dark? Have a meal, perhaps?" Ethan asked, seeing Samantha's look of panic and hearing his stomach growl for the tenth time that day. He still wasn't convinced the pirate would take them to Valencia—or anywhere else, for that matter.

Crawley seemed to mull over the idea. "Tell you what. Let me arrange for Miss Fitzsimmons to freshen up a bit. She would no doubt like a bath. A change of clothes. A light repast. She can do that in my cabin whilst I see to getting us headed for Spain."

Allowing his suspicion to show, Ethan shook his head. "I'll not let her out of my sight," he said in a whisper.

The captain let out a breath and turned his attention to Samantha. "I suppose you're going to have an audience for your ablutions," he said with an arched brow, his manner most teasing.

Samantha was quite sure her blush was evident, even in the gloom of the lower deck. "I accept your generous offer, Captain. If Mr. Range insists, I see no reason why he cannot ... guard the door on my behalf while he eats his luncheon."

Crawley nodded, giving Ethan that arched eyebrow again. "Then, if I may, I should like to invite my lady to dinner later this evening. In my cabin, of course." He seemed rather pleased at hearing Ethan's low groan. "And Mr. Range can guard the door on our behalf. Now, if you'll excuse me," he turned and clambered up the steep steps, shouting orders that included one to have hot water delivered to his cabin.

"I don't trust him," Ethan whispered as he led Samantha back to the companionway.

"I find I can," she countered as she reached for Ethan's arm. "There's something ... *familiar* about him. He seems to behave one way when his men are about and then, when they're not looking, he's completely different. I just can't put my finger on why."

Ethan's eyes widened. "Are you *daft?*" he asked in surprise. "He's a *pirate!*" This last was said with a good deal of emphasis, as if Samantha had somehow forgotten the man was engaged in illegal activities and didn't exactly have their welfare in mind.

"I know. I just ..."

"Miss Fitzsimmons, your bath awaits," Crawley said from the top of the companionway. He knelt down onto one knee and reached a hand down. "Here. Allow me to help you." He turned his attention to Ethan. "I must have been mistaken when I took you to be a gentleman."

Taking a deep breath, Ethan was about to respond when Samantha turned from her perch on the second step and kissed him on the mouth. "Whatever you were about to say ... don't," she whispered with a small shake of her head. Putting on a brilliant smile, she turned, looked up, and accepted the pirate's proffered hand. "Why, thank you, Captain Crawley."

Despite the kiss—what a wanton woman she was!—a stab of jealousy had Ethan suddenly seething. Didn't Samantha realize Crawley's intentions? The pirate was no doubt planning a seduction whilst they had dinner in his cabin! Ethan had half a mind to chase the chit down and bring her back to the hold—at least he would be able to keep an eye on her. He was pretty sure she wouldn't venture far from him given the likelihood of rats or other vermin down there.

Forcing himself to take a deep breath, he shoved his shirt into his breeches and donned the waistcoat, quickly buttoning it up in an effort to improve his appearance. At least his shirt had benefited from its morning rinse in the spring—it was certainly cleaner than any of the shirts the crew of the *Molly* wore.

If Samantha had no longer required the use of her sunshade, he would have unwound his cravat from it and added that to his attire as well. Unfortunately, she had taken it with her. When he popped his head through the opening of the companionway, he grimaced when he caught sight of her walking alongside Crawley with her hand on his arm. Following at a discrete distance—he had been invited to guard the captain's cabin door and intended to do so—Ethan glanced at the other pirates scurrying about on the upper deck. Two were scrubbing the deck rail, one scampered up the mainmast, releasing the ties as he went so the main sail soon filled with air, two others were raising the anchor, and several were involved with moving the barrels of brandywine into positions similar to the ones they had held on *The Fairweather*. From what he could tell, it appeared as if the crew numbered about a dozen.

"We're underway, Capt'n," the first mate announced from where he stood behind the wheel. Unlike *The Fairweather*, this ship's wheel was out in the open, mounted on a raised part of the deck.

"Take us due west-northwest. And keep us just out of sight of the coast as long as possible," Crawley ordered as he led Samantha to the only cabin on the deck—his. "Here we are, my lady," he said as he opened the door and allowed Samantha to precede him into the room.

Samantha hesitated, and glanced back to see Ethan appear from below deck. Once she assured herself he was close, she stepped over the threshold and was stunned. A bit roomier than the cabin she and Caroline had shared on *The Fairweather*, this one was far more elegant. The bed, covered with a deep navy velvet counterpane, was tucked against one wall, a burled maple table for two was anchored in the center of the room, and a settee and upholstered chair were along the other wall. Although the low table in front of the settee was small, it was large enough to accommodate a tea set. Along the back wall, a copper bathtub and a stand for a pitcher and water bowl were next to a shelf containing a stack of bath linens, and closest to the bed was a huge mahogany wardrobe.

Just as Samantha stepped inside and moved to one side, two crewman came in bearing pails filled with steaming water followed by a young boy who struggled with another pail. She watched in surprise as they dumped the water into the tub.

Jack Crawley moved behind her and to the wardrobe, opening both doors wide. He shuffled through several items and finally pulled out a gown. "I believe this should fit you, my lady," he said as he brought it to Samantha, the red silk de Naples fabric draped over his arms.

Samantha arched an eyebrow. "Won't your wife object to you loaning out her gowns?" she asked *sotto voce*. Without looking around, she knew Ethan was watching from the doorway. She hoped he wouldn't do something typically male. There was something just a bit ... *off* ... about Captain Crawley, and she was quite sure she would be able to figure it out if she could spend just a bit more time in the pirate's presence.

Ethan nodded to the three who took their leave of the captain's quarters, their buckets now empty. At least they, too, were barefoot. He glanced down at his own feet and grimaced at how dirty they'd become since his fishing expedition the day before.

He wondered if he and Samantha would still be stranded if he had known it was possible to get to the other island so easily. Their raft might have made the trip, but the thought of trying to steer it without the benefit of a sail or an oar had him afraid they would be swept back out to sea. Being on a ship was probably a step up from their previous situation, he considered, especially one that seemed in good repair.

Secretly, he was impressed with the captain's quarters. It had no doubt been furnished from the cabins of other ships. He had heard tales of the scoundrels raiding ships for their cargo—apparently the furnishings and the luggage of their passengers made for good booty, as well.

And maybe even the passengers themselves.

Ethan was reminded of their current situation when the captain suddenly let out a hearty laugh. "Oh, my lady, you are a breath of fresh air. There is, sadly, no Mrs. Crawley. But that doesn't mean I'm not in the market," he added, directing this last in Ethan's direction.

The marquess crossed his arms and leaned against the door frame, his usual scowl firmly in place. Having never seen a pirate in person, Ethan was having a hard time reconciling the painting he had seen of Blackbeard with the flamboyant dandy who stood before him. Perhaps the name of his ship was also his predilection.

But if the man was a molly, then why the overt attempt to impress Lady Samantha? Ethan would be keeping a close eye on the captain. A close eye, indeed.

CHAPTER 27

A MOST WELCOME BATH

Reluctantly, Samantha accepted the gown. Her own sapphire silk was beyond repair, and she had nothing else to wear. "It's most inappropriate, but I rather think what I'm wearing is even more so. If you insist," she finally said with a nod. "Thank you, Captain."

Crawley gave her a nod and stepped back. "I'll leave you to it. I'll expect you for dinner this evening, my lady," he turned his attention to Ethan, "While Mr. Range guards the door for us." This last was said with a cocked brow and a good deal of amusement. "When you're finished here, I must insist you go below deck. I'm afraid my men may ..." He left the comment unfinished, his implication clear.

Samantha's eyes widened. "Of course," she replied. Not looking forward to spending any time in the dark cargo hold, she realized she would be far more uncomfortable in the presence of his crew. At least Ethan would be with her. "And luncheon?"

Crawley appeared surprised by the query. "I'll have a tray brought to Mr. Range shortly," he agreed with a nod. His manner suddenly more serious, he gave Samantha a bow and took his leave of his cabin.

Confused, Samantha watched his departure and then finally

gave her attention to Ethan. "What an odd man," she whispered.

Ethan rolled his eyes. "I'll be right here," he said as he nodded toward the door.

Samantha returned the nod, half tempted to invite him to join her in the tub. Once he had the door shut, she quickly stripped her gown and undergarments from her body, wishing it were Ethan undoing the buttons and ties. She helped herself to several linens and a bar of what appeared to be French milled soap, planning to wash her hair. Gingerly, she stepped into the water, sighing with relief as warmth engulfed her. Laying back, she closed her eyes.

When she opened them, she was startled to find Ethan leaning over the tub, reaching for the bar of soap.

"When I didn't hear any sounds of splashing water, I thought perhaps you might have drowned," Ethan drawled as he wet the bar and began stroking it over her bent knees and down to her thighs. "But now I see there's not enough water in here for that to happen."

Gasping at Ethan's sudden appearance and his rather intimate work with the soap, Samantha straightened in the tub. She gave him a tentative grin. Had she fallen asleep? The feel of the soap skimming over her skin was heaven. "If this tub was a bit larger, I would have you join me," she whispered.

Ethan stilled the soap, his loins stirring with the thought of taking a bath with her. "Perhaps another time," he murmured, leaning over to kiss her temple. "Would you like me to help with your hair?"

Samantha's eyes widened. "You mean, with washing it?" she asked.

"Of course," the marquess answered with a shrug. He had come to realize their opportunities to be alone would soon be over. If Captain Crawley truly delivered them to Valencia as he claimed he would do, they would next need to board a ship bound for England. He had no intention of sending Samantha on alone—he would simply see her to London, deliver her to her uncle, and be on his way to Rome.

Once she had leaned back and soaked her hair, Ethan got to work massaging her scalp, the soap leaving tiny bubbles in its way.

"You've done this before," she accused, her eyes closed and her slight moans indicating the enjoyment she was experiencing.

Ethan stopped moving his fingers. "I tried once. Apparently I wasn't doing it right."

The comment had Samantha's eyes opening in disbelief. "Someone was mistaken," she countered, relaxing into his hold on her head and neck. "This is positively heaven." Despite her words of encouragement, she knew something had changed in Ethan just then. His manner had gone from playful to serious, and the lines of his forehead seemed to deepen. "A penny for your thoughts."

Remembering his one foray into Daisy's bath, Ethan shook his head. His mistress had been most insistent that he watch her bathe, presumedly to make him understand just how much effort went into her *toilette* to prepare for him. But in making him play lady's maid, she had also made him realize just how shallow she was, how poorly she behaved when he was present, especially toward the real lady's maid who he employed on her behalf. He wondered if she treated the girl that way when he wasn't around and had thought to increase the maid's pay as a reward for continuing in the position.

Perhaps it had been that bath that had first opened his eyes to Daisy's character faults. Perhaps it was during that bath when Daisy realized her mistake in insisting he attend her. Thinking he would soon end their liaison as a result of him paying witness to her poor behavior, she had made arrangements for another paramour to take his place.

Just thinking of it now had Ethan realizing he was no longer angry with Daisy for what she had done—she was merely looking out for herself. But the entire situation had hardened him, certainly made him suspicious of women, of their motives.

As an unmarried marquess, he knew there were women who would gladly marry him, but he also knew they would do so for the coronet of a marchioness and the purse that came with it.

Would it be worth it to marry a woman who only wanted the title, the money?

Once in Yorkshire, though, would she agree to live at Castle Keys? The place was a pile—a cold, dark, forbidding structure on the edge of a moor, a castle straight out of a gothic novel. Even if she did agree to move into the keep, he rather imagined she would soon make excuses to visit London, her stays in the capital becoming longer until she never returned.

The idea of being married and living apart had him avoiding the Marriage Mart and London in general. Did he really want to saddle an heir with the marquessate?

"Where were you just now?" Samantha whispered, watching his face as he completed his ablutions on her hair.

Ethan gave her a glance but returned his attention to rinsing her hair. "Castle Keys," he replied quietly. "Home, but not a very pleasant place."

Samantha waited for him to finish rinsing her hair before she said, "But it can be made so, can it not?"

Remembering her on the island wearing only her corset and pantaloons, Ethan imagined Samantha running about Castle Keys in the same attire. She would certainly brighten up the place, he considered with a grin, although she would probably freeze to death in the process. "It would take a good deal of effort, but I suppose it could be done." He watched as she gave him a grin, and he wondered what she was thinking.

"A penny for your thoughts, and then we'll be even," he offered, reaching for a linen in which to wrap her hair.

Smiling, Samantha reached out and touched his arm. "Your castle sounds like a very intriguing challenge," she replied as she took the linen and wrapped her long hair into it, settling it atop her head. "I can't imagine one would get bored there."

Ethan took a deep breath, amazed at her words. *Would she truly like living there?* he wondered, his chest clenching just a bit. *I've ruined her. I should do the honorable thing. Make her my wife.*

"I don't suppose you would," he finally answered, remembering her affinity for painting. "So, I am thinking we should ..."

The door to the cabin suddenly opened and Captain Crawley poked his head in. "There you are," he said with some delight as his eyes took in the sight of Samantha still in the tub —and clearly in sight of the marquess. "Your luncheon is out here on the deck."

Somewhat annoyed by the interruption, Ethan nodded to the captain and then gave Samantha a glance.

"Go eat. You're starving," she said as she held a linen over the top of the tub in a weak attempt at modesty.

"You're sure?" he replied, giving the captain a suspicious glance.

"Of course. I'll be out shortly," she said, hoping the pirate would take his leave at the same time. He did so, but not before making a comment about being a lady's maid should she need one.

When she was alone, Samantha stood up and dried herself off with the linen, grimacing at the thought of donning the corset she'd worn for a week. Almost tempted to check the wardrobe for a replacement, she instead pulled on the red silk gown and regarded her reflection in the small shaving mirror by the pitcher of water. A bit roomy, the gown didn't really require she wear a corset, she decided.

Pulling on the pantaloons and her stockings and boots, Samantha stood up and gave a sigh of relief. Once her hair was dry and pinned up, she would feel like a lady.

Somehow, the thought wasn't as comforting as it should have been.

CHAPTER 28

PARTING IS SUCH SWEET SORROW

*E*than regarded Samantha with an expression of surprise when she stepped out of the captain's quarters. Dressed in a red silk dinner gown that might have been a bit too large, she appeared rather regal with her hair pinned up in a simple chignon. "Are you sure this is a good idea?" he asked, glancing nervously about to see the reactions of the crew members on the deck.

Only one seemed to take notice of Samantha—the first mate—while the other two went about their business. Crawley had obviously said something to dissuade the men from making cat-calls or even looking in her direction.

"Of course not," she replied. "But what choice do we have?" she countered. The island was no longer in sight—indeed, no land could be seen on the horizon—and she certainly didn't want to offend the ship's captain.

The marquess finally nodded. "If he does anything untoward, so help me ..."

"He won't," Samantha replied. "I won't allow it. I promise." Secretly she felt a bit of a thrill at how protective Ethan seemed to be in their new environment. Jealous, almost. "We have to go below," she reminded him, noticing how the first mate was staring at them with an expression that suggested they had best take their leave of the deck. She quickly moved toward the companionway.

Ethan nodded and walked alongside her. "I'll go first, and then help you down," he said in a whisper.

Samantha stepped aside and followed him down the steep ladder, nearly cursing at how difficult it was to keep from stepping on her skirts as she descended. She still had several steps to go when Ethan simply lifted her from the ladder and set her down. "One more to go," he said as he led them to the opening for the cargo hold. He helped himself to a lantern hanging nearby. Kneeling so he could see down to the cargo hold below, he lowered the lantern through the hole. A few barrels lined the hull, but not nearly as many as he expected to find. For a pirate ship, it seemed to lack booty. Perhaps they had sold their cargo at their last port.

"Did you ever get anything to eat?" Samantha asked suddenly.

"Uh huh. Cook took pity on me," Ethan replied before disappearing into the cargo hold. "He mentioned something would be sent down here for you after you finished your toilette."

Samantha's eyes widened, wondering if the cook had actually used the word. Her stomach growling—she hadn't eaten anything since that morning's berries—Samantha followed him down the ladder. "What are we supposed to do until I'm summoned for dinner?" she whispered once she was on her own feet again.

Ethan could think of one thing they could be doing. The clean scent surrounding Samantha along with the darkness surrounding them had him aroused. His lips found hers and he kissed her until he had to pull away to breathe. Leaving his forehead pressed against hers, he whispered, "You temptress."

"Here?" she whispered in dismay. "I just got dressed!"

"It may be our last chance," Ethan replied, frowning when he realized how desperate he sounded. *Christ!* What had she done to him to make him want her so? The mere thought that they would no longer be able to spend their nights together had him in a near panic, had his chest clenching with pain.

Glancing around the hold, Ethan spotted a tub of brandywine. "Here," he said as he pulled her to stand before him as he sat on it. He had the fastenings of his breeches undone in an instant, his manhood springing forth.

Stunned at how quickly her body had responded to his kiss, Samantha gathered up her skirts and lifted them to her hips. Ethan had her pantaloons pulled down and off from around her feet before grasping her hips and pulling her onto his erection.

Samantha had to stifle a shriek as he impaled her, as his hands pulled down the sleeves of her dress to expose her breasts, as his lips took purchase on a nipple and his tongue laved it. "I'm going to miss this," he managed to get out as he lifted and lowered her hips. "Miss you," he murmured, his lips moving to her other breast.

Her breaths coming in gasps, Samantha clenched on his manhood, willing herself to hang onto her sanity for just a moment more.

Miss you?

He had said the words as if he would never see her again. She was about to ask him what he meant when one hand encased a breast and the perfectly placed thumb of the other sent her into an oblivion of pure pleasure. The stars behind her eyelids coalesced into a blinding light as her entire body seemed to shatter around her.

Samantha's suddenly arched back and the intense grip on his shoulders was enough to let Ethan know he could allow his own release, the spasms of pure pleasure drowning out everything around him. He buried his head between her breasts, breathing in the clean scent. He felt as well as heard the quick thud of her heart beat against his ear. Buried deep inside her— he could still feel her undulations around his manhood—he wished time could stop. He wished they could just remain this way forever.

Could anything be as heavenly as this?

He moved his arms to wrap around her waist, to hold her as hard as possible against the front of his body as her quiet moans subsided, as her body's reaction finally stilled. After a few moments, he fell asleep.

Aware of his hold having lessened from around her body, Samantha took a deep breath and put her gown to rights, wincing as the fabric abraded her tender nipples.

Would this truly be the last time they would be together like this? She should be ashamed, she knew, for ever giving herself to the marquess, for ever spending the nights on the island with him. But she wouldn't have been able to forgive herself if she hadn't. The way he had worshipped her body with his own, the words he had spoken, the kisses they had shared—she was quite sure she would never again experience them with another man.

When tears threatened, she slowly stood up, moving Ethan's head to rest against the barrel behind the one on which he sat. "I love you," she heard him whisper, although he gave no evidence he was awake. She kissed him on the forehead, whispering, "I love you, too."

She pulled on her pantaloons and shook out her skirts. Opening her reticule, she found her mirror and checked her reflection by the dim light of the lantern. Although her hair was still in perfect order, she looked as if she were about to cry. Like a woman who had just been tumbled and told it would be the last time.

At the sound of booted feet overhead, she glanced at the opening at the top of the ladder. When Captain Crawley's face appeared, she quickly moved so her body would hide Ethan from his immediate view. She held a finger to her lips. "He's asleep," she whispered.

Crawley smiled and gave her a nod. "My cook informs me dinner is nearly ready," he whispered.

Giving one last glance in Ethan's direction, Samantha gave the captain a nod and carefully made her way up the ladder.

CHAPTER 29

DINNER WITH A PIRATE

lthough she had been in the captain's quarters only an hour earlier, she was stunned to find the small dining table dressed in fine linen and set with china and crystal. A bottle of wine was already uncorked, and the scents of herbed beef and carrots drifted from the covered dishes. The captain had even dressed for dinner, his black topcoat worn over a black shirt and black cravat. A waistcoat embroidered with silver threads peeked above his topcoat.

"It smells delicious," Samantha said as she took the chair Captain Crawley held for her.

"As do you, my lady," Crawley replied with an teasing arch of his eyebrow. "I must apologize for your having to spend time in the cargo hold."

Samantha placed a napkin across her lap, the years of training as a lady coming back to her in an instant. "Oh, there's no need to apologize. I realize we must do as we must in these situations."

Crawley took his own seat and poured the wine. "My first mate tells me we're well on our way to Valencia," he commented.

Valencia. Samantha blinked as she tried to remember where on the map the port city was located. "Southwest of Barcelona?" she guessed, taking a sip of the red wine. Rather dry and robust, she thought it particularly good. Other than the brandywine, she hadn't had anything to drink other than the odd-tasting water while on the island.

"Yes," he replied, surprised she would know. "I take it you're familiar with the Mediterranean?" he asked as he served the sliced beef in gravy.

"Only from what I've read, and from ..." She was about to say 'Lord Everly', but decided not to bring up the earl and his travels to Minorca. "The little bit of it we sailed before ... before the wave took us overboard," she managed to get out.

"That must have been quite frightening," Crawley commented, wondering if he could have survived long enough to get onto a piece of wreckage. He figured the marquess had to be strong swimmer in order to save himself and the lady.

Samantha considered the question for a moment. "It was more shocking, I suppose. The water was so cold. But Ethan was quick to get us to safety," she said before taking a bite of the roast beef.

Other than fish, she hadn't eaten meat for over a week. Although it smelled wonderful, she found the flavor lacking. She wondered how long it would be before she could eat a regular meal again and not think of foraging for berries or using her sunshade to catch fish.

Crawley regarded his dinner guest, noting her sad visage. She certainly didn't seem anxious to return to civilization. "Well, your ordeal is nearly over. It won't be long now. We'll simply leave you with *The Fairweather* and be on our way ..."

Samantha's eyes widened in sudden alarm. "You're ... you're just going to ... just ... *drop* me overboard?" she asked, panic gripping her. *Ethan was right. We never should have left the island with these men!*

Crawley frowned. "Well, no. I mean, I was planning to *dock* first, so that you might use the ramp," he explained as he splayed one hand on the table top, his numerous rings shining in the lamplight.

Samantha blinked. And blinked again. "The ramp?"

The captain sat back and regarded Samantha for a moment.

"Yes. The ramp. It's customary to leave the ship ..."

"The gang plank, you mean," Samantha said, her breaths coming faster.

Captain Crawley blinked and a slow smile spread over his face. "I think there may be a ... misunderstanding here," he finally said with a nod. He suddenly understood a comment the marquess had said when they were back on the island. "Earlier, on the island, Mr. Range made mention of *The Fairweather*, implying it had been lost at sea."

Blinking back tears, Samantha nodded, imagining how difficult it was going to be to walk the gang plank, to fall—she would simply refuse to jump—back into the cold waters of the Mediterranean.

Well, this time she wouldn't fight the cold. She wouldn't try to swim. She would simply let the cold water envelope her, suck the warmth from her body, and drag her down to her death. A whimper escaped as she wondered if Ethan would be forced to go with her. Perhaps they could drown in each other's arms.

"My lady," Crawley whispered hoarsely. "I am not going to make you walk the gang plank, for God's sake. I'm going to take you to where *The Fairweather* is docked in Valencia. Once I am quite sure you have been safely returned to Viscount Fitzsimmons, and the *Molly* has taken on some more provisions, I'll be on my way. Wouldn't be good for my cover to look too terribly legitimate, now would it?" he wondered, his voice changing from the Continental accent he'd been using to one of an English gentleman.

Samantha blinked, wiping a tear from her cheek. "Cover?" she repeated. She straightened in her chair. "*Cover?*"

The captain nodded, his head angling to one side. "Bradley. Alex Bradley, Foreign Office operative, at your service," he said, standing and giving her a bow.

Blinking several times, Samantha stared at the captain. "Oh!" she managed to get out, pushing her chair back and rising suddenly. She stepped around the table and threw her arms around the startled captain. "I just *knew* I knew you from somewhere!" she claimed in delight.

Stunned to suddenly have his dinner guest in his arms, Alex allowed a smile. "I apologize for the way you and the marquess have been treated, Miss Fitzsimmons. I couldn't very well afford you the courtesies you deserved," he said quietly. "Most of my crew is unaware of my true identity, you see."

"Oh, there's no need to apologize," Samantha replied with a shake of her head.

"I say, I was quite surprised to find you with Lord Plymouth, as I was only directed by Lord Chamberlain to find him and return ..."

"You know he's a marquess?" Samantha interrupted, her brows furrowed in confusion. Then she realized the rest of what he had said. *Directed by Lord Chamberlain to find him.*

"Of course. I've been looking for him for a couple of days, in fact. I received a missive from Lord Chamberlain explaining Plymouth had been swept overboard whilst traveling on *The Fairweather*. Knowing the area well, I began a search of the islands near where Captain St. John said his ship was damaged, using the possibility of finding the lost cargo as my excuse. Found you and the marquess on the third island we stopped at.

"Thank you, by the way, for ..." He stopped, embarrassed at what he was about to say. "Being so easy to spot," he finally managed to get out.

Samantha brows furrowed, wondering just how much of her the man had been able to see whilst she dressed that morning. "But, my uncle didn't mention anything about me?" she wondered. *Did Matthew think I had simply perished? That it was only likely the marquess would survive?* A sob caused her to hiccup and she slumped against the front of the captain.

"The note was brief. It had to be," Alex replied quietly, one arm moving to Samantha's back. "I'm sure he'll be quite relieved to know you have survived."

Suddenly aware they weren't alone, he glanced up to find Ethan standing in the doorway, the man's expression fearsome. It was then Alex knew the meaning of 'eyes shooting daggers' just then, for the marquess had aimed his directly at him.

A stab of fear shot through him when he realized Ethan

Range was probably angry enough to kill him. But instead of stepping into the cabin and confronting him, the marquess simply closed the door, never having actually entered the cabin. Alex had no idea how long the door had been open, no idea how much Ethan had overheard, if anything.

Alex pulled himself away from Samantha. "I trust you'll tell Lord Plymouth what I've told you. Just ... be very quiet about it. I've got a crew of very loyal seamen aboard, and I shouldn't like them to find out I'm not really Captain Crawley," he whispered.

Samantha nodded. "I'll keep your secret, of course," she said, nodding, tears still streaming down her face. She moved back to her chair, almost slumping into it. As she continued to eat, her spirits rose with each bite she took, with each sip of wine she drank. When she was sure she had spent the right amount of time with the captain, she bade him her thanks, took her leave of his quarters, and hurried off to tell Ethan the good news.

At least, she intended to.

Finding him proved to be impossible, even after she returned to Crawley's cabin to report he wasn't in the cargo hold or on the deck. A thorough search of the ship turned up nothing but news that a packet was missing.

A packet and Lord Plymouth.

CHAPTER 30

A MARQUESS MAKES HIS ESCAPE

For at least the tenth time that night, Ethan remembered the sight of Samantha in the arms of Captain Crawley. He remembered how her arms were wrapped around his body. And he remembered the delight he had seen in her profile.

Delight not aimed at him, but at the man in whose arms she was being held.

The anger he felt fueled his arms as he rowed toward a shore that seemed to recede every time he looked over his shoulder. He knew the image was merely an optical illusion. He was getting closer to the coast of Spain. He had to be.

How could she have made love to him, and then, only an hour later, be in the arms of the pirate captain? Didn't she realize she was his? He had taken her virtue on the island. Taken her body with his own. Taken her kisses, and the berries she had picked, and the wine she offered in the shells she had collected. He had taken everything she offered and more.

But, like Daisy, she had transferred her affections to someone who offered her more. Someone who had promised her ... *what*, he did not know. For what could Captain Crawley offer but a life on a pirate ship? A life of crime and port cities and bad food?

Is that the life Samantha wanted?

Perhaps the man had a second life somewhere. Perhaps he had promised her a home rich with the spoils of his voyages, jewels galore, a coach-and-four, and gowns made from the finest fabrics.

Ethan stopped rowing a moment.

Someone had offered her more.

What had he offered her?

Nothing, he realized.

They hadn't discussed a future. They had spoken of marriage and children—but not their own. They hadn't talked about a home or where they would travel or …

Ethan lifted the water jug he had stolen from the ship and drank as much as he could. Tearing off a piece of jerky and stuffing it between his teeth, he took up the oars and continued the exhausting, repetitive motion that brought him closer to the shore.

He remembered the look on her face that morning when she sat in the packet—probably the same packet he was rowing to shore right now—a look of disappointment, of regret. As if she didn't want to leave the island.

At the time, he had thought her upset because they were being rescued by pirates. But perhaps she had realized something else.

Her mother was dead. Other than her uncle and her two close friends, she had no one else in London. What kind of life did she have to look forward to there?

A life much like his own, he supposed.

No wonder she had happily accepted whatever it was the captain had offered.

The sun had cleared the horizon and was nearly halfway up the bright blue sky when Ethan felt the boat's bottom snag on something underneath. Startled, he turned around to find very little water between the boat and the beach. Dropping the oars, he pulled on his waistcoat, reached for the water jug and jerky, slowly stood up and took his leave of the packet.

Barely able to walk, Ethan resisted the urge to kiss the

ground and instead made his way toward the buildings and docks he spotted to the north.

Along the way, as he once again remembered Samantha, he realized something rather profound. He had taken everything from her, but he had only given her a sunshade in exchange. Closing his eyes for a moment, he hoped she would at least keep the diamond pin that held it together.

CHAPTER 31

A SHIP DOCKS IN VALENCIA

*S*amantha knew something was different when she slowly opened her eyes and found herself staring at the ceiling of Captain Crawley's cabin. A bit of panic swept over her, but a quick look down her front confirmed she still wore the red silk de Naples gown Crawley had given her, and on top of that lay a wool blanket.

The sound of snoring had her redirecting her gaze. Captain Crawley was asleep in his bunk at the other end of the cabin. All at once, memories of the night before crashed into her consciousness.

Nightmares, actually.

Where had Ethan gone? And why? She remembered his words right after they had made love. He had held her so tenderly, his head pressed against her breast. *I'll miss this. Miss you.*

He must have known he would be leaving. Must have already planned to take a packet and row to shore. But why? They were on their way to Valencia, on their way to *The Fairweather*. To her mother and uncle.

But Ethan didn't know that.

Ethan didn't know Captain Crawley's true identity. He didn't know the man had been dispatched to find the marquess and return him to England.

"He'll have to row at least four miles," Crawley had said. Or rather, Alex Bradley had said. It was hard to think of the Foreign Office agent as anything other than a ship's captain. "But at least he left when we were closest to shore. With any luck, he'll make it to Costa Nova or perhaps Xábia sometime tomorrow."

Samantha shook her head. "Can't we ... go after him?" she asked, panicked and on the verge of tears, thinking the ship would be able to move fast enough to catch up to him. By the time they realized he had taken his leave of the *Molly*, he had only been gone an hour.

"My lady, it's too dark," the first mate had replied, his head shaking from side to side. "If we didn't see him in time, we could run right over him."

Feeling helpless and alone, Samantha had merely nodded her understanding and returned to the captain's quarters. Her back to the wall, she slowly slid to the floor and wept. Bradley had no doubt found her asleep and tossed the blanket over her when he retired for the night. At least he hadn't attempted to rouse her and make her move to the cargo hold!

Rising from the floor, Samantha stretched and dared a peek out of the cabin's only window. She blinked, wondering if she might still be dreaming. Land stretched out as far as she could see in both directions. Then beneath her feet, she felt the vibration of the rudder and felt the slight turn of the ship as it responded.

"We're about to dock," Bradley said from behind her.

Startled at the sound of his voice so close, Samantha gasped. "Oh! I didn't hear you get up," she said, giving him a quick glance. Afraid he might be in his nightclothes, she was relieved to see he was already in breeches, boots and a shirt opened at the neck.

"I apologize. I didn't mean to startle you," he replied. "And I'm sorry for the poor accommodations ..."

"Oh, you needn't be," she interrupted with a shake of her head. "I've been sleeping on the ground for a week now, so the floor was quite fine."

Alex Bradley furrowed his brows. "A *week?*" he repeated. "I didn't realize it had been so long," he whispered as he shook his head. He seemed to hesitate before he said, "About the marquess ..."

Samantha turned from where she had been watching the shore pass by. "Yes?" she whispered, reminded once again he had taken his leave the night before. Taken his leave without saying 'good-bye'.

"I have failed my mission," he said with a sigh. "I'm hoping returning you to your uncle will make up for it somehow."

Samantha recalled their conversation over dinner the night before. The agent had been dispatched by Lord Chamberlain to find Lord Plymouth. He had done that; he just hadn't kept the marquess on board so he could be delivered to the mainland.

"I promise I will put in a good word for you," Samantha said with a wan smile.

Hopefully Ethan had made it to the coast, she thought, determined not to allow any more tears to fall. He had obviously planned to go it alone when he had the chance. He had money to pay for new clothes, money to pay his passage to Rome and back to England. Money to buy the batteries he claimed he needed for his coal mines. The week they had spent on the island merely delayed him in his mission. She hoped he didn't regret their time together. She knew she never would.

Samantha wondered if she would ever see him again. At a ball or shopping in London, perhaps. What would she do if she ever saw him again? Act as if they had never met?

No. She couldn't do that, not while her entire body would be blushing, remembering how his kisses and caresses had brought her such pleasure. No. She would greet him, kiss him on the cheek, and treat him as a long lost friend. She could do nothing less.

"I know it's none of my business, my lady, but," Bradley said in a quiet voice, his British accent still evident. "I had the distinct impression he was in love with you."

Samantha angled her head and nodded. "As did I," she replied. The captain's words reminded her of Ethan's words after they had made love the night before. *Thank the gods I responded in kind.* She would have forever regretted not saying those three little words that now meant so much. *Or not enough.*

When the ship stuttered to a near stop, Samantha heard shouts and instructions coming from the deck. "I've got to go," Bradley said suddenly. His voice suddenly changing to that of the pirate captain, he said, "Can't allow my first mate to take all the credit of a perfect docking now, can I?" And with that, he took his leave of the cabin.

Samantha allowed a wan smile as she watched him go. Although she was tempted to step out on the deck, she didn't want to be in the way of the crew as they carried out their various duties. When it was time to go ashore, she was sure Captain Crawley would escort her down the ramp.

When it was time to disembark, it was the ship's first mate who came to fetch her from the captain's cabin. "My lady, it's time," he said, his words spoken in a distinct British accent.

Samantha angled her head before she nodded. She held out her right hand, "I am Samantha Fitzsimmons. May I inquire as to where you are from?" she asked, giving his hastily supplied hand a quick shake.

"Kent, my lady," he replied. In a lowered voice, he said, "I'm not really a pirate, but I think you already knew that," he added with a shrug.

"I didn't, actually," a surprised Samantha replied with a shake of her head. "But I'll keep your secret."

The man nodded. "I'm to see you to *The Fairweather*, my lady."

With that, the first mate escorted her across the deck and to a ramp that led to the dock below. They were nearly on the wooden boards when Samantha remembered the dress she wore didn't belong to her. "This is the captain's gown!" she whispered suddenly, turning to head back up the ramp.

The first mate shook his head. "Oh, no, my lady. Captain says you can keep it," he stated. At Samantha's look of confusion, he added, "Damned gown has gotten him into too much trouble. One of the crewmen found it and thought maybe the captain was really a molly. We nearly lost the ship over it," he explained.

Samantha nodded her understanding as she resumed the short walk to the slip that held *The Fairweather*. She was surprised it looked as good as it did. There was no evidence of storm damage—the wheelhouse had obviously been replaced—and it sported all its masts. "It doesn't look as if it nearly capsized," she breathed as they climbed aboard. No one seemed to be about, but it was early. The crew could still be abed. "Thank you for the escort. I'll just go down to my cabin now," she said as she curtsied to the first mate.

"Very well, my lady. Hope your man makes it home all right." And with that, the first mate headed back down *The Fairweather's* ramp and to the *Molly*.

My man? she wondered, closing her eyes for a moment to allow an image of Ethan to appear. Forcing herself to forget him for the time being, Samantha glanced about the deck before heading to the companionway. Carefully stepping down the shallow stairs, she was nearly to the cabin deck when she was suddenly face-to-face with Captain John St. John.

The man blinked and regarded her for a moment. "Jesus," he muttered, his head shaking from side to side.

"I am not a ghost, I assure you," Samantha said as she allowed a smile, rather happy to see the ship's captain still alive.

"Good God, however did you survive?" he asked as he led the way to her cabin.

"I was about to ask you the same thing," she countered. "Until ..." She stopped, realizing she couldn't tell Captain St. John about Alex Bradley. "I truly thought *The Fairweather* had sunk when the wave crashed onto the deck. Lord Plymouth said the mast broke ..."

"Cracked," St. John corrected. "Other than losing part of the wheelhouse and most of my maps ..."

"That reminds me," Samantha interrupted, opening her reticule to pull out the captain's log and map she had found on the island. "I think these are yours," she said as she passed the folded documents to the captain. "They are a bit faded, I'm afraid, but may still be of use." She paused a moment, rather enjoying the captain's look of disbelief. "Unfortunately, the three tubs of brandywine that landed with us were confiscated by pirates. One of the walls of your wheelhouse made an adequate raft. Got us to a small island where we stayed until the pirates showed up."

"Pirates?" St. John repeated, his brows furrowing and his head shaking as if he were having a hard time following her story.

"Yes. I was on the *Molly*. The ship that just pulled into a slip near here," she said with a nod.

Captain St. John blinked a couple of times. The only ship that had pulled into port that morning was flying British pennons. "I'll take my leave of you. When you're ready to go to the hotel, I'll be up on deck," he said. "I know your ... relatives will be very anxious to see you alive and well."

When the captain opened the door to the cabin she and her mother shared, she glanced in. "Where ...?"

"She stayed in a convent for a couple of days until a local aristocrat suggested she use his residence as a hotel. Lord Chamberlain joined her there a few days ago. I'd be honored to take you there," he offered.

Samantha glanced down at her gown and winced. Seeing her trunk still in the cabin, she gave the captain a nod. "I should change. Give me a few moments?" she replied.

"Take your time. But now that you've returned, we'll be heading back to England just as soon as the viscount and his lady return to the ship."

Surprised at hearing her uncle was in Valencia, Samantha nodded until she remembered Captain Crawley's comment about having been dispatched to the find the marquess.

Well, he had been found. Perhaps they would be able to find him again.

CHAPTER 32
REUNITED

Samantha took a turn in the small cabin, the memories of the few days she had spent there with Caroline coming back in vignettes. Back then, the woman had been her aunt, and the way they had played lady's maid to one another was merely an extension of how they behaved on the days their own maids were off back in London.

When Caroline's bout of seasickness started, Samantha had been concerned, of course, but she wondered how she would feel now knowing the woman was really her mother. Worried, probably. Certainly more sympathetic.

She replayed some conversations they had shared over the years in her head, the perspective now so different because Caroline was her mother and not just an aunt forced to be concerned for her welfare because she was her closest relative. How different everything seemed in this new light!

Why did she keep me in the dark? Was she ashamed of having borne me out-of-wedlock? Of course, that had to be the reason.

So, who is my father? Do I have sisters and brothers? Nieces and nephews? Cousins?

Feeling a bit overwhelmed, Samantha shook her head and realized she would soon learn some answers. She would demand them of her mother—just as soon as she was reunited with her and Uncle Matthew.

Moving to her trunk, she opened it to find everything just as she had left it. She pulled out a sprigged muslin day gown, chemise, corset and pantaloons, fresh petticoats and stockings. Thank the gods she had brought several sets, despite Caroline's claim they would have the benefit of a laundress in Rome!

Dressing quickly, her heart pounding in anticipation, Samantha still stopped to finger the soft cotton and silk garments as she pulled them on, the clean fabric welcome after so many days of wearing the same undergarments. Struggling with the corset, she was about to call for Captain St. John to help when she caught herself.

After a week in a man's company, had she really lost all sense of modesty? All sense of propriety?

"I can help you with your corset if you'd like."

Samantha spun around to find Caroline regarding her with tear-filled eyes. "Mother!" She rushed to the woman, her arms wrapping around her shoulders and pulling her into a hug.

Caroline, surprised at how Samantha had addressed her but more relieved to see her in one piece, pulled away after a time, tears dripping down her cheeks as she looked over her daughter. "You're well? You're all right?" she whispered. "You're certainly showing a bit of color!"

Samantha nodded, her own tear-filled eyes closing as she pulled Caroline back into the hug. "I thought you had died," she whispered, sniffling.

Caroline slowly pulled away from her. "Why ever would you think such a thing?" she asked in surprise.

Blinking at the surprising question, Samantha replied, "When we were washed off the ship, we were sure it capsized. Ethan heard the mast break ..."

Caroline blinked as she stared at her daughter. "Ethan?" she repeated. She shook her head. "You were with him, then?" she asked, her brow furrowing in concern.

Nodding, Samantha said, "Well, he was up on deck at the same time I was." She paused. "Smoking," she added with a roll of her eyes.

Caroline nodded, apparently relieved to hear her daughter

hadn't arranged a clandestine meeting with the man. "And where is Lord Plymouth now?"

Samantha took a deep breath and let it out slowly. She shook her head. "I ... I don't know, but ..." Tears started flowing down her cheeks. "I do hope he'll make it to shore today. If he hasn't already. I owe him my life," she whispered.

Allowing a wan smile, the viscountess angled her head and regarded her daughter. "Well, it seems we have much to talk about. Your uncle is here, of course. Let's get you dressed, and we can go to the place where we're staying. Have some luncheon."

Samantha nodded. "I'd like that," she agreed, her stomach growling, reminding her of the sounds Ethan's had made when they were on the island.

Once Caroline had her corset fastened, Samantha finished dressing and regarded her half boots. Poor things. Despite their dunking in the Mediterranean, they were still serviceable. Samantha cleaned them up with a linen from the basin and pulled them on as she made small talk.

"How did you know to come look for me here? Today?" Samantha suddenly asked, her attention on the sound of boots on the cabin deck.

A knock at the door and Matthew Fitzsimmons appeared around the edge of the door. "Now there's a sight for sore eyes," he said with a wide grin.

"Uncle!" Samantha rushed into his arms and hugged him. "Thank you. Thank you for sending Captain Crawley to find us," she murmured.

Matthew finally gave up his hold on her. "He ... he mentioned the marquess took his leave of the *Molly* last night." At Samantha's widening eyes, he added, "I went to his ship first."

"How did you know to come to the docks?" she asked as she sat down to finish fastening her half boots.

Her uncle moved to sit next to Caroline, giving her a kiss on her temple as he did so. "I've been watching for incoming ships. Saw the British pennons and hoped for the best."

Samantha sat up straight. "British pennons?" she repeated. "Not ... not the skull and ...?" She stopped, realizing that in port, Captain Crawley, or rather, Captain Bradley, wouldn't want his ship to be identified as that of a pirate's.

Matthew's head shook quickly. "I have been expecting him," he said then. "I rather hoped he would have arrived yesterday, but I suppose you weren't as easy to locate as I had hoped."

Furrowing her brows, Samantha regarded her uncle for a time. "So, you believed I survived?" she queried, rather surprised he would have that kind of faith.

"I had to. I'm married to your mother, you must know," he replied with a quirked lip.

Samantha allowed a smile. "A situation which makes me very happy," she said. Sobering a bit, she added, "I do hope you don't think Captain Bradley failed in his mission."

Matthew frowned, his expression suggesting he was a bit confused by the comment. "Mission?" he repeated.

"To find Lord Plymouth. Return him to British shores," Samantha explained.

"Oh, that," Matthew murmured. "Truth be told ... I may have used him as an excuse to find you, my dear. But given the circumstances, I couldn't very well send him on a wild goose chase, either. We had no idea if you lived, and if so, where you would end up."

Samantha nodded her understanding. "And with Lord Plymouth not having any heirs, I suppose there was concern his marquessate would end up with the Crown."

Matthew's look of surprise passed quickly. "Indeed. You have the gist of it," he replied. "Now, if you two ladies will indulge me, I should like very much to eat, and I'm sure you would, too," he said as he stood up and turned to assist Caroline.

Her stomach growling in response to his comment, Samantha giggled, tears once again streaming down her face.

CHAPTER 33

TRUTHS BE TOLD REDUX

Four days later

"You seem awfully anxious to get home," Caroline commented as she watched her daughter pull on a day gown. Captain St. John had said they would make London sometime in the afternoon, and for Samantha, that time couldn't come soon enough.

"I am," Samantha replied.

"And yet, a few weeks ago, you could hardly wait to reach Rome."

Samantha paused as she pulled on a pair of slippers, wincing at how uncomfortable they still seemed after a week of going barefoot. She gave her mother a slight shrug. She hadn't shared much about her experiences on the island, certainly none of the details of what she had done with Ethan. Now that she knew Caroline was really her mother, she found it more difficult to share her ordeal with the woman who she had only ever known as her aunt.

Samantha had spent hours on deck at the railing, staring at the water below and wondering about Ethan's fate. Had he made it to the mainland? If so, had he found a way to get to Rome? Or had he simply returned to England? And why had he left the *Molly?* Left her with a man he probably still believed was the captain of a pirate ship?

At first, she had been incensed Ethan would simply leave her with no word, no note. And then later, she had wept, worrying over his fate. By the following morning, she had been anxious but so excited to be reunited with Caroline and Matthew that she hadn't given Ethan much thought.

But these past few days, as *The Fairweather* made its way back to England, she'd had the time to reflect on the week she had spent with the marquess. Had time to remember the feel of walking barefoot in warm sand, of swimming in clear water, of picking berries and wild garlic and cooking fresh fish. She relived his kisses, remembered how they had made love in the dunes and watched shooting stars.

Make a wish.

She was sure he wished for a ship to rescue them from the island. Well, he got his wish, even if he didn't stay on board.

Her wish? *I wish I could wake up every morning in his arms.* Considering she had woken up on the floor of the cabin that morning, tangled in her night rail and a blanket, she knew *that* wish certainly hadn't come true.

Caroline moved to fasten the last few buttons on Samantha's gown. "Oh, Samantha. Please, tell me what's wrong," she whispered.

Samantha's eyes widened. "Nothing," she lied, giving her head a slight shake.

"You were on the *floor* this morning," the viscountess countered.

Sighing, Samantha realized she had to tell her mother something. "I'm used to sleeping on the ground, is all. I just ... need some time to get used to a comfortable bed again."

Caroline blinked, her mouth dropping open. "These bunks are far from *comfortable*," she argued with a shake of her head. She had sneaked into Matthew's cabin in the middle of the night, removed her night rail and spent several hours pressed against him, rather happy when he finally rolled atop her. They made slow, quiet love until the dim light of dawn intruded. His bunk was far more comfortable than the one she indicated with a wave, although she knew it had more to do with him being in it than the mattress.

"You hardly ate anything at dinner last night."

Samantha sighed again. "I spent a week eating berries and fish. It will just ... take some time to get used to beef again," she reasoned. Truth be told, she wasn't very hungry. With little room to move about the ship, she hadn't done much to work up an appetite. "I'm going up on deck to get some air," she added, grabbing her sunshade and hurrying to the door. She was out of the cabin and halfway up the companionway when Caroline poked her head out of their cabin and called, "But you haven't put up your hair!"

Pausing in her ascent, Samantha closed her eyes. Oh, how she missed the island!

Matthew Fitzsimmons emerged from his cabin and regarded his wife with an arched brow. He kissed her temple. "How is my beautiful mischief maker this morning?" he whispered, taking one of her hands in his. He turned her palm up and kissed it.

Caroline smiled despite her worry over Samantha. "I'm at a loss at what to do about Samantha," she whispered.

His brows furrowing, Matthew glanced in the direction of the companionway. "Give her time, Caro. She's been through hell," he said in a hoarse whisper. "Did you tell her yet? About Emma?"

Caroline shook her head. "I ... I was going to last night, but she ... she doesn't seem to want to talk. About anything. She won't tell me what happened on the island. Something had to have happened for her to be this ... quiet, though." Her eyes widened. "Do you suppose Plymouth ...?" She left the rest of her question unspoken, the pain in her face suggesting she thought the worst of the marquess.

Matthew shook his head. "She told me he was a perfect gentleman the entire time," he replied. He gave his wife another kiss. "I'll go up on deck, though. See if I can't ... draw her out a bit."

Her eyes widening, Caroline was about to protest but finally nodded. "I'll be out shortly. For breakfast," she replied.

Scrubbing his face with a hand, Matthew considered how best to approach his niece. So much had happened in just a couple of weeks. So much had come to light. He knew she deserved to know everything, though, and so he made his way up to the deck.

Blinking in the unusually bright sunshine, Matthew found Samantha leaning against the starboard deck rail, her makeshift sunshade propped up against the hull. The diamond-tipped pin winked in the light, nearly blinding him. "Quite the parasol you have there," he murmured as he stepped up and leaned his elbows on the rail next to Samantha.

His niece smiled. "Ethan made it for me," she replied, not giving a thought to her use of the marquess' given name.

"Out of what, exactly?" he wondered as he lifted it from where it stood. *Ethan?* Well, he supposed a week on a deserted island would have had the two castaways on a first-name basis. He examined the branch and the fabric, rather startled to find a diamond pin holding it all together.

"His cravat. And his pin," Samantha replied. "I'll need to return them to him just as soon as he returns to London," she added. *If he returns.* She blinked, realizing she had assumed the best.

Matthew nodded. "Rather sporting of him to give up his cravat on your behalf," he commented. "Did you have to give up anything in return?"

Samantha's eyes widened. "Whatever do you mean?"

The viscount offered her the sunshade, a hint that she needed to use it given the weather. "Your innocence?" he whispered, not able to make eye contact with his niece.

"Uncle Matthew!" she scolded. "Lord Plymouth was a perfect gentleman the entire time we were on the island." She shook her head, not quite believing she had just lied.

"Forgive me for thinking the worst," he replied. "I don't know the man well. He's rarely in London, and he hasn't yet taken his seat in Parliament."

Samantha considered his words. "I didn't like him at first," she said. At her uncle's raised eyebrow, she added, "He scowled the entire time we had dinner with him and the captain the first night we were underway. Although he answered questions when asked, he ..." She sighed. "He barely acknowledged us." *Because we're bad ton*, she remembered him saying on the island.

Matthew angled his head. "And once you were on the island?"

Samantha considered how to respond. "He ... He got foxed the first night. Some brandywine from this ship made its way to the same beach where we landed. We talked. After that, we simply did what we had to do to survive," she explained, not adding that their survival tactics included a good deal of kissing and spending their nights together. "Are you angry with her?" she asked then, wanting to deflect his attention from her ordeal.

"Angry?" Matthew repeated, his brows furrowing together.

"At Caro ... Mother, I mean," Samantha clarified. "You have every right to be furious with her," she whispered.

"Are you?" he asked quietly, noticing his niece was on the verge of tears.

Samantha gave a slight nod. "I'm three-and-twenty, and I had to find out from a marquess I barely know that I am a bastard," she whispered, "So, yes, I suppose I am a bit ... *disappointed* in her."

Matthew winced. "Sam, no," he said with a shake of his head, reaching his arms around her shoulders to pull her into a hug. "Never, never, never say that," he murmured.

"How long have you known she was my mother?"

The viscount took a deep breath. "I've suspected since the day she brought you home from Darbing Manor," he finally said. At Samantha's look of surprise, he shook his head. "But once we were betrothed, I found it didn't really matter. I knew she was a widow. I wasn't about to break the engagement. I ... I was smitten with her. Prettiest chit in all of London, and she agreed to be my wife."

"Because the Earl of Mayfield ... my *grandfather* ... forced her to," Samantha countered. "Or Uncle Stanley."

Matthew gave Samantha a quelling glance. "Mayfield didn't force her to do anything, and neither did her brother," he assured her. "Her mother, now she was the one who had her marrying that second son—the idiot who ended up dead after only a couple of weeks in France," he explained. "I think the dowager was afraid if she didn't get Caro settled right away, she wouldn't be biddable."

Samantha realized just then that the Dowager Countess of Mayfield was her grandmother. She had to resist the urge to shudder at the thought. But having Stanley Harrington as an uncle wasn't so bad. And his daughter, Julia, was her best friend. *And cousin!*

Her uncle had paused a moment, as if he were trying to decide how to broach another subject. "Little did Lady Mayfield know there were two of us who wanted your mother."

Samantha stilled herself, her gaze shifting to the horizon. Land was rising out of the waters, land she knew was England. "Was my father one of them?" she asked quietly.

"Indeed. A widower with a daughter," he replied, watching for Samantha's reaction. He wasn't disappointed when he saw comprehension and a mix of excitement and fear cross her features.

"Did you ... did you know him?" Samantha asked suddenly, her brows furrowed.

Resisting the urge to laugh, Matthew merely smiled. "Too well, I'm afraid," he said with a nod. "He was my brother, George."

Samantha blinked. And blinked again. "The hat maker," she said. "His daughter is ..." She paused as she tried to remember the name of the woman who had sold the hat shop and married the Earl of Trenton's cousin. In her younger years, the young woman had occasionally paid a call on Fitzsimmons Manor. She was Matthew's niece, after all, but had never been close.

"Emma," Matthew said with a nod. "She's Mrs. Wellingham now. A rather accomplished woman. She's an accomptant at Wellingham Imports. She and her husband live at Woodscastle with his sister and Grandby's cousin, Gregory. The outrageously rich man who helps the rest of us build our fortunes," he added with an arched brow. "If Lady Torrington doesn't deliver an heir,

Gregory stands to inherit the Torrington earldom," he explained.

Samantha pondered this bit of information before she realized Emma might not realize she had a sister. "Does she know about me?" she asked, realizing that perhaps the woman had probably known for a long time, maybe even all of Samantha's life.

Matthew nodded. "She does. She ... wants to meet you. Wants you to know she has followed your accomplishments. I believe she even has one of your paintings in her office," he said quietly.

Tears dripped down Samantha's cheeks. When she moved to open her reticule, she found the handle missing from around her wrist. *I left it in the cabin*, she realized. Matthew had a handkerchief held out for her, though. "Thank you ..." She hiccuped. "For telling me. I ..." She sobbed, dropping her head against Matthew's chest. "I rather like that I'm really your niece and not just one by marriage," she managed to get out.

Kissing the top of her head, Matthew felt his chest clench. "That's music to my ears," he murmured. "Especially since you're about to have another sister or brother who will also be your niece or nephew."

Samantha laughed, the tears flowing freely, tears for Emma as well as for Ethan and the baby her mother would deliver in six months or so. When she finally let go of Matthew, she saw her mother standing near the companionway, her own tears streaming down her face.

"Oh, dear," Samantha said as she gave a sideways glance in Matthew's direction.

Her uncle stepped away and joined his wife, wrapping his arm around her shoulders and pulling her against the front of his body. "All is well," he murmured.

Except, of course, it wasn't. Not really. Until Samantha learned of Ethan's fate, learned why he had left the *Molly*, she was sure she wouldn't sleep.

CHAPTER 34

LONDON WELCOMES A CASTAWAY

From the time *The Fairweather* docked in London, Samantha knew her life would be different, and not just because she was different. Much had happened in the seventeen days since she had been in England, and apparently word had already spread about some of it.

"Why are all these people here?" she asked as she stood at the deck railing. A crowd of people—she recognized many of them—were gathered at the dock. At first, she thought they were there to board another ship, but *The Fairweather* was the only passenger ship at his particular dock.

Matthew shook his head, his bushy eyebrows furrowing. "I'm not sure, but I have an idea," he murmured. Turning to Captain St. John, he arched one of those brows. "Who knows we were to arrive today?" he asked, not mentioning he knew of a few at the Foreign Office who had been apprised of his situation by a courier sent via a land route from Valencia. He wouldn't expect any of them to form a welcoming party, however.

The captain gave him a nod. "I was ordered by the ship's owner to send word just as soon as anyone was found. The courier obviously arrived before we did," he said with an arched brow.

"Ship's owner?" Matthew repeated.

"Nattersley," St. John responded. "A bit of a ... publicity hound, especially where the company is concerned. He was quite adamant that if any survivors were found, he was to be informed immediately."

Frowning, Matthew glanced out at the crowd. "Then he must have also shared the information that two passengers had gone missing, otherwise, there would be no welcoming party," he reasoned.

"He is an optimistic man," the captain said with a shrug. The forward movement of the ship suddenly ceased as the docking ropes were pulled taunt. "Excuse me, my lord," he added as he moved away from the railing, apparently to do whatever captains had to do when their ship made port.

"Evangeline is here," Samantha said, bouncing at bit as she lifted a hand and waved to her best friend. "And Julia and ..."

"Lady Torrington," Caroline breathed from where she stood on the other side of Samantha. "Samantha. We need to agree not to say anything about my being your mother," Caroline whispered. "If anyone finds out ..."

"I know, Aunt Caroline," Samantha replied with a nod. Indeed, if anyone in the *ton* discovered Caroline was really her mother, the scandal would be untenable. After all these years of being passed off as the daughter of Elizabeth and Edward Fitzsimmons, Samantha would become *persona non grata*, her illegitimacy a detriment to her and the rest of the Fitzsimmons. The scandal would also reach the Harringtons. She couldn't abide her uncle, Stanley Harrington, Earl of Mayfield, and his countess, Temperance, suffering as a result.

Thank the gods her sister, Emma, had kept their secret all these years. Samantha desperately wanted to meet the woman again, her only knowledge of the accomptant coming from Matthew and a brief introduction when Emma had paid a call on her uncle, a call meant to reestablish familial ties. Although he had been estranged from his brother when George opened his hat shop—against the wishes of his father and Matthew—Matthew at least welcomed Emma into his life.

"When was the last time you saw her?"

Samantha wondered how different her first night in Valencia might have been had she known about Emma, the night they were celebrating her return to civilization. Despite not knowing anyone in the port city, the arrival of Samantha had set off a celebration among those who had met her mother and Matthew while they waited for Samantha's fate to be determined. Soon, others joined the impromptu party, and by midnight, the entire town seemed to have joined in the drinking and merry making. Samantha had never been surrounded by such joy in all her life.

If only Ethan had been there, too! The thought had her heart clenching, and she fought back a sudden tear.

"Just a few weeks ago," her uncle replied with a shrug. "Had I any idea she was your sister, I assure you, I would have made arrangements for you two to meet when you were still a babe," he claimed, giving her a pat on the back. "Come. I think it's time we made our way off the ship."

Arm-in-arm, Caroline and Samantha led the way to the ramp that led down to the dock. Samantha spotted Alistair Comber and Jeffrey Sommers. Surprised her friends' husbands would have accompanied their wives to meet the ship, Samantha nearly stopped walking down the ramp. But the crowd had begun cheering, and Samantha was swept along in a wave of good tidings and cheer from everyone on the dock.

"You look as if you have been in the sun for an age!" Julia cried out as she pulled Samantha into a hug. She was replaced by her husband, Alistair, who planted a kiss on her cheek and murmured, "What a relief," into her ear.

Before she could even react to his comment, Jeffrey Sommers had his arms around her. "I'm going to write a novel based on your adventures," he yelled over the din of the crowd.

And then Evangeline had her arms around her, hugging her so tight she thought a rib or two might have cracked. "Don't you ever leave England again," the baroness whispered.

Tears spilled down Samantha's cheeks. "I won't. I promise," she managed to get out. "Goodness, but who are all these people?" she asked, turning to find her godfather holding out his arms to her.

"Grandby!" she shouted, holding her own arms out to hug the man. Caroline claimed that upon her appearance in London with Samantha when she was but a babe, Grandby had announced he was her godfather even before being asked to perform the honor.

"Scared me to death, you did," he said, a hint of a northern accent tingeing his voice. He held her at arm's length and then looked about. "We'll talk. Soon," he said, one eyebrow cocked up in a manner that suggested she had better call on the man post-haste.

"Of course," she managed to say before being pulled into another group of well-wishers.

A calling card was pressed into her hand. "I wish to speak with you on the morrow," a man said before disappearing into the crowd. Samantha dared a glance at the card, stunned to find the name of a reporter from *The Times*. Before she had a chance to tuck the card into her reticule, another was given to her. "I would appreciate an audience with you. Later today perhaps?" She caught the words, 'The Morning Chronicle', before the man was replaced by the Harringtons.

"My God, girl, you had us worried," Stanley said as he bussed her on the cheek.

"If you hadn't come today, I swear I would have had a fit of the vapors," Temperance claimed as she kissed the other cheek. "Do pay a call tomorrow, won't you?" she added before taking Samantha's hand and squeezing it.

Feeling a tug on her other hand, she suddenly found herself face-to-face with a man she had never met, a man who was rather handsome and probably not yet thirty. He lifted the hand to his lips and brushed his lips over her knuckles. "Sir James. James Moriarty, at your service," he said with a deep bow.

Samantha took the first breath she had in over five minutes and regarded the rather dashing young man for a moment. "Lady Samantha," she replied, managing a curtsy.

Sir James gave her a devastating smile. "Where have you been all my life?" he asked rhetorically.

Her eyebrows lifted in surprise, Samantha had no idea how

to respond to the man. "On a deserted island?" she replied with a smile.

"And the rest of your life?" he asked, his eyes bright and his face lit up with what could only be described as pure joy.

Samantha shook her head. "I've no idea," she replied.

"Marry me!" he shouted over the sounds of the crowd.

Blinking, Samantha thought she had heard him wrong. "What did you say?" she asked loudly.

"Marry me!" he repeated, his voice carrying over the other voices so that suddenly, everything and everyone was quiet. "Marry me," he repeated in a voice much lower but still heard by the entire crowd.

Samantha swallowed and wondered why the edges of her vision were suddenly gray, why the sounds of the crowd had diminished to low rumbles. A moment later, everything went black.

When Samantha came to, the odor of vinegar assaulting her nostrils from Lady Torrington's smelling salts, she was leaning against her uncle.

"There you are. Gave us a bit of a fright just then," he said, making sure she could stay standing before he let go his hold.

I've never fainted a day in my life!

"I just need some air," she said with a nod. And some answers. "Could we go to the office?" she asked as she pointed to the small building with the shipping company's shingle hanging above the door. "I need to make an inquiry."

Matthew followed her line of sight and nodded. "As do I," he said.

With the crowd dissipating, she and Caroline were able to follow Matthew as he made his way toward the wooden building.

They were barely in the door when Samantha inquired as to the fate of Lord Plymouth. The clerk excused himself, saying he needed to consult someone else. After a short wait, only one man at the shipping company could answer her query.

"Why, Lord Plymouth arrived yesterday on the *Bellingham*," William Nattersley replied with a happy nod, seeming rather pleased with himself. "I rather hoped he would arrive with you so he could be welcomed appropriately. Not much for crowds, apparently. Asked that his luggage be sent on to Yorkshire. Rather amazing you two survived, what with being tossed overboard and all. I rather imagine he's already on his way to Yorkshire. Would you like to send a note?"

Samantha felt a pang of regret and shook her head. "No, thank you," she said. She took her leave of the office with her uncle and mother, a sense of sadness settling over her that was soon replaced by something else entirely. Climbing into a hackney for the trip to Fitzsimmons Manor, Samantha couldn't shake the feeling she was being watched. When she scanned the crowd, hoping she would find Ethan, she instead only saw the young man who had proposed.

Marry me, he had said, and loud enough for everyone to hear.

The fool. What had he been trying to accomplish by proposing in front of so many people? Perhaps he was a candidate for Bedlam, and she was merely the unfortunate recipient of his misplaced attentions.

Except that when they reached Fitzsimmons Manor, the butler, Porter, informed her Sir James was waiting for her in the parlor.

"I explained you weren't in residence, but he insisted on staying," the older man said.

"Thank you, Porter." Samantha gave a wide-eyed glance in her mother's direction and then suddenly wondered about Lily Harkness. She hadn't been at the docks. "Is Lady Lily still in residence?" Samantha half expected the butler to inform her the girl was married and moved out. From what Ethan had said that night on *The Fairweather*, it was certainly possible, although Samantha didn't know how the marquess would have any knowledge of Lily's suitors except for what had been printed in *The Morning Chronicle.*

"No, milady," the butler replied with a shake of his head. "Lord Trenton sent his coach with a request that she pay a visit to the Trenton earldom in Staffordshire. Lady Lily left later that day and said to expect her return within the month."

Caroline frowned. "Interesting timing. She was considering so many offers before we left for Rome," she murmured, one eyebrow arched up.

Samantha angled her head and said, "Perhaps Trenton wanted to hear more about her choices before settling on an amount for the dowry," she suggested. Gabriel Wellingham, the Earl of Trenton, was quite insistent his half-sister be treated as if she were a Wellingham—born and bred—instead of the illegitimate daughter of a maid. She rather doubted the man would approve a match if the potential groom was anything less than a baronet. She was reminded of who waited for her in the parlor and briefly wondered if Sir James had proposed to Lily.

"Perhaps," Caroline agreed. "Meanwhile, it seems you have a caller. Let's not keep him waiting."

Samantha gave a nod and sighed before making her way to the parlor. Poking her head around the door frame, she was surprised to find the young man holding out a bouquet of hot house flowers in her direction.

"I apologize. I ... I didn't mean to make you faint, my lady," Sir James said as he hurried to take her hand. He brushed his lips over her knuckles.

Swallowing, Samantha took the flowers with a murmured, "Thank you," and indicated he should take a seat. "You're forgiven, of course," she said as she settled onto the settee, hoping the tea tray would arrive without her having to ring for it. "I was just taken by surprise."

She suddenly realized they had no chaperone. A week on a deserted island with a man had obviously made her lose all concern for propriety. She reached over and rang the bell, relieved when Porter appeared. "Could you bring a tea tray, please. And send my lady's maid?"

Porter nodded, his look of displeasure never so evident.

When he left the room, Samantha turned her attention back to her guest. Dressed impeccably in a superfine navy topcoat, a beautifully embroidered scarlet waistcoat, and black breeches,

Sir James looked like one of the gentlemen she had spotted in the bow window at White's as she walked by the men's club. She wondered if he was a cohort of Beau Brummel's, but decided not to ask if he knew the man who seemed to have taken the men's fashion scene by storm. Sir James' blond hair, a bit longer than the current fashion, was combed forward. Blue eyes watched her intently from above a typical aristocrat's nose. And his lips, well, Samantha had seen those lips on one other gentleman of late. They looked exactly like Ethan's!

"Were you knighted by the king?" she asked, wondering how he came by his title. He seemed entirely too young to have done something important.

"I am a baronet, actually," Sir James replied with a nod. "Inherited from my late father."

"Oh, I meant no offense," Samantha said quickly, remembering baronets were considered members of the gentry and ranked above knights.

Sir James leaned forward and gave her a brilliant smile. "None taken, I assure you. Might I ... call on you?" he asked then. "I know you have just returned from a trip. It's terribly rude of me to have called on you this soon after your return to England, but I simply had to be sure you were well. Perhaps we could go riding in the park. Tomorrow?"

Samantha considered the invitation for only a moment. "Of course. I look forward to it," she replied with a nod. She remembered she had ordered tea and was about to ask if he could stay when he moved to stand.

"I regret I must take my leave of you," he said as he stood up. "I've an appointment in New Bond Street."

Surprised by the sense of disappointment she felt, Samantha stood and gave him a curtsy. "Until tomorrow then," she replied.

"I'll come for you at four o'clock," he said, giving her a bow before taking his leave of the parlor just as her lady's maid appeared.

"Good day, my lady," Jenny said as she watched the baronet leave. When she turned back to regard Samantha, she found her mistress on the settee with a look of what could only be described as confusion on her face. "I'm too late, aren't I?" she murmured. "I had no idea you would be returning from your trip so soon."

Nodding, Samantha allowed a sigh. "No harm done, though." After all, she had spent a week on an island with a man, and by sometime tomorrow, everyone in London would know.

How much more could she be ruined?

CHAPTER 35

SISTERS REUNITED

Two days later

Peering from inside her uncle's ancient town coach, Samantha blinked as she took in the sight of the brick building that housed Wellingham Imports. Located near Puddle Dock, the structure seemed to be one giant box with a line of stables on one side. Friesians, Cleveland bays and even a Percheron or two were either being escorted to stalls by stable hands or led to drays and coaches to be harnessed. A large set of double doors set in the adjacent wall suddenly opened from inside, and a group of burly men emerged carrying crates and boxes. Soon drays were loaded, coaches were filled, and with the crack of whips, drivers led their teams away.

The trap door at the top of the coach suddenly opened and her driver poked his head down. "Sorry for the delay, milady, but there's a coach blocking the lane."

Samantha glanced out the window and realized it would be some time before they could move again. "I can get out here, Farley," she said, moving to undo the door latch.

"I'll be right down," Farley said before the trap door shut. In only a moment, he had the door opened and was assisting Samantha to the pavement. "I would offer escort, milady, but I don't see anyone to hold the horses."

Indeed, every man in the area was engaged in some sort of

work, either harnessing horses or loading crates. "It's all right," Samantha said with a shake of her head. "I believe the entrance is just around the corner of the building," she said as she pointed toward the river. "Perhaps you'll be able to park in front." With that, she took her leave of the Chamberlain coach, opened her parasol and made her way down the lane to the end of the building that faced the Thames.

Just the hour before, she had left Fitzsimmons Manor having informed her mother she was off to pay a call on her sister. Caroline's eyes betrayed her surprise. "Without Matthew?" she had asked, apparently thinking Samantha's uncle should make the introduction. "We're expecting callers this morning."

Still disappointed with her mother for not having told her about her parentage and not looking forward to another day of describing her time on the island—how many times could one proclaim the marquess was a perfect gentleman?—Samantha had merely shrugged and said, "Give them my regards, won't you?"

She remembered the pang of regret she felt at Caroline's look of hurt. Her stubbornness prevented her from apologizing, though. Stubbornness and her own hurt. She still hadn't heard anything from Ethan.

Samantha turned the corner at the end of the building and nearly stopped. While the sides of the structure concerned with housing horses and loading drays were utilitarian, the front of Wellingham Imports looked as nice as any shop in Oxford Street. Pots of flowers were positioned at both sides of the main entrance, windows sported shutters that had recently been painted, and the words 'Wellingham Imports, est. 1779' were painted in an arch on a large wooden sign. A shingle also hung above the front door, its decorative black wrought iron mount at odds with the nature of the business.

Her heart racing, Samantha paused before moving to the door. *Why am I so nervous?* It wasn't as if she had never met Emma Wellingham before. She had, although it had been many years ago. At the time, Emma was merely a distant cousin,

Matthew's niece come to pay her respects to a man from whom her late father had been estranged since before her birth.

All because of hats?

Samantha shook her head. She realized the estrangement had more to do with George Fitzsimmons opting to work in trade. As the son of a viscount, he should have embraced a life of leisure by attending *ton* events, staying out late at men's clubs, gambling, riding in the park, and socializing with others of the peerage. Instead, the man had made a career as one of the best hat makers in all of England. His original shop, now 'Fitzsimmons and Smith'—his younger partner had purchased the business from Emma prior to her marriage to Thomas Wellingham —was still in Oxford Street.

Taking a deep breath, Samantha moved to open the door when it suddenly opened from within. Startled, she stepped back and found herself staring at a young man in his mid-twenties. His eyes were wide, though, as if he were just as startled at nearly running into Samantha.

"Oh, I apologize, my lady," he said, a slight Cockney accent evident. His eyes traveled down and back up to take in the sight of her deep green walking ensemble, matching reticule, and short-brimmed hat.

Samantha regarded the brown-eyed man for a moment, noting his short-cropped hair, rolled-up sleeves, simple waistcoat and dark breeches. "'Tis quite all right," Samantha answered, wondering why the man was staring at her so intently.

"Forgive me, but ..." He suddenly removed his cap and gave her a bow. "I was just reminded of something that happened a long time ago. Just like this ..." His voice trailed off.

"I beg your pardon?" Samantha replied. She was sure she had never met the man before, but he looked at her as if he recognized her.

"Overby," he said as he held out his right hand. "Billy Overby. I'm a clerk here."

Samantha shook his hand. "Samantha Fitzsimmons," she said with a nod, managing a slight curtsy.

Billy's eyes widened. "Well, no wonder," he said with a shake of his head. "You look exactly the same as she did the first day I met her. Right here at this very door, in fact," he said with a brilliant smile. He suddenly sobered. "I scared her, actually. Back then I was just a caddy for Mr. Wellingham."

Her own eyes matching his in surprise, Samantha swallowed. "Are you referring to Emma Wellingham, perhaps?" she asked in a quiet voice.

"Oh, but of course. I'll take you to her if you'd like," he offered, opening the door wider.

"Thank you," Samantha replied with a nod, glad for the assistance. She had never visited such a business before and wondered how she would find the offices. She lowered her parasol and took the man's arm. "I do hope I'm not taking you from your duties," she remarked as he escorted her past a counter and a wide desk at which a man, presumedly a receptionist, was busy transcribing forms. They climbed a set of stairs that led to a long line of offices overlooking the warehouse space. "You looked as if you were on an errand."

Billy shook his head. "Not at all. I was just going out for a smoke," he replied. "Mr. Wellingham don't allow us to smoke in the warehouse. Too much danger of fire," he explained as he paused in front of one of the office doors and gave it a rap with his knuckles. The sound of a muffled 'Come in' made its way through the heavy wood.

Billy opened the door and stepped aside. "A visitor for Mrs. Wellingham," Billy announced before giving Samantha a nod. "Very nice to meet you," he said with another lift of his cap before he made his way back to the stairs.

Thomas Wellingham looked up from a rather messy desk and regarded his visitor with an expression that was much the same as the one Billy Overby had displayed. He stood up quickly, though, and gave her a bow. "Lady Samantha, I presume?" he said with a grin as he made his way around the desk.

Relief settled over Samantha just then. "Why, yes. You must be ..."

"Thomas Wellingham," he said as he took her hand and brushed his lips over the back of her gloved fingers. He didn't let go, but held onto her hand. "At your service." He turned his head to the side. "Emma, my sweeting, you have a caller," he said as he kept his eyes on his sister-in-law. Lowering his voice, he leaned over and murmured, "She'll be thrilled to see you again."

Samantha allowed a nervous smile. "I should have come years ago," she managed to say before realizing her sister was regarding her from a doorway at the back of the office.

"Lady Samantha?" Emma said, her smile widening. "Oh, it's been an age!" she breathed as she hurried to take Samantha's hands.

"Too long, I know. I've so much to say and ..." She was suddenly pulled into a hug. Tears pricked the corners of her eyes as Emma held her.

"She finally told you, then?" Emma half-asked, pulling away to regard her younger sister. "I cannot tell you how many times I nearly ..." She suddenly turned around and gave her husband an apologetic nod. "Would you allow Samantha to join me in my office?" she asked.

Thomas gave his wife a look of surprise. "*Allow?* Why, of course! And when you're done playing at being watering pots, I'll take you to luncheon at the Crown and Anchor," he teased. "'Bout time I can celebrate having another sister."

Arms locked, the two women headed into the office behind Thomas', where a large window looked over the Thames and two upholstered chairs were positioned in a corner. What stunned Samantha, though, was the landscape painting positioned above the chairs, a painting she had done while still in finishing school. "I seem to remember giving this to my godfather," she murmured. "He said he grew up there," she added as she pointed to the depiction of an area near Chiswick.

Emma glanced at the painting of the land behind Merriweather Manor, the household in which generations of Merriweathers and Grandbys had been raised. "As did his cousin,

Gregory, who managed to steal it from Lord Torrington. And then my husband saw to its acquisition and placed it here.

"I cannot tell you what a wonderful surprise it was to discover it had been painted by you. You paint beautifully."

Samantha shook her head, stunned at Emma's comments. "Your husband knows about me?" she whispered, tearing her eyes from the painting as she took a seat.

Emma nodded. "Since ... before we were married, I suppose," she said with a nod. "You've no need to be concerned, though. He has kept you a secret, as have I." She took the other chair. "I found Caroline's letters to my father when I was setting up the household in Kingly Street, but I didn't know at the time they were from her. They were tucked away in his desk," she explained. "You can imagine my shock when I found them. I ... I had no idea my father felt affection for another after my mother died—no idea he had another daughter."

Samantha's eyes widened. "Then, how did you discover they were from my ... from Aunt Caroline?"

Emma gave a slight shrug. "They were signed 'Caro', and she was the only Caroline I could find who was married to a viscount. The idea that the viscount was Uncle Matthew ..." She shook her head. "I often wondered if perhaps Caroline was the reason my father and Matthew didn't speak to one another."

Shaking her head, Samantha touched her hand to Emma's. "Matthew assures me it went back far before ... *me*," she said quietly. "Apparently they were both quite stubborn brothers."

Emma smiled. "I'm finding men are like that in general," she replied with no hint of humor. After a moment, she said, "Speaking of men, I am sure you are sick to death of telling the tale, but please, tell me, is it really true Sir James proposed to you when your ship docked the other day?"

Rolling her eyes, Samantha allowed a grin. "He did. Having never met him before, I was quite ... *shocked*. But I felt a bit ..." She paused, not quite sure how to describe how satisfying it had been to have a man's attention like that, especially in front of so many people. *Too bad it wasn't Ethan,* she thought.

"Vindicated?" Emma offered, knowing how long

Samantha had been on the Marriage Mart. "I was almost one-and-twenty when Thomas proposed. Back then, I was already on the shelf," she added when she saw Samantha's look of surprise.

"He seems ... like a good man," Samantha said, keeping her voice low. Thomas' desk was on the other side of the wall, and she wondered if he could hear their conversation.

"He is," Emma agreed. "Ours was a love match."

"How did you meet?"

Emma angled her head to one side. "I was his sister's roommate at Warwick's Grammar and Finishing School. I was about to finish a course in accounting when he hired me to audit the company's books."

Samantha's brow lifted. "Love at first sight?" she guessed.

"Not at all," Emma replied with a shake of her head. "He tried to play matchmaker. He and everyone else I knew at the time."

Shocked, Samantha leaned closer. "If not himself, then who did Mr. Wellingham have in mind for you?" she wondered.

Emma's eyes widened a fraction before a blush covered her face. She suddenly giggled. "His business partner, Mr. Vandermeer," she whispered. "He wasn't his partner at the time, thank goodness," she added with another giggle. "Mr. Vandermeer ended up married to my best friend, Deborah."

Tears pricked the corners of Samantha's eyes. "I so wish my marriage could be a love match," she murmured, trying to avoid sniffling.

Emma sobered, stunned at the sight of Samantha on the verge of tears. "You're quite sure it won't be?" she asked in surprise. There were rumors Samantha found Sir James rather agreeable, despite his unconventional proposal. "But, I thought ..."

"I'm in love with the marquess," Samantha blurted. "I cannot help myself."

Emma blinked. And blinked again. "The man with whom you were stranded on that deserted island?" she clarified. When she saw Samantha roll her eyes, she sighed. "I read about it in

The Times," she admitted. "Although I did not know how much of it to believe."

Samantha shrugged. "Most of it, I suppose. I despised him when I first met him. He is the one who told me Caro was my mother. Told me I was a bastard ..."

Emma gasped and straightened in her chair, rather stunned by her sister's words. "How did ...? How did *he* ...?"

"From when he was a child. He knew everything because he was there. At Darbing Manor, where I was born. But ... the week we were on the island ... he ..." Samantha sighed and took another deep breath, one hand waving in front of her face. "He said he loved me," she whispered. "When we were on the ship heading for Valencia. And, then, later that night, he disappeared. I've heard nothing from him since."

The tears began to flow, and Emma quickly pressed a hanky into Samantha's hand. "But he must have returned to these shores," she said as she placed a hand on Samantha's knee. "Why, just this morning, we had a note from the Earl of Torrington saying we should expect a visit from him at some point."

Samantha lifted her red-rimmed eyes to meet Emma's. "Why would Grandby send you a note about Lord Plymouth?" she asked in surprise.

Emma seemed to hedge a bit. "The earl is my brother-in-law's cousin. He knows we're capable of bringing in products from all over the world. Apparently your marquess is in need of ... something important."

Samantha stared at her sister for a moment, remembering Ethan's reason for making his trip to Rome. "Batteries," Samantha said with a nod. "For miner's lamps. He has coal mines in Yorkshire."

Emma nodded her understanding. "We already bring them in for Lord Bostwick," she said with a nod. "He has three mines in Sussex where they're used."

Samantha nodded. Having visited Elizabeth Bennett-Jones, Viscountess Bostwick, on occasion, she knew the viscount was always looking to improve his properties and ensure those in his employ weren't in danger. She rolled her eyes again. "My dear sister, you must think me the biggest fool. I am usually rather level-headed. I take things in stride. I look upon other watering pots with little in the way of sympathy, and yet, I haven't cried this much since I was a *babe!*"

Despite the seriousness of the situation, Emma smiled. She was finding she rather liked her sister, although she knew she would from the time she had met the girl when she was but five years old. "What do you *want*, Samantha?" she asked then, holding her hands in her lap. "You're three-and-twenty. You're old enough to make these decisions without having to consider the opinions of others, although I will tell you that if you love the marquess, and he has said he loves you, then perhaps you should follow your heart in this matter."

Samantha stared at her sister for a very long time. "Even if Lord Plymouth has not asked for my hand in marriage?"

Emma sighed. "Even if," she said with a nod. "Follow your heart, Samantha. It may hurt to do so, but you will forever wonder what your life could have been if you don't at least do what you can to marry the marquess."

Samantha stared at her sister, remembering the woman had thirteen years on her. "And if I have already accepted another's proposal?" she asked with a raised eyebrow. *I genuinely like Sir James,* she thought suddenly. *I just don't know yet if I can love him.*

Her sister regarded her for a long time before saying, "You needn't break an engagement simply to determine the heart of another," she hinted.

"Are you two ready for some luncheon?"

The sisters looked up to find Thomas regarding them from around the edge of the office door, his eyes going back and forth between the two of them. "You realize she looks exactly like you did when I married you," he said in awe, his attention directed to his wife.

"Do I have reason to be worried?" Emma replied with an arched eyebrow, her upturned lips a testament to her teasing question.

Thomas moved into the room and shook his head. "You, milady, do not," he replied with a shake of his head. "She, on the other hand, may have to from some young buck in the *ton*." He leaned over and kissed his wife on the forehead.

"Or from a baronet or a marquess, take your pick," Emma replied, taking her husband's hands in hers and kissing the palm.

Samantha watched the interplay between her sister and Thomas, amazed at the ease with which they spoke to one another. "How long have you been married?" she asked, deciding she wanted a marriage where she could be as comfortable with her husband as Emma was with hers. *Goodness! The two practically work in the same office with one another.*

Thomas and Emma glanced at one another. "Fifteen years," they said in unison.

Samantha smiled. "Mr. Wellingham ..."

"Thomas," he interrupted. "We are family," he said when he noted her look of surprise.

Nodding, Samantha began again. "Thomas, I do believe I am ready for luncheon, although I cannot speak for my sister," she added.

Emma nodded. "Oh, yes you can. I'm starved." Glancing over at Samantha, she said, "I tried to have breakfast with some of Christiana and Gregory's brood this morning, but I spent more time feeding children than I did myself," she murmured. "We'll have you for dinner soon, and then you can meet my sister-in-law and her husband."

"And all their children," Thomas put in with a roll of his eyes.

Her attention darting back and forth between Thomas and Emma, Samantha asked, "How many children do they have?" she asked carefully.

Thomas and Emma exchanged a glance before Thomas erupted into laughter. "Five, six, seven?" he replied with a shake of his head. "I've lost count."

"Depends on if you count the one or two that are on their

way," Emma said with a grin. "I believe they still plan to have ten."

Samantha smiled, her mood considerably brighter than it had been earlier that morning. "I look forward to meeting each and every one of them, as well as those who are on their way," she said with grin.

"They'll love having another aunt," Emma murmured as she moved to stand up. "Come. Let's go have some lunch. My husband is treating us," she said as she allowed Thomas to help her to her feet. He then turned his attention to Samantha.

"My lady," he said as he gave Samantha a nod.

"Sam," she replied as she stood up. "You should call me 'Sam'," she said, "Seeing as how you're my brother."

Thomas gave his sister-in-law a grin. "Sam, it is."

The three took their leave of Wellingham Imports and made their way to the Crown and Anchor for luncheon, the Chamberlain coach their mode of transport.

Later, when Samantha was alone again and on her way back to Fitzsimmons Manor, she considered everything her sister had said. Her heart a bit lighter but her mind more troubled, Samantha decided she had a bit of time before she needed to give Sir James an answer in response to his unusual proposal. In the meantime, she could hold out hope Ethan would send word.

Or better yet, show up and ask for her hand.

CHAPTER 36

AN AGENT OF DECEPTION AT WORK

*D*aisy listened intently at the snippets of conversation she could hear as she leaned against the wall separating the study from the salon Myles Longburn allowed her to use when she was in residence. His voice rather distinctive, Myles was directing one of his visitors to make a delivery to his downtown office while another seemed to interrupt frequently with concerns about being caught.

"You won't be caught if you act like you know what you're doing," Myles replied, his clipped tones suggesting he was becoming impatient with the naysayer.

"There are more barrels than will fit in a single dray," a different man commented. "We'll need at least one more cart and another team of horses."

"I can arrange it."

Myles voice, she was sure.

"What time?"

Yes, indeed. What time? And day? If she could just get that little bit of information, she could report her findings to Felix, arrange for the arrest, and be on her way back to London within a fortnight.

This assignment had already lasted far longer than the six months she had been told to expect by the Home Office. Some of the extension had been due to spending time on a suspect who turned out to be entirely innocent. In the meantime, she had discovered at least two other suspects—Myles Longburn being one of them—and had to work her wiles to be hired by him as his mistress.

As with most men, an appeal to his manhood, both mental and physical, seemed to have the tradesman eating out of her hand—and giving her expensive gifts for her trouble.

She fingered the jewel that lay in the hollow of her throat. *How had Myles been able to afford the huge sapphire?* Her research had shown he wasn't rich enough to own such a bauble, nor was there any evidence it had been inherited, which could only mean the jewel was stolen or used in payment for some kind of service. *Certainly not to the Crown.* She hoped she was about to find out exactly what kind of service.

"It can't be too late. Say ... five o'clock. Tomorrow." That was the man who mentioned the need for another cart.

"Make it six. The shops won't be as crowded, and the streets won't have as much traffic," said the man who was the naysayer.

"Done. I'll have your payment ready on delivery. Don't disappointment me, gentlemen. I've come to count on you for a bit of extra pin money, and I'm quite sure you're ready for a nice payday."

Daisy realized the conversation was complete and she best take a seat in the salon in case Myles came for her.

Or perhaps she should move to a different room.

His bedchamber? Just down the broad hall of the Longburn mansion, the huge room housed what had to be one of the most ostentatious collections of furnishings ever found in a private home, including the giant bed on a platform tall enough to require stairs on all sides.

She pitied the chamber maid who was forced to make the bed every day. Between Myles' thrashing about in his sleep and their frequent conjugal couplings—the man seemed insatiable when it came to sex—the bed linens were rarely still on the bed in the morning.

She had just closed the door to the bedchamber when she heard the door to the study open and the voices suddenly grow louder. "Good evening, gentlemen. Do keep it down as you leave. I shouldn't want the neighbors disturbed."

There was a bit of laughter, probably due to the fact that Myles Longburn lived outside of Scarborough, and the nearest house was nearly a half-mile away. A moment later, and the butler had closed the door. The house was suddenly silent.

Shedding her gown and petticoats, Daisy was about to roll down her stockings when she heard Myles calling for her. Moving quickly to the door, she opened it and struck a provocative pose on the threshold, leaning her back against the wide door frame and bending one knee so her foot was pointed down. She leaned her head into the hallway. "Yes, dear?"

One thing she had learned in her short time with the trader —his regard for one head seemed to ensure the other was usually stupid.

"There you are, you wanton woman," he said with a broad smile, his hands held out so he could cup her corseted breasts when he reached her. Besides the corset, her only other clothing was a pair of stockings tied with ribbons above her knees and a pair of slippers.

"You wouldn't have it any other way," she replied with an arched eyebrow, reaching up with a finger to trace the whorl of his ear.

He imitated the growl of a wild animal, and it took all of her acting skills to keep from breaking into laughter. She was able to turn her growing grin into a sultry smile. "Are your guests finally gone? I was getting impatient," she complained, her lower lip protruding into a pout.

"All gone," he said with a nod, moving into the room. Daisy shut the door, wondering if she dare drug him. If the delivery of the liquor was truly happening on the morrow, she would need to get word to her fellow operative that night. She moved to pull the pin from his perfectly tied cravat but gave him an arched eyebrow first.

Sometimes Myles liked to undress himself.

She wondered if he thought she might try to steal the diamond-tipped pins he wore, although she couldn't think why given they weren't nearly as nice—or as valuable—as those the Marquess of Plymouth wore in his cravats.

A stab of disappointment hit as she thought of Ethan Range. Secretly, she was glad the man wasn't guilty of assisting the smugglers who were delivering boatloads of illegal liquor into Yorkshire. But she did miss his company. He truly seemed to appreciate her—in every sense of the word. Not that anything could ever come of their liaisons, though.

When she completed this assignment, there would be another, probably down the coast. At just over thirty, she figured she had at least five years of posing as a mistress before she would have to either retire from the service or take a desk job in Whitehall.

"Help yourself," Myles said as his eyelids lowered to her corset and the décolletage displayed at the top of the busk.

"I could say the same to you," she murmured, her voice pitched to appeal to his ego.

Although she had rules against kissing on the mouth, she allowed Myles to kiss her everywhere else. He was using his lips to good effect on her shoulder and neck as she undid his cravat and the fastenings of his breeches. "What would you like as an aperitif?" she whispered, aware of his erection just behind the placket of his breeches.

As was his custom when faced with a decision he couldn't possibly make—his brain seemed to shut down in moments like this—he said, "Whatever you wish to feed me," he murmured, moving his lips to the tops of her breasts.

The man will never learn, she thought as she reached for the crystal decanter and a tumbler. The sleeping powder tumbled from one of the trinkets on her bracelet as she poured the scotch. "Then let's start with a drink," she suggested, handing him the glass of spiked scotch, "And then I'll feed you."

Myles grinned and downed the finger of scotch in one gulp. Daisy led him by the last remnant of his cravat until they reached the stairs to the bed. Pulling down the counterpane and bed linens—she made sure to arch her back so her bottom was thrust up—she tossed a few pillows together at the head of the bed. She managed a sultry look when Myles pressed himself against her bottom, one of his hands fumbling for a breast to hang onto.

As Myles wobbled a bit, his giddy grin getting larger, Daisy carefully turned him so his back was to the bed and pulled off his shirt. She pushed on his chest so he fell back on the bed, and then she pulled off his breeches. His eyelids slowly closed. Arranging the bed linens over his prone body, Daisy gave Myles one last glance to ensure he was out cold before redressing and taking her leave of the bedchamber.

An hour later, Daisy Albright was able to contact Felix Snelling, the Scarborough-based operative who would arrange the sting operation and the arrests. The following evening, a ring of smugglers along with Myles Longburn were caught and arrested for their part in a scheme to import illegal brandywine and scotch into Yorkshire. A week later, Daisy was on her way to London and her next assignment.

As Daisy stepped out of a mail coach in Cambridge, she was stunned to find Ethan Range, Marquess of Plymouth, as he was about to board a coach making its way north.

"My lord," she said as she curtsied. Her eyes took in the sight of the rather suntanned man, and she allowed a sigh.

Ethan regarded his former mistress for a moment, unsure of what to say. "My lady. I hope you're in good health," he managed to get out. Only a few months ago, the sight of Daisy Albright would have him feeling a bit of lust, would have him thinking of when he might next bed the woman who had been his mistress for nearly a year.

But not now.

Not after having spent a week on a deserted island with Samantha Fitzsimmons. His time with her was still too fresh, too precious to sully by spending time with a different woman, especially one who had thrown him over for another man.

"I am," she replied, her mouth a bit slack. "And you? You look as if you've spent time in the sun," she managed to get out.

"Yes. On an island. I'm on my way back to Castle Keys.

And you?" he asked, thinking she was dressed rather conservatively. He rather doubted he had ever seen her in a gown that completely covered her as her scarlet traveling gown did.

"On my way to London. My ... *work* ... is done in Yorkshire," she said, managing a wink as she said the word 'work.'

Ethan frowned. "Myles Longburn isn't ...?" He stopped, realizing his question was wholly inappropriate. What business was it of his if Longburn could no longer afford her? *And I'm certainly not about to rehire her.*

Daisy angled her head. "Mr. Longburn has been arrested and is awaiting trial on smuggling charges," she replied, a prim smile indicating she was rather pleased with the turn of events.

"Oh," Ethan replied, his brows furrowing in question. "I always wondered where he seemed to get all his blunt," he mused for a moment. He angled his head. "For what it's worth, I did ... enjoy our time together," he admitted, thinking it better to leave on good terms with the woman.

Daisy inhaled at his words, a wan smile appearing. "As did I," she replied with a nod.

When Ethan gave her a bow, she responded with a curtsy and the two took their leave of one another.

Neither looked back as they walked away.

CHAPTER 37

A MARQUESS ARRIVES IN YORKSHIRE

Ethan regarded the front door of Castle Keys with a frown. Despite having been gone only a few weeks, the Portland stone building with its array of ivy and circle of shrubs at its base appeared, well, *shabby*. The windows needed a good wash, the front door needed a new coat of paint—preferably one of a color other than the drab green it currently sported— and the half-circle drive could do with a fresh layer of pea gravel.

At least the front lawn looked as if it had been recently cut. There were some flowers in the pots on either side of the front steps to add a bit of color, but otherwise the castle looked far more like a dungeon than a home. Other than a staff of servants, no one else lived there.

The front door opened even before he reached the top step.

"Evans," he said with a nod, wondering how the man had known to be on the lookout for him.

"My lord," the butler said with a hint of surprise on his face. "You're back ... early," he added, immediately regretting the comment. His master appeared suntanned, nearly sunburned, in fact, and a bit gaunt. "Is everything ... all right?" he wondered. "I heard horses ..."

Ethan regarded his butler for a moment and finally angled his head to one side. "The mail coach," he said with chagrin.

What marquess had ever been forced to travel by mail coach? "Except for having been shipwrecked on an island for a week and unable to purchase the batteries I intended to bring back with me ..." He almost added something about having taken a lady's virtue, but decided his manservant really didn't need to know that tidbit—he was quite determined that no one but he and the lady in question know anything about it. "I am ... *miserable*," he finally answered, his shoulders slumping as if he carried the weight of the world.

Atlas would certainly understand.

Back in Spain, he had almost ... *almost* ... sought passage on a ship bound for Rome so he could complete his quest. But his concern about Lady Samantha's fate had him deciding to return to England as soon as possible. Although he had spent his entire trip from the *Molly* to the Spanish shore angry at the chit for having turned her affections on Jack Crawley, he found himself worried about her once he reached Gandia, a small town on the coast of Spain. If the pirate did take her to Valencia, then she would no doubt return to England on the next available ship.

Once in London, he thought about finding a berth on another ship bound for Rome. But every ship leaving Wapping was either full or unable to take passengers. *Three weeks*, he was told. Too long to simply stay in London— although there were plenty of amusements he might enjoy during those weeks—he didn't have the desire to remain in town. Besides, news had reached London that Samantha had been rescued and would arrive the following day. A mixture of relief and pain had Ethan deciding to leave London just as soon as he could confirm her arrival on English shores. The possibility that their paths would cross during his stay was too much to bear.

Coward! he thought, his body betraying him as he thought about Lady Samantha Fitzsimmons. She had been so different from the other daughters of the *ton*. Although her dowry was probably more than adequate, she seemed to understand her place in the hierarchy of available chits. She was older than most, and perhaps a bit more resigned to a possible life as a spinster. But she seemed to accept her fate. Maybe even embrace it.

A memory of her writhing beneath his body had his own responding suddenly, his manhood hardening in anticipation. Her golden brown hair, streaked with gold from the sun and splayed out over the sand, came to mind. *And those fingers!* She had used them to good effect, caressing his skin with just the right amount of pressure. Her eyes, wide and curious and ever so green, their gold flecks dancing in the sunlight, seemed to see right through him. He couldn't tell a lie when those eyes beheld him. She would know, he was sure.

And then there was her wit.

When the pirate had implied he could fill his hand with her one of her breasts—had Ethan been able, he would have killed the man with his own bare hands at his callous remarks—she had countered with an observation that the man's hand was far too large. The sound of the pirate's laughter had been as amusing as it was a relief. How had she known he wouldn't make good on his threat to bed her?

Or had she? And with her affections so obviously transferred to the pirate, had she since warmed his bed?

Nearly cursing, Ethan shut his eyes tight and willed himself to forget Lady Samantha. Forget what she had done to him. What he had done to her. What they had shared during their brief stay on the small island.

How he ever thought he could forget such a force of nature, though, was beyond his comprehension. Lady Samantha was as vital as the air he breathed. As necessary as food. As important as the hours he slept and the longer hours he was awake.

The love of his life.

Damnation! How could he have allowed this to happen? Especially now? Now that matters at the mines were at a critical junction? Now that everything he did—or didn't do—mattered so much?

Well, Lady Samantha didn't matter when it came to the problems of the Plymouth marquessate. The marquessate was his responsibility. His burden. And acquiring the batteries and seeing to their continued delivery was still necessary, which meant he would simply make the trek back to Rome in a few weeks. He had time. Very little, but enough to make the trip there and back.

Evans managed an expression of concern. "My lord?" he asked as he watched the changing expressions on the marquess' face. "It seems a glass of scotch might be in order," the butler suggested, one eyebrow cocked in query.

Ethan considered the offer. Although it would only delay the inevitable, a glass of scotch sounded rather capital just then. "Yes, Evans, scotch is in order. My study, of course," he murmured, surrendering his hat to the butler as he made his way through the vestibule and down the wide hall to his study.

The pile of envelopes and notes on the silver salver was higher than he had ever seen it. So high, in fact, he was sure they would tumble to the floor if Evans so much as tilted the salver one way or the other. Of course, he did not, for Evans was a butler of the old school. He had lived his life in service and had from the time he was old enough to be a footman.

"Good God, are all those for me?" Ethan asked as the salver landed on the edge of his massive mahogany desk. He had often wondered why the desk was so large; it wasn't as if he could reach the front nor the sides of it if he opened his arms as wide as they could go and stretched out his fingers. The edges were always just beyond his reach. *Like this damned marquessate.*

Evans seemed confused by the query. "Unless there is another 'Lord Plymouth', they are, indeed, all for you, my lord," he replied as he pushed the salver closer to the middle of the desktop. He set down the glass of scotch well within reach of his master. "Will there be anything else, my lord," he asked, his hands moving to rest at his back.

Ethan considered the question for a moment. "Let cook know I'll eat in here," he finally said as he reached for the scotch.

"Yes, milord," Evans replied before he took his leave of the study.

Sighing, Ethan considered the amber liquid and swirled it

before taking a sip. His eyes closed as he held the liquor in his mouth, breathing its fumes and allowing his tongue to feel a bit of burn before finally swallowing the smooth, smoky elixir. *Bowmore?* he wondered. *Or Strathisla?* It mattered not, he supposed, but damn it felt good going down.

He reached for the note at the very top of the pile on the salver, deciding it was past time he saw to the business of the marquessate. The note wasn't from anyone in Yorkshire, though. The seal was that of the Earl of Torrington.

Ethan popped the wax and unfolded the note.

Plymouth, As per your request, I have seen to it your luggage was sent to Yorkshire. As per your other news, well, I have a mind to call you out. Although my goddaughter claims you were a perfect gentleman whilst on that island, I am of the opinion she is lying to protect you. God knows why.

Lifting his head, Ethan frowned. *Why would Samantha feel the need to protect me? And what about her affections for the pirate captain?* Shouldn't the earl be more concerned about Crawley?

He returned his attention to the missive.

As for the man who is courting her, I will see to it he's not allowed to marry her, even if I have to be the one to challenge the banns.

The man who was courting her had to be the captain, Ethan figured.

If there's any chance you should be the one, then I suggest you return to London post-haste. Grandby.

Ethan scrubbed his face with a hand, wondering what gave the earl the right to scold him. Frowning, he read the rest of the note.

Post scriptum. I have heard you intended to meet with Count Volta regarding his batteries. Please note that there is no need for you to make the trip to Como for the devices. My cousin's brother-in-law, Thomas Wellingham of Wellingham Imports can import them on your behalf. You're welcome.

Leaning back in his leather chair, Ethan stared at the wall across from his desk. *Wellingham Imports.* He hadn't even considered there might be others who would know about the batteries Volta had invented.

His thoughts returned to Samantha, to when she had been in the arms of Captain Jack Crawley.

Was she worth fighting for? he asked himself.

Perhaps.

He leaned over and took another note from the pile on the salver. Once he was through dealing with the mail and any other business that had come up during his absence, he would consider what to do.

Until then, Ethan Range was at the mercy of the Plymouth marquessate.

CHAPTER 38

AN EARL AND HIS COUNTESS DISCUSS A GODDAUGHTER

Milton Grandby, Earl of Torrington, was reading that morning's edition of *The Times* when his wife, Adele, waddled into the breakfast parlor. "Good morning, my beautiful," he said as put down the paper and gave her an appreciative glance.

Adele responded with a quelling look. "Oh, Milton," she scolded him. "I'm as big as a *house*," she complained as she struggled to sit in the chair a footman had pulled out for her. Unable to sit up at the table—her seven-month pregnancy bump prevented her from doing so—Adele sat at an angle to the table and sighed.

"Careful, sweeting. You're speaking of my daughter," he replied as he motioned to the footman to deliver their breakfast. The footman quickly took his leave of the parlor and returned a moment later with china plates filled with steaming food.

Shaking her head, Adele allowed a grin. "You mean your *heir*, I should hope," she replied as she regarded the assortment of breakfast foods arranged on her plate. Every morning's servings seemed to grow larger, but then, she always seemed able to clean her plate.

Although the earl had put voice to his preference for a daughter several times over the months since he figured out his wife was carrying his child, Milton Grandby had come to realize this might be their only opportunity to have a baby. If Adele did give birth to a girl, the Torrington earldom would be without an immediate heir—Milton had no brothers— although there were cousins aplenty who were next in line to the Torrington earldom. The next oldest in line would be perfect in the role.

Gregory Grandby, a man of considerable wealth and the father of at least seven children—Milton had lost count after the fifth—had married Christiana Wellingham, a cousin to Gabriel Wellingham and the current Earl of Trenton, back in '02. Christiana's brother, Thomas, owned Wellingham Imports and was married to Lord Chamberlain's niece, Emma Fitzsimmons. Although all were on the fringe of the aristocracy, they were good people. And it didn't hurt they had built a thriving business with Wellingham Imports and an impressive home in Chiswick.

"The earldom will survive quite fine, and perhaps even better, if Gregory inherits," Milton finally replied. He tucked into his breakfast, occasionally waggling an eyebrow in his wife's direction.

"Milton!" Adele demurred.

"I can't help it!" he replied. "I happen to ... enjoy you like this. All round and soft and ... so ..." *Beddable!* It didn't seem to matter the time of the day or the place, Adele's body was always ripe and ready for him. Although she sometimes complained about his randy behavior, she was soon accommodating him and always seemed rather glad she had done so afterward. Milton thought it helped to take her mind off her growing body and the aches and pains she seemed to be suffering.

Thank goodness Viscount Bostwick had suggested Grandby rub her feet at night. That simple gesture had Adele begging him to join her in her bed every night. In the process of washing and drying her feet and massaging them until the swelling subsided, Milton had developed a fondness for her toes. Nibbling one or two on each foot would have Adele giggling like a schoolgirl until she begged for him to stop. The giggling had the side effect of causing the baby to kick, a phenomenon Milton found rather profound.

Until the first time he was kicked in the stomach while making love to his wife.

Because, until then, the idea of a baby had been just that—an idea. The night he took the kick changed his perspective, even changed his entire attitude toward impending fatherhood. "I think she just kicked me!" he had said as he stilled his movements, leaving Adele on the verge of divine pleasure.

Frustrated and yet suddenly humored by her husband's reaction, Adele burst into a fit of giggles. She finally cursed and announced that it was about time he took the brunt of a kick as she had been the target of too many of them that week.

"Why didn't you tell me?" he asked, incredulous, still holding his body suspended over hers. "You didn't say a word about it!" He placed a hand on her belly, barely touching the smooth skin.

Lowering her feet to the mattress, Adele sighed. "Would you have believed me?" she wondered in exasperation. "If this baby is truly a girl, she'll be a *hoyden*," she complained.

Milton had smiled down on her, lowered his face to hers and kissed her sweetly. "I'll love you both no matter if she is a hoyden," he whispered, thinking it might be rather fun to have a tomboy for a daughter. At least until she needed to behave like a lady. Then he would have to see to it she was suitably educated for life as an earl's daughter.

"Now. Where were we?" he asked rhetorically, kissing Adele's bump. Slowly, carefully, he pushed himself into Adele and even more slowly pulled himself out. At some point, he realized they would have to take a different approach to lovemaking. His next thrust was a bit deeper. He wondered if she would be comfortable on the chaise lounge. The next thrust was a bit more forceful. Perhaps they could do it from the edge of the bed. He continued increasing the speed of his thrusts until their rhythm had Adele's body bowing, her breaths turning to pants, her eyes closing and his name on her lips as the waves of pleasure replaced her aches and pains and seemed to pull him farther into her body.

Or perhaps they could do it on their sides.

On the verge of his own orgasm, Milton held himself as still as possible. He wasn't sure if it was the kick in the groin that set off his release or simply the manner in which Adele held his buttocks or the sensation of waves pulling on his manhood, but his release had been so sudden, so intense, he was quite sure the neighbors heard his curse.

"Milton," Adele had murmured in rebuke before a fit of giggles had her body bucking beneath his. He took another kick to the belly before he, too, burst into laughter.

"A penny for your thoughts," Adele said quietly.

Milton looked up from his plate and regarded his wife with a grin. "I can hardly wait to be a father," he replied.

Adele's eyes widened. "Oh." A bit embarrassed she had assumed the worst—that he was merely plotting how to get her into bed after breakfast—Adele sighed. "You'll make an excellent father," she said. "And you have friends who have already been through it. Surely they can provide guidance when needed."

Nodding his agreement, his face took on a darker expression. "Speaking of friends who are fathers," he said, one eyebrow furrowing. "I received word from a courier last night. It seems Chamberlain is a bit concerned about the attention Lady Samantha has been receiving since their return from the Mediterranean."

Adele straightened in her chair. "She has been receiving an inordinate number of invitations and callers," she agreed. "Especially a particular gentleman. Caro is rather concerned. And Caro looks a bit peaked, which is to be expected, I suppose, given she spent most of the voyage with seasickness." She paused, wondering if she dare ask after the marquess. "Has there been any word as to the fate of Plymouth? Samantha is beside herself with worry."

Milton frowned but nodded. "He sent me a note with instructions. It came from here in London, but he has no doubt left for Yorkshire by now. Apparently he didn't join the Fitzsimmons in Valencia because he was on a different vessel and landed somewhere else in Spain. He took a land route to the

Channel and arrived on the *Bellingham* the day before *The Fair-weather.*"

Adele's eyes widened. "But ... why didn't I hear anything of this when I was paying calls this week?" she asked, thinking the Mayfair gossips usually had the important news spread through parlors quicker than it appeared in the papers.

"Because Plymouth didn't tell anyone. I don't think he real-ized he was missed. Apparently, he simply reported to *The Fair-weather's* owner, asked that his trunk and other possessions be sent on, and then he arranged for transport up to Yorkshire. He was gone before anyone even knew he was in London." He shrugged. "The only reason he sent me the note is because he wanted someone to follow up with Mr. Nattersley at the ship-ping company to be sure his trunk was sent on."

Adele shook her head. "But, why would Plymouth send *you* to follow up with the shipping company?" she wondered. "I wasn't aware you knew each other."

Milton gave her a quick glance, his brows furrowing in confusion. "I don't know. It's true we've never been friends ..." He suddenly stood up from the table and left the breakfast parlor. Adele watched him leave, her look of confusion matching his. When he returned only a moment later, she asked, "What was that all about?"

Milton shook his head. "I didn't read the entire message," he said as he unfolded the parchment he carried. He took his seat at the table. "I stopped so I could write a note about his luggage and dispatch a footman with it to Nattersley," he explained. "And then it was time to go to White's." He always visited the men's club in the late afternoon, his visits perfectly timed so he would be home just as the dinner bell chimed.

Milton returned his attention to the note, reading quickly until he reached the line with the instructions. Reading aloud, he said, "I am sure you are probably wondering why I would request this of you since we are but slight acquaintances ..." Milton glanced up from the note. "He's got that right. I think I only met the man once." He resumed reading. "I wish to inform you I spent a week with one of your goddaughters. Lady

Samantha is a commendable example of the kind of woman with whom one should spend a week on a deserted island. Resourceful, good-natured and optimistic, she never complained about our unfortunate circumstances. I regret her affections were transferred to another, a situation I simply could not again abide."

Wondering who the marquess could be writing about, he earl looked up from the note. *Affections transferred to another?* "Do you suppose Samantha felt affection for the marquess? Before they were rescued?" he asked absently.

Adele angled her head to one side. "They were on an island for a week. He is a rather handsome man ... when he's not scowling. And he is a marquess," she answered, as if she thought the question didn't warrant asking.

But what did the man mean when he inferred Samantha's affections were transferred to another? *He's been jilted before*, Adele realized, wondering to whom Samantha's affections had been 'transferred'.

Milton shrugged and returned to reading. "I committed an unforgivable act by abandoning her to the protection of the pirate ship's captain, a man named Jack Crawley. The first mate of the *Molly* assured me, however, that he would see to her safe return to civilization and Lord Chamberlain post-haste (a situation I have since confirmed did, indeed, occur). She is probably better off with the captain as life on the sea may suit her far better than life in Yorkshire. Please accept my humblest apologies. Plymouth."

Milton set the note aside and regarded his wife with an expression of astonishment. "My God! He thinks she should end up with the captain of a pirate ship!" he said with a good deal of disbelief. "Can you believe this?" He straightened when he realized Adele was waving her hands in front of her and shaking her head.

"Something's not right here," Adele replied in dismay. "Does Lady Samantha *know* the marquess has returned to England?" she asked, hoping the poor girl had heard something directly from Plymouth. Although Samantha had put on a brave face during tea, Adele was quite sure the girl spent the afternoon on the verge of tears. And she certainly didn't seem as if she were pining for a ship's captain—pirate or otherwise. And then there was the baronet who had proposed on the dock. Adele was quite certain Samantha had never seen the man before in her life.

Milton shrugged. "I doubt it. I let Chamberlain know as soon as I received the note, but I don't think he's particularly pleased that the marquess left his daughter without protection on a pirate ship." He leaned forward. "Have you heard what happened on the island? From Lady Samantha directly?" he asked in a hoarse whisper.

Glancing about as if she just then realized Milton didn't want any of the servants to overhear their conversation, she nodded. "I paid a call on Fitzsimmons Manor the day after their arrival. Samantha looked ... quite healthy, if a bit ... sun kissed," she said.

Milton blinked. "Sun kissed?" he repeated, not familiar with the term.

Adele shook her head. "You saw her!" she accused. "Her skin is ... *golden*, poor thing. Although, given her hair color, it's a rather becoming look on her."

Giving his head a shake, as if her response was unexpected, Milton asked, "But what happened on the *island?* She spent a week with Plymouth. Did he ...?"

"Ruin her?" Adele finished for him. "Apparently not. She claims he was a perfect gentleman the entire time."

Milton's shoulders slumped. "*Damn!*"

"Milton!" Adele admonished him. "You make it sound as if you wanted her to be ..." Her eyes suddenly widened and she sat up as straight as her belly would allow. "You did want her ruined," she realized just then. "But, ... but, *why?*"

The earl looked suitably guilty for all of about five seconds.

"Well, it's about time Plymouth married, and I rather doubt he's going to find a suitable wife up in that hell-hole he lives in," Milton explained with a shrug. "Sam needs to be settled. She's ..." He stopped, trying to figure out her age based on when he had announced he was her godfather.

"Three-and-twenty," Adele finished for him, her expression softening. "Caro said that before they left for the Continent, she thought Samantha had decided life as a spinster wouldn't be so awful, but apparently Samantha now has a serious suitor."

At this bit of news, Milton Grandby straightened. "Who? Or are you speaking of that fool that yelled out a proposal to her on the docks?" he asked, not particularly pleased at hearing the news since he'd had nothing to do with arranging said suitor.

The Earl of Torrington took great pride in having helped several of his goddaughters in their choice of husbands, either because he had nudged the gentlemen in their direction or because he had set up circumstances to favor a particular man. He hadn't yet turned his attention to Samantha because she and her aunt were to have been on the Continent for several months. With the unfortunate accident that had Samantha stranded on an island with the Marquess of Plymouth and her early return to London, however, lining up a husband for Samantha was now a priority.

"Sir James." Adele whispered. "Moriarty," she added when Milton's expression didn't indicate he recognized the name of Samantha's suitor.

Milton Grandby was up and out of his seat so quickly, Adele nearly jumped from hers. "What is it?"

Her husband shook his head. "He's a *baronet*. He's a … gambler. An *opportunist*." This last was said with enough vehemence, Adele thought her husband might suffer a heart attack.

Her eyebrows rising in surprise, Adele bit her lower lip. "Surely someone will inform her," she replied, thinking she could certainly let Caroline Fitzsimmons know when she paid her a call later that afternoon. The viscountess certainly wouldn't allow her niece … her *daughter* …

"Milton," she said suddenly. "There's something you need to know. About Samantha," she said as she slowly stood up and faced her husband. "Caro told me the day after their return from Valencia. I promised to keep it a secret, but …"

"Caroline is her real mother," he finished for her, noting her look of relief at his simple words. "Which means our dear Samantha is illegitimate."

"Yes," she murmured sadly. "How ...?"

"Chamberlain informed me. It's rather good news, really. I think he has suspected as much these past few years."

Adele lowered her eyes, wondering how learning someone was illegitimate could be good news. "And he knows who the father was?" she whispered.

The earl nodded. "His brother, yes, but you mustn't say a word to anyone," he whispered. "Promise me ..."

"I won't say a word to anyone," Adele assured him. "But will you and Chamberlain be contacting the marquess? I really think ..."

"Something's not right?" Milton finished for her.

Adele nodded. "I cannot abide her ending up with a baronet. I don't care if she's illegitimate and the *ton* thinks she was ruined whilst on that island, she deserves better than an opportunist as a husband."

The earl nodded. "I couldn't agree more."

CHAPTER 39

A SOIRÉE SAYS IT ALL

*J*ulia Harrington Comber regarded her best friend with a shake of her head. "Oh, Sam, I cannot fathom how you could have survived such conditions," she whispered, the look of worry on her face so unlike the usual joy she displayed. She was at least a few months with child, her skin glowing as result.

"Well, I wasn't alone," Samantha said with a shake of her head. Oh, how she wished she could tell Julia she was her cousin! "The marquess helped to get us on a raft, we made it to an island, and we were rescued by pirates."

She rather liked how that sounded. She had been using it as a preamble to telling the tale in all the parlors of Mayfair. A passing thought had her wondering what the Earl of Everly would think of her adventure. Would he be impressed? She hadn't seen the man since her return and wondered if he had already left London on another expedition.

"There were plenty of berries to eat," she added with a shrug. "And fish. Lord Plymouth was quite adept at catching them in a net he fashioned from his cravat."

Julia arched an eyebrow. "Is he truly as mean as he looks?" she replied, leaning in to be sure her words weren't overhead. The soirée at Lord and Lady Morganfield's Mayfair mansion was a crush, and Samantha had an audience no matter which direction she turned.

She gave Julia a look of surprise. "Not in the least," she replied with a shake of her head. She attempted to take a deep breath, her tight corset preventing her from doing so. She silently cursed Jenny, sure her lady's maid had deliberately pulled the ties too tight so that the mounds of her breasts would show above the neckline of her bodice.

"Alistair claims he attended Oxford with the man—before he was a marquess—and that he was quite ill-humored," Julia said, her eyes darting around the room.

"He was quite agreeable," Samantha countered, wondering how many times she would have to defend the marquess. *Where was he? He should be here,* she thought, even though she knew he would never make an appearance at such a *ton* gathering.

"If I might have a word with this goddaughter?" Milton Grandby said as he directed his comment to Julia, another one of his goddaughters. He placed a hand at Samantha's elbow.

Mrs. Comber gave him a brilliant smile and a kiss on the cheek. "Of course, my lord," she said as she gave Samantha an arched eyebrow and stepped away.

"Is there another room we can go to?" Samantha asked, feeling a bit faint.

Grandby escorted her to an adjacent room—the library— and shut the door behind him. He leaned over and kissed her on the temple. "I wish to know everything," he said, his manner suddenly quite serious.

Samantha blinked and shook her head, realizing she would need to be careful in how she responded to the Earl of Torrington. The man might be her godfather and concerned for her welfare, but he was also a powerful man. "A wave washed us off *The Fairweather,* the marquess helped to get us on a raft, we made it to an island, and we were rescued by pirates," she said quickly, hoping he didn't ask about the six days in between.

He asked about the six days in between.

"Besides the fact that you were on deck with him—

unescorted—when the wave hit, what exactly did you two *do* the rest of the time you were together?"

Samantha gave a nonchalant shrug. "Picked berries, found water, fished, watched for ships, cooked fish, ate, slept ..."

"Together?" he asked, one eyebrow arching up, as if he dared her to tell him otherwise.

"Lord Torrington!" she admonished him, managing to display a look of offense with her arched eyebrows and wide eyes. "He was a perfect gentleman the entire time," she claimed, using almost the same words she had used with her uncle. She had a feeling Matthew didn't believe her, but he hadn't pressed the issue.

Grandby did.

"Ethan Range is a *man*. Are you trying to tell me he didn't ...?"

"Of course not!" Samantha replied with a shake of her head. "And I do not believe he would be so inclined as he was rather ..." She sighed and allowed her shoulders to slump. "Incensed," she finally managed.

The Earl of Torrington regarded her for a long time, his manner softening. "And why would *he* be incensed?" he queried.

Tears formed at the corners of her eyes, but Samantha didn't allow them to fall. "He claimed I was a bastard," she said in a whisper. She dared a glance at the earl, hoping her simple words would deflect his attention from her situation on the island.

Having been told by Matthew about Caroline and Samantha, Grandby dropped his gaze to the floor. "How did *he* know?" he asked quietly.

Her sudden inhalation of breath the only sound in the room, Samantha clutched her fingers at her waist.

Grandby already knows. But who told him?

"He was there. In Yorkshire. At Darbing Manor, where I was born." When Grandby lifted his eyes to hers, she added, "He was a child, but he knows Caroline was pregnant. He knows Liza lost all her babies. He saw me when I was a babe."

"*Christ!*" Grandby spat out, his eyes raised to the ceiling.

"He won't tell anyone," Samantha said with a shake of her

head. "He might have considered doing so before ... but I do not believe he will do so now."

Grandby shook his head and sighed. "Even if he didn't ruin you ..."

"I know," Samantha replied, realizing just then that if William Nattersley had simply kept the fate of *The Fairweather* to himself, none of this would be happening. No one would know she had been tossed off a ship and stuck on a deserted island for nearly a week with a marquess. "But I don't know where Ethan is ..." Samantha sucked in a breath, realizing she had used the marquess' given name.

Grandby stared at her for a long moment. "By now, back in Yorkshire. He arrived in London the day before you," he said with an arched brow.

Although Samantha had heard the same information from the owner of the shipping company, she had hoped he was mistaken. She couldn't help but hope he had been present when she arrived in London. Even through the crush of people at the dock, she thought he would be there. Somewhere.

"He didn't leave for Yorkshire until he was sure you were home safe," Grandby said quietly.

Samantha closed her eyes, no longer able to prevent the tears from falling. "Oh," she cried, her hands coming up to her face. *He was there. Watching.*

Her godfather's arms were around her in an instant. "Do you love him?" he asked in a whisper.

Stunned the earl would ask such a thing, Samantha angled her head before nodding. "Yes," she said with a hiccup. "But I rather think it doesn't matter," she added after taking a deep breath.

"Oh?" Grandby replied. "And why is that?"

Samantha put on a brave face. "I finally have a suitor, you see. Sir James. Sir James Moriarty."

Grandby stared at her, his face rather expressionless. So, it was true she was considering marrying Sir James. Well, Grandby was quite sure he knew exactly why Sir James would be interested in marrying his goddaughter, and it had nothing to do with affection. "Do you love *him?*" he asked, daring her to answer his bold question.

Samantha sighed before giving her head a shake. "I don't yet know," she answered carefully. "We only just met. The day on the dock, when he made his rather public proposal."

Nodding, the Earl of Torrington gave her a quick peck on the cheek. "Do let me know how it goes," he said with a nod. And with that, he took his leave of the Morganfield library.

He had to speak with a certain viscount.

CHAPTER 40

AN ENGAGEMENT IS UNDER DISCUSSION

"The baronet was quite insistent I plan to attend his mother's fête," Samantha said as she took a seat at the small metal table in the conservatory of Sommers Place.

Evangeline Tennison Sommers regarded her friend with a look of surprise. "You seem to be spending a good deal of time in the man's company," she remarked as she took the chair directly across from her friend. A footman was quick to assist her; although Evangeline had only been the mistress of Sommers Place for a month, the servants seemed ever so helpful, as if they feared for their positions if they didn't immediately see to her every request. Evangeline often wondered if Jeffrey had said something to make them think she was a mean, nasty tyrant along the lines of Lady St. Clair.

Now there was a woman who could strike fear in the hearts of servants as well as nearly everyone in the *ton*.

Samantha gave her friend a shrug. "I'm only ever with him when there are others present," she claimed with a wave of her hand. Indeed, she could not remember a moment, other than when the baronet had appeared at Fitzsimmons Manor the same day she had returned from her trip, when the two had been alone. Completely alone. Even at Lord Weatherstone's ball, when they had sneaked into the library for the few minutes James claimed he wanted to see her, they had not really been alone. Another couple waited outside the doors, intending to use the same room for their *tête-a-tête*.

For some reason, Lord Weatherstone's library—and sometimes his gardens—had become the *de facto* location in which to kiss or propose marriage.

"Not like you when you used to read in Grosvenor Square," Samantha added with an arched eyebrow.

Evangeline colored up. *What had Samantha heard?* She had told Samantha and Julia about reading *The Story of a Baron* in Finsbury Square with the baron the day she had purchased the book, but she hadn't said anything about her and Jeffrey Sommers reading it together in Grosvenor Square. "What do you know of Grosvenor Square?" she asked with a raised eyebrow.

Realizing she had said too much, Samantha shrugged and then sighed. It was useless to make up a story—Evangeline was a smart woman. She would figure it out even if Samantha didn't own up to how she knew. "Julia and I may have paid witness to your presence there whilst you read the book with Lord Sommers," she admitted with a shrug, attempting to make light of the day they had spied on Evangeline and the baron.

Her eyes widening in alarm, Evangeline sucked in a breath. "You *spied* on us?" she whispered, lest a servant overhear her accusation.

Shifting in her chair, Samantha's face took on a pink blush. "Well, I wouldn't call it *spying* exactly," she replied hastily. "'Ensuring your safety' is perhaps a better explanation," she responded with a nod, hoping Evangeline would drop the subject.

"Ensuring my safety?" Evangeline repeated, not the least bit humored nor satisfied with the explanation. Why, that day in the square was probably the day she had nearly fallen into the baron's lap!

Sensing Evangeline's impending anger, her friend straightened and countered the comment. "For example, you nearly fell into the baron's lap," Samantha accused. "One minute you were reading thigh to thigh and shoulder to shoulder," she said in a breathy voice, "And the next, you were suddenly leaning over Lord Sommers! And then you were executing a perfect pirouette!"

Evangeline's eyes widened in alarm. *Damnation!* Samantha and Julia had seen it all!

"I thought my pirouette was quite pretty," Evangeline remarked with a nod, deciding not to address the rest of what Samantha had said. She was wont to change the subject, though, and thought bringing up Samantha's recent engagement would do the trick.

"So, you must tell me more about your baronet," Evangeline said as she reached for the teapot. "And you're to tell me *everything*. All the details. I hear he's a rather agreeable man," she claimed as she refilled both cups. She leaned over to add honey to her own and gave Samantha a glance. "Is he?"

Samantha couldn't fight the blush that suddenly colored her face. "Not ... not especially," she answered carefully. How much should she admit to her best friend? That she'd had a life-changing adventure with a man whom she found rather despicable at first and then ... and then rather *lovable* when all was said and done?

Once they were aboard the *Molly*, though, something had changed. Ethan disappeared. Captain Crawley saw to it Samantha was reunited with Lord and Lady Chamberlain in Valencia, and a week later, she was home safe in England. Somehow, the Marquess of Plymouth had returned to his castle in Yorkshire as if nothing untoward had happened, although she took a bit of satisfaction in learning he stayed in London until he could ensure she was home safe. *He was the one I felt watching me,* she remembered suddenly, rather likely that he would spy on her from somewhere nearby.

There was that, at least.

It was only the sudden interest by Sir James Moriarty, a baronet, that had Samantha attending every late summer ball and soirée in London. He was nice enough. Blonde, pleasant in appearance, well-spoken, and Eton and Cambridge-educated, Baronet Moriarty seemed enamored with Samantha from the moment she stepped off *The Fairweather*. The tale of the ship-wreck and subsequent life on the island off the coast of Spain had the *ton* in a twitter. Questions abounded whenever she entered a parlor or salon.

How had she survived?

Well, she was only there a week, and water, fish and berries had been readily available. Had their time on the island lasted longer, she thought they might attempt a trip to one of the neighboring islands on their makeshift raft in the hopes of finding more food sources.

How did she fair with the despicable marquess?

"Despicable?" she repeated, blinking at the description provided by the reporter from *The Times*. "He was not in the least, I assure you," she had answered with a shake of her head. "In fact, he was most helpful. I am quite sure I would have drowned had he not assisted me in swimming to a remnant of the ship on which I could float," she had explained. Ethan was obviously a good swimmer, but anyone who had seen him without his topcoat and waistcoat and shirt would have been able to determine that for themselves. The man had the most amazing physique! Like a Greek god come to life. Muscles rippled beneath his skin with every move he made. Muscles that belied his station as a marquess. *What had the man done to build such an appealing body?* Perhaps he plowed his own fields, or mined his own coal or pulled his own carriage ...

Samantha shook herself from her reverie. Of course the marquess didn't pull his own carriage! He had the best horses from Tattersall's for that. And he employed the very best servants and tailors and boot makers and tradesmen.

Why would he be interested in me?

The worst of the questions left her the most perplexed.

Did he ruin you?

At her surprised expression, the reporter merely raised his eyebrows, as if he had already decided the marquess had taken advantage of the situation and taken her virtue. The two were alone on an island for an entire week, after all.

"Of course not!" Samantha had replied, indignation

apparent in her voice. "He was a perfect gentleman the entire time." Which was a complete and utter lie, but she wasn't about to tell the reporter of how they spent their nights. After all, she hadn't done anything to dissuade Lord Plymouth from kissing her, from taking her into his arms and holding her close whilst they slept under the stars. Or in the tower. Or under the broad-leafed palm tree that provided the best shade in the afternoon.

She had encouraged it!

Even now, the thought of his arms around her brought a shiver of delight. A pang of regret. A feeling of sadness. A sense of loss.

She had rather hoped the marquess would seek her out once they were back on British shores, pay a call and ask how she was faring. But her godfather explained the man had left for Castle Keys the day after the Fitzsimmons arrived in London on *The Fairweather*.

So much for a possible match to a marquess!

"What kind of a man is he?"

Samantha blinked when she looked up to find Evangeline waiting for an answer to her simple question.

"He is ... driven, I suppose," she offered. "More a tradesman than an aristocrat. Which is a relief since it was he who claimed we would make it back to civilization. He knew a passing ship would eventually find us." Although the marquess knew very little about how to survive on the island, he had been a source of consolation, a willing companion who valued her insights about the island despite his apparent dislike of Lord Everly, the source of most of her information about the area in which they were stranded. "I owe him so much. He saved my life."

Evangeline stared at Samantha for nearly ten seconds before she said, "I thought we were talking about James Moriarty. The *baronet*," she added with an arched eyebrow.

Samantha couldn't help but drop her head into her hands.

"Oh. Of course. I ... I don't know what I was thinking ..."

"You were thinking about Lord Plymouth," Evangeline accused in a whisper. After a pause, she placed a hand on

Samantha's arm. "I cannot blame you. The man saved your life. Of course, you would think of him on occasion."

Samantha's eyes widened a bit. *On occasion?*

Good grief! She was thinking about him at breakfast, during luncheon, while she was riding in the park during the fashionable hour, all through supper, at night, when she was about to fall asleep ... even her dreams were filled with images of him.

"Tell me, Eva. When you are apart from Lord Sommers, do you think about him every waking minute of the day?" Samantha asked suddenly. Tears threatened. Her eyes were bright with them.

Evangeline regarded her friend with a sudden frown. Sitting back, she dared a glance around the conservatory to be sure no servants were lurking behind the potted palms or orange trees. "Not *every* waking moment, no," she answered carefully, not about to admit she thought of Jeffrey Sommers at least half of her waking hours. "Is that ... is that what's happening to you?" she whispered, leaning in close. Perhaps her carnal thoughts of the man who was now her husband were not so unusual.

Samantha nodded, her eyes darting about as if she were quite nervous. "I feel so guilty," she said quietly. "I should be thinking about *James*. I should be dreaming about James. I should be looking forward to our wedding, our life together ... but I find I ... I cannot." A small sob interrupted the statement as Samantha moved a hand to cover her eyes.

Lady Sommers regarded her friend for a long time before rubbing her arm. "Time will help, Sam. I know it will. But if you have given your heart to the marquess, perhaps you should tell the baronet ..."

Samantha gasped, her eyes wide. "I couldn't!"

"It's not as if you two have known each other long enough to even be *engaged*," Evangeline continued, not remembering just then that her own engagement had been but a few weeks.

"Although the *ton* can be rather hard on broken engagements,

they will give you latitude. You have been through so much ..."

"No!" Samantha protested.

Evangeline stared at her best friend for several moments, thinking something stronger than tea might be necessary.

And Julia.

Perhaps Julia Harrington Comber could provide a bit of perspective. She was the one married to a second son of an earl, a man who had taken employment as a groom in the Harrington House stables in order to earn his way in life. Now he was in charge of the stables—and a breeding program that had the Harrington horses producing some of the best horse-flesh in England. Everyone expected the daughter of an earl to marry at least equal to her rank, and instead she had married a groom.

How had Julia found the treatment by the *ton* since marrying a man who was proud to be known as a horse breeder? Who mucked stalls along with the lowliest stable boys? Who shod horses as expertly as he rode them? Who had become a consultant to Tattersall's, for if they didn't employ him, they knew their buyers would to their detriment?

The Combers were invited to all the *ton* events as if Alistair were a peer, but Evangeline thought perhaps it was due to how genuinely agreeable Alistair seemed to all who met him. And perhaps because Julia sang his praises whenever she was in the company of others. A more supportive wife could almost not be found among the peerage. Almost, because Evangeline was equally supportive of her baron. His latest novel was nearly finished and could boast a far larger expected print run than *The Story of a Baron*.

"I do believe we require a third party to help in this," Evangeline said quietly. "I shall send a note to Julia. The three of us will have this sorted in no time," she said with as much authority as she could muster.

Samantha regarded her friend with a look of surprise. "Are *you* of the opinion I need to break off my engagement to Sir James?" she whispered, tears threatening again.

Evangeline shifted in her chair, finally lifting her eyes to meet Samantha's. "I am."

Samantha's cry had Evangeline leaning forward and grabbing one of her hands. "I *adore* my husband. I cannot imagine my life without him," she whispered hoarsely. "Julia is of the same opinion about her Alistair. Should you end up in a loveless marriage, we will spend our days feeling ever so guilty about not having intervened before it was too late," she explained in harsh tones, her own eyes brightening with tears. "You cannot marry Sir James. Not when you love another."

Samantha stared at her best friend for several moments, finally swallowing a sob. "I ... I cannot break it off," she replied with a shake of her head. "There may never be another ..."

"Poppycock," Evangeline interrupted suddenly. "I am inclined to believe my husband when he says there is a soul mate for everyone," she explained with a nod. "Yours may be Lord Plymouth. Or perhaps you haven't yet met him," she added with widened eyes. "But if you marry Sir James, a man who only wants you for your notoriety, you will never know what might have been."

Her shoulders sagging, Samantha stared at Evangeline as a single tear made its way down her cheek. "Notoriety?" she repeated.

Was that really why James had taken such an interest in her? Because she was the current *on-dit* in a way that was exciting? In a way that could provide him some celebrity simply by association?

The man did seem overly excited by the invitations he had been receiving of late. A bit too concerned about his waistcoats and breeches and his boots. Too occupied with what he drove and the horses that pulled it. And sometimes a bit critical of Samantha's style of dress or bonnet. The comments hadn't bothered her much at the time, but seen in light of Evangeline's cutting remarks, she was suddenly offended by her fiancé's manner.

"What will happen when you are no longer the *on-dit?*" Evangeline asked as she angled her head. A thought struck her and she leaned over the table. "Perhaps *he* will be the one to end the engagement," she said with a bit too much hope. "Then you won't have to!" This last had her nearly bouncing in her chair, as if her friend considered her being thrown over would somehow be a good thing.

"Eva!" Samantha countered with a frown. "Have a care," she said with a sigh.

In the end, it didn't matter if she was thrown over or if she was the one to end the engagement—the outcome would not reflect well on her. *I am doomed*, she thought with a sinking heart.

"Simply doomed."

CHAPTER 41

TEA FOR THREE

The following day, Samantha and Evangeline arrived arm-in-arm for tea at the Earl of Mayfield's London residence. Julia Harrington Comber regarded her callers from the settee in the parlor, one hand resting at her middle. "Finally! I was beginning to wonder if you would ever take pity on me and pay a call," she teased as her visitors took the upholstered chairs across from her. "Although I'm not that far along, I feel as if I've already gained a stone!" she complained as she poured the tea. She offered the cup to Samantha. "What is it?" she asked, wondering at Samantha's odd gaze in her direction.

Samantha smiled. "Nothing. You just ..." She couldn't tell Julia they were cousins—not without admitting she was the illegitimate daughter of Julia's aunt, Caroline. But now that she did know, she saw the resemblance in her eyes, in the shape of her nose, her lips. Julia could pass as her sister. "You look so happy," Samantha finally said with a sigh.

A pink blush covering her cheeks, Julia allowed a shrug. "Why, thank you. I'm sure it's due to the baby. And Alistair is rather free with his compliments. Tells me everyday how pretty I am," she said with a smirk, as if she didn't necessarily believe her husband's words.

Evangeline accepted a cup of tea and added some honey. "Of course, he does. Because you are," she said with a grin. She suddenly sobered. "Speaking of husbands," she said with an arched brow. "Samantha is about to gain one."

Julia arched an eyebrow, her attention turning to Samantha. "So, the rumors are true? Sir James really did propose marriage?" she half-questioned. "Have you given your answer? Already?" she asked, setting her own teacup on the low table between them.

Samantha dared a glance at Evangeline before nodding to Julia. "At Lord Weatherstone's ball. In his library," she admitted with a sigh. "He's quite pleasant and ... rather good looking. And there may never be another, so ..." She shrugged as if she were resigned to her fate.

Evangeline rolled her eyes. "He's rather critical of our dear Sam, isn't nearly as pleasant as she claims, and is only marrying her for her notoriety," she countered. "Or maybe her dowry."

Stunned at Evangeline's harsh words, Julia dared a glance at Samantha before saying, "How do you know he's marrying her for ... her notoriety?"

Sighing, Evangeline looked to Samantha before saying, "He's an opportunist. And Jeffrey claims Sir James gambles. Poorly. I don't want to see Sam hurt. Especially when her heart is set on another."

Julia's inhalation of breath had Samantha giving her a look of concern. "What is it? Is it the baby?" she asked in alarm.

Blinking, Julia shook her head. "No, of course not. It's far too early for that. Now, pray tell, who has your heart?"

Samantha slumped in her chair, realizing she couldn't keep the news from Julia. "Plymouth," she admitted sadly.

Julia's face brightened with her huge smile. "Oh, thank goodness," she said happily. "Alistair was quite beside himself when he heard of your stay on the island with the man."

"He was?" Samantha replied, her eyes wide. "But, why?"

Shrugging one shoulder, Julia lowered her voice. "They attended university together. Apparently Lord Plymouth had a horrible father, and the marquessate is quite troublesome. Alistair is of the opinion the poor man could use a good wife, and although he said it wouldn't be fair to Samantha for her to have to be his marchioness, he couldn't imagine a woman better suited to the position."

Evangeline and Samantha dared a glance at each other, not sure how to respond to such a claim. "That's rather ... generous of him," Samantha managed, not having thought of the title that would come with marriage to a marquess. She had to admit she was only interested in Ethan for the time they could spend together when he wasn't working on matters of the marquessate.

"Can you imagine our Samantha, the niece of a viscount, the Marchioness of Plymouth?" Julia asked, her brilliant smile lighting up the entire room. "I can!"

A bit stunned by her friend's comment—and that of her husband's—Samantha sighed. "Can you imagine me as the wife of Sir James Moriarty? A baronet's wife?" Samantha asked with a grin, her head nodding in the hopes that her friends would agree it could be a good match.

Julia and Evangeline exchanged a glance, their brows furrowed in confusion. Or perhaps it was concern.

"Who?" Julia asked.

Although she allowed the barest hint of a grin, Julia gave a slight shake of her head while Evangeline simply shook hers back and forth.

Samantha regarded her two best friends and sighed. *Damnation!*

CHAPTER 42

A PIRATE PAYS A VISIT

*E*vans stood in front of the large desk of the marquess, knowing the man wouldn't welcome the interruption. Ever since his return from the Mediterranean, his master had been short-tempered, his moods darker than the shortening days. But more disturbing was overhearing the man talk whilst he slept. Evans could swear he heard his master say the name 'Sam' at least a few times.

Who is Sam?

At least Ethan Range had been spared another trip to the Mediterranean. Lord Torrington's suggestion that he pursue his shipment of batteries using Wellingham Imports had not only saved the marquess the trouble, but kept him off a sailing ship, a mode of transportation Evans was quite sure the marquess wouldn't plan to use for rest of his life.

"My lord, a gentleman named Alex Bradley wishes to have a word with you," he said, his hands clasped behind his back.

Ethan raised his head from the ledger he had been reviewing, his brows furrowing. "I don't know anyone named Alex Bradley," he said, but not with much conviction. These days, he barely remembered what he'd had for breakfast let alone the names of anyone he had met when he was last in London—or wherever Alex Bradley might have been.

Evans repositioned his feet and took a deep breath. "I am to mention you know him better as Captain Jack Crawley, my lord."

The name had Ethan's head popping up so quickly, Evans was quite sure the marquess sprained his neck. "The pirate?" Ethan responded in disbelief. He watched as the butler's eyebrows shot up to the middle of his forehead. Had Ethan been in a better mood, he might have found some humor in seeing the normally staid servant discomfited.

"He did not introduce himself as such," Evans hedged carefully.

Ethan set aside the ledger and regarded his butler for a moment. "Bring the scotch ..." He paused a moment. "No. Make it brandy. And send him in."

Evans gave a nod. "Very well, my lord."

Alex Bradley regarded the ancient decor in the vestibule of Castle Keys with a frown. Not a very welcoming home—the battlements appeared to be intact as did all the gray walls of the stout stone structure—Castle Keys stood at the edge of one of the many moors scattered throughout this part of Yorkshire. At least it was close to the bay where Alex had left the *Molly*. The ship, now manned by a crew of only six, was being used for less nefarious purposes by the Foreign Office. Although it was still his home, at some point soon, Alex planned to return to London and to his office in Whitehall.

He was studying a rather large painting of a bloody medieval battle when the butler returned from his trip to confer with the marquess. "Let me guess. He didn't know me," Alex said with a quirked lip. Opening his topcoat, he pulled out a newspaper clipping.

Evans gave a sideways nod. "Your *nom de plume* seemed to do the trick," the butler acknowledged. "This way, sir."

Following the butler through the massive hall, Alex wondered when last a woman had been within the castle. The place could certainly use one. He had one in mind, although he knew convincing the marquess of her value to him might prove impossible.

Alex stepped into the massive study of the Marquess of

Plymouth and gave a bow in the direction of the man who sat behind a desk so large, Alex was quite sure his outstretched arms wouldn't have reached from one end to the other. "It's good to see you again, Lord Plymouth," he said as he took a step toward the desk.

Ethan regarded the clean-shaven, short-haired man claiming to be Captain Jack Crawley and shook his head in reply. "Forgive me. I was expecting someone else. What's this about?" he asked, allowing his voice to betray his annoyance.

Noting how the marquess' familiar scowl was now punctuated with deep lines across his forehead, Alex took a breath and let it out slowly. Adopting the manner of speech he used as the captain of a pirate ship, Alex put his hands on his hips and said, "I must have been mistaken when I took you to be a gentleman."

Ethan's eyes widened and he slowly stood up from the desk. "I'll be damned," he breathed. "What the ...?"

"Alex Bradley, Foreign Office. I've been working undercover as Jack Crawley for a couple of years," he explained quickly. "I could have written with my concerns, I suppose, but I thought a visit would be more ... effective."

Evans appeared on the threshold of the study with the brandy and crystal balloons. "My lord," he intoned as he moved to set them on the desk. He poured a bit into each glass, set one in front of their guest and the other next to the ledger, and took his leave of the study.

Indicating one of the chairs across from his desk, Ethan moved back to his and sank into it, his attention on the operative the entire time. "Am I in some kind of trouble?" Ethan ventured, wondering as to the purpose of the man's visit.

"Depends," Alex replied. "When you left my ship, where did you go?"

Ethan settled into his chair, deciding it couldn't hurt to tell the man what he had done that night when he had taken his leave of the *Molly*. "To shore. I knew we were close, so I waited until it was dark enough and took a packet. Got to Gandia.

Bought some boots and a coat. A cravat." This last was said

with a hint of bitterness. "Found a courier who could speak English and sent off notes to a few who might have heard word that *The Fairweather* had gone down ..."

"It didn't, you know," Alex interrupted with a shake of his head.

The marquess regarded his guest for several moments before taking a sip of the brandy. The sensation of warmth spread down his throat and filled his insides, a warmth he hadn't felt since his days on the island. "I didn't know. You're saying ... you're saying the ship made it to Rome?" he asked in surprise, just then realizing it was *The Fairweather* from which Samantha disembarked when she returned to England.

Shaking his head, Alex inhaled the fumes from the brandy balloon and let out a sigh. "Much better than the stuff we got from *The Fairweather*," he added before taking a sip. "Which, by the way, only made it to Valencia before it returned to London." At Ethan's widened eyes, he added, "Captain St. John knew you and Miss Fitzsimmons were missing and feared dead. His shipping company sent word to Lord Chamberlain about your disappearance. My orders were to find you and deliver you to Valencia," he said with a bit of derision. "Back to *The Fairweather*. So, after making the fastest run I could from Marseilles, I find you on the third island we searched in two days, and, blast and damn, I wait until it's safe to let you in on the plan, and you've gone and disappeared from the ship!"

His brows arched in anger, Ethan slammed his balloon onto the desk. "You mean you waited until after you compromised Miss Fitzsimmons ..."

"I did no such thing!" Alex countered as he leaned forward.

"I saw her in your arms, I heard her ... whimpering!"

"Because I had just told her who I really was and about how her uncle had me looking for you!" Alex countered, suddenly realizing his anger was getting the better of him. He took a deep breath in an attempt to calm his temper. "Anyway, I delivered her to *The Fairweather*, where she was reunited with her aunt ..."

"*Aunt?*" Ethan repeated, taking too large a sip of the brandy and nearly choking on it.

Alex sighed. "Yes, *aunt*. I paid witness to the entire family reunion. Valencia was the location of a rather boisterous party following her return. My men talked of it for days afterward."

Ethan frowned, the expression making him appear ten years older. He sighed. *Of course, there would have been a party.* And Samantha would have been the center of it, her smile lighting up the dark, her happy countenance attracting everyone like a bee to honey. *My honey.* "She's back in London now, though," he half-asked, trying with all his might to get her image out of his mind. He had stayed in London until he had seen with his own eyes that she had arrived safely, and then he had left for Yorkshire.

"Oh, she's back and quite the center of attention. Including that of Sir James Moriarty." Alex slid the newspaper clipping across the desk as far as he could reach.

His attention on the operative while he picked up the clipping, Ethan asked, "Who is Sir James?"

Alex took another deep breath, almost responding with, "Not you," but decided against it. "A baronet who seems to gravitate toward ... notoriety," he said with some derision. "And who is in desperate need of a lady's dowry." At Ethan's deepening frown, he added, "According to one of the agents in the Home Office, he is in serious debt due to excessive gambling. The rake apparently can't win at faro."

Ethan hissed at the words, his eyes closing for a moment. "And why would this baronet's debts be of any concern to me?" Ethan asked. "He doesn't owe me anything."

Alex sat back in his chair and studied his brandy. "I was hoping you might intervene on the lady's behalf," he said quietly.

Ethan swallowed, finally realizing just why Alex Bradley was paying him a visit. "Seems to me, *you* should be the one to save Sam from the rake. If you came here seeking my ... *permission* to do so, by all means. Make her an offer."

Alex blinked, angling his head to one side. He hadn't missed the marquess' use of Miss Fitzsimmons' given name, but it was the rest of his comment that had him confused. "I beg your pardon? Why ever would you suppose *I* should offer for Miss Fitzsimmons?" he asked, his brows furrowing. "I certainly have no claim to the lady."

Slumping back into his leather chair, Ethan continued to scowl at the operative-cum-pirate. "When last I saw her, she was in *your* arms, looking quite ... *comfortable*," he ground out, his anger building so it was quite evident to his visitor.

Shaking his head, Alex gave a frustrated sigh. "What you saw was a young woman who had just learned *The Fairweather* was still in one piece and docked at Valencia. That her aunt was still alive. And that her ... *uncle* had dispatched me to find you but hadn't bothered to mention I might find her with you." He said the last in a quieter voice, hoping to make the marquess understand there wasn't anything untoward in what he had seen before he shut the door to the pirate's cabin on the *Molly* and disappeared.

Ethan stared at the operative for a long time, his scowl turning into an expression of pain.

"Why wouldn't Viscount Chamberlain mention his niece was missing from *The Fairweather?*"

Alex sighed. "It would have looked suspicious, I suppose, if he had mentioned that Miss Fitzsimmons had gone missing at the same time as you. I believe he was saving you from the scandal," Alex continued, realizing how it would have looked to the gossips in London. "A man and a woman go missing from a sailing ship in the Mediterranean at exactly the same time ..."

"It wasn't like that," Ethan argued as he leaned forward over the desk. "We both got caught in the same wave that took the brandywine from the deck. We both ended up in the water. We were able to swim to a piece of the wreckage ..." He stopped as he realized what Alex originally meant by his comment. "*Damn you!*"

Alex shook his head. "For stating the obvious? You were on the deck ... together. Apparently the only two on the deck at the time you were washed off of it. Seems to me and everyone else who might have heard the tale that you two were having a tryst."

Rolling his eyes, Ethan let out a groan of frustration. "It wasn't like that. I was up there to smoke. She was there to take the air. Her aunt ... mother ... *whomever* ... had been ill the entire trip ..."

"She was experiencing morning sickness, according to the viscount," Alex stated with a nod.

"And we were merely having a conversation ..." He allowed the sentence to trail off, his brows furrowing when he realized what Alex had said. He straightened in his chair. "Lady Chamberlain is expecting a *baby?*" he whispered, rather stunned by the news. *Good God!* The woman had to be ... well, *at least in her early forties*, he thought. And Lord Chamberlain was far older than that!

Alex nodded, his eyes narrowing a bit. "Now, I'm wondering if Miss Fitzsimmons has found herself in the same condition."

Ethan's eyes rounded and he pushed his chair back a bit. "How *dare* you?" But even as he said the words, he realized Samantha really could be expecting a baby.

My baby.

The image of Samantha, her skin golden from the sun and her brown hair with its glints of gold splayed out on her sapphire silk gown, had him taking a breath. The thought of her, belly round with his child, had him exhaling slowly. Something clenched in his chest. Something painful and pleasant and oh, so reminiscent of a similar sensation he had felt on the island, on those mornings when he woke to find her snuggled up against his body, her skin so soft and her body so willing, so wanton.

Even if she wasn't carrying his child, he owed her a life better than the one she would have with a rake, with a gambler who would probably spend her dowry and end up in debtor's prison.

Perhaps she would agree to move to Yorkshire. Even if she couldn't be his wife—the thought of his father's edict that he avoid bad *ton* resonated in his brain—perhaps she would agree to be his mistress. If not his mistress, then maybe an artist-in-residence, painting landscapes for the drab walls in Castle Keys.

Would life at Castle Keys be any better for her, though?

It would have to be, he considered, for if Jack Crawley—Ethan shook his head and regarded the agent opposite his desk—*Alex Bradley* didn't have a claim on Samantha, then he sure as hell was going to. He had to save her from a gambler. He owed her that much. Oh, and a gown, too.

"By the way, you owe me a packet," Alex said as he finished his brandy. He took his leave of Castle Keys without saying another word.

CHAPTER 43

CALLING ON A MOTHER

he very next day
"You scowl exactly like your father did," Margaret Range, Dowager Marchioness of Plymouth, claimed as she greeted her son in her salon at Plymouth Park. The widow's cottage, an entailed manor located just northwest of Scarborough, featured no fewer than six guest bedchambers, modern plumbing, an extensive formal garden and a folly next to a pond.

At one time, Ethan had thought to move there, but his mother had made it clear in her younger years that she planned to occupy the estate. "After all those years in that drafty castle, I believe I have earned the right to have a comfortable place in which to live in my old age," she had said when his father died. As far as 'old age' was concerned, the woman wasn't yet fifty.

"You look as if you've had entirely too much sun. Did you finally make the trip to Italy?" she asked, noting how morose her son seemed at the moment. *Something is wrong,* she realized. She thought she might know what, but decided to allow her son to broach the topic.

"Not exactly," Ethan replied with a shake of his head. "I didn't just wake you, I hope," he added as he leaned over and kissed his mother on her cheek. She wore only a dressing gown and feather-trimmed slippers. Her dark hair was down and a bit tousled, as if she had been abed when the butler announced her son's arrival.

Margaret tittered as she waved a hand and took a seat in a floral upholstered chair, its higher-than-usual back making it appear as if it might be her throne. "Goodness, no. I've been awake for hours. It's getting *out* of bed that can be a bit ... *problematic* sometimes." At Ethan's furrowed brow and look of concern, she giggled, which only seemed to make her son's scowl more intense.

"Are you ... well?" he asked, realizing she was nothing like she had been when his father was alive. An air of joy seemed to surround her, as if widowhood suited her far better than life as his father's wife. He rather imagined being Charles Xavier Range's wife would have been difficult. Being his son had certainly been no picnic.

Ethan took the chair across from her, wincing when he realized it wasn't nearly as hard as he hoped. Ever since his return from the island, he was finding it difficult to find comfort in furniture.

Margaret regarded her son for a moment before responding. "I am. In fact, I think it's best you know so you don't hear it from some village gossip. I have taken a lover," she explained with an arched brow.

Despite already knowing of his mother's tryst with a local widower—a member of the landed gentry who owned several thousand acres of forest—Ethan still colored up at this mother's admission. "Does he treat you well?" he asked, not sure what else to ask just then.

The butler appeared with a tea tray, setting it on the low table in front of the marchioness. "I'll serve, Maxwell. If you could just let my guest know I may be awhile?"

Bowing, the butler said, "Very well, my lady," before taking his leave of the salon.

Ethan waited until the door closed. "I didn't mean to interrupt, Mother. I can certainly ..."

"Darling. He's my lover, not my husband. And you are a marquess. You have paid a call at a perfectly acceptable time ..."

She glanced at the ornate mantle clock over the fireplace and arched a brow in surprise. "Of eleven o'clock. Oliver can wait," she said as she poured tea and handed him a cup. "About time he learned some patience."

Sighing, Ethan finally nodded and accepted the tea, grateful for the refreshment. He had left Castle Keys without having had a cup of coffee or tea, intent on arriving at Plymouth Park before luncheon. Depending on what his mother's advice might be, he would either be returning to Castle Keys that afternoon, or arranging transport to London.

"Now, tell me. What has you visiting me when I know damn well you're still supposed to be in Italy?" she asked, her bit of a smile indicating she was rather proud of including a curse in her question.

Ethan was struck by how unapologetic his mother was using the word 'damn'. Of course, she had spent all those years living with a man who did nothing but curse all day and never apologized for it. *I don't either,* he realized, wondering how many times he had cursed on the island and never asked for forgiveness from Samantha.

"Actually, I never made it to Rome," Ethan finally responded. "I ended up ... tossed off the ship and stranded on an island for a week." He made the comment in an off-hand manner, hoping she wouldn't overreact to the explanation.

Margaret's eyes widened. "Oh, my God. Then the rumors are true?" she whispered in reply, her teacup landing on her saucer with a clatter. "I thought perhaps ..." She didn't finish that sentence but rather straightened in her chair and regarded him a moment. "Your ... companion? Is it true you were stranded there with a ... a lady?"

Ethan nodded, realizing that news of his and Samantha's adventure had made the rags. *Good God!* What had been written about them? About their time on the island? He felt rather sorry for Samantha just then. Living in London as she did meant she was probably being hounded for information. *What had she said? Or did it even matter?* The *ton* would take whatever she said and twist it into something lurid. Her reputation ...

He averted his eyes for a moment, surprised how his mother's simple question could cause him to feel such pain just then.

Despite his every effort to forget about Lady Samantha, he had been unable to get her out of his mind. He thought of her when he was about to fall asleep at night, he dreamed about her whilst he slept, he woke up wanting her next to him in his bed. He was driven to distraction by thoughts of her when he was in his study attempting to do the business of the marquessate.

He simply couldn't get her out of his head.

When he glanced up to regard his mother, he found her staring at him, her head angled to one side and an expression of awe on her face.

"You fell in love with her, didn't you?" she asked in a whisper, her voice filled with wonder.

Ethan felt as if he had been punched in the gut. "I don't ... know about that," he stammered, his breathing suddenly difficult. "I ..." He closed his eyes a moment, attempting to calm himself so that he might ask her what he came to discover. Certainly she would know the answer. He couldn't be the only one to know the truth. "I am hoping you can shed some light. On the family ..."

Margaret leaned forward, her hands clasped together as her elbows rested on her crossed legs. "Are we speaking of Lady Caroline now?" she asked in a quiet voice, rather liking how her son, normally so staid and serious, could be so discombobulated by a woman. "Or Lady Samantha?"

Straightening suddenly, Ethan stared at his mother. "How ... How do you know who ...?"

Lady Plymouth rolled her eyes and stood up from her chair. "We do get news of London up here, Ethan," she replied with a bit of indignation. "I read *The Times*."

Caught off-guard, Ethan struggled to stand as his mother strode over to her escritoire and picked up a folded letter. She returned to her chair and settled into it, opening the parchment. "And I still correspond with my friends," she added as she waved the letter. Shedding her feathered slippers, she tucked her bare feet beneath her as she folded her legs up onto the chair and leaned to one side, one elbow supporting her on the upholstered arm.

Ethan blinked, the sight of her bare feet reminding him so much of Samantha's, of how the chit had spent day after day barefoot as they made their way up and down the dunes of the island. "Friends?" he repeated, tearing his gaze from where her feet ended up on the chair.

"Well, one, in particular," Margaret said as she nodded. Turning to the letter, she scanned the feminine script and read aloud, "My poor Samantha is quite beside herself, a bit surprised at her sudden celebrity and rather shocked that it took such an accident to gain the attention of a suitor. Of course, he is not good enough for my only daughter, and I have doubts her late father would find him acceptable, either. As for his brother, well, Matthew cannot abide the thought of her marrying a baronet anymore than I can." She stopped reading when she heard Ethan's sudden inhalation of breath. "Lady Samantha is truly a Fitzsimmons, if that's what you were wondering," Margaret said quietly.

Ethan stared at his mother for a long time. "How long have you known?" he asked quietly.

Margaret shrugged. "Since before Lady Samantha was born, I suppose," she replied with a sigh. "Caroline was one of my best friends, after all."

Squeezing his eyes shut, Ethan considered the information. "Yet, she bore an illegitimate child," he whispered, struggling with the fact that his mother had known Caroline's secret. He had thought he was the only one in the family who knew Samantha wasn't the daughter of Liza and Edward Fitzsimmons.

"And what would you have her do instead?" his mother replied carefully. "Ethan, Caroline is an earl's daughter, an earl's sister. She's married to a viscount. Her only crime was falling in love with a man who loved her." Margaret stopped, shaking her head as she decided there was nothing more she could say to her son to make him see reason—at least not as it applied to Caroline Fitzsimmons. "What would you have had *me* do?" she asked then, straightening on the chair so her bare feet were on the floor.

Ethan frowned. "What do mean?" he asked, his scowl reappearing.

Margaret leaned over to touch the spot between his brows where the skin furrowed, shaking her head as she did so. "Darling, had you been born three days earlier than you were, *you* would be a bastard," she answered with a sigh. "And if you tell anyone I told you that, I will deny it."

Staring at his mother for several seconds, his look of shock almost comical, Ethan groaned. "You jest," he accused.

Arching an eyebrow as she gave him a teasing smile, Margaret regarded him for a moment. "Your father proposed marriage, bedded me, and then left for the Continent the very next day. For his Grand Tour. An opportunity to sow his wild oats and see all the sights. When he returned, I was living in the country with an aunt, and I was ..." She held out her hands in front of her "... *Round* with child—with *you*. But Charles had already secured the marriage license and was ready to marry. I think he actually missed me whilst on his travels," she explained with a wan smile. "So, you missed being born a bastard by just a few days."

Unable to abide his mother's gaze just then, Ethan scrubbed his face with an open hand. His father had been forced to marry, although he had proposed before leaving on his Grand Tour. That was a point in his favor, at least. "Probably why he was so mean," he murmured.

Margaret shook her head. "He was actually a rather pleasant fellow in those days," she replied. "But he didn't wear his title very well. When the troubles started in the mines, and the farmers had problems with crops, and the villagers demanded more, more, more, he ... he turned into someone else. The man *you* remember, unfortunately," she said sadly. After a moment, she added, "She paints beautifully."

Ethan blinked. "Beg pardon?" he murmured, his thoughts still on the story his mother had just told. He was still trying to determine if any of it were true.

"Lady Samantha. She's a painter. Does beautiful landscapes that appear as if they're lit from within. Castle Keys could use a few of them," she said with an arched eyebrow. "Castle Keys could use *her*," she amended with a nod. "You ... you *need* her." After a pause and another sigh, Margaret straightened in her chair. "Now. What else brought you to my humble abode on this glorious day?" she asked brightly.

Having made his decision as to where he would be going upon leaving Plymouth Park, Ethan shook his head. "Why, just the opportunity to spend some time with you, mother," he said. He finished off his tea and leaned over to take his mother's hand. He kissed the back of it. "I think you might have kept Oliver waiting quite long enough."

Margaret grinned as she regarded her son. "Don't make her wait," she warned with a shake of her head.

One brow cocking up, Ethan regarded his mother with a quirked lip. "Doesn't she need to learn patience?"

Her grin turning into a scowl, Margaret shook her head. "How long has it been since you last saw her?" she countered.

Ethan swallowed. Hard. *Too long.*

He took his leave of Plymouth Park and left for London that afternoon.

CHAPTER 44

A MARQUESS PAYS A CALL

hree days later

Ethan stepped down from a hackney and regarded Fitzsimmons Manor from the half-circle drive. Nearly every window on the lower level was lit, an indication—he hoped—that the viscount and Lady Samantha were in residence. The front door opened before he reached the top step.

"Lord Plymouth for Lady Samantha," Ethan stated as he removed his top hat and stepped over the threshold of Fitzsimmons Manor.

Porter, the butler, nodded, but hesitated to take the hat. "Lady Samantha is not in residence, my lord."

Impatient and not the least bit happy about waiting, Ethan forced himself to take a deep breath. "Lord Chamberlain, then," he said, deciding it would be better to speak with the viscount first.

Shaking his head, the ancient butler replied, "Lord Chamberlain is not in residence either, my lord. I expect he'll return within the hour, however."

Taking another breath and letting it out, Ethan wondered at his lightheadedness. "I'll wait for his return."

I suppose it's time I learn some patience.

Porter blinked but nodded and took the proffered hat. "Very

well, my lord." Leading the marquess to the parlor, Porter regarded the younger man and noted his nervousness.

"May I pour you a brandy? Or a scotch, perhaps?"

Ethan nodded and nearly said, "Both." Instead, he replied, "Tea, if you would."

His eyes widening a fraction, Porter nodded. "Of course, my lord." He took his leave of the parlor and hurried off to the kitchen, not too surprised a marquess was calling on Lady Samantha. Her recent adventure had obviously stirred up interest in the chit, given the number of guests Fitzsimmons Manor had hosted since her return from the Mediterranean.

Ethan Range paced for a moment, chastising himself for expecting to find anyone in residence in the late afternoon when Lady Samantha was no doubt paying calls and Matthew Fitzsimmons would be at the Foreign Office. *I should have gone there first,* he considered.

But to say what?

I'll be paying a call on your niece and wish to take her with me to Yorkshire on the morrow? Do I have your permission? Or should I be asking your wife?

How much did Lord Chamberlain know about Samantha? Did he know she had a sister? His older niece, in fact?

Seeing Emma Wellingham at Wellingham Imports earlier that day had been like seeing a slightly older version of Samantha. Although Mrs. Wellingham's hair was lighter, her features were nearly identical to Samantha's.

At Grandby's suggestion, he had paid a call at the import company first thing that morning to place his order for the batteries. Although he had been escorted to Thomas Wellingham's office and had been conversing with the man for several minutes about his needs, he could see Mrs. Wellingham working at a smaller desk farther back in her husband's office.

He knew he had been staring too long when she finally regarded him with an arched eyebrow. "Do I have something on my face?" she asked, lifting an ink-stained hand to wave over one of her cheeks.

Knowing he had been caught staring but unable to tear his gaze away, Ethan had simply shaken his head. At that point, Emma's husband, Thomas, stood up from his desk. "Lord Plymouth, this is my wife, Emma. She is an accomptant here at Wellingham Imports. You look as if ... as if you recognize her," he said, his voice cautious.

"I apologize, my lady," Ethan said as he stood and reached for her hand. He leaned over to brush his lips over her knuckles. "I thought for a moment you were ..." He stopped, unable to say Samantha's name.

Emma's eyes widened at having her hand taken, but she quickly recovered. "'Tis very good to meet you, Lord Plymouth," she responded. Giving her husband a glance, she angled her head. "Lady Samantha, perhaps?" she offered, unaware of any other woman she might resemble. Or any other woman he might be curious about. After all, Samantha had been stranded on a deserted island with the man.

It was Ethan's turn to widen his eyes. "Yes," he responded. "Are you ... related, perhaps?" he asked, his brows furrowing.

Emma and Thomas exchanged glances, a hint of nervousness appearing on Emma's face as she decided how much to admit. Samantha's secret wasn't really hers to tell, but something told her the marquess needed to know. His look was so intent. "We had the same father, yes," she finally answered, a blush coloring her cheeks. "George Fitzsimmons. Known for 'hats that make the gentleman'," she added, thinking that although the marquess would be too young to remember her father—George had been dead for twenty years—he might be familiar with the shop where his hat designs were still being sold. 'Fitzsimmons and Smith' enjoyed a well-earned reputation as a premium hat maker and a milliner of hats and bonnets for ladies.

But why would the marquess ask such a question?

Ethan regarded the woman with a wan smile, deciding she should know what he had finally admitted to himself. "I find myself in love with your sister."

He would never forget Emma's expression of stunned happiness, never forget how her eyes lit up and her head angled much like Samantha's did when she was delighted by something. "She will make you an excellent marchioness," Emma had said in response. "And I have always wanted a brother."

Never once had he said he would *marry* Samantha, but at least he knew he had her sister's blessing.

The sound of the front door closing brought Ethan out of his reverie. Listening carefully, he heard feminine voices and then the butler's before the tap-tap of boots on the marble floors indicated someone was on their way to the parlor. Stilling himself, Ethan took a deep breath and pretended to pay attention to his cup of tea.

At the sight of the viscountess, Ethan's eyes widened. "My lady," he said with a nod. "It's very good to see you again."

"Why, Lord Plymouth, what a pleasant surprise," Caroline said as a genuine smile appeared. She hurried to the marquess and offered her hand.

Ethan bowed over it and brushed his lips over her gloved knuckles. "Forgive me. I ... I thought you had perished with *The Fairweather*," he murmured, deciding not to let on he knew she had survived but only because Alex Bradley had told him.

Still smiling as she regarded the impeccably dressed marquess, Caroline shook her head. "I'm most certain I am not the first to say that the rumors of my demise were greatly exaggerated. *The Fairweather* made it to Valencia for repairs the day after that terrible storm."

She glanced at her daughter, heartened to see Samantha staring at the marquess rather than fleeing for her bedchamber. "But I don't believe you are here to pay a call on me," she said. "Would you excuse me? I'm expecting my husband shortly, and I should like to look my best."

Before Ethan could reply, the viscountess gave a slight curtsy and took her leave of the parlor. He bowed and turned his attention to Samantha.

Looking luminescent, Samantha stood staring at him. Her skin, still golden from their days on the island, glowed.

Although she was dressed far more conservatively in a sprigged muslin gown and dark green spencer, he remembered her in her corset and pantaloons and had to tamp down the sudden desire he felt in his loins. "You look ... beautiful," he breathed, not sure where to start or what he would need to say to convince her to listen.

There was so much he needed tell her!

Samantha regarded Ethan as if she were seeing a ghost. A tall, rather well-built ghost who was wearing black evening clothes and a gold waistcoat embroidered with metallic thread. He had unbuttoned his topcoat, so his chronometer was visible and hung from a gold chain attached to his waistcoat. "Were you able to have it repaired?" Samantha wondered, a gloved finger lifting from her side to indicate the pocket watch.

Ethan at first wondered what she meant and then remembered the chronometer. He nodded. "A goldsmith in Ludgate Hill saw to it today, whilst I was at Wellingham Imports, seeing to the batteries," he answered, taking a step toward Samantha. "Are you ... well?"

Swallowing, Samantha fought the bit of disappointment she felt at hearing he had seen to his pocket watch before paying a call on Fitzsimmons Manor. *Priorities*, she thought, realizing the marquess didn't consider her very high on his list. She nodded. "I am," she finally replied with a sigh. Samantha took another breath in an attempt to stave off the tears she could feel forming in the corners of her eyes. "Tell me something, please ..."

"Anything, my lady," Ethan responded with a nod as he took another step closer.

Her eyes wide with his reply, she asked, "How did you ...?"

"I took a packet and rowed to shore."

"It must have taken .."

"The entire night, yes, and most of the following morning, but the *Molly* was far closer to shore than Captain Crawley indicated. A current helped as well, I suppose," Ethan added when he noted her look of disbelief.

Samantha pressed her lips together, fighting the urge to simply run to him, to wrap her arms around him and kiss him.

"Why?" she managed to get out, a tear finally escaping the corner of her eye and streaming down her cheek.

Ethan took another step closer. "I thought your ... affections ... had been redirected ... onto Mr. Bradley ..."

"Who?" Samantha interrupted, her chin rising at his words.

"Mr. Bradley. Uh, Captain Crawley," he corrected himself, thinking that she must know about the Foreign Office agent who had been posing as a pirate. *Wouldn't her uncle have told her?*

Suddenly indignant, Samantha showed a look of shock. "*Affections?*" she repeated. "How in heaven's name could you have ever thought ...?" But Ethan was suddenly in front of her, suddenly so close she could smell his amber cologne and feel the heat from his body.

"I saw you in his arms," he interrupted, keeping his face as impassive as possible.

Ethan's words had Samantha's brows furrowing, but after another moment of staring at one another, his lips took purchase on hers, silencing any rebuttal she might have provided.

Although she gave into the kiss for the first moment—*oh, how I have missed this bit of intimacy with the marquess!*—she remembered where they were, remembered her situation, and pulled her herself away. Slightly unsteady on her feet, Samantha shook her head. "I am ... *betrothed*," she managed to get out. Tears filling her eyes, she turned and fled the library, her half-booted feet nearly tripping on her gown as she ascended the stairs to her bedchamber.

Ethan remained standing where he was in the parlor, rather surprised at Samantha's sudden disappearance.

I am betrothed, she had said.

Damnation!

So Alex Bradley hadn't been lying when he spoke of the baronet. Ethan had left for London thinking that perhaps the captain of the *Molly* was merely playing matchmaker. That by claiming Samantha was engaged to the baronet, Ethan would be compelled to do right by her and offer for her hand.

The ploy had worked, he supposed. There was no way he was going to allow Samantha to marry a baronet. And there was also no way he could continue his life without her. The weeks since his return from Spain had been miserable. Castle Keys, already a dark and foreboding pile, had been more so. Immersing himself in the management of the marquessate had done little to keep his mind off the week spent on the island— the best week of his life.

"Frustrating creatures, aren't they?"

Ethan blinked, stunned to find Matthew Fitzsimmons standing before him. "Aye," Ethan replied with a slight nod. "Good afternoon, Lord Chamberlain. I hope you don't mind. I told your butler I would wait for your return."

Matthew gave a shrug. "Not a bit. Truth be told, I was hoping you would get here sooner," he added with an arched brow. "Porter tells me you only accepted tea when you arrived. Perhaps you'll join me for a scotch?"

Giving the viscount a nod, Ethan replied, "I could use one," he agreed.

The viscount waved a hand toward the door. "Let's go to the study. A bit more conducive to discussing important matters."

Ethan moved into the hallway, but turned to regard Matthew. "Important matters?" he repeated.

The viscount shrugged as he led them across the wide hall to the study, a cozy room decorated in dark mahogany paneling and royal blue fabrics. Matthew indicated one of the overstuffed chairs next to a small table as he moved to a sideboard and poured scotch into two crystal tumblers. He turned and gave one to Ethan. "Of course. My niece. Her dowry. Her future." He tapped the rim of his glass against the one a rather stunned Ethan held. "Cheers," he murmured.

"Cheers," Ethan repeated, almost falling into the chair. "I came today with the intention of asking permission to marry your niece, but ..."

"Well, don't let Sir James get in the way of that," Matthew replied, taking the chair opposite. He took a sip of the scotch and held it on his tongue, inhaling the fumes before swallowing the smoky liquid. "My favorite," he murmured as he settled back in the chair.

"But, if Lady Samantha has already accepted another's proposal ..." Ethan started to say.

"He didn't ask permission for her hand," Matthew cut in, his expression of contentment suddenly changing to one bordering on anger. "And her godfather has made it quite clear he won't abide her marrying Sir James," he added. "The baronet is an opportunist, nothing more," he stated with a shake of his head.

Ethan remembered the strange missive he had received from the earl and wondered if he had earned the man's wrath. The man could be fearsome if events didn't go his way. "Opportunist?" Ethan repeated, realizing that apparently everything Alex Bradley had told him was turning out to be true. *So the captain-cum-pirate hadn't simply shown up with a tall tale in an attempt to rid himself of an obligation to marry the chit as I had surmised.*

Samantha really was engaged to be married to a baronet. The part about the gambling debts was probably also true.

Matthew gave Ethan a look indicating his frustration. "Didn't Bradley explain all this when he was in Yorkshire?" Matthew asked. He leaned forward. "I sent him up there to apprise you of the situation ..."

"He did," Ethan replied with a nod of his head, rather surprised the man had been dispatched to Castle Keys. "I ... I apologize ... I misunderstood his intentions." He scrubbed his face with a hand. "And hers."

Settling back into his chair, Lord Chamberlain regarded the marquess for a long moment. "Are you willing to marry her?"

"Of course," Ethan replied a bit too quickly. At Matthew's raised eyebrow, Ethan sighed. "I ... I ruined her. But even if I hadn't, we were on that island a long time, and on a raft before that, and on the deck of the ship without benefit of a chaperone when the wave hit ..." He stopped when he noticed Matthew holding up a hand. "My lord?"

"You *ruined* her?" Matthew repeated, his expression impassive.

Ethan stilled himself, realizing too late what he was admitting to with his words. It was also too late to come up with a different explanation, too late to claim he had been a perfect gentleman whilst on the island. And Alex Bradley had paid witness to a few moments when Ethan had been at Samantha's side while she bathed in the captain's quarters. If the agent had said anything to the viscount about that incident, it would have been more than enough to force a wedding. "Yes." His eyes suddenly widened. "But not against her will, I assure you," he claimed, rather fearful as to what the viscount might do to him.

Or what he might have the Foreign Office to do him.

"Good," Matthew responded with a nod. "Do you suppose you could ever come to feel affection for my niece? You see, I recently confirmed she really is my niece, and not just by marriage, and on behalf of my late brother, I would like for her to be settled with a man who can appreciate her talents, her ..."

"I can," Ethan interrupted. "I do," he amended when he saw the viscount's raised eyebrow. "I believe I have her sister's blessing, as well," he added, thinking that a mention of having spoken with Emma Fitzsimmons Wellingham could only help his cause.

Matthew's brows furrowed and he stared at Ethan for a long time. "How ...?"

"My mother, and then Mrs. Wellingham told me. Not ... not directly, but I knew about Samantha's real mother from when I was eavesdropping as a child, and ..." He shut up when he realized Matthew was once again holding up his hand.

"You knew Samantha's mother was really ... my viscountess?" the viscount asked, a hint of alarm on his face.

Ethan sighed, coloring up a bit. "Yes," he admitted. "I used to hide in cupboards and listen in on the conversations taking place in Darbing Manor. Wrong, I know, but ... little pitchers have big ears."

Matthew's attention was directed beyond Ethan, as if he were thinking, as if he were remembering incidences from long ago. "Who else knows? Whom did you tell?" he finally whispered, his eyes clearing to regard the marquess with obvious curiosity.

Of course, Ethan realized, a man who had worked in the Foreign Office as long as Lord Chamberlain had been employed there would be concerned with who might know such information. Perhaps the man had only recently learned of it himself.

Giving a slight shrug, Ethan replied, "My mother knows, but as a friend of your wife's, she has kept the secret. I have only ever told Lady Samantha. When we were up on the deck of *The Fairweather* that last night on board. I thought she knew. I was …"

He shook his head, wondering why he had been in such a foul mood that night. As soon as he had seen Samantha appear at the top of the companionway, he had felt annoyance. Not anger certainly, but *bothered* that a chit could be so unaware of the truth of her existence. Bothered that her real mother could be so heartless as to keep her daughter in the dark as to her real parentage. "I was annoyed, I suppose," Ethan finally managed to get out. At Matthew's questioning glance, Ethan added, "Lady Samantha was raised as a lady, but because of what I knew about her, I figured her father was a commoner …"

"He was my *brother*," Matthew interrupted, a hint of warning in his voice, as if he were defending the man. After a moment, though, he seemed to calm himself, and he sighed. "Caro was a very young widow and fancied herself in love with George. Although there were times I wished they had never met, it all happened before we were married. As a result, she has Samantha, and she's been true to me ever since."

Ethan regarded the viscount for a moment, realizing he spoke the truth. Had Caroline been unfaithful to Matthew, the man would no doubt have learned of it from one of his operatives. "So, Samantha is the granddaughter of a viscount and the granddaughter of an earl," Ethan said with a nod, thinking the viscount wanted to make a point of her position within the peerage. *Samantha's not such bad ton, after all,* he thought, a bit annoyed with himself—with his father—for ever thinking it was important in the first place.

"Indeed," the viscount responded. "I believe she would make you an excellent marchioness, but you'll need to decide that for yourself. But I beg you, don't ask for her hand if you intend to marry her and leave her here in London."

Ethan frowned, a bit stunned by Lord Chamberlain's words. "I've already decided I want her as my *wife*," he countered, not about to admit he hadn't considered the ramifications of the rank she would hold. "And I have no intention of leaving her here. Why would you even suggest ...?"

"Your mistress," Matthew interrupted, the words sounding like an accusation.

Ethan's eyes narrowed to slits. Had the Foreign Office been spying on him? Or the Home Office? If so, why? Or was the viscount merely implying he had a mistress because so many members of the peerage did so? "Your ... *reconnaissance* is sorely out of date," Ethan replied in clipped tones. "I haven't had a mistress for several months, nor do I intend to employ another," he stated in no uncertain terms. He felt a bit of satisfaction as he watched Matthew's expression change suddenly.

"You must trust me when I say you've not been the target of any investigation by the *Foreign* Office," Matthew replied carefully. "At least, not to my knowledge."

"Then how ...?"

"I asked about you at Boodle's when I returned to London a few weeks ago. It seems one or two members think you still employ a Miss Daisy Albright. I must say, I'm relieved to hear you no longer use her services."

Ethan realized immediately that the viscount's comment wasn't made with his niece in mind but rather from something else. His brows furrowing with the comment, Ethan was forced to ask, "Pray tell, why?"

Matthew finished off his scotch and then hesitated before replying. "Not a word to anyone about this," he said in hushed tones. "I'm not at liberty to speak about what the Home Office might have at one time thought about you. Rest assured, they've been set to rights. However, you should know it's possible Miss Albright is operating as a spy for the Home Office ..."

"Daisy?" Ethan interrupted, his face displaying his disbelief. "I hardly think a woman who is as spoiled and emotional as Daisy Albright could be a *spy*," he responded with a shake of his head. But even as he said the words, Ethan realized Daisy could have merely been acting the part of a spoiled tart. Her behavior could be rather erratic, her manner somewhat flighty. *Why spy on me, though? And why quit me for a man engaged in trade?* When he had seen her in Cambridge, Daisy had said she had finished her work. And when he had asked about Myles Longburn, she had said, *He's been arrested and is awaiting trial on smuggling charges.*

Ethan's eyes widened when he realized what she really meant.

Matthew settled back in his chair and allowed the marquess to come to his own conclusions before finally offering an explanation. "Your coastline is a perfect hiding place for smugglers. There's been some concern that you might have been involved ..." Even before Ethan could rise from his chair in protest, Matthew held out a hand and waved him down. "... But it's become apparent there is another party under consideration now, and Miss Albright has simply moved her investigation to him."

Ethan stared at the viscount for a long time, stunned by the implication of his words. Daisy had claimed she accepted a better offer from Myles Longburn because he had given her jewels worthy of royalty. If so, where had Longburn obtained the jewels? Or had she merely told him that to gain her freedom? To ensure she could take Longburn as a client? But if Longburn hadn't given her an expensive bauble, from where had he obtained the funds to pay for a better house? Provide more pin money? Finding out Longburn was involved in smuggling along the marquessate's Yorkshire coastline certainly explained the man's sudden wealth. Knowing from Daisy that the man had been arrested on smuggling charges had Ethan suddenly feeling a bit superior.

"Myles Longburn," Ethan said quietly, his attention on his glass. "I'd never heard of the man before Daisy told me she had accepted his offer. And a rather large bauble," he said, finally lifting his eyes to meet Matthew's.

The viscount took a sip of his scotch and nodded. "I'm certain the Home Office will act when she's provided the necessary information to convict him," he assured Ethan. "If there is a smuggling ring working off your shores, the authorities will see to it the rascals are arrested," he continued, speaking the words as if he were convincing himself rather than Ethan.

"He's already been arrested," Ethan murmured. "Accused of smuggling. I believe Miss Albright's work in Yorkshire is done."

Matthew angled his head a moment and took a breath. "Well, then I suppose there's only one other matter we need to clear up."

Ethan finished his scotch, his mind still reeling at the thought that someone in the Home Office thought him involved in smuggling. And what other matter could Lord Chamberlain want to discuss? "What might that be?" Ethan asked carefully, not sure he wanted to know just then.

"Lady Samantha's dowry, of course," Matthew replied, apparently surprised Ethan hadn't brought it up first.

Shaking his head, Ethan set his tumbler on the small table. "I hardly care. I plan to marry her no matter the amount of her dowry," Ethan replied, leaning his elbows on his knees. "Provided I have your permission, of course," he added, just then remembering Matthew's comment about Sir James not having asked permission.

Lord Chamberlain regarded the marquess for some time. "Hardly the words of a man who feels forced to marry out of a sense of honor," he finally replied, one eyebrow arching up.

Ethan frowned, his own brows furrowing at the words. "I am not looking to marry her out of some sense of honor," he countered, his ire showing. "I want to marry her because ..." He stopped then, realizing he was about to admit something to the viscount he hadn't yet admitted to Samantha.

Or to himself.

"Because I wish her to be my wife," he finished finally, taking a breath and letting it out in a huff. "Will you give your blessing to the match? I paid a visit to Doctors' Commons earlier today. I've a special license," he said as he reached into his top coat to pull out the paper he had paid twenty-one pounds to secure.

The corner of Matthew's lip curled up as he pretended to think about Ethan's question. The man was a marquess, for God's sake.

Of course I'm going to give my blessing!

"Of course, you have my permission," Matthew said with a grin. He frowned suddenly, though. "It's really none of my business," Matthew began in reply, "But may I ask if you'll bring her back to London on occasion? I only ask because my viscountess has informed me she's expecting a child in about six months, and I would like it very much if Samantha could meet her brother or sister. I would hate for her to be separated from this one like she was from Emma all these years."

Ethan blinked. And blinked again when he remembered Alex Bradley's comment about the viscount expecting a child. Pretending the news was new to him, he affected an air of surprise. "She's going to have a *baby?*" he whispered, his mind going back to the days on board *The Fairweather*. At Matthew's eager nod, Ethan shook his head. "She wasn't seasick," he said with awe in his voice.

Matthew grinned, one shoulder coming up a bit. "Morning sickness, apparently. Although she's well past that now," he said with a genuine smile. "And I seem to be the beneficiary of ..." He stopped suddenly, his face sobering as well as turning bright red as he straightened in his chair. "Well, let's just say, I rather enjoy my wife in her current condition."

Ethan wasn't quite sure he knew what the viscount meant, but figured it had something to do with marital bliss.

The viscount suddenly remembered their conversation about Samantha's dowry and leaned forward. A bit offended that her dowry didn't seem to matter to the marquess, Matthew spoke with some force. "You claim the amount of her dowry doesn't matter, but it damn well does to *me*." He had given the matter a great deal of consideration. Twenty-thousand would be suitable for a girl who wasn't even his daughter. Fifty-thousand would be far more than the marquess would expect. But this was Caroline's daughter—his niece—and he wasn't about to settle just any amount on the marquess.

"Will one-hundred-thousand pounds be enough?" he asked.

Ethan blinked. *A hundred-thousand pounds?* He blinked again. "Of course," he replied with a shake of his head. "I can ... I'll be sure to settle it on her and the children for when I ..." He stopped, surprised he had even thought about the children they might have.

He imagined a small brood of golden-brown-haired, green-eyed tykes running about Castle Keys, their giggles and shrieks bringing life to the otherwise somber keep. Imagined Samantha, round with child, painting their portraits and reading to them as they sat spell-bound around her skirts. Imagined them gathered around the dining table, where chaos would no doubt reign at every meal, but Samantha would simply take it in stride as she did everything else.

Ethan swallowed, fighting to maintain a semblance of control on his face. "In answer to your other question; yes, I'll be sure to bring her back to London. For the Season. I think it's past time for me to claim my seat in Parliament," he said, his gaze on something far away.

Matthew nodded. "Very good then."

Ethan regarded the viscount for another moment. "Might I be allowed to visit Lady Samantha ... on the morrow? I have some additional business I need to see to before I press my case with the lady."

Viscount Chamberlain gave the marquess a nod, wondering what business might trump the man's proposal. "By all means. I'll let Porter know to let you in. Second door on the left up the stairs," Matthew said with a nod. "If for some reason you're not able to talk some sense into her, I can certainly ..."

"If she spurns me, Lord Chamberlain, I shall take my leave

and never return," Ethan replied with a rather stern look on his face.

"If she spurns you, Lord Plymouth, I shall see to it she enters a convent," Matthew countered, his own stern expression making him appear rather formidable.

The Marquess of Plymouth stood up and gave the viscount a nod. "My lord. Thank you for the ... advice. And the scotch," he said, realizing he had actually downed the entire serving of the amber liquid.

It had been far better than the brandywine on the island.

CHAPTER 45

A MOTHER-DAUGHTER TALK

eanwhile, upstairs

Caroline Fitzsimmons fussed in front of her vanity mirror, determined to bring her hair into perfect order before allowing her husband to see her. Matthew's transformation from a man who occasionally paid her a conjugal visit to a man who shared her bed every night of the week and doted on her as if she were incapable of taking care of herself was nothing short of a miracle. She couldn't even be sure just what it was that had him behaving so. He had been attentive even before she told him she expected his child.

Had it been all her doing? Because she had learned a bit about seduction and wrested his attention from matters of state? Or had Matthew realized he was getting old, and needed to spend time with her if there was any hope of producing an heir?

Placing a hand on her belly, she took a deep breath and sighed. If only Matthew had been home more in the earlier years of their marriage! She was sure she would have borne him a child far sooner if only ...

Caroline shook her head. They may not have spent their younger years as they should have, but at least they were making up for it now.

The sound of Samantha's door closing had Caroline straightening on the vanity chair. Faint sounds of crying had her up and out of the mistress suite in a few strides, her long legs carrying her across the hall and into her daughter's room in mere seconds.

Caroline found her daughter on her bed, her forehead resting on her crossed arms as she lay sobbing. It looked as if Samantha had simply thrown herself onto the counterpane and landed in an elegant heap of sprigged muslin and velvet.

"Oh, my darling daughter," Caroline said with a shake of her head as she moved to the bed and took a seat behind Samantha. "Whatever did the marquess say to have you so upset?" she wondered, at first rather annoyed the man would cause her daughter pain.

"He thought my affections were with Captain Crawley," she said between hiccups, her sobs becoming more pronounced with the pronouncement.

Caroline straightened on the bed, her legs dangling over the side of the mattress. "Oh," she replied, her brows furrowing in confusion. "And were they? You never mentioned a Captain Crawley," she ventured, not intending to tease Samantha. "Telling Sir James you're throwing him over for the captain of a pirate ship will be a bit of a conversation, but one you'll manage just fine, I'm sure," she added with a genuine smile.

Samantha raised herself onto her elbows and glanced back at her mother. "*What?*" she replied, not believing her mother's words. "No! My affections were never with Captain Crawley. They were always with Ethan. But you're suggesting I break an engagement for a man who ... who *abandoned* me whilst on a pirate ship?"

Caroline considered the question and realized Samantha did have a point, but she replied, "Why, yes, I guess I am, dear."

"Who ... who *ruined* me while we were on that island?"

Caroline's eyes widened a bit at the change in Samantha's story, but she gave a shrug. "Well, I should hope so. You were on that island for an entire *week*," she countered. "And on a raft before that. I do hope you two found comfort in each other's arms whilst you waited for rescue."

Samantha sat up on the bed and regarded her mother with astonishment. "*Mother!*"

Giving an innocent shrug, Caroline regarded her tear-stained daughter for a long time. "I cannot make this decision for you, but know that I am here and willing to talk about it. I'll still love you no matter what you decide."

With that, Caroline took her leave of Samantha's room.

Samantha stared at her bedchamber door, wondering at her mother's parting words. Moving to her vanity, she took the seat in front of the looking glass and regarded her reflection. She attempted a smile, one she thought suitable for a woman betrothed. She thought of Sir James and immediately regretted it. The mere thought of the baronet had Samantha's reflection sobering.

What if the claims about Sir James were true? That he was an opportunist only out for her dowry? That he was a gambler and needed her dowry to pay off debts? Once he used up the money, how long would it be before he was in debt again?

The man seemed to genuinely care for her, although he was a bit critical of how she wore her hair, of how she dressed. The thought of him didn't have her insides all fluttery and excited, not like she was a moment ago when Ethan had appeared at her door.

Perhaps ... she remembered how just two month ago, she considered spinsterhood. Would it be preferable to a loveless marriage? Hire a companion, buy a townhouse, travel ...

Ugh! The thought of setting sail for the Continent didn't have the same appeal it had when she and her mother had boarded *The Fairweather*. What if she and her companion didn't become fast friends? If the woman proved difficult to live with? Or her beliefs clashed, or ...?

Samantha sighed. Spinsterhood had certainly lost its appeal since her time on the island. A time during which she realized she rather liked the company of a man. The freedom from the constant censure of the *ton*. Being out of doors. Carrying a sunshade fashioned from a silk cravat and a diamond pin. Wearing almost nothing. Swimming.

A light blinked on the vanity top, and Samantha turned to regard the diamond-tipped cravat pin. *I should have given it to him when he was here,* she thought as another tear traced its way down her cheek. Through the lens of her wet eyes, the diamond continued winking. Was it making fun of her? Or was it merely trying to tell her something

Dropping her head into her hands, Samantha wept.

CHAPTER 46

A VISIT TO WHITE'S

*T*he *following afternoon*
James Moriarty lounged in one of the overstuffed chairs in the bow window at White's, one leg haphazardly draped over the other. "Now there's a brilliant one," he announced to no one in particular as his eyes followed a young woman who walked past the window, apparently unaware of the baronet's gaze. His hips made a thrusting motion to emphasize his point.

"Too bad she's already married," a voice sounded behind James. "Else you could pursue *her* for her dowry."

The baronet straightened, uncrossing his legs as he turned to discover the identity of his interloper. "Know the chit, do you?" he replied, wondering if the well-dressed man who towered over him might be the woman's husband.

Ethan Range, Marquess of Plymouth, shook his head. "I do not," he responded as he indicated the empty chair opposite the one in which James sat. "But the bump under her left glove suggests a rather large stone on her wedding ring."

James shrugged, making it apparent he wasn't particularly impressed. "Take it, please. You can watch the chits coming from the other direction," he said as he retrieved his lit cheroot from a porcelain ash tray. "Sir James Moriarty," he introduced himself before taking a draw on the cheroot.

Settling himself into the proffered chair, Ethan regarded the blond-haired baronet who pretended to be bored. "Ethan Range, Marquess of Plymouth," he stated. "And the holder of all your debt." He felt a great deal of satisfaction when Sir James' eyes widened for a fraction of a second before returning to their previous heavy-lidded gaze.

"Indeed?" the baronet replied, finally leaning forward after his eyes flicked to the side, as if he wanted to ensure no one else was within earshot.

"According to Frank O'Laughlin over at The Jack of Spades, faro doesn't seem to favor you," Ethan said as he pulled out several markers from his topcoat pocket. He pulled another from the opposite pocket. "And neither does whist." Spreading out the markers on the small table that separated him from the baronet, Ethan leaned back in his chair and crossed his legs. "Gambling, in fact, doesn't seem to favor you at all."

James continued his air of detachment, giving a slight shrug in response. "I enjoy it, however. It's ... a bit of a *thrill.*"

Ethan pulled out a cheroot. A footman was at his side in an instant, holding a candle from which he could light it. "Thank you," Ethan acknowledged with a nod. He turned his attention back to the baronet. "And a bit of an *expensive* thrill, given how much you owe me."

Sir James studied a fingernail, his sport of watching and commenting on the passing women forgotten. "What, ten-thousand pounds or thereabouts?" he replied, sounding as bored as he looked.

"Thirty-two-thousand, five-hundred and fifty-two," Ethan countered as he lifted one of the stacks of markers. "Oh, and a dueling pistol and a *horse,*" he added as he nudged the other stack.

The look of boredom quickly disappeared from the baronet's face. "Thirty-two?" he repeated, apparently astonished. "But ..."

"I believe interest has upped the ante considerably," Ethan said before taking a long draw on his cheroot. He couldn't ever remember having smoked in White's. As a member of Boodle's, he rarely darkened the door of the men's club populated by the younger aristocrats and the older ones who liked to place bets on others' misfortunes.

Sir James regarded Ethan for a moment. "Are you here to ... collect?" he asked carefully, wondering how he could possibly pay even a portion of the debt. Rent on his bachelor apartments would be due in short order, he no longer had the horse, but he was fairly sure he could locate the dueling pistol if he looked hard enough. "I could probably get you the pistol by the end of the day," he said with an arched eyebrow. "As for the horse, I already gave it up to cover that particular debt," he commented, not bothering to mention that he had used the horse twice as collateral. He left the obvious unsaid.

A feeling of dread was slowly building in the baronet. His entire plan had been to marry an aristocrat's daughter, use the dowry to cover the existing debt and have enough leftover to live on for the rest of his life. He had thought Lady Samantha's dowry to be worth around twenty-five-thousand pounds; now he realized it would have to be more.

Much more.

He wondered how much he could demand from Viscount Chamberlain. Forty-thousand? Fifty-thousand? He would need every pence if he had any hope of coming out of this alive, he realized. The gaze of the marquess was positively deadly.

Ethan picked up the marker for the dueling pistol and glanced at the baronet. He then took the two ends of the marker and ripped it in half. "I have an excellent pair of dueling pistols, so I don't particularly want yours," he said. He tossed the torn marker onto the table. "As for the horse, I have several, and again, I don't particularly want the one you used as collateral. Twice." He held up the marker and slowly tore it in half.

Sir James swallowed. He glanced to his right, wondering how far he could make it if he tried to take his leave of the men's club. There was an open path to vestibule if he could just ...

"I have two Bow Street Runners guarding the front doors," Ethan said in a voice that had the baronet settling back into his chair.

Swallowing hard, the baronet stared at Ethan. "How much time ...?"

"None."

"None? But how am I ...?"

"You should have thought of that when you were at the faro tables," Ethan interrupted. He stared at Sir James until the man was forced to glance away, feeling a good deal of satisfaction when he saw how the man actually squirmed in his chair. "But since you didn't, I find myself forced to make you a deal."

Sir James stared at the marquess. "A deal?" he repeated, one eyebrow furrowing in confusion.

"Yes," Ethan replied. He took another draw from his cheroot before leaning forward. "Are you interested in a deal? The terms may be hard for you to accept ..."

"What is it? What's the deal?"

Ethan had to suppress the smile he felt at the man's discomfort. *What a rake!* An irresponsible, despicable rake! *How had Samantha ever agreed to marry the man?* he wondered.

Because you abandoned her on a pirate ship, he answered himself. Left her ruined and with no other options but to accept the attentions of a man wholly unworthy of her.

Well, he wasn't about to allow Lady Samantha to marry this sorry excuse for a baronet, no matter how agreeable the guy was supposed to be.

"You're going to walk away from your betrothal to Lady Samantha," Ethan stated in no uncertain terms.

Sir James blinked. He blinked again as his brows furrowed into a single caterpillar. "Come again?" he whispered, his eyes once again on the lookout for interlopers.

Ethan sighed and rolled his eyes. "You heard me. Give up your claim to Lady Samantha, and all these markers are yours to do with as you please. Given your sorry excuse for an existence, they might provide enough fuel for your fireplace on a cold night," he added with as much disdain as he could manage.

The baronet shook his head. "And?" There had to be something else. Something more to the deal than to simply call off his engagement to Lady Samantha.

"And, nothing," Ethan replied, stubbing out his cheroot in the porcelain ash tray. "Do we have a deal?" He hesitated before reaching out with his right hand.

His head seeming to shake and nod all at the same time, Sir James regarded the marquess for a moment. "But, *why?*" he asked in confusion.

Ethan dropped his arm to the table in a huff. "Because I won't allow her to end up with a *rake*," he replied, annoyance evident in his voice. "So, what's it to be? Do we have a deal, or do you wish to spend your remaining days in Newgate?"

At the mention of the prison, Sir James held out his hand. "We have a deal," he nearly yelled, grabbing Ethan's hand to shake it twice.

Recoiling, Ethan frowned and pulled his hand back to grasp the stack of markers and shove them across the small table. "Speak to her again, and it will be pistols at dawn. Do I make myself clear?" he asked in his most venomous voice.

Sir James nodded. "Crystal," he answered with a nod. He reached over and grabbed the markers from the table, hovering them over the open flame on the table's candle lamp. Within moments, the markers were nothing more than ash.

When Sir James looked up to give his thanks to the marquess, he found the man's chair empty.

CHAPTER 47

A HEART-TO-HEART

The next day

Hearing Samantha's bout of tears first thing in the morning, Caroline Fitzsimmons did what any mother would do. She gathered her daughter in her arms and scolded her.

"Your eyes are going to be red and puffy, and you have a soirée to attend with Sir James this evening," the viscountess stated, offering her daughter a hanky from her pocket.

Samantha blinked. She had completely forgotten about the soirée, her thoughts entirely on the Marquess of Plymouth and how he had appeared at her door the day before. How sad he looked. How contrite. And then he had kissed her, and she was suddenly back on the island, back in a time when soirées didn't exist and she had Ethan at her side every night.

She was quite sure he had been in her dreams, as well, for she had awakened feeling the same contentment as she had on the island, her body satiated and a smile on her face.

Then she remembered where she was and truly woke up—on her bedroom floor.

Breakfast held no appeal. Even a cup of chocolate did little to restore her to that sense of contentment she had felt first thing that morning. Despite her listless constitution, she accepted callers throughout the day and even smiled at some of their comments. By late afternoon, though, she was once again a watering pot.

"I think I shall send my regrets," Samantha said between her quiet sobs. "I'm not feeling well."

Caroline held her hand up to Samantha's forehead, one eyebrow arching up when she detected what could be a fever. "Are you sure you're not suffering from cold feet?" she asked as she moved to sit on the edge of the bed. "All these tears are not what one would expect of a girl about to marry the man of her dreams."

Samantha considered the question. Of course, she was suffering from cold feet! Sir James Moriarty was hardly the man of her dreams. Not even the man of her daydreams. But did she dare admit it to her mother? The woman had already begun wedding plans. Their modiste was making wedding clothes. And at some point in the next few months, she would be wed. She would become the baronet's wife.

"You could be with child."

Caroline's words were said with a wan smile, and Samantha gasped when she realized her mother might *want* her to be pregnant.

"You'd like that, wouldn't you?" Samantha replied, her breaths suddenly coming a bit too fast. "For us to be expecting at the same time?" Incredulous, Samantha planted her hands on her hips. "Well, I don't think *I* would like it one bit!"

Caroline grinned as she angled her head. "I know I shouldn't allow you to speak to me like that, but I find I'm rather enjoying this," she said happily. "We have a lot of catching up to do as mother and daughter."

Samantha stomped a slipper-clad foot and then winced when she felt the impact all the way up her leg despite the Aubusson carpet that covered her bedchamber floor. "Ow!" she groaned, wiggling the foot to shake off the pain. When she looked up, she found Ethan Range standing beyond the threshold of the open door. He was regarding her with the same smile her mother was displaying and held a rather large box under one arm.

"I could kiss it and make it better," he offered, the smile fading when he saw she had been crying.

"If you two will excuse me, I'm expecting my husband's return any moment now," Caroline said in a quiet voice, knowing she wouldn't be missed if she simply took her leave of the bedchamber.

Ethan managed a bow in the viscountess' direction as she scooted out of the room and down the stairs. When he returned his attention to Samantha, she was still where she was when she had stomped her foot. "Did you hurt yourself?" he asked quietly, still just outside her door.

Samantha shrugged and tried to stifle a sob. "No."

Ethan nodded. "Are you well?"

Sighing, Samantha realized she felt exhausted. "As well as can be expected, I suppose," she finally answered. "And you?" she queried, noticing there were dark circles around his eyes.

"I'm sleeping on the floor."

Samantha blinked, wondering if the marquess was merely teasing her or if he truly intended to sleep on the floor of her bedchamber. "I rather doubt my uncle will allow that," she replied with a shake of her head.

Or perhaps he would, just so he could discover Ethan and claim the marquess had ruined her and force him to marry her.

A bit late for that, though.

But she could hope.

Ethan shook his own head, a grimace showing on his face. "I meant, in my bedchamber of course. I ... I can't sleep. I find I ..."

"Can't sleep in a soft bed," Samantha finished for him. At his surprised nod, she took a step toward him. "I find myself doing the same," she said in a whisper, "Although I'm quite sure I'll be able to at some point." *I'll have to*, she thought. She was about to be married. Her husband would expect to find her in her bed when he visited her bedchamber—not down on the floor with only a blanket beneath her.

A sense of melancholy settled over Ethan just then. "I don't suppose you would be willing to try a different bed, perhaps," he said hopefully.

Samantha's eyes widened. "Did you have one in mind?" she asked, taking another step toward him.

Ethan nodded, a bit heartened by her sudden interest. "Two, in fact," he said with a slight nod. "You would have your choice, of course," he added, thinking if the bed in the mistress suite at Castle Keys didn't suit her, she was certainly welcome to sleep in his. And if she chose the mistress suite, well, then he would have to hope she would invite him to spend the night with her. Or maybe he could just sneak in quietly while she was sleeping and ... Ethan shook his head in an effort to wipe away the image of her sleeping in his arms.

Closing the remaining distance between them, Samantha angled her head and regarded the marquess for a time. "It sounds positively charming," she whispered.

"Oh, it's not," he replied with a shake of his head. "Well, the *beds* are, I suppose," he corrected himself, noticing her crestfallen expression. "Usually rather comfortable, too. But the place they're in is just a big, dark, cold pile of rocks near the coast. There are moors not too far off, and fog, and rain." He suddenly swallowed, chastising himself for painting such a bleak picture of Castle Keys.

"Not like Darbing Manor, then," Samantha replied, remembering his description of the house in which she had been born.

Ethan shook his head, surprised she would bring up the home where he had spent so much of his childhood. "No," he agreed, his eyes downcast.

Samantha reached up a finger to his cheek. "My uncle has threatened to send me back to Darbing Manor," she said quietly. "He's none too happy with my impending nuptials, you see," she explained, her lip curling up when Ethan's gaze suddenly lifted.

"If he's done so to make it some sort of ... sentence, I do hope you realize it's not," he insisted. "Darbing is rather cheery and bright. There's a lake and gardens and ..."

"Lots of cupboards and wardrobes in which to hide?" Samantha finished for him.

Ethan nodded, remembering just then that Darbing Manor had belonged to a viscountcy. Edward and Elizabeth had merely been allowed to live there, probably as stewards. "It belongs to your uncle, doesn't it?" he asked, his manner suddenly not so serious.

"The Chamberlain viscountcy, in fact," Samantha answered. "But I don't think it's entailed," she added with a shake of her head.

An idea flashed through Ethan's mind just then. He lifted a finger as he quickly worked out a few details in his head. "Might I take my leave of you for just a moment?" he asked suddenly, stepping backwards from the door. He suddenly stepped forward again, though, and held out the box. "This is for you, by the way."

Samantha swallowed and blinked in alarm, reluctantly taking the flat box. "Are you coming back?" she asked, rather startled by his retreat. She was quite sure he was about to kiss her.

"Of course," he answered. "I still have a proposition to make," he added, and he disappeared from the room.

Samantha regarded the box, a bit stunned by Ethan's parting words. *I still have a proposition to make.*

Marriage?

All at once, Samantha felt a myriad of emotions, all due to the confounded marquess. She found herself feeling a bit sorry for him, for it was evident he didn't particularly like his home. Nor his bed, although she was quite sure he would eventually come to sleep in it again.

She rather liked the way his entire face had lit up at the mention of Darbing Manor. Then she thought of his comment about her being an ugly baby. But then she remembered him saying she smelled wonderful. Then she recalled how he had put to voice such uncharitable thoughts of Caroline, such anger over Samantha being passed off as the daughter of her aunt and uncle that Samantha was left feeling rather offended.

Am I bad ton? she suddenly wondered. *Is my mother?*

I'm illegitimate.

Although she wanted to remain angry with Ethan for having abandoned her on the pirate ship, he had seen her in the arms of the captain and had obviously thought her a wanton, especially after what they had done together on the island!

What would she have done had she seen him in the arms of another woman?

A stab of jealousy had her clutching her belly just then, jealousy so intense, she felt sick to her stomach. Taking a deep breath, she was able to settle herself so the nausea passed.

Had Ethan felt that way when he had seen her in Captain Crawley's arms?

Samantha moved to the bed and placed the box on the counterpane. She wrested the top from it and pulled apart layers of tissue paper. A gown of sapphire blue lay folded in the bottom, its sleeves and color a near-match for the one she had worn on the island. Pulling it from the box, she shook out the skirts and held it against the front of her body. Turning toward her vanity, she regarded her reflection. She appeared no different than she had that morning, but the thought of Ethan proposing made her light up. She glanced down at the diamond pin and her smile widened.

And what of Sir James?

Who?

She changed gowns as quickly as she dared, grinning as the blue silk of the new gown settled onto her body. Spinning in front of the cheval mirror, Samantha smiled and reached for the cravat pin. Then she moved to the very spot where she had been when Ethan took his leave of her and took a deep breath.

Ethan had only been gone a few moments when he suddenly reappeared in Samantha's bedchamber doorway. He found Samantha standing where he had left her, wearing the sapphire gown he had purchased earlier that day and looking so much like she had when they were on the island that he had to stop and take a breath. "God, you're beautiful," he managed to get out before he noticed she was wringing her hands together. "What's wrong?" he asked.

"I did something rather ... stupid," Samantha said, fighting back the tears that threatened to replace the joy she had felt only moments ago.

Ethan shook his head. "I can't imagine you ever doing anything stupid," he replied.

"Oh, but I did," she countered, her eyes closing to stave off the tears. "I ... accepted an offer of marriage ..."

"Because you felt you had to," Ethan responded.

Samantha nodded. "Yes, but to a man I have reason to believe ..."

"Is a rake," Ethan interrupted.

Frowning, Samantha shook her head. "No. An opportunist," she replied. "And a gambler. He may only be marrying me for my dowry. And the notoriety he gains by being associated with me."

Ethan rolled his eyes and closed the distance between the two of them. "All of the above," he said as he lowered his forehead so it touched hers. "I have seen to it he will no longer darken your door," he whispered.

Samantha gasped, pulling her head from his as her eyes caught his gaze. "Whatever have you done?" she asked, stunned by his words.

Was that hope he heard in her response, he wondered. It certainly didn't sound like concern. "I didn't kill him, if that's what you're wondering," Ethan said with a shake of his head. "But I rather wish I had."

Samantha's eyes widened. "Really?" she replied with a bit too much enthusiasm, rather liking the idea of Ethan putting an end to the man who Samantha realized had taken advantage of her situation. Her notoriety. And her vulnerability.

Perhaps the inflection of her voice made her sound as if she agreed with the idea—Ethan wasn't quite sure—but her response had him fighting a chuckle. "It can still be arranged," he offered. "I told him if he ever spoke to you again, it would be pistols at dawn."

Shocked at his comment, Samantha's mouth rounded into an 'O'. "I suppose that means he won't be paying a call on me to break our betrothal," she said in a whisper.

But where did that leave her?

"He will not. But rest assured, my lady, it is broken," Ethan replied as he once again lowered his forehead to hers and felt her nod.

Samantha blinked back tears. "Thank you," she said, not meeting his gaze.

Ethan frowned. *Thank you?* Well, it wasn't exactly the response he expected, but it was certainly better than a 'how dare you?' or 'I hate you' or 'take your leave and never see me again.'

"I believe this is yours," she whispered as she held up the diamond pin.

Wrapping a hand around hers, he regarded the diamond for a moment and shook his head. "I very clearly recall giving it to you," he replied in a whisper. He wrapped his arms around her waist and pulled her against the front of his body, his hand moving up to hold her head against his chest. "I miss our time together on the island," he said in a whisper. "I miss this," he continued as he tightened his grip. "I miss you."

Samantha melted against him, her curves filling his voids. "I miss you, too," she whispered. Before she realized what was happening, his lips were on hers, tentative and tender and oh, so warm and inviting. When she responded in kind, her lips barely touching his, she sighed his name.

"I still have a wish that hasn't come true," he murmured.

Samantha sucked in a breath. "As do I."

"I wish you would sleep with me every night," he whispered against her lips.

"I wish I could wake up in your arms every morning," she countered.

"Then marry me," they said in unison.

The two pulled away from each other in surprise, each staring at the other.

"Truly?" they asked in unison, smiles replacing their expressions of pain.

"Truly."

EPILOGUE

*W*edding Trip Wonders
    Ethan didn't say a word when he suddenly appeared in the doorway of her salon in Darbing Manor. As Samantha glanced up from the book she had been reading next to the west window, her eyes widened in surprise. The book fell from her hand as she stood, a mix of excitement and fear gripping her. The look on his face was so intent, so determined, she felt her body react before her mind realized quite what was happening. Her insides seemed to liquefy and her breasts swelled, and even though the instinct to take flight and flee the room came from some part of her brain, another more powerful sensation—desire—kept her rooted in place.

Her lips parted as he strode into her salon, one arm wrapping around her waist when he was directly in front of her, pulling her so she was nearly on her toes. His eyes, usually a rich brown, seemed almost black, almost predatory. She angled her head even as his lips moved to take possession of hers, his kiss hard and demanding. The moan she heard might have come from her own throat or from his, but it mattered not. With his body pressed into the curves of her body, she felt his desire, felt the evidence of his erection against her belly. The moment was thrilling, so unexpected, she wondered if perhaps he would take her on the Grecian chaise on which she had been reading. Instead, he swept her into his arms and moved quickly to his bedchamber, slamming the door with a quick kick.

"I rather like it when you've decided you've been in your study long enough," Samantha murmured. She lay back in the soft bed linens, a wan smile spreading into a grin. Although it was late afternoon, dappled sunlight spilled into his bedchamber in Darbing Manor, making the room appear golden.

"Me, too. I'm thinking of spending less time there and far more time here," he replied with a sigh. "This was an excellent idea, by the way."

Samantha sighed, realizing he referred to their decision to live in Darbing Manor while she saw to renovations at Castle Keys. Eventually, they would probably live in Castle Keys, but until then, Darbing Manor was large enough for the two of them and a few servants.

"Thank you for arranging it with Uncle Matthew," she murmured, remembering how stunned Matthew had been when Ethan requested the house in exchange for her dowry.

"Thank you for telling me it was his," Ethan replied in a whisper. "I never bothered to learn who owned the place." One of his hands still encompassed one of Samantha's breasts, his palm covering most of it while his fingers danced about the edges. He lifted himself onto an elbow, his brows furrowing as his hand moved to her other breast.

"What has you perplexed?" Samantha wondered in a whisper.

Ethan leaned over and kissed a nipple. "When we were on the island and Crawley appeared, you implied your breasts weren't large enough to fill his hands," he murmured, a slight smile appearing when he remembered how indignant Samantha sounded with her retort, how positively adorable she had looked with her hands on her hips and her chin raised in defiance.

"That's because they weren't," Samantha replied, inhaling sharply as he gently pinched a nipple between his thumb and forefinger.

"But ... my hands are certainly as large as his, and I can barely hold one of your breasts in it," he replied as he hefted the soft flesh.

Samantha smiled. "Well, they do tend to ... swell a bit when a woman is expecting," she admitted, watching carefully for his reaction.

Succumbing to his post-coital exhaustion, Ethan sank down to the bedding and took a deep breath, his hand moving to her side so he could pull her against his body. "Oh," he murmured, his eyes closing. A moment passed before his eyes suddenly opened and he was back up on his elbow. "What did you say?" he asked in alarm.

Giggling, Samantha pressed her face into his chest and placed a kiss on his sternum. "I'm going to have a baby," she said quietly.

Ethan stared down at his wife, his expression unreadable. His hand moved from her side to her belly, the fingers lightly skimming over her smooth skin and setting off frissons beneath the surface. "A baby?" he repeated.

Samantha nodded as she pressed a hand over his. "Your heir, I'm hoping," she whispered before his lips were suddenly over hers, kissing her urgently. He moved them down her cheek, sprinkling kisses to her neck, to her shoulder and finally to a breast.

"How can you already ... *know?*" he asked when he came up for air. "We only just ..." Then his eyes widened. "The island," he whispered before he leaned over to kiss her belly. Then he pressed his ear there and listened for a moment.

Reaching a hand to the side of his face, Samantha cupped his jaw. "Yes," she said quietly. "But I'm not sure which day ... or night," she added. She had spent a good deal of time thinking of just when the baby had been conceived, but in the end, it really didn't matter. Their time on the island, although fraught with unknowns and some hunger, had been the happiest of her life. These early days of her marriage to Ethan were proving happier, though.

"If I hadn't gone to London for you ..." Ethan stopped and sat up in bed, his hands clasped together in front of him. "I shudder to think of my ... progeny ... with Sir James' name," he said in a voice that suggested he was near panic.

Samantha lifted herself onto one elbow and placed a hand over his. "I wasn't going to be the wife of a baronet. And I would have come to Yorkshire for you," she said with a sigh. "I would have had to." At his lifted brow, she added, "I have a very persuasive aunt who turns out is really my mother, a very insistent best friend in Eva, a rather demanding cousin in Julia, and a very loving sister in Emma."

Ethan's look of offense was nearly comical. "You're saying you were *coerced* into marrying me? It took ... *four* women to convince you to accept my offer?" he responded, incredulous. Then he remembered that she had proposed to him, too.

Samantha giggled, the sound reminding Ethan of their time on the island when she had found such joy in small things. "Not at all. For you see, in the end, I really had no choice in the matter. I love you, Ethan Range. And despite having sworn off travel by sea, I do believe I would have gotten right back on a ship and sailed here to Yorkshire to ask for your hand in marriage."

Letting out the breath he had been holding, Ethan regarded Samantha for a long moment. "Indeed?"

Nodding, Samantha leaned over and kissed him on the cheek.

"And not just because you're carrying the heir to the Plymouth marquessate?" he pressed.

Smiling, Samantha shook her head. "Although, I must admit, it gave me that much more incentive."

Ethan pulled his hands out from under hers and wrapped an arm around her shoulders, pulling her to him. "Does this mean a wedding trip to the Continent is out of the question?" he asked with some amusement.

Samantha considered his query for a moment. "I suppose I could abide a Channel crossing, although I may have morning sickness," she said with some concern.

At the reminder of his mother-in-law's condition whilst on *The Fairweather*, Ethan frowned. Remembering her comment about wanting to paint in Scotland, he said, "Perhaps a trip to …"

"Scotland!" Samantha finished for him, her eyes wide. She smiled and gave her husband a kiss. "Oh, aye."

EXCERPT

Read on for an excerpt from Linda Rae Sande's
Book 3 in "The Sisters of the Aristocracy" series
The Desire of a Lady

Sarah Wellingham, Countess of Trenton, speared her fingers through her husband's butter blond curls. "Why, give me a glance with those beautiful blue eyes and toss me a sovereign, and I'll give you a tumble right here and now."

Gabriel Wellingham, Earl of Trenton, straightened at his desk and regarded his wife with widened eyes. "What?" he replied in shock. "It didn't cost me anything last night!" he claimed in mock dismay.

Grinning in delight, Sarah shrugged. "It's those blue eyes and that blond hair," she whispered as she ruffled up his hair with her long fingers. A gold filigree bracelet dotted with sapphires encircled the wrist at the base of her hand. Although the piece of jewelry was more appropriately worn at balls and the opera, Gabriel had insisted she wear it everyday. "You'll need a reminder you're a countess now, and no longer a commoner," he had said when he first wrapped it around her wrist.

Sarah tore her eyes away from the winking blue jewels and settled them back on her husband's blue eyes. "And speaking of your very best trait, you must know your sister is receiving a good deal of attention, and not all of it because of those blue eyes and blond curls of hers," she said with an arched eyebrow. "She was mentioned again in *The Morning Chronicle*."

The earl sighed. "I am a bit concerned about that," he admitted, "Which is why I sent the coach to London for her. I expect her arrival at any time."

Sarah nodded her understanding. Although she was still the manager of the Spread Eagle in Stretton, she had arranged for Margery Higgins, her eventual replacement, to see to the operation of the coaching inn while she prepared for her sister-in-law's arrival. At some point, probably sooner than later, Margery would simply take over and run the inn, but Sarah had promised the owner she would continue her involvement until Margery was truly ready to assume command. With a toddler hanging onto her skirts and what she was sure was another baby on the way, Sarah hoped it would be sooner.

"I fear those who pay her such attendance don't necessarily have her best interests at heart," Sarah said as she took the chair across from her husband's desk. Although she had only been his countess for over a year, Sarah had settled into her role much like she had when she agreed to manage the Spread Eagle. Running an earldom, as it turned out, was very much like running a business.

Gabriel frowned. "You think they mean to ruin her and ... what?" he asked in alarm.

Allowing a sigh, Sarah leaned forward and lowered her voice. "Ruin her and *marry* her," she clarified. "She's a very pretty chit, but there is another reason all the young bucks, and some *not* so young ones, are interested in taking her as their wife."

His blue eyes widening in alarm, Gabriel shook his head. "Her dowry, do you suppose?" he asked finally.

It took everything Sarah had not to roll her eyes. Although Gabriel was usually a smart man—he hadn't always been, but that had more to do with blind ambition and youth than brains—he sometimes seemed a bit dense when it came to matters of finance. "I suppose," she replied with a hint of derision. "Gabe, every man vying for her may only be doing so because they expect their wedding day to be the means to pay off their gambling debts, hire another mistress, buy a yellow phaeton, and enjoy an auction or two at Tattersall's," she admonished him.

Visibly wincing, Gabriel slumped in his chair. He had been guilty of everything she mentioned when he had inherited the Trenton earldom three years ago. "Don't you think she'll be able to discern the fortune hunters from the … *legitimate* suitors?" he countered, thinking his half-sister was smarter than Sarah might be implying with her comment.

Just fifteen months ago, Lily Harkness had been a lady's maid for Lady Samantha Fitzsimmons. The illegitimate daughter of a house maid, Lily knew the identity of her real father, but given the Earl of Trenton never acknowledged her as his daughter, she never expected any consideration from him— nor from his estate. So imagine her surprise when Gabriel showed up at Fitzsimmons Manor and announced he was recognizing her as his sister! Gabriel made it clear he intended for her to enjoy all the comforts afforded to one who was a member of a rich earldom.

The fact that Lady Samantha had stepped forward and volunteered to take Lily under her wing and see her through her first Season was a testament to his sister's pleasant demeanor and willingness to learn everything she needed to know to succeed among the fickle *ton*. Gabriel often wondered if Lily did it simply to prove to him she could. She certainly hadn't seemed very pleased to learn she was being acknowledged as a Wellingham.

Sarah considered her husband's question for a long time. "I cannot speak for Lady Lily when I say this," she hedged carefully, "But I do not believe sincerity is always so easy to determine."

Gabriel leaned back in his chair and rested his head against the soft leather back. "I suppose you are right," he replied. "When she arrives, the first thing I'll have her do is provide a list of every suitor …"

"The first thing you're going to do is *greet* her," Sarah interrupted, one finger extended into the air. "And then you're going to kiss her on the cheek and allow her to go to her suite so that she may refresh herself and perhaps take a nap ..."

"And have a spot of tea and biscuits," Gabriel chimed in with a roll of his eyes.

"And *then* you can ask about her suitors," Sarah finished with a nod.

"I love you," Gabriel stated as he leaned forward and reached over the desk for one of Sarah's hands.

"Of course, you do," Sarah replied with a wink. "You wouldn't put up with me otherwise," she added as Gabriel kissed the back of the hand he held. "Oh, and against by better judgement, I suppose I love you, too," she added gleefully.

Gabriel was about to feign offense, but he was interrupted by a knock at the door to the study. "Come!" he called out.

Fitzroy, the butler, appeared at the threshold. "Your carriage just pulled into the drive, my lord," he stated in a baritone worthy of an opera singer.

Both Sarah and Gabriel were out of their chairs in an instant. "She must not have required the coach to stop very often," Gabriel murmured with a hint of awe.

"She's not as spoiled as you," Sarah countered with a grin, hurrying to the vestibule with her husband at her side. When she suddenly stopped, Gabriel took another step or two before realizing he needed to stop. He whirled around to face his wife. Before he could ask as to why she had suddenly halted in the grand hall, Sarah's lips were suddenly on his, and one of her arms had circled his neck.

Rather surprised by Sarah's assault of affection, Gabriel returned the brief kiss before slowly pulling away, apparently unaware of the stares of the footmen poised to meet the coach. "I must ask why you would afford me such a display of affection," he whispered, his forehead pressed against hers.

"I do love you," Sarah whispered in reply. "Please, do not be offended by my teasing," she added with a slight shake of her head against his.

Gabriel kissed her nose. "I would be offended if you did not occasionally remind me I am a mortal," he replied with a wink.

"I spent the entire carriage ride here thinking I might be better off *not* marrying," a feminine voice called out from the vestibule, "But then I pay witness to you two and think I should become a wife post-haste!"

The earl and countess whirled around to find Lady Lily standing at the end of the great hall with one hand on her hip and a huge grin on her face.

"Lily!" Sarah called out as she hurried to join her sister-in-law. The two hugged before leaning back to regard one another.

"Marriage certainly agrees with you," Lily stated as her brother joined them. "And you," she added as she gave her brother a thorough look. She reached up and kissed his cheek.

A bit startled at his sister's comment, Gabriel gave Lily a kiss on the cheek and regarded her for a moment. "It's my sincerest wish it will agree with you as well, although I have learned the choice of a spouse is paramount ..." Gabriel stopped when he realized his wife was giving him a quelling glance. He suddenly sobered. "You must be exhausted from your trip. Allow me to escort you to your bedchamber so you can take a nap and freshen up before dinner," he suggested, remembering Sarah's edict.

Lily grinned and turned to Sarah. "My, how well you've trained my brother," she whispered with an arched brow.

Sarah nodded. "A bit of work, but well worth the effort," she whispered back.

"I heard that," Gabriel said with feigned offense, one open hand pressed against his chest. "How I'll manage the two of you whilst you join forces is beyond my comprehension."

The two women exchanged innocent glances before Lily shook her head. "Dear brother, you should know by now that you cannot manage a woman," she said in a whisper filled with delight. "It's the woman who manages the man."

And with that, Lady Lily and Lady Trenton made their way up the steps and to the guest bedchamber.

ABOUT THE AUTHOR

A self-described nerd and lover of science, Linda Rae spent many years as a published technical writer specializing in 3D graphics workstations, software and 3D animation (her movie credits include SHREK and SHREK 2). An interest in genealogy led to years of research on the Regency era and a desire to write fiction based in that time.

A fan of action-adventure movies, she can frequently be found at the local cinema. Although she no longer has any tropical fish, she does follow the San Jose Sharks. She makes her home in Cody, Wyoming.

For more information:
www.lindaraesande.com